Legends of PAUL BUNYAN

. . . he had woven a flexible handle. . . .

LEGENDS
OF
PAUL BUNYAN

Harold W. Felton, Editor

Illustrations by Richard Bennett

Foreword by James Stevens

University of Minnesota Press
Minneapolis • London

The Fesler–Lampert Minnesota Heritage Book Series

This series reprints significant books that enhance our understanding and appreciation of Minnesota and the Upper Midwest. It is supported by the generous assistance of the John K. and Elsie Lampert Fesler Fund and the interest and contribution of Elizabeth P. Fesler and the late David R. Fesler.

Publisher's Note

Our knowledge and appreciation of the culture and history of Minnesota have advanced considerably since this book was first published, and the attitudes and opinions expressed in it may strike the contemporary reader as inappropriate. This classic has been reprinted in its original form as a contribution to the state's heritage.

First University of Minnesota Press edition, 2008

Reprinted by arrangement with the University of Nebraska Foundation

Published by the University of Minnesota Press
111 Third Avenue South, Suite 290
Minneapolis, MN 55401-2520
http://www.upress.umn.edu

Library of Congress Cataloging-in-Publication Data

Legends of Paul Bunyan / Harold W. Felton, editor ; illustrations by Richard Bennett ; foreword by James Stevens. — 1st University of Minnesota Press ed., 2008.
   p. cm. — (The Fesler-Lampert Minnesota heritage book series)
   Originally published: New York : A. A. Knopf, 1947.
   Includes bibliographical references.
   ISBN 978-0-8166-5460-4 (pb : alk. paper)
   1. Bunyan, Paul (Legendary character). 2. Legends—Minnesota. 3. Loggers—Minnesota. 4. Legends—United States. I. Felton, Harold W., 1902– II. Bennett, Richard, 1899–1971, illus.
   PS461.B8L45   2008
   398.20973'02—dc22
   [E]   2008016683

Printed in the United States of America on acid-free paper

The University of Minnesota is an equal-opportunity educator and employer.

15 14 13 12 11 10 09 08   10 9 8 7 6 5 4 3 2 1

DEDICATION

ONCE upon a time there was a very big man. He was very wise and could do wonderful things. He never made a giant dinner horn like Paul Bunyan did, but he could make wonderful whistles. He never tracked an old moose back to its birthplace, but he could always prove that there was a rabbit at the end of each rabbit track. He had nothing to do with the Pacific Ocean nor with the creation of the Japanese current, but he taught almost every kid in town to swim, and while he had no occasion to tame wild water, he knew where the best swimming holes were.

No tall tales were told about him, but he could tell them. He didn't plant and cut down great forests, but he had a way with a garden. Even Paul Bunyan could not have raised larger cabbages. It almost took a Paul Bunyan to harvest them. The big asters he was so proud of were quite as large as Babe the Blue Ox's eyes, and fully as blue.

His name was Dad. This book is dedicated to him.

CONTENTS

THE WONDERFUL BIG BLUE OX, BABE

FOOD AND THE KITCHEN

PAUL'S FELLOW WORKERS, PALS, AND FRIENDS

PAUL MADE GEOGRAPHY

PAUL HAD A WAY WITH WATER

PAUL MADE AND MET THE WEATHER

THE SPIRIT OF PAUL BUNYAN WILL STAY IN AMERICA

AN OLD LOGGER'S FOREWORD

In the year of old, 1904, I was twelve. Then I worked as a summertime choreboy in a little logging camp. It was in the piney mountains of Southern Idaho. I did not hear of Paul Bunyan in that camp, but I did hear tall tales of the woods.

Like every Idaho ranch boy of that time, I knew many stories about Indians, cowboys, outlaws and other strong characters of early Western life. A neighbor was a veteran of the Indian wars. He told stories in which Coyote was the hero, always smarter than man. I learned the legend of the great Thunderbird, who could carry a buffalo, or even a whale in his talons, and who flew belted with a monster snake that made the lightning.

My grandfather had met Buffalo Bill, Kit Carson and Jim Bridger, all mighty men of the Western plains and mountains. He said that Buffalo Bill was the biggest liar he had ever met and that Jim Bridger could tell the biggest stories. There was a difference, grandpa said.

One of Jim Bridger's stories was of a petrified forest in the Yellowstone country.

"It is the most petrified place ever known," he told. "Not only the trees are petrified, but up in their boughs are purty little petrified birds, all singing sweet little petrified songs!"

Nature in the wilderness held no terrors for such men as Jim Bridger and Kit Carson or for Davy Crockett, another man who lived as a brave pioneer. A hundred years ago many big stories, or tall tales, about Davy Crockett were printed. In each he was the storyteller. Here is an example:

Davy tells that he and his friend, Ben Hardin,' were sitting in the stern of a Mississippi River steamer, when a big storm blew along. Then—"the noise got bigger, and the water begun to squirm about like a stirred-up punch bowl, and the boats begun playin' rock and seesaw at such an etarnal rate that even I couldn't hold 'em still. . . . The boats begun to play smash with one another, and the ribs of ourn got stove in clar to the biler. A gray streak of lightnin' come passin' along, so jist as it come I grabbed it by the fork and sprung on it. Ben follered, and held on to my hair . . . and the way we streaked it and left the tornado behind was astonishin' to all natur."

At the same time the French woodsmen and rivermen in Canada were making up tales and songs which still live as folklore in Quebec and Ontario. Irish workers came to this country in great numbers after 1848, and many went to work in the pineries of the Lake States. They brought with them wonderful legends and ballads about giants and wee folk, wicked weather and queer creatures. In the shanty camps the Irish and the French met. It goes without saying that there they repeated old big stories and invented new tall tales, just as Davy Crockett and Jim Bridger and the Indians had done.

Nobody can prove it that I know of, and I lived and studied in Michigan for two years trying to prove it, but the best authorities agree that the Irish and French lumberjacks of the Lake States started the stories of Paul Bunyan and Babe, the Blue Ox in the woods. If I said I knew, it would be a lie. I am not too good to tell a lie, but I don't dare to, for when I lie my neck swells to Size 27.

But I can tell big stories, for that is only fooling and not deceiving. I learned to tell tall tales about Paul Bunyan in the year of old, 1910. The place was a pine-woods logging camp in Northern California. I drove a team of horses. There were old-time lumberjacks from Michigan, Wisconsin and Minnesota in the camp. Some of them wore beards. A few liked to argue about Paul Bunyan. An after-supper argument would go something like this:

One old-timer would remark, "Too many folks have the notion that all of Paul Bunyan's loggers were powerful big men. I recollect he had a slew of runts for swampers. One of the runtiest was Peewee Riley. One winter he broke his leg three feet below the knee, and——"

Then another would chop in with "Let's get this straight. A lineal foot in Paul Bunyan's time ain't what a lineal foot is today. Sam, you specify what you mean by 'three feet below the knee.' "

"Well, to put it rough, Luke, Peewee Riley measured an axhandle from his knee down to where he broke his leg."

"But Sam, blast it, that ain't real specifyin', either. Anybody knows that a Paul Bunyan axhandle was longer'n any known today. Come on, now, and get down to facts and figgers."

"Why, Luke McGluke, you know that the standard Bunyan axhandle was measured by the lower front middle tooth of Babe, the Blue Ox."

"But Sam, Babe never had any lower teeth—not in front, anyhow!"

"Who ever told you that there? Babe had three full sets of teeth—lower, upper and a spare. He had to change teeth, like they do saws in a mill, because Babe loved to chaw spruce timber and it was hard on his grinders. It was from one of Babe's spruce-timber cuds that Paul Bunyan got the notion of inventin' the pulp industry."

And so it would go, until somebody would change the subject. In my own experience no lengthy Paul Bunyan stories were heard in the logging camps. The old-timers would simply argue about the stock characters, Paul Bunyan, Johnny Inkslinger, the Big Swede, and Babe, the Blue Ox, and make up odd "gags" about them. Well used to tall tales, in 1910 I did not think of the Bunyan bits I heard as things extra and rare.

But by 1914 thousands of camp tale-tellers had contributed their bits to the lore of Paul Bunyan. Through many years in the woods of the Lake States and the West those bits of lore had grown into a giant body that the imagination of a poet was able to visualize—to see as though the giant truly lived.

Douglas Malloch was a poet. He wrote poems for a journal, *The American Lumberman*. He knew the lumber woods and lumberjacks. In 1914 he saw an American giant in the sum of the odd bits of lore he had heard for so long in the tall talk of rugged woodsmen. So Douglas Malloch was inspired to write the poem, "The Round River Drive," and *The American Lumberman* was proud to print it.

From that time on various contributors "sent in" Paul Bunyan tales to the lumber-trade magazines, and numerous good ones were printed. During the period W. B. Laughead, a brilliant young advertising writer and artist, began to use the Paul Bunyan material in the advertisements of the Red River Lumber Company. With Poet Malloch, he was a pioneer in writing the big Bunyan stories, and in "improving" on them.

In 1920 Lee J. Smits, who had grown up in the Michigan woods to become a newspaper man, traveled to Seattle to work for the *Star* newspaper. He remembered the Paul Bunyan stories he had heard in his boyhood, and he wondered if they were told in the tall timber of the West Coast. So he wrote a story on the subject and asked for Paul Bunyan contributions. Many were sent him, and the *Star* ran a series of the tall tales for two weeks. This was the introduction of Paul Bunyan to the general public—to readers outside the lumber industry. A booklet of the grand Laughead anecdotes and drawings was widely distributed. A series of brief Bunyan tales was run on the editorial page of the Portland *Oregonian,* by the columnist, DeWitt Harry, in 1922.

Then the gold rush was on. Hundreds of articles and dozens of books on the life and times of Paul Bunyan have been published since 1923. In December of that year, while working in a Bend, Oregon, sawmill, I wrote "The Black Duck Dinner," the first full-length magazine story on a Paul Bunyan theme. The core of it was a real bit of folklore from the pine woods. Most of it I made up. I did this naturally. My grandfather and a hundred other old-timers of the West had shown me how. Other writers of Paul Bunyan tales have had to invent as I did, or else borrow from the stock of Paul Bunyan material already in print.

While the original genuine Paul Bunyan legends of the woods are few, with each no more than an anecdote, the printed stock of stories is now mountainous. Mr. Harold W. Felton has worked hard and well to harvest samples of the published material that represents the heart and soul of the grand old timber tales. It is high time for the publication of a Paul Bunyan collection of this kind, and I glory in it.

Herein is the traditional stuff for argufying and wits-fighting, or for simple fireside yarning on stormy evenings; here are imaginings to enjoy as Sam Whidby and Luke McGluke used to enjoy them in that year of the good old times, 1910. Here you can see America working and winning in the old way; bragging, whooping and snorting; joking and laughing; taking everything in giant's stride.

And here are remnants of a lost life, shadows of a fallen

day. Out of the great times of the woods, when the axmen harvested their way across the timberlands as their part in the building of America, we keep a few stories, we cherish a little lore. The past truly touches us with its life and speaks to us from these tales.

JAMES STEVENS

Seattle, November 10, 1946.

INTRODUCTION

Too little—much too little is known of Paul Bunyan, The Great American.

For many years, voices in every part of the land have been singing his praises. Some of the voices were heard, as songs were sung for the amazement and amusement of the few, gathered around a camp stove or at work. Other voices have reached larger audiences. This book attempts to bring some of them together, with the hope that a pleasing choir will be the result.

The voices are American. They sing American words and they sing with American spirit. The theme is work. I am sure you will find that each song has its individual charm. They have one common characteristic. Each is distinguished by its enthusiasm. I hope you will find that they go well together, and add suitably to the honor and the glory of the Great American.

If some of the stories indicate that the same event appears to have occurred in different ways or at different times, it is understandable. History is that way. If observers disagree as to facts, it may be well to recall that Paul was a big man. An event viewed from a vantage point on the toe of his boot might well appear to have occurred in an entirely different way when viewed from the towering height of his mackinaw pocket. Remember the blind men and the elephant. The very differences create room for explanation. Naturally, one who understands Mr. Bunyan can explain.

xix

Thus it is clear that what may seem to be inconsistency, is not inconsistency at all. Every historian when writing about the Great Paul Bunyan has not only the right, but the duty to disclose what he actually saw or heard.

If differences appear as to basic historical facts, it is not surprising that there may be some discrepancy in the relatively minor details of spelling, punctuation and the like. Similarly, these differences should cause no concern. If historians can disagree, so can artists.

There are but few unchanging and unchangeable realities. One is Mr. Bunyan himself. The Great Blue Ox is another. Paul and his works are marked by certain events that have already occurred, and therefore cannot be changed. Notably, these are the Winter of the Blue Snow, The Year of the Hot Winter, and others less well known, but nevertheless established beyond all doubt.

For those who have not met Paul Bunyan, this introduction may well be concluded by this excerpt from *Fortune Magazine,* July, 1944 issue, page 148:

"Paul Bunyan is a genuine American folk character, created by the people themselves. He is one of the few characters, among the mythical heroes of the earth, whose stories do not spring from the gray depths of antiquity. The great folk heroes of Europe and Asia were born before history. They lived in the dim universal wonderland of the earth's beginning, breathing fire and changing their shapes, slaying their dragons and conquering their wizards in the days before learning and facts and statistics placed their gentle curbs on man's imagination.

"But Paul Bunyan was born when almost everyone could read and write. He was created in a bunkhouse, in an ordinary logging camp. His deeds were made up by grown men. They sat around the stove, after working all day in the woods —woods that were just as dangerous, with their toppling trunks and falling widow-makers, as the Black Forests whence came European fairy tales—and told stories of spontaneous exaggeration and odd combination of practical work and extravagant fantasy. It was the loggers, by reputation the most violent roughnecks of all industry, who made up the innocent legend of Paul Bunyan, a lumberman the size of a Douglas fir.

"Paul Bunyan's task was not to create, invent, govern, or reform. It was to clear the ground so that a new America could spread itself upon it. His size is the measure of the task that the pioneers undertook. His spirit is the reflection of the vitality and exuberance with which they made their country grow. Paul Bunyan's task is complete. But a land of machines, cities, and slums needs Paul Bunyan's overbrimming energy and spirit even more than a land of mountains, timber, and plains."

H.W.F.

Legends of PAUL BUNYAN

THE SPIRIT OF PAUL BUNYAN
IS IN AMERICA

Louise Leighton:

I HEAR PAUL BUNYAN

When the night is still and the wind, that ancient squatter
Claiming the timeless land of the sky-blue water,
Sleeps in his weathered wigwam of birch bark,
I hear Paul Bunyan tramping through the dark.
I hear the sibilance of aspens quaking,
I feel the tremor his mighty feet are making,
I can almost see him striding by
Parting the Norway pines to clear the sky.
Between the boughs the star-combed waters glisten,
And vibrant, breathing forests pause to listen,
As throb, throb, throbbing through the night,
Paul Bunyan haunts the land of his delight.

🌲🌲🌲🌲🌲🌲🌲

Carl Sandburg.

WHO MADE PAUL BUNYAN?

Wʜᴏ ᴍᴀᴅᴇ Paul Bunyan, who gave him birth as a myth, who joked him into life as the Master Lumberjack, who fashioned him forth as an apparition easing the hours of men amid axes and trees, saws and lumber? The people, the bookless people, they made Paul and had him alive long before he got into the books for those who read. He grew up in shanties, around the hot stoves of winter, among socks and mittens drying, in the smell of tobacco smoke and the roar of laughter mocking the outside weather. And some of Paul came overseas in wooden bunks below decks in sailing vessels. And some of Paul is as old as the hills, young as the alphabet.

The Pacific Ocean froze over in the winter of the Blue Snow and Paul Bunyan had long teams of oxen hauling regular white snow over from China. This was the winter Paul gave a party to the Seven Axmen. Paul fixed a granite floor sunk two hundred feet deep for them to dance on. Still, it tipped and tilted as the dance went on. And because the Seven Axmen refused to take off their hobnailed boots, the sparks from the nails of their dancing feet lit up the place so that Paul didn't light the kerosene lamps. No women being on the Big Onion river at that time the Seven Axmen had to dance with each other, the one left over in each set taking Paul as a partner. The commotion of the dancing that night brought on an earthquake and the Big Onion river moved over three counties to the east.

One year when it rained from St. Patrick's Day till the Fourth of July, Paul Bunyan got disgusted because his celebration of the Fourth was spoiled. He dived into Lake Superior and swam to where a solid pillar of water was coming down. He dived under this pillar, swam up into it and climbed with powerful swimming strokes, was gone about an hour, came splashing down, and as the rain stopped, he explained, "I turned the dam thing off." This is told in the Big North Woods and on the Great Lakes, with many particulars.

Two mosquitoes lighted on one of Paul Bunyan's oxen, killed it, ate it, cleaned the bones, and sat on a grub shanty picking their teeth as Paul came along. Paul sent to Australia for two special bumblebees to kill these mosquitoes. But the bees and the mosquitoes intermarried; their children had stingers on both ends. And things kept getting worse till Paul brought a big boatload of sorghum up from Louisiana and while all the bee-mosquitoes were eating at the sweet sorghum he floated them down to the Gulf of Mexico. They got so fat that it was easy to drown them all between New Orleans and Galveston.

Paul logged on the Little Gimlet in Oregon one winter. The cookstove at that camp covered an acre of ground. They fastened the side of a hog on each snowshoe and four men used to skate on the griddle while the cook flipped the pancakes. The eating table was three miles long; elevators carried the cakes to the ends of the table where boys on bicycles rode back and forth on a path down the center of the table dropping the cakes where called for.

Benny, the Little Blue Ox of Paul Bunyan, grew two feet every time Paul looked at him, when a youngster. The barn was gone one morning and they found it on Benny's back; he grew out of it in a night. One night he kept pawing and bellowing for more pancakes, till there were two hundred men at the cook shanty stove trying to keep him fed. About breakfast time Benny broke loose, tore down the cook shanty, ate all the pancakes piled up for the loggers' breakfast. And after that Benny made his mistake; he ate the red-hot stove; and that finished him.

🌲🌲🌲🌲🌲🌲🌲

Thomas G. Alvord, Jr.:

THE FIVE-STORK BIRTH

It was when I was workin' on Stony Brook drive,
  For Angus McDougal MacNally;
We'd broke down the rolls, and pushed the sticks in
  About sixty miles north of the Scally,
When one evenin' in camp, on the banks of the stream,
  After supper we lay around smokin',
A-dryin' our socks and a-peggin' our boots,
  And a-swattin' mosquitoes, and jokin',
Big Michael O'Leary,—we called him "the Squirrel,"
  On account of his bein' so agile—
And Glass Eye McBride, whom we dubbed "Glass" for
      short—
  Him bein' in parts rather fragile—
Was arguin' some about big "cuts" and such,
  The drive years before on the Onion,
And the talk got around where we all spun a yarn,
  And had somethin' to say about Bunyan.

Says I to the Squirrel;—it was him I addressed,
  For it seemed that he'd given some study
To matters pertainin' to Bunyan's career,
  And I figured, although rather muddy,

His knowledge, perhaps, since his grandpap O'Shane
    As a young feller knew Bunyan well,
Might enable him some, if he'd be so inclined,
    To review what he knew, and to tell
Both the tales he'd heard through his grandpappy's talk,
    And the ones which he'd gathered in camps,
The sum of the twain such as might make a book,
    Or a pen-pusher ill with the cramps.

As I say, I spoke up and addressed my old friend,
    And I says to him: "Squirrel, do you know
"As regards to the birth of this Paul Bunyan chap,
    "Of his kin, of his parents?—If so,
"I'd certainly like to get straight in my mind
    "Some facts upon which to depend,
"For all that I've heard are conflictin' reports,
    "Which leads me, of course, to contend,
"That Paul was a fake; but a fantastic dream
    "The feats which, it's claimed, he performed.
"But it's just as I say, there's good reason to think
    "That I've been a lot misinformed."

            .   .   .

" 'Twas a night some like this," so continues the Squirrel,
    As he peers through the spruce at the moon,
Which is risin' up full off across the muskeg,
    Like a mammoth inflated balloon,
"When a feller named Hodgins,—a native back Maine—
    "A bit over-loaded and weary,
"Comes weavin' along with his jug and his jag,
    "A-eyein' the tote-road some bleary.
"He's singin' a song, which he chants mou'nful-like,
    "Regardin' his Slaughter-house Lily;
"A right mou'nful tune, but it seems that it suits,
    "His mood on this drunken occasion,

"For he's rounded it off for the fifty-sixth time
  "When he sees him a sight that's hair-raisin'
"Loomin' up 'fore his eyes, 'twixt the swamp and the moon,
  "And this Hodgins comes near to chokin'
"For the strange things he sees, high over the trees,
  "Is a pacel o' five storks a-flappin',
"And 'twixt them a blanket, in which there's a child,
  "Unusually boisterous and strappin'.
"It's no wonder this Hodgins stands froze in his tracks;
  "Then fixes to light out o' there,
"It bein' they's queer things took place with his knees,
  "And they's somethin' which tugs at his hair,
"But he notes while he gapes, with his eyes bulgin' big,
  "That the storks are a-fixin' to light,
"So hidin' himself in the brush close at hand—
  "Where he's certain to be out o' sight—
"He watches and waits, and it w'ant very long
  " 'Till sure enough, down all kerthud,
"Them storks and their freight comes a-bustin' thru space,
  "And lands in a heap in the mud.
"Well them natal birds, with their wings about broke,
  "And exhausted from strenuous flight,
"Of course are ashamed a great deal by the fact
  "That they've fallen some short of the site
"Where the Bunyans abide in the big timber near,
  "And in council decide that they'll try
"By effort supreme and by will most superb
  "To continue their journey, or die.
"But this infant—this lad—who, you must know, was Paul,
  "From his blanket kicks loose in a hurry,
"And stands up erect and addresses his crew,
  "And, says he, 'My good fellows, don't worry.
" 'I'm able, indeed, and I wish to proceed,
  " 'But a stranger I am in this section,

" 'So give me a guide to walk by my side,
  " 'To show me the proper direction.'
"Quite unusual, unique, and I might say sublime,
  "Was the conduct of Paul this particular time,
"For upon his arrival at Bunyan's abode,
  "He said naught to his ma, but deliberately strode
"To the pantry where victuals piled high on the shelf,
  "Permitted his gettin' a meal for his-self."

9

The Spirit
of
Paul
Bunyan

PAUL, THE BABY AND THE BOY

Esther Shephard:

PAUL'S CRADLE

IF WHAT they say is true Paul Bunyan was born down in Maine. And he must of been a pretty husky baby too, just like you'd expect him to be, from knowin' him afterwards.

When he was only three weeks old he rolled around so much in his sleep that he knocked down four square miles of standin' timber and the goverment got after his folks and told 'em they'd have to move him away.

So then they got some timbers together and made a floatin' cradle for Paul and anchored it off Eastport, but every time Paul rocked in his cradle, if he rocked shoreward, it made such a swell it come near drownin' out all the villages on the coast of Maine, and the waves was so high Nova Scotia come pretty near becomin' an island instead of a peninsula.

And so that wouldn't do, of course, and the goverment got after 'em again and told 'em they'd have to do somethin' about it. They'd have to move him out of there and put him somewheres else, they was told, and so they figgured they'd better take him home again and keep him in the house for a spell.

But it happened Paul was asleep in his cradle when they

went to get him, and they had to send for the British navy and it took seven hours of bombardin' to wake him up. And then when Paul stepped out of his cradle it made such a swell it caused a seventy-five-foot tide in the Bay of Fundy and several villages was swept away and seven of the invincible English warships was sunk to the bottom of the sea.

Well, Paul got out of his cradle then, and that saved Nova Scotia from becomin' an island, but the tides in the Bay of Fundy is just as high as they ever was.

And so I guess the old folks must of had their hands full with him all right. And I ought to say, the king of England sent over and confiscated the timbers in Paul's cradle and built seven new warships to take the place of the ones he'd lost.

When Paul was only seven months old he sawed off the legs from under his dad's bed one night.

The old man noticed when he woke up in the mornin' that his bed seemed considerable lower than it used to be, and so he got up and investigated, and, sure enough, there was the legs all sawed off from under it and the pieces layin' out on the floor.

And then he remembered he'd felt somethin' the night before, but he'd thought he must be dreamin'—the way you do dream that you're fallin' down sometimes when you first go off to sleep.

And he looked around to see who could of done it and there was Paul layin' there sound asleep with his dad's cross-cut saw still held tight in his fist and smilin' in his sleep as pretty as anythin'.

And he called his wife and when she come in he says to her:

"Did you feel anythin' in the night?" he says.

"No," she says. "Is anythin' wrong?"

"Well, just look here," he says. And he showed her the four-by-eights layin' there on the floor and the saw in the kid's hand.

"I didn't light the lamp when I went to get up this mornin'," she says, "and I guess I didn't notice it."

"Well, it's Paul's done it," the old man says. "And I'll bet that boy of ourn is goin' to be a great logger some day. If he lives to grow up he's goin' to do some great loggin' by and by, you just see—a whole lot bigger than any of the men around here has ever done."

And they was right, all right. There ain't never been loggin' before nor since like Paul Bunyan done.

Charles E. Brown:

HIS BOYHOOD

VERY LITTLE romance attaches to Paul's babyhood. Three hours after his birth, as confirmed by several of the old French women present, Paul was a "chunk of a boy" weighing a full eighty pounds. He soon made himself heard in the humble home, his baby voice, "A sort of a cross between a buzz saw and a bass drum," fairly "raised the roof" of the little cottage. The first time he yelled "maa" (in French of course) every lifeboat along the coast for forty miles put to sea thinking that the whole fishing fleets were in distress, and the steeple on the village church turned upside down.

Paul grew so very fast, that, although all of the island women kept their looms working day and night, they could not weave cloth fast enough to keep the child supplied with clothes and blankets. Some of the looms got redhot. It was a problem to get buttons big enough to fasten his garments, but finally the Ladies' Aid Society prevailed upon the men to contribute the wheels of their wheelbarrows.

An old lumber wagon was used as his baby carriage. Because the island roads were narrow, his nurses had to tie his arms down to keep them from knocking down the rail fences and other structures along the highway. His large feet would get over the end of the wagon and tear up the road surface.

This was not the child's fault because his feet were so far from his head that he but seldom, or never saw them. One day a fly settled on his nose. To get rid of it he blew so hard that he completely wrecked several clouds that were floating above.

Paul's christening was a big event. The islanders came from many miles around to attend. Malpeause Bay was the only place along the coast which was big enough for the baptismal ceremony.

He was lowered into the water with a steam crane, but one of the chains broke and the child hit the water with such a great splash that it started a tidal wave on the Bay of Fundy which has not entirely subsided yet.

🌲🌲🌲🌲🌲🌲

Charles E. Brown:

A BIG FEEDER

Even as a child Paul Bunyan was a very heavy feeder. The nurse was given orders to keep count of the amount of food he ate in order to safeguard his health. This girl was poorly educated and could only count up to thirty-two. After that number she lost count and the child ate seventy-four buckets of oatmeal porridge and almost bloated himself. The girl was discharged and Paul's worried mother then invented the card index system now in such general use. After that there was less trouble about his diet.

Charles E. Brown:

SCHOOL DAYS

Pᴀᴜʟ's ғᴏɴᴅ ғᴀᴛʜᴇʀ thought that something ought to be done to give his son an education. He wrote to the Canadian government asking help. All that he received in reply was an autographed photograph of the Governor General and some agricultural pamphlets of small value. He was advised to carry the matter higher up to Queen Victoria but he felt no hope of success and did not carry out the idea. He finally decided to send him to the parish school, but, luckily perhaps for the boy, he contracted a bad case of mumps. He was sick for eleven years, and it took three doctors, an osteopath, twelve chiropractors and a mind-reader to pull him through.

After his recovery he started school in the eighth grade. He carried a tin bucket which his indulgent mother filled with bread, meat and other food. One day he sat down on it, and that authorities say, is the way the hamburger sandwich was invented.

His teachers were always complaining about Paul, and the school board began protesting also. Every time he wrote his name he wore out a lead pencil. As he could not get more than one letter on each page of his copybook his teacher would not let him spell words of more than four letters, except on his birthday. It took a strong ox team to bring his geography to school. He could only study one subject a day in order to keep the schoolyard from being jammed with teams. He was too big to be thrashed when he was unruly.

Paul never did get very much satisfaction out of his schooling. All of the pretty girls were afraid of him, and he seldom got a chance to carry home their books. The boys would not fight him unless he tied his feet at the ankles and his hands behind his back.

⚜⚜⚜⚜⚜⚜

Esther Shephard:

PAUL WRITES FIGGURS

THEY USED to tell how Paul went to school part of a day when he was a kid, back in Maine. His father and mother

got him a slate—cleaved out of a mountain-side in Vermont—
and a pencil imported from Germany that would be big
enough for him, and then they sent him to school to learn
to read, and write, and cipher. The schoolmaster was an old
man whose mother lived to be over a hundred years old.

Well, the first thing the teacher started Paul in on was
to write the figgurs, "1, 2, 3, 4," on his slate, and Paul grabbed
his slate pencil and went to work.

He was tryin' his best to make the curlycues just right, but
the figgurs was so big that all the lines looked straight to
the old man, who couldn't only see but part of 'em at a time.
And so he got mad at Paul, and I don't know what he was
goin' to try to do to him, but anyway Paul picked him up
and threw him in the stove—it was one of them big ones
they used to have in the middle of the room in them old-
time schoolhouses.

And then Paul started for the door. But he tripped on the
stove and knocked it over, and the stove-door come open,
and the old man got out, and took after Paul.

Well, Paul kept a-goin' up the road as hard as he could
leg it with his breath comin' out in puffs like the exhaust of
an ocean liner and freezin' all around him—for it was a cold
November day. He'd left the old schoolmaster miles behind
at the start, but he was goin' so hard he couldn't stop, and
kept right on goin' over hill and down dale, like they say
in the song, till he got pretty near to the Gulf of St.
Lawrence.

Then he stopped, and quit puffin' so hard, but them frost
breaths of his that froze trailin' behind him that cold November day is still hangin' round the Maine coast. Sometimes
they get out to sea and then they're called fog, and they
hang around the big icebergs, and the big ships get lost in
'em and get on the rocks and ice, like the *Titanic* done.

✿✿✿✿✿✿✿

Esther Shephard:

THE YOUNG DAY-BREAKER

AT LOGGIN' he was A-1 right from the start, I guess, for they say he cut his teeth on a peavey and drove logs down the Kennebec in his first pair of pants. He went to work for his uncle up in Ontario when he was still just a kid, and because he was so much quicker and bigger and stronger than any of the men even then, they used to give him several jobs that nobody else in camp could do. One job he had was day-breaker. The cook used to send him up in the Blue Mountains with an ax to break day and Paul was so quick he could always get his job done and get back to camp and call the men to breakfast long before the daylight got there. And another job he had was blowin' the dinnerhorn for the cook. When Paul'd blow, the noise was always so loud the men could ride in out of the woods on the echo.

I ain't never surprised to hear anythin' like that about Paul when he was a kid from them that knowed him then, for I know he must of been a great kid to grow to be the kind of logger he was. And he was a great logger, that's sure —and I guess there ain't nobody pretends there ever was anybody like him.

I remember in the old time when we used to be gettin' out squared timbers for the British trade how Paul used to go out a half mile in the woods and begin squarin' the trees up.

Four cuts was all Paul ever made to a tree—one on each side and it was done. And he'd work a half hour or so, and then when he'd get 'em all standin' like that clean and white, he'd get his ax on the wove grass handle and swing

And another job he had was blowin' the dinnerhorn for the cook.

it around and cut 'em all down, a third of an acre at a time, and hitch the Blue Ox to 'em and snake 'em down to the river, and they'd float away, a raft fourteen miles long of clean, white timbers. Course squared timbers always floats on their edge, and that made it a plaguy hard job to stick on 'em when we had to drive 'em down the river, the way we used to, down the Ottawa in the old time. The British buyers was mighty partikkelar and didn't want 'em marked up with shoe calks nor nothin', but Paul knowed what to do about that all right. What he done was, he just had the calks took out of the men's shoes and put in the timbers instead, and got wooden shoes for the men to wear on the drive, and that way they never got 'em cut up so bad.

I logged for Paul for a good many years, and it was fine loggin' too them old times. Not like it is now. When the trees used to be standin' tall and thick so that the only way you could look was straight up, and all you could see was a little patch of blue right above you, and all you could smell was the smell of the firs and balsam and pine around you, and all you could hear was the squirrels and chickadees, and the scrape of the lumberjacks' saws and the bite of their axes. That was fine loggin'. Not like the measly little stump tracts we got here now to log, with small scraggly trees and lonesome-lookin' burnt trunks standin' around. You can't log in that there kind of country.

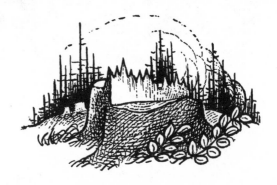

✝✝✝✝✝✝✝

Charles E. Brown:

PAUL'S MUSICAL TALENT

Eᴀʀʟʏ ɪɴ ᴄʜɪʟᴅʜᴏᴏᴅ Paul began to take an interest in lobster factory music. It was very difficult to keep him away from the lobster factories. Here many of the witty sayings of the Island and many of its songs were originated. He became very musical, so his father bought all of the instruments of a German band that went broke in Maine. He had the village blacksmith hammer them all together into a single instrument. While he was doing this a bumblebee and a screech owl flew into one of the big horns and he welded them into the mass. That is how the saxophone came into existence.

Paul liked to go down to the beach to play on his saxophone. By doing this he completely ruined the commerce of the Island. The ships' captains heard his playing and thought it was a foghorn and sailed up the St. Lawrence or went to Halifax instead of landing there. One schooner that got directly in the path of the wind of his horn sailed clear down to the south end of South America before it could stop, even with all of its sails furled and its anchors down. During this swift passage the captain and mates aged twenty years through the fear of sailing over an island or two, or wrecking a Brazilian coffee plantation.

✤✤✤✤✤✤✤

Wallace Wadsworth:

PAUL AS A BOY

PAUL WAS VERY BIG for his age, of course, but he was never clumsy as many big boys are. Once—the first time he ever went hunting—he sneaked his father's old shotgun out of the house and set forth to see what he could find. He kept his sharp eyes wide open, and at last he saw a deer stick its head around a tree four or five miles away. He blazed away at the animal with the old gun, and then was so anxious to see if he had killed it that he started for the spot, lippity-cut. He ran so fast that he outran the load he had fired from the gun, with the result that he got the full charge of buckshot in the seat of his breeches.

So, as one can readily see, his size did not in the least interfere with his spryness. Even when he was an old man, or what would be old for most men, he was so quick on his feet that he could blow out the light in the bunkhouse at night, and be in bed and asleep before the room got dark.

As the years of his boyhood went on he continued to get bigger and stronger and quicker of action, as well as becoming better versed in everything that pertained to the woods. He was learning that he seldom dared to exert his full strength, so powerful was he in every way, for fear of the damage he might do. He was only about fourteen or fifteen years old when he found out that he could kill a whole pond full of bullfrogs just with one yell, and as his voice was getting stronger all the time, he had to watch closely and always speak softly, or else the tremendous sound would stun every one within hearing or perhaps flatten out a few houses.

Thomas G. Alvord, Jr.:

HIS MOTHER HAD TROUBLE
With His Clothes

"Now it's hard to believe," says Wallace D. Steve,
 "That just a mere sprout of a lad,
"When he's hardly turned ten and is less than half-grown,
 "Could be taller a lot than his dad.
"And old Bunyan, his-self, in his moccasin feet,
 "Although he's some stooped and knock-kneed,
"Ain't what you'd call runtish, or stunted a lot,
 "Nor failin' to hold up the breed.
"But it's Paul takes the prize when it comes to physique,
 "For he keeps on a-growin' each way—
"Straight up and straight out, and a lot in between—
 "Until it's not long to the day
"When the old folks at home is plumb pushed out o' bed,
 "And find they must still further yield;
"So they give up the house, and move out where there's
  room,
 "And set up a camp in the field.

"Did I speak of his growin'? Young Paul grew so fast,
 "A-spreadin' out every direction,
"That his ma had to sew in his breeches, each week—
 "After makin' most careful inspection—
"Both gussets and Vs, out of rubber she'd saved
 "From the gum-rubber boots of his daddy,
"And this to allow for the daily increase
 "In the growth of her gigantic laddy.

"And Paul never wore shoes from the day of his birth,
  "Until his splay-feet stopped a-spreadin',
"But in winter wore kegs, with his snow-shoes attached,
  "And socks which were made out o' beddin'.

"As for learnin'—that is, such as comes out o' books—
  "Paul gets but a spare bit of schoolin',
"On account of his bein' so mightiful big
  "That the Board bars him out, through a rulin',
"Prohibits his squeezin' himself into schools,
  "And crowdin' out all other scholars;
"Which rulin' results from parental complaints,
  "And the general disruption which follers,
"So Paul gets his learnin' at home through his ma,
  "Who teaches him figures and verbs,
"And the chemistry taught by Dame Nature herself,
  "Such as values in grasses and herbs.
"His pa lends a hand, and reveals what he knows,
  "Of the stars overhead in the trillions,
"And teaches him how to tell lumber from punk,
  "And figure board feet in the millions.

"Well in due course of time, after years on the farm,
  "Paul naturally feels an ambition,
"To seek out his fortune and further fulfill,
  "As well as he might, life's commission.
"So he makes up his mind that he'll outwardly state,
  "Declare, and at once, his intention,
"To live his own life in a more tasteful way,
  "And this without heed to convention.
"So he speaks to his father, Horatius B.,
  "And his father in lieu of a blessing,
"Is inclined to deliver a boot in the seat,
  "But instead he resorts to a 'dressing.'

"But it's all in good form, and in due course of time,
    "The old man comes around to Paul's views,
"Provides his young son with such gold as he has,
    "Much advice, and his first pair of shoes.
"Says he to young Paul, who was cheerin' his ma
    "With a playful-like smack on the chin,
"That comes near to tippin' her over a cheer
    "And into an open flour-bin,
"Says his father: 'My boy, both myself and your ma
    " 'Are rejoicin' to know you're a man,
" 'But you leave with our hearts a bit heavy today,
    " 'So be sure to come back when you can.
" 'Out yonder I've tied the white bull to the post;
    " 'It's Babe, which you've raised from a calf;
" 'You're to have him, my lad, as companion for life;'
    "And with that the old man had to laugh.

" 'It's grateful I am, and I thank you,' says Paul,
    " 'And if fate will only be kind,
" 'I'll be comin' back soon from the big loggin' woods,
    " 'With me pockets right properly lined.'
"So a-pinnin' his ears back tight to his skull,
    "And slappin' bear's grease in his hair,
"Paul Bunyan starts out with ambition to burn,
    "His big feet a-walkin' on air."

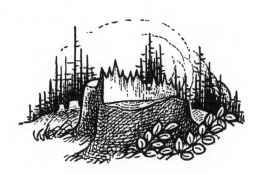

PAUL, THE MAN

Wallace Wadsworth:

THE HIRSUTE BUNYAN

PAUL BUNYAN was of tremendous size and strength, the strongest man that ever swung an ax. He had curly black hair which his loving wife used to comb for him every morning with a great crosscut saw, after first parting it nicely with a broadax, and a big black beard that was as long as it was wide and as wide as it was long. He was rather proud of this beard, and took great care of it. Several times every day he would pull up a young pine tree by the roots and use its stiff branches in combing and brushing it smooth.

De Witt Harry:

THE BIG BLOW

MUCH OF THE EARLY history of Paul Bunyan, hero of all woodsmen, is shrouded in mystery. Who were his parents? Were his manifold talents inherent or were they developed by the hardy woods life? Did he have any advantages when a boy or did he just grow up?

These are but a few of the many questions most frequently

asked about this immortal logger. A letter from an old lumberman, who does not want his name mentioned, may shed some light on Paul's earlier days:

"Paul Bunyan (accent on last syllable) was of French descent and was born on the bank of the Chippewa River, Canada. Quite young he developed traits that have since gained for him notoriety. It is said, when only 9 years of age, he could catch a squirrel on the frame of a barn.

"In the early '50's Battise Doe was rafting logs across the lakes, then down the river. There was great strife among the loggers as to who would get their drive into Quebec first. Sometimes, with adverse winds, they would cross the lakes with the aid of a windlass anchored ahead and turned by the lumberjacks as they joyfully sang their chanty songs.

"Battise Doe was apparently losing in the race and an employee, Joe LaFleur, asked permission to secure the service of Bunyan. Request was granted and young Paul hastened to the raft. Taking a batteau and anchoring it behind Battise Doe's raft, he blew against the raft with such force that it crossed the lake ahead of all rivals, reaching Quebec far in the lead."

🌲🌲🌲🌲🌲🌲

Earl Clifton Beck:

PAUL'S DINNER

I⊤ was in the early part of the year 1860 that I first met the very lovable but much maligned and lied-about character known to every Michigander as Paul Bunyan.

I was chief cook for old Charlie Backus of the Backus Lumber Company doing business on the Au Sable River. The camp was a big one, and the crew was equally big, consisting of 180 big men. When I say big men I mean just that: big men. Not a man of that memorable crew was under 7 feet in height, and none weighed less than 350 pounds.

To get back to my friend, Paul Bunyan. It was in the month of February, 1860. The snow was twenty feet deep, on the level. It was, undoubtedly, the worst winter known in the annals of history. I had just finished peeling 180 bushels of potatoes, a chore which had taken me over an hour. I was at that time the fastest undresser of spuds in the north woods.

I can hear you ask: "Why 180 bushels of potatoes?" Now, I answered that question before you asked it. Didn't I say we had 180 men? Each man's allowance of potatoes was a bushel a day.

As I finished the chore I glanced through the window, and the sight which met my eyes made me gasp. Accustomed as I was to seeing big men, I was totally unprepared for the sight which I saw. What first appeared to be two of our pine trees began moving towards the cook camp door. Hastily grasping the long knife, which I had been using to peel the spuds, in one hand and a huge cleaver in the other, I opened the door and stepped out to meet the giant. Slowly my eyes began to travel upward to the man's head. Never had I seen such a sight. In my amazement I dropped the knife and cleaver. I was positive I was dreaming until I heard a rumbling sound and realized that the man was speaking.

I am not a small man myself, being 6 feet 14 inches and tipping the scale at 333 pounds. But this man . . . well . . . what's the use of trying to explain to you tyros of the woods? You wouldn't believe me anyhow. Still, at the risk of being called a prevaricator, I will endeavor to give you an idea of the size of the real Paul Bunyan, something no other man has been able to give the public without resorting to untruths.

From the soles of his feet to the roots of his hair he split the atmosphere exactly 12 feet 11 inches. His weight, he told me—and I don't doubt his word for a moment—was 888 pounds.

The rest of his body was built in proportion. Around his hips he measured 12 feet 9 inches; waist, 9 feet 11 inches; shoulders, 14 feet 10 inches; thighs, 6 feet 6 inches; calf, 4 feet 7 inches; and his reach, from here to there, 17 feet 11 inches.

But what interested me most was his face. He had the most unusual eyes I ever have seen. The distance between his eyes was 17 inches. They were the size of ordinary saucers. His nose resembled a fresh leg of mutton. When he opened his mouth in one of his prodigious yawns one could have inserted a ten-quart pail.

He had, as I afterwards learned, three distinct voices. One, which he used while speaking inside a room, was well modulated, somewhat resembling a twenty-mile gale of wind. The second voice, which he used while working outside, reminded me of a well-developed thunderstorm. The third voice he used for his swearing and cussing. I will not try to describe this voice for fear of setting fire to my paper. Seven times during my association with Paul Bunyan did I hear him use that third voice; and six of the seven times his hot words set forest fires raging, fires which took five hundred men about a week to extinguish. For that reason all men refrained from antagonizing him.

Strangely, I was not afraid of Paul. His size meant nothing to me. A camp cook feared no man, for the simple reason that all men feared the camp cook. Make no mistakes, my friends. Every lumberjack knew who buttered his bread; therefore, the cook had nothing to fear from any man, big or small. I was supreme in my cook shack.

I invited Paul Bunyan into the cook shack, and he accepted with alacrity. We had fine talks, and he amused me greatly with stories of his exploits and feats of strength. He was very hungry and a wee bit tired, though he would not admit the latter. No true lumberjack ever would admit that he was tired.

During our conversation Paul explained that he had walked from Marquette, a town on Lake Superior which was discovered by a priest of the same name, which sounded to me like a queer coincidence. I often intended asking Paul whether the priest or the town had arrived there first, but the thought escaped me at the proper moment.

But here was Paul, and he was hungry. And was Paul hungry? I'll tell the cockeyed world he was. I had a crew of twenty-two men in the cook shack, and I put them all to work preparing food for our distinguished guest. To this day you probably will hear some old woods cook tell how he was there when I fed Paul Bunyan his first meal in the Lower Peninsula. But pay no heed to such tales. All of my helpers are dead, have been for forty years. I am the lone survivor of that eventful day; so you will have to take my word for the menu that was served to Paul.

We worked for three hours to prepare the meal. It consisted of 33 pounds of beef, 1 whole venison, 2 bushels of fried potatoes, 12 loaves of bread each weighing 4 pounds, 7 gallons of coffee, 6 hams, 12 dozen eggs, 678 pancakes made with exactly 1 barrel of buckwheat flour, topped off with 6 gallons of pure maple syrup. Paul Bunyan was hungry.

He stayed with us for three months. I was sorry to see the big feller go when he made up his mind to leave us. I could write all night on some of the great things which our camp accomplished while he was in our midst; but I fear you would not appreciate the tales I could tell. And to be quite frank with you, I am afraid you would not believe me if I did tell you.

Don't make the mistake that many readers of Paul Bunyan tales have made. Most of the stuff and nonsense which has been written about him have been deliberate lies. What I write is authentic and truthful, as I am the only man living who knew Paul.

❦❦❦❦❦❦❦

James Cloyd Bowman:

PAUL'S AX

THERE WAS ONE thing about Paul Bunyan that everybody admired. He no sooner thought of a thing than he immediately set about doing it.

"Now that I know I'm going to be a famous lumberjack, I've got to invent some tools to suit me. These axes I've been using are a nuisance because I never dare swing them for a hard blow. When I do want to try my strength, the handle flies into splinters as fine as match-wood, and then the axes themselves are so very small. What I need is an ax that will slash off twenty trees at a single stroke." As quick as a flash, he threw a dozen of the largest pine-trees into his fireplace. Then he took the seventy-seven axes that he had been using, and threw all of them, with their broken handles, into the midst of the intense heat. Soon he had hammered out an ax that was an ax. Its cutting edge measured fifteen feet across.

But where was he to get a suitable handle or helve for this new ax? Suddenly he remembered, and went bounding from his shanty, across the fast-disappearing snow. He had seen an enormous ironwood tree when he was out one day gathering moss for Babe. In his excitement he bounded off like a snow-shoe rabbit pursued by a timber-wolf.

He grabbed hold of the tree, close to the ground, and with a single twist uprooted it. As he galloped back to his shanty, he slashed off the roots and the limbs with his great jack-knife. Next day he had made the largest ax-helve that had ever been known. It measured forty-seven feet and seventeen inches, and weighed nearly a ton.

"Now—by the bull-moose call!—I'll go out and see what I can do. By the jumping Jehoshaphat! the trees that get into my way had better be careful!"

How proudly he walked with the great ax across his swaying shoulder! When he came to the thickest spot in the forest, he stopped and gave the ax a mighty swing. He whacked off thirty-one trees as if they had been stalks of wheat before the swinging cradle.

The calamity was that the ax-helve snapped in two, and the ax itself flew half a mile through the forest without ever striking another tree. As the trees crashed to the ground, Paul let out a roar of mingled delight and disgust.

"Ha! you can't beat me!" he shouted. "I know where the largest and toughest hickory trees grow this side of Kingdom Come."

But the hickory handle was no better. At the first mighty stroke, it shivered into a thousand splinters, at which Paul was much disappointed. He was so disappointed, in fact, that he could say nothing. Instead, he put his chin in his hand and thought hard for a whole half-day.

At last his face suddenly relaxed, and the dimple in his left cheek quivered with joy. Paul laughed an enormous laugh that shook the trees for miles.

"I have it at last—by the leaping buck deer!—and there's no doubt about it. There is a tall grass that grows in the swamp behind the crest of Hog Back Mountain. It's three times as tough as rubber and twice as strong as tempered steel. Don't I know, for didn't I get my left moccasin tangled in it one day when I was out gathering moss for Babe, and didn't it take me half a day to pull myself loose? By gravy! that'll make me an ax-helve!"

Immediately Paul was off on the jump, and next day he had woven a flexible handle fifty-one feet long and two feet and a half through, on the end of which were two hand-holds.

After practicing for a day and two nights outside his shanty, Paul finally learned how to swing the ax with the flexible handle. He swung the ax two or three times above his head to get it in motion, and then with a mighty swirl of his body, threw it like a flash of lightning into the trees. When, years later, an athletic coach from Harvard College happened to stray into the woods, he saw Paul still swinging his ax. And so this may be considered the invention of the method which is still used in the hammer-throw at a track meet.

☨☨☨☨☨☨

Dell J. McCormick:

ELMER AND THE PHANTOM FOX

The summer Paul had his camp on Tadpole Creek the cooks complained of the shortage of fresh eggs, so Paul went to work and built the largest chicken coop in the world and stocked it with eight thousand chickens. The chickens worked in three shifts, the last shift finding the nests by the aid of kerosene lamps.

Some idea of the size of this chicken coop can be gathered from a story Shot Gunderson tells of the painter who painted the roof. It seems Paul told this man to paint the roof white and make a good job of it no matter how long it took. So he

. . . he had woven a flexible handle. . . .

went up with his ladders, and nothing more was heard of him for several years.

Johnnie Inkslinger counted the chickens every morning, and one day he found three or four missing. He talked it over with Paul Bunyan, and they decided to place a guard around the chicken coop at night and find out who was stealing the chickens. Around midnight the men on guard heard a noise and rushed inside, expecting to catch Sourdough Sam red handed. Instead they caught a glimpse of a small red fox leaping nimbly through the window with a plump chicken in its mouth.

The whole camp was aroused and plans made to capture the fox. Ole suggested they spread a path of flour all around the outside of the camp the next night. In that way, if the fox returned, he would leave his footprints in the flour and they could trace him to his lair. The following night four more chickens were missing. But the strangest thing of all was that there were no footprints in the flour! The fox had not gone into the woods at all. He was still in the camp!

There was a wild scramble to look under flour bins, in wood piles and under bunkhouses, but no trace of the Phantom Fox could be found.

Suddenly Johnnie Inkslinger had a brilliant idea.

"Let's get Elmer the Moose Hound to track him to his hiding place!" he said.

Everybody thought that was a good idea, for Elmer had the keenest nose of any dog in the North Woods. He could track a fox even if the fox wore overshoes and walked backwards, as foxes sometimes do. Elmer would just sniff the ground and know exactly where the fox lived and who his father was and what he had had for breakfast the last three days.

Sourdough Sam said he remembered the day he took an apple out of the apple bin and started peeling it. Elmer, who was at the other end of camp five miles away, lifted his nose in the air and sniffed. In five minutes he was sitting happily outside the cook shanty door licking his chops, for he was very fond of apple pie. Another time Elmer was tracking a weasel, and the weasel jumped into Tadpole Creek and waded half a mile downstream to throw Elmer off the scent. Then he swam five miles upstream and came out on the opposite side of the creek—and there was Elmer sitting on his haunches waiting for him!

With a great crowd of loggers at his heels Elmer was taken over to the chicken coop. Excitement ran high, and many bets were made as to how long it would take Elmer to find the fox. It was going to be a big day for Elmer and his educated nose! But something seemed to be wrong. After sniffing around a bit he sort of gave up and quietly trotted back to Paul. They took him back to the chicken coop again and again. They showed him the window the fox jumped through. They pointed to the tracks outside. But Elmer didn't seem to be paying much attention. After a casual sniff or two he went back to Paul and refused to have anything more to do with the hunt. It was all very sad. They tried to reason with him but he just sat there looking at Paul with his great sad eyes. Everybody decided that as a fox hunter Elmer was not worth his board and keep.

Paul called a meeting, and they all sat down to discuss the matter. Everybody had a theory, and one after another they talked and talked. It was pretty hot and Paul got tired of listening to them argue, so he lay down and soon fell asleep. On and on talked the fox hunters. The Phantom Fox was some place in camp, but no one knew where.

Brimstone Bill stood looking quietly at Elmer. Suddenly he found the answer.

"I got it! I got it! Elmer was right all along. We just didn't understand what he was trying to tell us."

Without waiting to explain he armed three or four men with rakes and clubs and told them to follow him. A ladder was placed against Paul's chest as he lay peacefully sleeping on the ground. Up climbed Brimstone Bill until he was standing knee-deep in Paul's beard.

Soon the men spread out and began beating around and poking through the heavy beard with their clubs and rakes. In less time than it takes to tell they flushed out a bevy of quail and three small chipmunks! Then suddenly a badger appeared, surly and peevish. He had built himself a nice nest in the beard and expected to stay there the rest of the summer. Up near Paul's left ear a family of small rabbits were driven from cover and went bounding off through the woods. Two raccoons scurried by as the men prowled around in the dense undergrowth of the heavy black beard.

Suddenly Brimstone Bill heard a faint rustling in the depth of the beard right under Paul's chin. He motioned to the men to gather around him. Carefully they went ahead. Sure enough, there was the Phantom Fox hiding at the very bottom where he had thought he would be forever safe from prowling eyes.

By the time Paul woke up the fox was caught and tightly tied and thrown in a cage where he would never again have a chance to steal chickens.

Elmer the Moose Hound was the hero of the camp! Wasn't he the one who had led the men straight to the spot where the Phantom Fox was hiding? It was lucky, of course, that Brimstone Bill had thought of looking through Paul's beard. Otherwise they would never have found him.

Paul admitted he had been very careless lately about combing his beard and that this would be a lesson to him. Every morning after that he would take a large jack pine and carefully comb his beard as Elmer the faithful Moose Hound sat happily beside him.

James Stevens:

THE MIGHTY FISHERMAN

"THERE IS NO such fishin' nowadays as men knew in the long ago time of Paul Bunyan and Babe the Blue Ox." So speaks Larrity, the old logger, to the boy by the pinewoods campfire. "It was for the fishin', indeed, that little men first came over to America—the wee men they were, not one of them more than 11 feet tall, or toe-high to Paul Bunyan.

"Never was a land so friendly to fishermen. Even the worms of the place were hospitable and kind. In the mulberry groves they not only spun silk but wove it into the finest lines. In the earth there were hookworms of all sizes, so strong they'd hold the toughest trout, and every sod was a nest of bait. The great ants of the valley swarmed to serve the fishermen. They put on aprons and washed the dishes and swept out the camp when the fishin' day was done. Then, at eventide, came the mosquitoes, never to bite at all, but only to hum lullaby songs, singin' the happy, happy fishermen to sleep.

"The trout of Paradise River, like the fish of the sea, swam in great schools. Each school had for itself a prime scout whose job it was to look for fishermen along the riverbanks. These scouts were eels. Up and down the river an eel would waggle along, ever and again h'istin' his snout high from the water and oglin' about. When he sighted a fisherman, off the eel would streak to his trout school with the glad news: then all would tear back after him, in a great rush to beat the rival schools of the river.

"Bulldog the trout of Paradise River were called, for once one of them had taken a bite, he'd never let go. When a school of them rushed a fisherman's hook, it was both a race and a fight to get first to the bait. And when one would grab it and hang on like grim death, would the others turn tail and go off in corners to sulk? Indeed they would not. They never quit. A second trout would grab the tail of the one on the hook, a third would grab his tail, and so on, till always a fisherman would reel in at the least 17 trout for every cast.

"The boss of all the river fish was a lone trout so big that he was truly a fresh-water whale. The great Paul Bunyan fished for him alone. When he caught the boss at last the mighty woodsman made a pet of the mighty fish. Each day he would take the boss trout from the water, for a longer time each day, till finally the great fish lived always on land. But Babe the Blue Ox got jealous of him. One time Paul and the boss trout was on the riverbank; the fish was settin' up on his hind fins, and Paul ticklin' his ears; and the jealous ox charged, he did, and butted the boss trout into the deep river. So used to the land, the poor fish drowned to his death."

🌲🌲🌲🌲🌲🌲🌲

Wallace Wadsworth:

PAUL WAS A WHITE WATER MAN

IN ADDITION to the stories of his great logging feats in Maine, there are also several interesting things told about Paul Bunyan at this time which are conducive to a clearer understanding of his exceptional powers and show his remarkable ability for doing big things in a big way. For instance, he could ride logs through water which ran so fast that it would tear in two any ordinary man who might try to drink of it. It is said of him also that he was the greatest log-roller that ever wore calked boots.

A favorite lumberjack sport is rolling a log. A man stands on a big log afloat in the water and starts turning it with his feet, keeping his feet going so that he is always on top and standing safely upright, no matter how fast he gets the log to whirling under him. Paul Bunyan could roll a log so fast that it made foam on the water solid enough for him to walk ashore on, and he is known to have crossed wide rivers in this way. Not all of this foam which he thus caused has disappeared to this day, and occasionally small bits of it may still be seen floating down many streams after a heavy rain.

As a white-water man, though, probably the greatest and hardest task which Paul ever had was when he poled a big raft of logs upstream over Niagara Falls. He came very near losing out several times on that adventure, but he stuck to it as only he could do and eventually succeeded, as usual, in finishing what he had started. He was nearly fagged out, however, for a few minutes afterwards.

Along with his hard work, the great logger enjoyed a little sport now and then. Best of all, he liked to hunt, and no one has ever equaled him as a hunter.

Once, when Paul was out hunting, he spotted a deer five miles or so away, sticking its head over a fallen tree, and taking careful aim with his trusty rifle, he fired at it. The deer disappeared, but to his great surprise, a second later it again stuck its head into view. "My aim must be getting poor," grumbled Paul as he rubbed his eyes, and then he let drive at the animal again. To his even greater astonishment, the deer's head had no more than dropped out of sight from his second shot than it lifted up in the same place again. The exasperated hunter kept on firing, and each time the strange performance was repeated the deer bobbed up into view again after each shot. He had only twenty-eight cartridges, and he fired them all. It was not until he had used his last one that the deer's head went down and stayed out of sight.

"Well, I got him at last, but that was certainly poor shooting," Paul muttered sadly to himself as he walked ahead to pick up the carcass of the animal. He was feeling very badly over his poor marksmanship, as was quite natural, since he was always before able to hit whatever he aimed at, no matter how poor the shooting conditions were. One can imagine how surprised he was, and how reassured, when he looked behind the fallen tree and found twenty-eight dead deer there, every one with a bullet hole exactly between the eyes. The whole herd had taken turns at peeping over the deadfall and Paul had thought that it was the same animal reappearing each time. When he got back to camp, he sent the Little Chore Boy out to bring in the game—which he was able to do in one load—and that evening for supper the crew enjoyed a feast of fresh venison. The remarkable thing about the whole proceeding is that the number of cartridges which Paul had with him should have so exactly coincided with the number of deer in the herd.

🌲🌲🌲🌲🌲🌲

Harold W. Felton:

THE ATHLETE

Paul was the hero and the friend
 Of all the lumber jacks.
They came for miles to see him use
 His homemade, two-edged ax.

Paul Bunyan could roll a log so fast that it made foam on the water solid enough for him to walk ashore on. . . .

For thus equipped, he cut a tree
    With one great powerful smack;
And with no loss of energy,
    Another coming back.

And sometimes, after work, the men
    Would sit around on stumps
And watch him cross a river, which
    He did in three short jumps.

The world's greatest lumberjack
    Would sometimes play a prank,
And jump across, and then jump back
    And not touch either bank.

And fast, the man was speed itself!
    Why he could just about
Blow out the lamp and jump in bed
    Before the light went out.

To go as fast as he could go
    Would have been most unkind.
For if he had, he would have left
    His shadow far behind.

🌲🌲🌲🌲🌲🌲🌲

De Witt Harry:

THE WORLD'S CHAMPION FALLER

HAVING WORKED with Paul Bunyan on some of his biggest jobs, it gets under my skin to read some of the atrocious suggestions that have been written about him of late. Any one with half an eye can see that they are absolutely impossible. Back in 1820 I was with him when he wrecked the Bridge of the Gods, because it had been condemned as a menace to river traffic.

The biggest job I ever saw him do, though, was in a contest with an Irish woods boss from one of the southern pine camps. This Irishman had worked up a local reputation and thought he was riding astride the world until he sent a challenge to Paul stating that he was the better faller of the two and demanding a match. They decided to meet in the redwoods. Thousands flocked there to see these two supermen.

The referee picked out two big redwoods, each 34 feet in diameter and 240 feet high, and the men took their places. The starter's pistol popped and before the echo died away Paul had burned out three saws and flattened the edges of five axes putting in his undercut. Grabbing a new 40-foot saw he started cutting her down. So fast did he saw that it took 17 men to keep him supplied with saws, and there was a stream of melted steel pouring out of the saw cut. As fast as one melted Paul put in a new one. He perspired so much that the spectators had to take to the trees to keep dry, and finally when the tree cracked the sweat was so deep that Paul was treading water and sawing.

Well, when that tree leaned to an angle of 65 degrees Paul grabbed a bucking saw and ran up it 20 feet and bucked a log, then another 20 feet, and by the time the tree was down it was all bucked up into 20 foot logs, and Paul had done a swan dive from the last one 80 feet in the air. They looked around and were surprised to see the Irishman's tree still standing with a cut about 20 feet deep in it, and him missing. However, he had written on a paper the following: "As a logger I'm good bull cook."

James Stevens:

BULL OF THE WOODS

Wʜᴇɴ ɪɴ ᴀ playful humor Paul would frolic with two-ton boulders, tossing them one at a time with his left hand, then pulverizing them into powder as he batted with his right fist. Paul pulled stumps with his teeth when he felt like it.

And that wasn't all. Paul Bunyan not only had hair on his chest but he owned kindness in his heart. In the first place he invented logging mainly for the sake of his Blue Ox, Babe, who measured forty-two ax handles and a pair of peaveys between the horns and was born for log skidding. Babe could pull anything that had two ends, except Paul Bunyan. Paul could never be pulled at all, and he could be pushed just so far.

Hels Helson, the Big Swede, was Paul's foreman. Hels himself was a mighty man. His boots were so big that jackpines were always being snagged into their tops and worked down to his toes, where they tickled him silly. Hels also had a great head. He kept his hair clipped short, and the Blue Ox often mistook his head for a bale of hay. So Hels Helson was forever suffering from ox bites.

The camp timekeeper was Johnny Inkslinger. He was nearly the size of the Big Swede, but not so bully. Johnny also served as camp doctor and was famous for his pills as well as his figures. He swung a razor to shave the spots off Paul's men when they had the measles, and he was such a mighty man with ink that he used a gallon every time he made a figure 8.

A host of regular little men was used by Paul Bunyan for choppers, swampers, peavey men and river drivers. These jacks were bugs beside Paul and Babe, Johnny and Hels. Not a man among them measured more than three feet from hock to kneecap. But they were strong and willing. They got out the logs.

Hels Helson got wind of the North Pole one summer and took a trip over the ice to take it for a pikepole. But Paul Bunyan had been there first. The Big Swede followed the trail and finally fought Paul for possession of the North Pole. In the earth-shaking combat Paul made slivers of the famous pole in a vain attempt to drive a dent in Hels Helson's head. Paul eventually won, of course, but the trophy of victory was beyond repair. So woodsmen scoff when they hear of explorers searching for the North Pole.

"They've got to find Paul Bunyan first," the woodsmen solemnly declare.

Johnny Inkslinger, the great figurer, invaded America to stake it out for the King of Europe, according to one story. Paul won him to his side by offering Johnny a timekeeping job and presenting him with a pen fed by hose lines from thirty-seven barrels of ink. Johnny Inkslinger became the foremost patriot of the camp, and the bards unite in crediting him with the invention of the "Fourther July" and all other American holidays.

Babe the Blue Ox was never a mere beast of burden. His main job was log skidding, of course, but Babe had many other responsibilities and chores. At night he was the watch ox of the camp. When danger drew nigh Babe's warning moo would roll through the shanties with such force that every 'jack would be heaved high from his bunk, turned over four times, dropped back, and then have his blankets tucked neatly about him again. A yell from Hels Helson would sometimes lift men and turn them over, but only Babe's moo had the power to tuck blankets. Whenever Paul went out gunning for game to give the shanty boys a rare Sunday dinner Babe would trot along as a hunting ox. When he froze to a point the temperature would drop to zero for a mile around, even in a blazing summer day. Babe was useful to Paul in a hundred other ways. His main trouble was his omnivorous appetite. Babe would eat anything he could swallow, and he had a gullet like a mammoth cave. Once a Fourther July celebration was ruined when Babe broke loose in the night before and devoured the cannonballs and black powder stacked for the morrow's uproar. He might have digested them peacefully, had it not been for the fireweeds in his hay at this time. They set off the powder in his stomach, and Babe belched cannonballs for three days and nights.

Many mighty timber beasts haunted the timberlands in the time of Paul Bunyan. Some were naturally enemies to the bull of the woods. Chief among this grim group was the pine-eating hodag, a beast with saw teeth, ax prong horns, a bark hide and calks in its paws. The hodags ravaged the timber, preying on all varieties, and making many regions unfit for logging. There was endless war between the hodags of the hills and the saugers of the swamps. At last these two tribes of timber beasts exterminated each other, to the prodigious relief of Paul Bunyan.

The swamp sauger was the dismalest animal on earth. When he emerged from the depths of his home to hunt conks or to engage in battle with a hodag, the sauger put a spell on all life in the forest with the dismalness of his croak and the drip of scummy swamp water from his cypress hair. Every creature simply wanted to lie down and die when hearing the sauger in a wet, weird night. So the saugers would bewitch the hodags and put an end to them. Their trouble was that they had to go too far from the swamps on a hodag hunt. Saugers were the bulkiest of beasts. When they stayed out in the night air too long they were apt to catch chest colds. A sauger's chest was so tremendous that a cold in it was certain to make him cough himself to death. So, even as he put a dismal spell on the last hodag, the lone survivor of the saugers coughed himself into a violent end. As the last hack shook the woods Paul Bunyan thanked his stars.

· The atmosphere of myth envelops many of Paul Bunyan's little men, his shanty boys, in the old stories. There was a prize crew of choppers famously known as the Seven Axmen. They were bigger than the average. In the Spring of the Mud Rain the chief of the crew broke a leg three feet below the knee. Each of the Seven scorned common hickory ax handles. They used rope handles and twirled the blades until they flashed like the teeth of circular saws. Three circles, and an axman would slash through the toughest tree. The Seven never paused for lunch. After a breakfast each axman took a huge, specially prepared flapjack, chopped a hole in the center, pulled the flapjack over his head so that it would rest like a ruff around his neck; and at noontime he would continue to chop, merely heaving his shoulders to keep the great cake moving in a circle, and so munch it down to the rim. That was one of Paul's shrewdest inventions. No industrialist has ever equaled him in saving the golden minutes.

Paul Bunyan's wars with the weather were always accorded solemn attention by the camboose circle. In the Michigan woods weather was of prime importance to those who lived by logging. A perfect round of seasons called for a moist summer, a dry, frosty autumn, a winter of snow which would keep the skid trails packed until deep in March, and a cool, rainless spring. But the weather of course seldom met these requirements. Most autumns were wet, and roads had to be built over bogs. Often a lack of snow would make heavy skidding from the woods to the banking grounds impossible, and logs would be left to the heat and worms of summer. Slack water usually hampered the spring drives.

Naturally the bards made a deep-dyed villain out of the weather of Paul Bunyan's time. Then it showed itself to be a rabid enemy of all woodsmen. It scrambled its seasons without rhyme or reason. There was the Year of the One Month, for example. Then spring came one week, summer the next, autumn in the third, and the last week of the month was frozen solid in winter's grip. One Further July the weather heaved all four seasons down at once, and every man 'jack in camp was smitten with sunstroke, chilblains and spring fever at the same instant. But that time the weather overreached itself. Autumn took a solid hold on the timber country and forced the other three seasons out. So Paul and his men had fine cool days all July and August instead of blazing ones, and the weather was foiled.

Numberless wicked seasons followed the mild and beautiful Winter of the Blue Snow, until the Spring Rain Came Up from China. The Year of the Twin Winters was characteristic of the weather's malicious deviltry against Paul Bunyan. Two winters came at once that year, and each one alone would have been nearly the hardest ever heard of. Two such winters at once were well-nigh intolerable. That was the time the boiling tea froze in the shanties and the 'jacks were all scalded by hot ice. Ax blades freeze to anything frosty in winter weather, and in that terrible season they would freeze in an instant to the frosty air. Let a chopper rest an ax for a second on his shoulder, and there it would stick until his mates came running up, swinging their own axes to chop the frozen air from his blade and free it. In the Year of the Twin Winters Babe's moos froze solidly as soon as he emitted them. Whenever Hels Helson bumped into a frozen moo he would pocket it. When the first spring thaw blazed down the moos melted, and Hels was scared witless as a chorus of moos bellowed from his hip pockets. He thought an ox ghost was haunting him.

The Spring of the Mud Rain was another characteristic attack by the weather on Paul Bunyan. Just when he was ready to make a spring drive the weather rolled up black cloud packs and the mud began to fall in sheets. In a day and night the creeks and the big river were oozing along in a muddy flow which promised to founder any logs that Paul might roll into them. At that time there were fresh water whales in the Great Lakes, and Paul broke a huge herd to the bridle and packsaddle. The leviathans heaved through the mud with little trouble. Paul piled his logs on them, and the whales took the drive down in fine style. The weather had used up all its energy in making a mud rain, and for a long time Paul Bunyan and his men enjoyed mild seasons.

The weather made charge after charge on Paul before his logging days were done, and all were repulsed. The rain that popped up from China occurred after the weather had been weakened into its present state. Timber country weather is not blamed for that reverse rain. The authorities pronounce it a plain freak of nature.

The most celebrated rivers of Paul Bunyan's time were the Big Auger and the Big Onion. Their tributaries were the Little Gimlet and the Little Garlic. Each valley was the scene of a mammoth logging operation by Paul and was the site of a great headquarters camp. The two prime rivers served as models for the camboose bards when a story of log driving was in order.

As its name implies, the Big Auger flowed like a giant turning screw. Deep grooves in the river's hard-rock bed steadily maintained its spiral flow. In the spring freshets the Big Auger would deepen its turning grooves, and a ridge of hard-rock shavings rose high above each bank. Only screw-fish could live in this powerful river, and it successfully resisted many attempts to drive logs down its course. Once Paul Bunyan dammed the river and tried to tame it down. The Big Auger bored through to freedom in a night. At last Paul invented his great river-drag, which was simply the logs from a season of chopping stacked and bound into a log mountain. Babe the Blue Ox was hitched to it and hauled the mountain down the Big Auger, flattening the stream into a smooth ribbon of a river. It was the one spring in which the bull of the woods made a log drag instead of a log drive, thus throwing his 'jacks out of work. But he had to do it to tame the Big Auger.

The Big Onion flowed in a seemly style; in fact it was too sluggish and slow to give Paul's white-water buckos much excitement. It saddened them up, however, until all the drives were jammed. The trees of this valley were onion pines. The bush was garlic scrub. All the brooks and creeks ran with water that had only to be dipped and boiled and salted to make onion soup. Paul's 'jacks were as strong for onions as onions were strong for them, but this was too much of a good thing. More strong men shed tears on the Big Onion drive than at any other time of history. That was the great trouble. As the spring sun blazed down, powerful fumes would rise from the Big Onion, and in no time the 'jacks were blinded by their tears and had to leave the logs. Paul Bunyan beat the river by straining it above the jam. There he packed the fragrant stream with moss for seven miles. The moss absorbed all onion matter as the river oozed on, and soon a crystal stream was gushing through the logs. The 'jacks blew their noses and dried their tears, pried the jam apart, and the drive went down.

"The like of the rivers of Paul Bunyan's time has never been seen since, either on lands or sea," say the old lumberjacks.

There was the Big Rubber, a river ten miles long and ninety miles wide. Paul managed to stretch that stream into a river five feet wide, which permitted him to keep the limber pines in line as he drove them down. His great trouble this trip was when the overstretched river snapped apart in the middle of the drive, leaving the logs low and dry. Paul had to work all summer stretching the snapped halves of Big Rubber River together again and patching them up. A forest fire helped him a lot. It melted the upper half down just as Paul had all the stretch worked out of the lower one. That year he did not make a drive until autumn, but he made it.

Round River was a famous Bunyan stream, flowing in a continuous circle. The only trouble with the Round was that it would take a log drive nowhere. But that did not bother Paul Bunyan much. His purpose was to make the drives, and if they got nowhere it made little difference. Paul Bunyan had one aim in logging.

"I aim to please," the bull of the woods always answered when some busybody would ask him what his aim in logging was.

Wherever a river flows in the woods any old-timer who happens to be around will tell what a strange and wonderful river it was before Paul Bunyan tamed it down. He never missed a one. Logging was his business, and river taming his specialty.

The limber timber of the Big Rubber country was a characteristic kind. In that land they were self-chopping pines. When an axman set himself for chopping, he only had to take care that he was in a position to pivot in a half circle. For the resilient fibers of a pine would give before the cutting blade of a chopper's ax, then violently snap back into place. The force of the snap would hurl the ax blade out. Keeping a stout grip on the handle, the chopper would let the blade blaze around to the other side of the tree, while he pivoted on his toes. Again the limber pine would send the blade flying. Soon the chopper would have his ax going like a shuttle in its half circle. All he had to do was to hang on like grim death. So all the pines of Big Rubber Valley chopped themselves down.

The Seven Axmen first adopted rope ax handles in place of conventional hickory while felling onion pines. Every ax blow made the powerful sap of these trees spurt seven ways. A chopper working near one would soon be blinded, or else the tears would pour with such force that mud puddles would form about his boots and bog him down. The Seven Axmen were gruff and grim, entirely without sentiment, so they shook their tears off like showers. But not a one of them liked to work in mud. So at last Paul rigged up long rope ax handles for them; and then a chopper could stand seventy feet from an onion pine and fell it by making casts with his ax. They shed no tears now.

The layer and the tower pines were of the same species, but they grew in dissimilar fashion. The former grew in groups of nine. All of the pines were horizontal. The bottom boughs of the first one had root systems which were anchored in the earth. Its top boughs joined the lower ones of the second pine, and so on up to the ninth, which was the only tree of a group to wave green boughs in the air. The tower pines grew in groups of five. The largest tree of a group was rooted in the ground like a pine of our own time, but its crown held the roots of the second tree, and so on to the top pine. Paul preferred the tower pines to all others, as a chopper could fell five at a shot. The layer pines took too much trimming.

The pacing pines were roving trees. Each pine had four powerful jointed roots which it could unearth at will, and then pace off to any part of the timberland. When Paul started to log the pacing pine country he saw how lucky he was that his Seven Axmen had become rope experts. When the pines tried to pace away from the choppers the mighty Seven easily roped the roots and brought the pines down for log-making.

✝✝✝✝✝✝✝

James Stevens:

THE GREAT HUNTER
of the Woods

"I WAS THINKIN' of the most famous hunt of history," said old Larrity the bull cook. "That was when Paul Bunyan, the first great hunter of the woods, shouldered his scatter-cannon to bring down the wing-tailed turkey that had ravaged the Round River country of its game. A terrible turkey that was indade, for even such hunters as Paul Bunyan and Dublin, the wire-haired terror who was tall as any tree. Such huntin' there was in that time long ago, a time too far away for even mention in the history books."

The old logger stopped there for a shrewd glance at the two by his side. They were Jeff Gavin, whose grandfather was the owner of the logging camp, and Mike, the boy's wire-haired terrier pup. Both were staring mournfully at the flaming leaves of dogwood thickets up the creek. There three men in red caps and brown coats with big spotted dogs sniffing and scampering at their heels, had vanished a few moments before.

"Whist, now, and you should be glad your grandpa left you with me. Pheasants they will be shootin'," said Larrity scornfully. "And the huntin' of chickens is too triflin' for the bother of old woodsmen like us, so it is. How much better,

Jeff, to sun ourselves here on the creek bank and talk of the days of real huntin'."

Curiosity lightened the boy's eyes. On other Saturday afternoons he had listened to stories of Paul Bunyan from old Larrity, who had learned them many years ago in the faraway Michigan woods. Here in the Oregon timber the stories would come to life. The Gavin grandson forgot his grief at being left in camp by the hunters. Mike, the terrier pup, also seemed resigned, as he stretched himself out in the rusty grass of the creek bank, crossed his paws, rested his chin on them and shut his eyes.

Old Larrity was telling of the great hunter of the woods. As his voice drawled on, the boy saw a mighty figure rising dimly among the shadows of the trees. . . . Paul Bunyan, whose curly black beard brushed the tree tops . . . and at his heels trotted Dublin, wire-haired terror of the hunting trails. . . .

On the first day of a certain Christmas week (said old Larrity) the great hunter of the woods and his dog, Dublin, marched into the Round River country. This was the game country in the time when Ameriky was all one big timberland, and Paul Bunyan was the ruler of it and all the rest. In the black wild woods circled by Round River the famous logger always did his Christmas huntin'. That was only to provide rare holiday dinners for his seven hun'erd bully men. This huntin' season the reg'lar game was ruined. And all because the terrible turkey, the most ferocious fowl of the tall timber, had at last migrated to Round River from the mountains of the North.

Paul Bunyan had no hint of the trouble and grief ahead as he tramped through the autumn woods for Round River. He saw nothin' but a promise of cheer in the keen, bright mornin'. Above him shone the clean blue sky and about him blazed the fire colors of leaves. The frost made his breath steam till white clouds trailed him. Sunlight glinted from the forty-seven barrels of his scatter-cannon. At his heels the tremendous terror was a gay dog, ever waggin' his tree of a tail.

For Paul Bunyan talked to Dublin, even as you talk to your Mike when the two of you walk together. It was all gladness in the mighty voice, for Paul Bunyan spoke of the men in the camp behind. Of Johnny Inkslinger Paul spoke, that timekeeper who was such a big figger that his pens were made of peeled trees. He had kind words also for the Big Swede, his foreman, and a man with legs so much like sawlogs that the reg'lar sized loggers were forever goin' after them with crosscuts and axes. Paul Bunyan spoke fondly to Dublin of Babe the Blue Ox, a beast that was even bigger than the dog, measurin' forty-two ax handles and a barrel of pickles betwixt the horns.

Of all these big figgers Paul Bunyan spoke kindly and well, but his best words were for his seven hun'erd men, who were no bigger than me or your grandfather. Never had his men done such fine loggin' as in this season. And for a reward they should have the grandest Christmas dinner ever heard of at all.

"What game shall it be for such a dinner?" said Paul Bunyan to Dublin, when they were to the bank of Round River. "The best meat will be none too good for my loggers' Christmas dinner, no sir! Should we bag some fat bucks for rabbit stews, Dublin? Or deer, to make a great steak dinner? Or cinnamon bears for the spicy roasts the loggers like so well? What do you say, you wire-haired terror, you?"

Dublin acted for all the world like he understood every one of Paul Bunyan's words. He sat down, and slowly scratched his ear with his left foot, seemin' to be in the deepest thought.

"I know what you want to be huntin', first, last and all the time, Dublin, I do." Paul Bunyan smiled down through his beard. "Yes, sir, mince-hunter that you are. You would have us go back with nothin' but mince meat for the Christmas pies, you would. But we must hunt other game than minces."

Sayin' that, he leaned restfully on his scatter-cannon and gazed into the black wild woods across the river. Now he began to notice that they were silent, almost. Every other autumn the woods had been roarin' with sounds of wild life. The game of the country had never migrated beyond the river that circled their home.

We would think such a stream as Round River most peculiar nowadays, but sure, in the time of Paul Bunyan rivers were young and wild, and each one would run to suit itself. It suited this river to run always in a circle, bein' too proud, no doubt, to run into another river, or even into the great salt ocean.

Whatever the reason, I'm telling you now, that river was round. In its circle lived timber beasts like the hodag and sauger, which are remembered only by old loggers. And there were creatures like our deer, rabbits, bobcats and bears, only mind you they all had tails in those times when the timberlands were young.

Fine and flourishin' tails were on all of them. The roarin' rabbit of the Round River woods was no such timorious, cowerin' and cringin' beastie as the rabbit of our time. Before he lost his tail the Round River rabbit would tackle a panther, he would, noosin' his powerful, long tail about the beast's neck, jerkin' him down, then kickin' the life out of the panther with both hind feet. In them days the blood-curdlin' roar of a rabbit was the most awful of all the wild woods sounds. The rabbits had run all the panthers out of the woods when the terrible turkey come to Round River.

The deer of them woods also had a fine tail for himself,

one like a plume and the brightest spot of beauty in the forest. The bobcat's tail was more of a fightin' kind, like you'd expect. It was a fang tail, with sharp teeth in the tip, and with them the bobcat would strike like a snake at birds and small beasts for his prey. The black and cinnamon bears had stiff brushy tails which they used mostly for the sweepin' of their caves. There were never cleaner creatures than the cave bears of Paul Bunyan's time; always hustlin' and bustlin' in every nook and cranny, keepin' everything spick and span.

Paul Bunyan did not dream that such a course had befallen the timber beasts as the loss of their tails. He had never even heard of the wing-tailed terrible turkey, so of course he did not know how this ferocious fowl made its meals. The dismal quiet of the black wild woods was all a mystery to Paul Bunyan, a quiet broken only by a whisperin' moan like the rustle of wind in trees at night. But this was no wind, indade; it was the timber beasts of Round River, hidin' away, and sighin' in sorrow and sadness for the lost tails of them.

Paul Bunyan wondered and worried, as he forded the river. Not even the mutter of a mince was heard, for that little beast, whose meat was so good for pies, was entirely gone. On no other huntin' trip had Paul Bunyan and Dublin come into the woods without hearin' minces mutterin' from their lairs. For the minces of Round River always muttered, so they did, just as the rabbits roared and the bears bellowed and growled. That mutter was the sweetest of music to the wire-haired terror's ears.

At last Dublin thought he heard it, when they had reached the inside bank of Round River. Paul Bunyan leaned on his scatter-cannon again, and wondered and worried still more about the dismal quiet of the black wild woods, with only that whisperin' moan to break it at all.

But something else was soundin' in the terror's ears. He perked them up and made himself believe that this was a mince mutterin' out of the woods. So he came to a point, with the blunt muzzle of himself stuck out, and his tail wavin' and waggin' in the wind. For Dublin could never point a mince without h'istin' and waggin' his fine tail, such a gay dog he was when huntin' his favorite game.

Then it happened. What Dublin thought was the mutter of a mince suddenly growed into growlin' thunder. Paul Bunyan stiffened up, but before he could bring the scatter-cannon to his shoulder a coppery streak touched with red at the head of it and with a whirlin' blur behind, flashed from sight along the circle of the river. In the same instant there rose a fearful howl of grief from the wire-haired terror.

Pore dog, indeed pore Dublin, sure he had a right to howl, for all but a stub of his tail was gone, clipped clean away before he could wink an eye. Now he was a sad dog, with tears tricklin' from his eyes as he looked up at Paul Bunyan. He whimpered and moaned with a sound which melted into that whisperin' from the forest, and now that was a mystery no longer to Paul Bunyan. He knew the reason for the sorrowful sound. Certainly all the timber beasts had been denuded of their tails, and like Dublin all were bemoanin' their loss. And the robber of all was none other than this red-headed thunderbolt in coppery feathers, this ferocious fowl who drove like lightnin' through the air by the power of his whirlin' wing tail.

Paul Bunyan figgered that out as he doctored Dublin's hurt with arnicky, stanched it and bound it. Then with kind words he comforted the grievin' terror. As he did so, he again heard that sound like the mutter of a mince from its lair; and it soon growed into rolls of thunder.

The great hunter of the woods stared up at the sound, his head turnin' back till the tip of his curly black beard waved at the sky. And here was the roar and the rush again; but now it was Paul Bunyan's time to howl; for all of his beard was gone, so it was, nipped and clipped slick away from his chin.

But Paul Bunyan did not howl with grief, nor did he roar with rage or sigh with sorrow or anything like that at all. Paul Bunyan was not that kind of a man. Enough had happened, indade, to drive anybody distracted—the ruin of the game, the loss of the grand Christmas dinner he had planned for his men, the thievery of Dublin's fine tail, and the snippin' and pluckin' away of his famous beard. Disaster and disgrace it all was, enough to make even a hero like Paul Bunyan despair.

But sure the great hunter would not give up, not even when he realized that he could do no thinkin' until his beard growed out again. Paul Bunyan could think only when he brushed his beard with a young pine tree. Now he had no beard to brush at all.

"If I cannot think, then I must act," said Paul Bunyan, makin' the best of things. "And I'll do that soon and sudden."

What to do was plain enough. Paul Bunyan could see it all without thinkin'. Both times the wing-tailed terrible turkey had flown in a perfect circle, follyin' the course of Round River. To get the feathered thunderbolt on the wing, he must shoot in a circle. So Paul Bunyan first bent the forty-seven barrels of his scatter-cannon so that they would do just that—shoot their loads of cannon balls in an in-curve that would exactly folly the course of Round River.

Next, it was plain that he must set up a lure, to bring the ferocious fowl swoopin' down again. Paul Bunyan fixed a lure by pluckin' a colossyal cattail from the riverbank and bindin' it to the pore stump left to Dublin. The dog whimpered, and he shed more tears at such a fake of a tail; he felt disgraced, indade, to have a cattail foisted on such a tremenjus dog as himself, and would have stuck it betwixt his hind legs and crept off in shame. But Paul Bunyan spoke to him stern-like, and Dublin, obejient wire-haired terror that he was, set up and took notice, flourishin' the shameful fake of a tail to please his master.

Well, the fake fooled the terrible turkey, who had no more brains than the small gobblers of our own time. Soon there was the mutter again, and then the thunder. A coppery streak bolted down from the blue sky, and the false tail was snipped up like lightnin'. So fast was it grabbed and gobbled that Paul Bunyan's scatter-cannon would have been no use at all, had not the terrible turkey gone red with wrath over the deceit played on him. He stopped in mid air to spit the cattail out of his beak, and also to strut and pout—and that was the chance for the great hunter to bring him down.

For two seconds Paul Bunyan took careful aim. The terrible turkey hovered low, and so was on a level with Paul Bunyan's shoulders. While he hovered, he puffed and swelled, the terrible turkey did, till only his wattles showed like flames from his ruffle of coppery feathers. His wrathy gobbles sounded like the stormiest thunder now. The wing tail of him, spread like a windmill, whirled slow, just holdin' him above the trees.

Paul Bunyan's aim was set. He squeezed the trigger, and the forty-seven barrels roared as one cannon. The balls whistled and screamed, powder smoke fogged up like a storm cloud, the earth shook, the timber shivered, and waves rolled over the river from the mighty blast of Paul Bunyan's scatter-cannon. The terrible turkey took alarm in the instant of an instant, so he did.

The cloud of balls was hardly out of the muzzles before he was off at full speed, his side wings spread, his wing tail a whirlin' blur again, his body a red-headed coppery streak.

"A second too late," groaned Paul Bunyan. "He is out-flyin'

my cannon balls, a curse on me now for bein' too careful and slow!"

The terrible turkey was gone. The streak and blur of him disappeared around the curve of the river. The cloud of cannon balls curved after him, but slower, and they were soon left behind.

Paul Bunyan was like to give up at that. He was minded to turn his back on the huntin' woods at once and return to his loggers with an empty bag. Never had he been so grieved, to know that this year he could give his loggers no fine Christmas dinner. Dublin stood by him and licked his hand, tryin' also, pore dog, to wag the stub of a tail which was left to him.

"So we must go back, Dublin," said Paul Bunyan sadly, "without even a mince for the loggers. Dear, oh, dear, and such a curse!"

He swung his gun over his shoulder to go. Just then the terrible turkey thundered down the river again. It was roarin' thunder indade this trip, for the fowl had his wing tail whirlin' at the speed limit. Down the river he curved, and was gone. And now, from away back up the river, sounded the whistle and screech of the cannon balls, too slow indade for that feathered thunderbolt. Paul Bunyan blushed with shame to see them so far behind.

Now they were beginnin' to fall. White spouts of water and foam gushed up from the river as spent cannon balls dropped, the spray flashin' in the sunlight, makin' rainbows bright to see. But Paul Bunyan took no joy in the sight. He was ashamed to think that his cannon balls were so slow that the terrible turkey might catch 'em from behind in the great circle of the river.

Paul Bunyan raised his eyes, to look behind the cannon balls which still whistled and whined down the river. And now Paul Bunyan got a hope, a flimsy and scrawny hope, but he needed no more. Paul Bunyan was that kind of a man.

"Up and ready, Dublin!" he roared. "Sic 'em, boy! *Up the river!*"

That was enough for Dublin. What was up the wire-haired terror didn't know, but he lepped up river. And with that Paul Bunyan threw up his scatter-cannon with the forty-seven barrels of it curved like a hoop; and he let fly. After the terrible turkey? Not at all. Sure, he'd tried that once. The bird was too fast for that. Paul Bunyan turned his back and fired in the opposite direction. For when he said to Dublin, "*Up* the river, boy," he'd bent the forty-seven barrels to the other side. Down the river curved the big bird and was gone. So *up* the river curved the shot, whistling and screeching. And Dublin after them.

There was a great sound as the terrible turkey flew head on into them new cannon balls. Feathers flew in clouds, and the river boiled and foamed as the cannon balls splashed down. The terrible turkey fell, but in a great rainbow curve, for his speed carried him on, turnin' him over and over, while the dog lepped in frantic chase of him.

Paul Bunyan, runnin' after both, saw the terrible turkey sail down like a coppery cloud, while Dublin lunged up like a black-spotted white cloud to meet him. The great hunter reached the death-grapple just in time. With one snap Dublin had taken off the terrible turkey's head in return for his tail and was goin' after the rest of him. Paul Bunyan had to grope his way to the dog through a snowstorm of feathers, but he got there in time.

Dublin soon had the terrible turkey well plucked. And when Paul Bunyan saw the royal drumsticks of the fowl, the rich meat of his breast, the grandeur of his giblets, and all the rest, his gladness was so great that he was like to sheddin' tears of joy.

"Would you but look at the drumsticks of him, Dublin!"

cried Paul Bunyan. "What logger would ask for a rabbit stew, deer steak or cinnamon bear roast, when he can have such fine eatin' as this for his Christmas dinner? Tender and plump, juicy and drippin', crisped to a fine golden brown, stuffed till he bulges, this behemoth of a bird will be enough for twice seven hun'erd men. Here is the meat for the finest Christmas dinner ever heard of; yes, sir!"

Yet the Dublin dog looked troubled. And Paul Bunyan knew why.

"Never mind," said the great logger cheerily. "I'll invent a recipe for mince meat which will beat that from the mutterin' minces of the Round River woods. You leave it to me, Dublin."

And so Paul Bunyan did. He invented such fine mince meat that cooks have used it ever since, and minces are never hunted any more for their meat at all. And the dinner from the terrible turkey was so ravishin' to Paul Bunyan's seven hun'erd men that they took his breast bone and made a mountain out of it, to stand as a moniment to the first Christmas turkey dinner.

And so we have had turkey dinners for Christmas ever since. To be sure, they are not terrible turkeys nowadays, for Paul Bunyan glued up the tails of all the young ones of the turkey tribe, and soon they had forgot how to fly with any but their side wings. But even our tame turkeys of to-day will pout and strut and spread their stiff tails, just like the terrible turkey of old. And their tails look like windmills, but never can they twist and turn, to make turkeys fly like lightnin' and thunder. Nor can our tame turkeys bite off dogs' tails, but they will peck at them every chance, in memory of what the daddy of 'em all used to do.

There is a bit of sadness to remember, too. For the rabbit was made a coward by the loss of the tail with which he choked panthers in the old times, and the rabbit roars no more. Nor did deer, bobcats and bears ever grow fine tails again. Neither do you see tails worth the mention on wire-haired terrors, these tiny descendants of Dublin, the tremendous terror who follied the first great hunter of the woods.

But sure it was worth it all to discover the glory of turkey for Christmas dinner. For that you must ever remember Paul Bunyan.

Old Larrity was silent. Jeff stroked his dog's head and stared out into the timber. Now, here in the autumn woods, he could imagine that he was Paul Bunyan and that Mike the pup was Dublin, a wire-haired terrier as tall as a tree.

🌲🌲🌲🌲🌲🌲🌲

Dell J. McCormick:

PAUL GOES HUNTING

IT WAS quite a sight to see Paul with his homemade shotgun that Ole the Big Swede gave him for his birthday. It took two dishpans full of nuts and bolts to load it and used a gallon can of powder every time it was fired. On special occasions, he loaded it with a keg of nails and not only killed ducks by the hundreds but hung them pinned to trees where they could be plucked easily by the cookhouse crew.

His sight was very sharp. He once shot ducks that were flying so high in the air they spoiled before reaching the ground. He spared himself that afterwards by loading his shotgun with some rock salt which kept the birds fresh until they could be picked up by the cooks. One fall, he shot some mallards so high in the air they fell across the state line and the game warden told him to quit firing at ducks so far away unless he was certain which state they were flying over.

It used to take a lot of venison to supply the camp, and Paul had quite a system for hunting deer that saved the cooks many hours of hard work. Instead of hunting them like an ordinary hunter, he would go out with Elmer the Moosehound and round up all the deer in the forests near the camp. Then he would drive them lickety-split through the woods toward the camp and shoot them one by one as they dashed by the cook shanty. In that way Sourdough Sam had a nice fresh supply of meat right at his back door without having to send the bull cooks out in the woods to carry it in.

Elmer was getting pretty old for deer hunting though, and Paul finally had to rig up a hammock on the gun to carry Elmer. Every time the old dog smelled deer, however, he would raise up and point the direction and naturally swing the barrel in that direction too, so Paul hardly ever missed a shot even if he couldn't see the deer. When Elmer finally died, Paul got a new hunting dog that was a cross between a kangaroo and an English bull. Paul called him old High Pockets.

His front legs were only about a foot long but his hind quarters were well over six feet high. His hind legs were long and powerful like a kangaroo which made his back slope down toward his head at quite an angle. In that way, of course, he was always running downhill which made it easier for him. In fact, he never tired and could run after deer and moose for days without the slightest sign of fatigue. The deer could not get away running on the level while old High Pockets was always running downhill.

Paul used to hunt coyotes when he first came West. The state had a bounty for each one shot, but they soon had to stop that, for Paul shot so many the first day they had to mortgage the state capitol to pay him off. It was the same way with timber wolves only Paul didn't waste any gun powder shooting them. He scared them to death just hollering at 'em.

Ole the Big Swede borrowed Paul's shotgun one day and went out hunting ducks. He took just one shot, and it hurt Ole more than the ducks. The gun of course kicked back with great force and knocked Ole eighteen feet backward into some wild blackberry bushes, and it took six men to carry him back into camp. The United States Government finally mounted the gun up near Fort Casey and used it to guard the coast until the barrel wore out.

Old-timers still talk about the time Paul went hunting caribou up in Canada one winter. It was so cold everybody wore seventeen vests under their mackinaws and the thermometer dropped to four feet below zero and then froze. It was the coldest winter on record. Even the shadows froze to the ground and had to be pried loose with pickaxes. Paul put on his snowshoes one morning and went out hunting. He didn't find any caribou but he ran into some snowshoe tracks in the snow and started following them. He couldn't figure out why anybody else would be out in such weather.

After following them for miles, he saw where they were joined by a second party on snowshoes and still later on by a third. More and more snowshoe tracks appeared in the snow until he was following a well-beaten trail. Paul followed the trail for two weeks without finding a soul and then found that one of his snowshoes had become warped because of the freezing weather and he had been walking around in a circle following his own tracks.

He finally ran into a herd of caribou, though, and got them all. They were two miles away when he first sighted them, and he tried a shot, but his gun froze. So he made a bow and arrow out of a jack pine thirty feet high and drove the arrows through their horns. In that way, he got three or four with each shot and the arrows held them together so he could swing them up on his back and carry them back to camp without much trouble. It was quite a sight to see Paul coming back over the snow with thirty-two caribou slung across his shoulders.

✝✝✝✝✝✝✝

Samuel Richardson Davenport:

PAUL'S LOST CAMP

W<small>RITE</small>? Ho! Zat jus' for Jean Eengsleengier! Not for me. I was logger, by Gar! Neeck Roche, I am hees great-grand-pere, he say I talk to hees leetle secretair'. You was 'er? Zen put my words on ze—w'at you call heem—notebuke.

You was dam' purty gurl, too. Een my day, you no 'ave to write, write, write. You fin' beeg strong man to work for you. Eef I was not ol' feller—

Oui, Ma'mselle, I 'ave marry five times. Neeck tell me I got plentee chil'ren—all boys. He can no count my grand-fils weethout machine. How ol' I be? Poof! You mak' figure. Le's see. I 'ave ze twenty-five years w'en Paul Bunyan cut t'rough dozain trees an' my leg, all at once. He feel vair-ry bad for zat 'cause I hees frien', so he mak' me wuden leg from live oak a hunnert year ol'. 'Ow many reengs eet got now? Hun-nert seventy-five? Hunnert seventy-seex? What? Only hun-nert seventy-*four*? I jus' ninety-nine? Voila! I am ze yo'ng man. Maybe, I get marry some more. You was purty gurl, Ma'mselle. How you lak' my moostache? Not so good, eh? Well, maybe, I not so yo'ng. I get tired othaire day w'en I 'old up back end o' Neeck's car w'ile he feex blow-out.

You want I should talk 'bout ol' Paul? By Gar, I talk. Zey mak' heem beeg feller now. I 'ear zey 'ave fete day for heem een Clear Rivaire, an' I walk feefty mile t'rough deep snow to see eet. All ze store windows she ees full weeth peekture of ol' Paul; an' you should see the dam' fin' p'rade zey 'ave. Mais non! Zees leetle men are no lak' heem. Eet mak' me seeck. Neeck he set me up with bar'l o' beer, bar'l o' wine, an' bar'l o' wheesky—steell, I no feel good. He show me—what you call heem—ze Paul Bunyan camp. Sacrebleu! Eet ees lot lak' ol' times weeth pikes, axes, blacksmeeth shop, an' bonk 'ouse. But, eet ees leetle—jus' play-'ouse for ol' Paul w'en he was babee.

I 'ear plentee story zere; yet, not a theeng I 'ave no 'ear before. Zat mak' me some more seeck, so mooch I 'ave 'ard time to walk ze feefty mile back to my cabin. You say Neeck wants I should tell new story, ze story zat no one 'ear 'cept me? You will write w'at I say, Ma'mselle? Zen, listen. I tell heem.

Non. He was not born een Maine. Ol' Paul was born een Canada. 'Ow do I know? He tol' me, by Gar! Long time 'go, Le Bon Dieu look ovaire ze United States. Not 'nuff room zere; too many people. He peeck Canada for Paul Bunyan.

You 'ear 'bout 'ow boats change from sail to steam. You know w'y? Zey 'ave no othaire way to go w'en ol' Paul get born. Hees fathaire 'ave to tak' all sails from Yankee Clippaires to mak' di'pers for hees boy; an' zere was only one place beeg 'nuff to 'ang zem out to dry—ze *boundry* line 'tween Canada an' ze United States. Ol' Paul was not lak' babee zeese day. Now, Canada pay mooch money for to keep babees: ol' Paul he keep Canada. W'en he jus' two year ol' he gif hees cradle to hees frien', ze Governeur-Generale. W'at zey mak' of eet? By Gar! Zere no be Canadien-Paceefeec Railroad today eef zey no use ol' Paul's cradle for zeir road-bed.

Oui. You go 'head an' ask question. 'Ow was eet ol' Paul peeck out Norske swampers an' pikers? Mordieu! Eet was one beeg lie! Johnny Eenksleenger's real name was Jean

Eengsleengier, an' Lars Larson's name was Loires Loireson. Zey jus' mak' out zey was Norske for joke. Even Babe, he was Canadien lak' me an' ol' Paul an' ze othaires.

Babe? Mais oui. He was ol' Paul's ox. You 'ear 'bout heem? He ees one beeg ox. 'Ow he get so beeg? Poof! Zat ees eas-y. He learn 'ow to grow an' forget 'ow to stop. By 'n by, hees skeen get so tight eet mos' let eenside bu'st out. W'at ol' Paul do 'bout zat? He tak' hide from rubbaire-neck moose, an' cut off streep of Babe's skeen, an' sew rubbaire-neck moose hide een eet's place. Purty soon, Babe grow so he ees seexty t'ree axe handles across at ze meedle; but, he stay feex.

I feel vair-y bad 'bout Babe, 'specially een Lost Camp. You no 'ear 'bout Lost Camp? I no theenk you deed. I tell.

Ol' Paul he fin' place een—what you call heem—Uppaire Meechegaine w'aire zey 'ave spruce four hunnert feet 'igh. Nobody else know 'bout eet, an' ol' Paul no want zey should know. One night, he get all us loggers togethaire een bonk-'ouse. He 'ave to 'ave guards for feefteen mile 'cause he want nobody should 'ear heem. An' zen, he only wheespaire. Eef he talk out loud on Isle Royale w'en day break, he wake up people on St. Lawrence. Zat's ze kin' of man ol' Paul ees! I no get down to business? I no tell 'bout Lost Camp? All right, I tell. Mak' holt o' your horses.

"My leetle ones," ol' Paul wheespaire as he peench our ears, "we want for to s'prise meels weeth more lumbaire zan zey evaire see. We mak' secret w'aire we get eet, eh? Now zat eet ees night, follow me an' mak' no noise."

We do jus' as he say. He go down to canoes an' get een. We do jus' lak' he do. Ol' Paul he point up-rivaire. We mak' lak' we paddle, but we no need to for ze rivaire eet start flow-eeng up-heell. We 'ad to paddle jus' the same, by Gar, so's not to go so sweeft. Purty soon, ze lead-canoe she come to point of land, an' ol' Paul sen' 'er nose on shore. He go 'bout seexty pike-lengths eento woods.

"Bettaire stop dreenkeeng, Babe," ol' Paul yells. "We 'ere all right."

I look ovaire toward moon an' see beeg shadow. Certain! Eet ees zat dam' fin' ox! He dreenk ze rivaire at ze source an' mak' eet turn back so we get zere weethout makeeng ze paddle. Sacrebleu! Eet was lucky zat ol' Paul 'ave Babe stop dreenkeeng. Eef he not do eet, we end up een ze stomach of zat ox.

What you theenk we do now? I not let you guess; I tell. We walk feefty mile eento woods before sun come up. Zen, ol' Paul sen' me an' Loires Loireson weeth sled to peeck up footprints, w'ile he an' ze othaires peetch een to mak' camp. By Gar! We 'aul seexteen t'ousan' loads o' footprints weeth seexteen hunnert footprints to a load. By ze time cookie call, "Come an' get eet!" we 'ave feell een seexteen square acres 'round Lost Camp with jus' footprints, een piles seex feet 'igh.

Dam' good theeng we do eet, too. By 'n by, eet get so col' zat ol' Paul 'ave to splice seexty-seex thermometers togethaire to fin' out 'ow mooch below zero we get. He no want to burn up timbaire, so we use ze footprints for fuel all wintaire. Come spreeng an' our grub get low, cookie mak' footprint flapjacks. You no got good grub lak' zat zeese days.

Mais non. Zat ees *not* all, Ma'mselle. I no say theeng 'bout zat pauvre bete, Babe. He jus' grow an' grow een zat wintaire een Lost Camp. Ol' Paul breeng 'long plentee 'ide o' rubbaire-neck moose; but, he no theenk 'bout Babe's teeth. Evairy time Babe eat, hees teeth ees so wide apart seence hees mout' grow zat he can no keep hees food eenside. Zere ees 'ole beeg as twenty-four plugs o' t'bacco between each tooth. Hees belly get so theen eet ees only forty-t'ree axe handles across. Zen me, I get ze idea.

"Ol' Paul," I say, "jus' geeve me chance. I feex Babe. Purty soon, by 'n by, he be good as new."

He say I should go 'head. I get sled-load o' footprints an'

nail zem togethaire. Zey froze so steef zey lak' ze rock. W'at do I do? I jus' ave Babe open hees mout' an' I fasten ze steef footprints between hees teeth weeth pike hooks. Notheeng leak out from zem, by Gar! Babe was so 'appy he steeck out hees tongue an' leeck my face. He bu'st my nose an' my jaw weeth hees tongue; but me, I am 'appy jus' ze same. I have done ze great deed.

Oui. Eet was one 'ell of a col' wintaire, Ma'mselle. W'en eet get feefty degrees below zero eet feel so warm zat us loggers get out weeth no shirt, an' sweat w'en we cut down ze tree. An' w'en eet get twenty-five below, ze ice she break een Lac Meechegaine. An' w'en eet get zero zere ees open wataire.

W'at we do zen? W'y, zen eet ees time for to mak' ze drive. We cut so mooch timbaire we no can mak' 'nuff sleds to carry eet out. Zat mak' no bothaire to ol' Paul. He jus' spleet teep of Babe's tail down leetle ways—'bout hunnert feet—an' spread eet out. Zat no 'urt Babe for hees tail was froze steef 'cause he no 'ave eet eenside all wintaire. Hees shed ees jus' beeg 'nuff for Babe, so hees tail 'ave to stay outside. Zen, ol' Paul tak' some lef' ovaire streeps o' rubbaire-neck moose 'ide an' tie zem to each side o' Babe's spleet tail. By Gar! He *shoot* ze logs out eento Lac Meechegaine lak' leetle boy shoot weeth sleengshot. Zat was all zere was to eet.

W'en we go from Lost Camp, ze men peeck up zeir footprints as zey go 'long, an' t'row zem eento sled. Purty soon, we come to ze Lac. Zen, we t'row ze footprints eento ze wataire. At first, we no can see ze othaire side, but after ze leetle w'ile ze footprints feell up ze Lac an' mak' land. Ze shore 'most get togethaire. Ol' Paul scratch hees 'ead to theenk of good name for place.

"By Gar, men!" he say, "I got eet. We call zees place ze Sault Ste Marie. Zat ees one dam' fine name!"

An' zat, Ma'mselle, ees eet's name zees vairy day.

But, some o' ze men zey mak' fun an' t'row ze footprints

'long ways. Zey all 'bout ze same strong so ze footprints pile up an' mak' islands. Neeck say he catch ze leetle feefty pound lac trout up zere.

W'en we get down by Bay Verde we fin' zere ees not 'nuff meells to plane our logs, so we mak' our own out of ze logs we drive. We built two hunnert meells. Eet tak' zem t'ree week, workeeng t'irty-t'ree hour a day, to mak' lumbaire out of our timbaire. Zen, we t'ar down ze meells, one by one, an' sen' zem t'rough our othaires. By 'n by, we come to ze las' meell. 'Ow we mak' zat one eento smooth boards? Poof! Jus' lac' zat, ol' Paul tak' out hees jackknife an' begeen wheetle. Seexteen meenutes lataire, all ze work she feeneesh.

Oui, Ma'mselle. Zat ees all of Lost Camp Drive. 'Cours, zere was more of zem—Onion Rivaire, Round Rivaire, Skunk Rivaire—on all of zem I was weeth ol' Paul. W'y do I not tell of ze othaires? You 'ave 'ear zeir story, an' you want I should talk of w'at no one 'as 'ear. Write zees las' one down vair-ry careful, for I want zat eet shall no be forget.

Zere come time w'en ze men zat work for ol' Paul theenk zey are purty beeg zemselves. Zey want for to work on zeir own, to cut down zeir own trees, to mak' zeir own drives. Ol' Paul he jus' shrug hees shouldaires an' let zem do w'at zey please. Loires Loireson stay een Meechegaine. Jean Eengsleengier an' L'Ole D'Olesoin go West. Ze othaires go East. Ol' Paul an' me, we start south t'rough Weesconsin.

By 'n by, we come to a beeg stone heell. Ol' Paul he seet down on ze stumps o' feefty trees.

"Jules, my frien'," he say, "I go no farthaire."

"W'at you mean?" I ask.

"I 'ave leeve 'ard an' work 'ard. My bones she get tired same as bear's. I feel lak' I mak' sleep."

"W'aire you sleep?"

"Zere ees good place." He point to beeg stone heell. "I theenk I sleep un'ner zat. Don't look so s'prise. Ze bear she crawl een cave. I jus' peeck up top of heell, deeg a 'ole, an' crawl een eet. I prop up top of heell weeth tree. W'en get 'een, you jus' keeck tree out an' ze heell she settle down."

" 'Ow you get out? W'en—"

"I get out w'en I get dam' good an' ready," ol' Paul say. "All I got t' do ees lif' up top an' step out. Theenk you can keeck out tree, Jules?"

"Poof! I keeck out seexty trees. But, w'en you wake up?"

"Een long time. Ze bear she jus' sleep *one* wintaire, an' she do no work an' she ees no tired. I work 'ard, so I sleep many wintaires. W'aire you be w'en I wake?"

"I got idea I mak' cabin on Chippewa Rivaire; feesh a leetle, hunt a leetle, maybe cut down tree a leetle—jus' to keep my 'and een. You sure you come an' get me w'en you dam' good an' ready, Paul?"

"Eet ees a promees, Jules."

Ol' Paul he shook my 'and an' bu'st evairy one of my feengaires t'ree times. But, zat don' mak' no mattaire. Ol' Paul he ees my frien'.

So, he tak' top off of stone heell an' prop eet up. By 'n by, after he deeg deep 'ole an' lie down een eet, I keeck ze prop out. Ze top come down an' lock heem een.

Zen, I come up 'ere an' get marry to five womans an' 'ave plentee chil'ren—an' more grandfils zan Neeck can count weeth hees machine—to put een time 'teel ol' Paul come an' get me for 'nothaire drive. Eef anybody say ol' Paul es dead; tell zem for me, Ma'mselle, zat zey lie, an' zat ol' Jules knock zeir teeth out! Bien! Zat ees all!

You want for to go 'ome, Ma'mselle? Your—w'at you call eet—car, eet not go? You got—date? Oh, I see. You mak' meet weeth yo'ng man back een town. Ol' Jules feex zat. 'Ere! Put your coat on. I wrap you een warm blanket an' carry you. But, zen I am so sorr-y. I am no so strong to tak' bot' you *an'* ze car zees treep. Voila! I breeng your car een, too, before night. Eet ees jus' feefteen mile to town. You are ready? Fin'. Allons, Ma'mselle!

✢✢✢✢✢✢

Robert Frost:

PAUL'S WIFE

To drive Paul out of any lumber-camp
All that was needed was to say to him,
"How is the wife, Paul?" and he'd disappear.
Some said it was because he had no wife
And hated to be twitted on the subject.
Others because he'd come within a day
Or so of having one and then been jilted.
Others because he'd had one once, a good one,
Who'd run away with some one else and left him.
And others still because he had one now
He only had to be reminded of;
He was all duty to her in a minute;
He had to run right off to look her up,
As if to say: "That's so, how *is* my wife?
I hope she isn't getting into mischief."
No one was anxious to get rid of Paul.
He'd been the hero of the mountain camps
Ever since, just to show them, he had slipped
The bark of a whole tamarack off whole,
As clean as boys do off a willow twig
To make a willow whistle on a Sunday
In April by subsiding meadow brooks.
They seemed to ask him just to see him go,
"How is the wife, Paul?" and he always went.

He never stopped to murder any one
Who asked the question. He just disappeared,
Nobody knew in what direction,
Although it wasn't usually long
Before they heard of him in some new camp,
The same Paul at the same old feats of logging.
The question everywhere was, Why should Paul
Object to being asked a civil question—
A man you could say almost anything to
Short of a fighting word? You have the answers.
And there was one more not so fair to Paul:
That Paul had married a wife not his equal.
Paul was ashamed of her. To match a hero,
She would have had to be a heroine;
Instead of which she was some half-breed squaw.
But if the story Murphy told was true,
She wasn't anyone to be ashamed of.

You know, Paul could do wonders. Everyone's
Heard how he thrashed the horses on a load
That wouldn't budge until they simply stretched
Their rawhide harness from the load to camp.
Paul told the boss the load would be all right.
"The sun will bring your load in," and it did—
By shrinking the rawhide to natural length.
That's what is called a stretcher. But I guess
The one about his jumping so's to land
With both his feet at once against the ceiling,
And then land safely, right side up again,
Back on the floor is fact or pretty near fact.
Well, this is such a yarn. Paul sawed his wife
Out of a white-pine log. Murphy was there,
And, as you might say, saw the lady born.
Paul worked at anything in lumbering.

He'd been hard at it taking boards away
For I forget—the last ambitious sawyer
To want to find out if he couldn't pile
The lumber on Paul till Paul begged for mercy.
They'd sliced the first slab off a big butt log,
And the sawyer had slammed the carriage back
To slam end on again against the saw-teeth.
To judge them by the way they caught themselves
When they saw what had happened to the log,
They must have had a guilty expectation
Something was going to go with their slam-banging.
Something had left a long black streak of grease
On the new wood the whole length of the log
Except perhaps a foot at either end.
But when Paul put his finger in the grease,
It wasn't grease at all, but a long slot.
The log was hollow. They were sawing pine.
"First time I ever saw a hollow pine.
That comes of having Paul around the place.
Take it to hell for me," the sawyer said.
Everyone had to have a look at it,
And tell Paul what he ought to do about it.
(They treated it as his.) "You take a jackknife
And spread the opening, and you've got a dugout
All dug to go a-fishing in." To Paul
The hollow looked too sound and clean and empty
Ever to have housed birds or beasts or bees.
There was no entrance for them to get in by.
It looked to him like some new kind of hollow
He thought he'd *better* take his jackknife to.
So after work that evening he came back
And let enough light into it by cutting
To see if it was empty. He made out in there
A slender length of pith—or was it pith?

It might have been the skin a snake had cast
And left stood up on end inside the tree
The hundred years the tree must have been growing.
More cutting, and he had this in both hands,
And looking from it to the pond near by,
Paul wondered how it would respond to water.
Not a breeze stirred, but just the breath of air
He made in walking slowly to the beach
Blew it once off his hands and almost broke it.
He laid it at the edge, where it could drink.
At the first drink it rustled and grew limp;
At the next drink it grew invisible.
Paul dragged the shallows for it with his fingers,
And thought it must have melted. It was gone.
And then beyond the open water, dim with midges
Where the log drive lay pressed against the boom,
It slowly rose a person, rose a girl,
Her wet hair heavy on her like a helmet,
Who, leaning on a log, looked back at Paul.
And that made Paul in turn look back
To see if it was anyone behind him
That she was looking at instead of him.
(Murphy had been there watching all the time,
But from a shed where neither of them could see him.)
There was a moment of suspense in birth,
When the girl seemed too water-logged to live,
Before she caught her first breath with a gasp
And laughed. Then she climbed slowly to her feet
And walked off, talking to herself or Paul,
Across the logs like backs of alligators,
Paul taking after her around the pond.
Next evening Murphy and some other fellows
Got drunk and tracked the pair up Catamount,
From the bare top of which there is a view

To other hills across a kettle valley.
And there, well after dark, let Murphy tell it,
They saw Paul and his creature keeping house.
It was the only glimpse that anyone
Has had of Paul and her since Murphy saw them
Falling in love across the twilight millpond.
More than a mile across the wilderness
They sat together half-way up a cliff
In a small niche let into it, the girl
Brightly, as if a star played on the place,
Paul darkly, like her shadow. All the light
Was from the girl herself, though not a star,
As was apparent from what happened next.
All those great ruffians put their throats together
And let out a loud yell, and threw a bottle
As a brute tribute of respect to beauty.
Of course the bottle fell short by a mile.
But the shout reached the girl and put her light out.
She went out like a firefly, and that was all.
So there were witnesses that Paul was married,
And not to any one to be ashamed of.
Every one had been wrong in judging Paul.
Murphy told me Paul put on all those airs
About his wife to keep her to himself.
Paul was what's called a terrible possessor:
Owning a wife with him meant owning her.
She wasn't anybody else's business
Either to praise her or so much as name her,
And he'd thank people not to think of her.
Murphy's idea was that a man like Paul
Wouldn't be spoken to about a wife
In any way the world knew how to speak in.

THE WONDERFUL
BIG BLUE OX, BABE

James Stevens:

THE WINTER OF THE BLUE SNOW

So PAUL BUNYAN fared well on the moose meat which Niagara brought him, and he lived contentedly as a student in his cave at Tonnere Bay. Each day he studied, and far into the night he figured. Taking a trimmed pine tree for a pencil, he would char its end in the fire and use the cave floor for a slate. He was not long in learning all the history worth knowing, and he became as good a figurer as any man could be.

Vague ambitions began to stir in his soul after this and he often deserted his studies to dream about them. He knew he would not spend his days forever in the cave at Tonnere Bay. Somewhere in the future a great Work was waiting to be done by him. Now it was only a dream; but he was sure that it would be a reality; and he came to think more and more about it. The books were opened less and less; the pine tree pencil was seldom brought from its corner. Paul Bunyan now used another pine tree which still had its boughs; it was a young one, and he brushed his curly black beard with it as he dreamed. But he was still a contented man at the time of the Winter of the Blue Snow, for his dreams had not yet blazed up in a desire for any certain attainment.

On the first day of the blue snow, Paul Bunyan was in a particularly contented mood. He sat all that day before his fire; so charmed with drowsy thoughts was he that he did not once look out. It had been dark a long time before he rolled into his blankets. He awoke at the dawn of a day that had scarcely more light than the night. He was cold, and he got up to throw an armful of trees on the fire. Then he saw the blue drifts which had piled up before the cave, and he saw the fog of the blue blizzard. He heard the roar of a terrific wind, too, and he knew that the storm was perilous as well as strange. But Paul Bunyan thought gladly of the blue snow, for it was a beautiful event, and the historians he liked most would write wonderful books about it.

He kicked the drifts away from the cave entrance, but the usual pile of slain moose was not under them. Paul Bunyan was a little worried, as he thought that Niagara [his faithful dog] might have lost himself in the blue blizzard. The possibility that the unnatural color of the storm might send the fauna of the forest, and Niagara as well, into panicky flight did not occur to him. He was sure that Niagara would return with a grand supply of moose meat when the blue blizzard had passed.

But the moose herds were now far to the North, fleeing blindly from the blue snow. The bruins galloped after them. Before the day was over, Niagara had overtaken the bruins and was gaining on the moose. At nightfall his lunging strides had carried him far ahead of all the fauna of the forest. He galloped yet faster as he reached the blacker darkness of the Arctic winter. Now the darkness was so heavy that even his powerful eyes could not see in it. . . . Niagara at last ran head-on into the North Pole; the terrific speed at which he was traveling threw his body whirling high in the air; when Niagara fell he crashed through ninety feet of ice, and the polar fields cracked explosively as his struggles convulsed the waters under them. . . . Then only mournful blasts of wind sounded in the night of the Farthest North.

The moose were wearied out before they reached the white Arctic, and hordes of them fell and perished in the blizzard; many others died from fright, and only a tiny remnant of the great herds survived. Some of the bruins reached the polar fields, and they have lived there since. Their hair had turned white from fright, and their descendants still wear that mark of fear. Others were not frightened so much, and their hair only turned gray. They did not run out of the timber, and their descendants, the silver-tip grizzlies, still live in the Northern woods. The baby bruins were only scared out of their growth, and their black descendants now grow no larger than the cubs of Paul Bunyan's time.

Being ignorant of this disaster, Paul Bunyan was comfortable enough while the blizzard lasted. He had a good store of trees on hand and his cave was warm in the storm. He got hungry in the last days; but this emotion, or any emotion, for that matter, could have but little power over him when he was dreaming. And he dreamed deeply now of great enterprises; his dreams were formless, without any substance of reality; but they had brilliant colors, and they made him very hopeful.

The sun shone at last from a whitish blue sky, and the strange snow fell no more. A snapping cold was in the land; and pine boughs were bangled and brocaded with glittering blue crystals, and crusty blue snow crackled underfoot.

Paul Bunyan strapped on his snowshoes and started out through the Border forests in search of Niagara. His was a kingly figure as he mushed through the pine trees, looming above all but the very tallest of them. He wore a wine-red hunting cap, and his glossy hair and beard shone under it with a blackness that blended with the cap's color perfectly.

His unique eyebrows were black also; covering a fourth of his forehead above the eyes, they narrowed where they arched down under his temples, and they ended in thin curls just in front of his ears. His mustache had natural twirls and he never disturbed it. He wore a yellow muffler this morning under his virile curly beard. His mackinaw coat was of huge orange and purple checks. His mackinaw pants were sober-seeming, having tan and light gray checks, but some small crimson dots and crosses brightened them. Green wool socks showed above his black boots, which had buckskin laces and big brass eyelets and hooks. And he wore striped mittens of white and plum color. Paul Bunyan was a gorgeous picture this morning in the frozen fields and forests, all covered with blue snow which sparkled in a pale gold light.

That day and the next, and for five more days, he searched in vain for Niagara; and neither did he see any moose herds in the woods. Only the frost crackles broke the silences of the deserted blue forests: and at last Paul Bunyan returned to his cave, feeling depressed and lonely. He had not thought that the companionship of Niagara could mean so much to him. In his mood of depression he forgot his hunger and made no further effort to find food.

Lonely Paul Bunyan lay sleepless in his blankets this night, his eyes gleaming through hedgelike eyelashes as their gaze restlessly followed the red flares that shot from the fire and streaked the walls and roof of the cave. He did not realize that his first creative idea was now struggling for birth. He could yet feel no shape of it. He was only conscious of an unaccustomed turmoil of mind. Wearied with fruitless thought, he at last fell into a doze. But Paul Bunyan was not fated to sleep this night. A sustained crashing roar, as of the splintering of millions of timbers, brought him up suddenly; it was hushed for a short second; then a thudding boom sounded from Tonnere Bay. Paul Bunyan leaped to the cave door, and in the moonlight he saw a white wave of water rolling over the blue beach. It came near to the cave before it stopped and receded. He pulled on his boots, and two strides brought him down to the bay. It had been covered with ice seven feet thick, and the cakes of this broken ice were now tossing on heaving waters. Now Paul Bunyan saw two ears show sometimes above the billows; they were of the shape of moose ears, but enormous as his two forefingers. Paul Bunyan waded out into the waters, and he reached these ears a mile from shore. He seized them without fear and he lifted . . . now a head with closed eyes appeared . . . shoulders and forelegs . . . body and hips . . . rear legs and curled tail. It was a calf, newborn apparently, though it was of such a size that Paul Bunyan had to use both arms to carry it.

"*Nom d'un nom!*" exclaimed Paul Bunyan. "*Pauvre petite bleue bête!*"

For this great baby calf was of a bright blue hue which was neither darker nor lighter than the color of the beautiful strange snow. A blue baby ox calf. For such was its sex. Its ears drooped pitifully, and its scrawny, big-jointed legs hung limply below Paul Bunyan's arms. A spasmodic shiver ran from its head to its tail, and its savior was glad to feel this shiver, for it showed that life remained. Paul Bunyan was touched with a tenderness that drove out his loneliness. "*Ma bête,*" he said. "*Mon cher bleu bébé ausha.*"

He turned back through the waters, and the ice cakes pounded each other into bits as they rolled together in his wake. In thirty seconds Paul Bunyan was back in his cave. He spread out his blankets in front of the fire, and he laid Bébé upon them.

Through the night Paul Bunyan worked over the blue ox calf, nursing him back to warm life; and in the morning

Bébé was breathing regularly and seemed to rest. Paul Bunyan leaned over to hear his exhalations, and the blue ox calf suddenly opened his mouth and caressed Paul Bunyan's neck with his tongue. Paul Bunyan then discovered that he was ticklish in this region, for the caress impelled him to roll and laugh. The serious student Paul Bunyan had never laughed before; and he now enjoyed the new pleasure to the utmost.

"*Eh, Bébé!*" he chuckled. "*Eh, Bébé! Sacre bleu! Bon bleu, mon cher!*" Bébé raised his eyelids with astonishment upon hearing this cave-shaking chuckle, revealing large, bulging orbs which were of even a heavenlier blue than his silken hair. Such affection and intelligence shone in his eyes that Paul Bunyan wished he would keep his eyes opened. But Bébé was weary and weak, and he closed them again.

He is hungry, thought Paul Bunyan; and he went out to find him food. None of the animals he knew about could supply milk for such a calf as this blue Bébé. But he was newborn and his parents should be somewhere in the neighborhood. Paul Bunyan stepped up on the cliff over which Bébé had bounced when he fell into Tonnere Bay. From here a wide swath of smashed timber ran straight up the side of the tallest northern mountain. It was here that Bébé had made his thunderous roll of the night before.

Six strides brought Paul Bunyan to the mountaintop. One of its jagged peaks was broken off, showing where Bébé had stumbled over it and fallen. Then Paul Bunyan followed the calf tracks down the land side of the mountain. For two hours he trailed them, but they grew fainter as he went on, and in the Big Bay country the last fall of the blue snow had covered them. Paul Bunyan now had no doubt that Bébé's mother had been frightened by the strange color of the snow and that his blueness was a birthmark. Like Niagara and the fauna of the forest, the parents had stampeded, forgetting the little one. It was no use to search for them.

Paul Bunyan circled back through the forest and gathered a great load of moose moss before he returned to the cave. This rich food would meet the lack of milk. Bébé was asleep before the fireplace when Paul Bunyan returned, and he still slumbered while his friend prepared him some moose moss soup. But when a kettle full of steaming odorous food was set before him, he opened his eyes with amazing energy and sat up. It was then that Bébé first showed the depth and circumference of his natural appetite, an appetite which was to have its effect on history. He drank most of the moose moss soup at three gulps, he seized the rim of the kettle in his teeth and tilted it up until even the last ten gallons were drained out of it; then, looking roguishly at Paul Bunyan the while, he bit off a large section of the kettle rim and chewed it down, switching his pretty tail to show his enjoyment.

"*Eh, Bébé!*" roared Paul Bunyan, doubling up with laughter for the second time in his life. And he praised the blue snow for giving him such a creature, and did not mourn Niagara, who had never been amusing. But now, as Paul Bunyan doubled over for another rare roar of laughter, he got one more surprise. He was struck with terrifical force from the rear and knocked flat. Paul Bunyan hit the cave floor so hard that its walls were shaken, and a cloud of stones dropped from the roof, covering him from his hips to his thighs. Paul Bunyan dug himself out with no displeasure. He was marveling too much to be wrathful.

There is strength in this baby animal, he thought; surely he has the muscle and energy for great deeds; for that was such a tremendous butting he gave me that I am more comfortable standing than sitting. So he stood and admired this strong and energetic ox calf, who was calmly seated on his haunches before the fireplace, now throwing his head to the right as he licked his right shoulder, now throwing his head to the left as he licked his left shoulder.

If he was to keep this blue ox calf, action was truly necessary. Bébé had shown that his super-abundance of vitality made him dangerous as well as delightful and amusing. This inexhaustible energy of his must be put to work; this vast store of power in an ox-hide should be developed and harnessed to give reality to some one of Paul Bunyan's vague dreams.

Soon the well-fed blue ox calf lay down and slept contentedly.

Bébé grew wonderfully as the weeks went by, and the moose moss made him saucy as well as fat. His bulging blue eyes got a jovial look that was never to leave them. His bellow already had bass tones in it. He would paw and snort and lift his tail as vigorously as any ordinary ox ten times his age. His chest deepened, his back widened, muscle-masses began to swell and quiver under the fat of his shoulders and haunches. The drifts of the beautiful unnatural snow melted away in streams of blue water, and the marvelous color of this historical winter vanished, but the glittering blue of Bébé's silken hair remained. His tail brush was of a darker blue; it looked like a heavily foliaged cypress bough in purple twilight; and Bébé was proud of this wonderful tail brush that belonged to him, for he would twist it from behind him and turn his head and stare at it by the hour.

THE WONDERFUL OX

THE GREAT BLUE OX was so strong that he could pull any-thing that had two ends and some things that had no ends at all, which made him very valuable at times, as one can easily understand.

Babe was remarkable in a number of ways besides that of his color, which was a bright blue. His size is rather a matter of doubt, some people holding that he was twenty-four ax-handles and a plug of tobacco wide between the eyes, and others saying that he was forty-two ax-handles across the forehead. It may be that both are wrong, for the story goes that Jim, the pet crow, who always roosted on Babe's left horn, one day decided to fly across to the tip of the other horn. He got lost on the way, and didn't get to the other horn until after the spring thaw, and he had started in the dead of winter.

The Great Blue Ox was so long in the body that an ordi-nary person, standing at his head, would have had to use a pair of field glasses in order to see what the animal was doing with his hind feet.

Babe had a great love for Paul, and a peculiar way of showing it which discovered the great logger's only weak-ness. Paul was ticklish, especially around the neck, and the Ox had a strong passion for licking him there with his tongue. His master good-naturedly avoided such outbursts of affection from his pet whenever possible.

One day Paul took the Blue Ox with him to town, and there he loaded him with all the supplies that would be needed for the camp and crew during the winter. When everything had been packed on Babe's back, the animal was so heavily laden that on the way back to camp he sank to his knees in the solid rock at nearly every step. These footprints later filled with water and became the countless lakes which are to be found to-day scattered throughout the state of Maine.

Babe was compelled to go slowly, of course, on account of the great load he carried, and so Paul had to camp overnight along the way. He took the packs from the Ox's back, turned the big animal out to graze, and after eating supper he and Ole lay down to sleep.

The Blue Ox, however, was for some strange reason in a restless mood that night, and after feeding all that he cared to, he wandered away for many miles before he finally found a place that suited his particular idea of what a bedding ground should be. There he lay down, and it is quite possible that he was very much amused in thinking of the trouble which his master would have in finding him the next morning. The Ox was a very wise creature, and every now and then he liked to play a little joke on Paul.

Along about dawn Paul Bunyan awoke and looked about for his pet. Not a glimpse of him could he get in any direction, though he whistled so loudly for him that the near-by trees were shattered into bits. At last, after he and Ole had eaten their breakfast and Babe still did not appear, Paul knew that the joke was on him. "He thinks he has put up a little trick on me," he said to Ole with a grin. "You go ahead and make up the packs again, while I play hide-and-seek for a while," and as the Big Swede started gathering everything together again he set off trailing the missing animal.

Babe's tracks were so large that it took three men, standing close together, to see across one of them, and they were so far apart that no one could follow them but Paul, who was an expert trailer, no one else ever being able to equal him in this ability. So remarkable was he in this respect that he could follow any tracks that were ever made, no matter how old or how faint they were. It is told of him that he once came across the carcass of a bull moose that had died of old age, and having a couple of hours to spare, and being also of an inquiring turn of mind, he followed the tracks of the moose back to the place where it had been born.

Being such an expert, therefore, it did not take him very long to locate Babe. The Great Blue Ox, when he at last came across him, was lying down contentedly chewing his cud, and waiting for his master to come and find him. "You worthless critter!" Paul said to him, and thwacked him good-naturedly with his hand. "Look at the trouble you have put me to, and just look at the damage you have done here," and he pointed to the great hollow place in the ground which Babe had wallowed out while lying there. The Ox's only reply was to smother Paul for a moment with a loving, juicy lick of his great tongue, and then together they set off to where Ole was waiting for them.

Any one, by looking at a map of the state of Maine, can easily locate Moosehead Lake, which is, as history shows, the place where the Great Blue Ox lay down.

No one, certainly, could be expected to copy him in the matter of straightening out crooked logging trails. It was all wild country where Paul did his logging, and about the only roads which he found through the woods were the trails and paths made by the wild animals that had traveled over them for hundreds of years. Paul decided to use these game trails as logging roads, but they twisted and turned in every direction and were all so crooked that they had to be straightened before any use could be made of them. It is well known that the Great Blue Ox was so powerful that he could pull anything that had two ends, and so when Paul wanted a crooked logging trail straightened out, he would just hitch Babe up to one end of it, tell his pet to go ahead, and, lo and behold! the crooked trail would be pulled out perfectly straight.

There was one particularly bad stretch of road, about twenty or thirty miles long, that gave Babe and Paul a lot of trouble before they finally got all the crooks pulled out of it. It certainly must have been the crookedest road in the world—it twisted and turned so much that it spelled out every letter of the alphabet, some of the letters two or three times. Paul taught Babe how to read just by leading him over it a few times, and men going along it met themselves coming from the other direction so often that the whole camp was near crazy before long.

So Paul decided that the road would have to be straightened out without any further delay, and with that end in view he ordered Ole to make for him the strongest chain he knew how. The Big Swede set to work with a will, and when the chain was completed it had links four feet long and two feet across and the steel they were made of was thirteen inches thick.

The chain being ready, Paul hitched Babe up to one end of the road with it. At his master's word the Great Blue Ox began to puff and pull and strain away as he had never done before, and at last he got the end pulled out a little ways. Paul chirped to him again, and he pulled away harder than ever. With every tug he made one of the twists in the road would straighten out, and then Babe would pull away again, hind legs straight out behind and belly to the ground. It was the hardest job Babe had ever been put up against, but he stuck to it most admirably.

When the task was finally done the Ox was nearly fagged out, a condition that he had never known before, and that big chain had been pulled on so hard that it was pulled out into a solid steel bar. The road was straightened out, however, which was the thing Paul wanted, and he considered the time and energy expended as well worth while, since the nuisance had been transformed into something useful. He found, though, that since all the kinks and twists had been pulled out, there was now a whole lot more of the road than was needed, but—never being a person who could stand to waste anything which might be useful—he rolled up all the extra length and laid it down in a place where there had never been a road before but where one might come in handy some time.

Nor was the straightening of crooked roads the only useful work which the Great Blue Ox did. It was also his task to skid or drag the logs from the stumps to the rollways by the streams, where they were stored for the drives. Babe was always obedient, and a tireless and patient worker. It is said that the timber of nineteen states, except a few scant sections here and there which Paul Bunyan did not touch, was skidded from the stumps by the all-powerful Great Blue Ox. He was docile and willing, and could be depended upon for the performance of almost any task set him, except that once in a while he would develop a sudden streak of mischief and drink a river dry behind a drive or run off into the woods. Sometimes he would step on a ridge that formed the bank of the river, and smash it down so that the river would start running out through his tracks, thus changing its course entirely from what Paul had counted on.

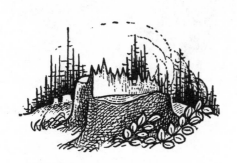

Harold W. Felton:

BABE'S BARN

The blue ox grew so fast that Paul
  Did not know what to do;
For every time he turned around
  Babe grew a foot or two.

One day Paul built the biggest barn
  In all the country side.
Babe rolled his eyes and licked Paul's neck
  And proudly walked inside.

When morning came Paul found the barn
Perched 'way up on Babe's back.
Babe went on growing all night long
And had outgrown the shack.

✝✝✝✝✝✝✝

K. Bernice Stewart and Homer A. Watt:

BABE AND THE LOG JAM

ONE TALE of the blue ox had best be told in the words of the lumberjack who sent it to a friend of Miss Stewart in a letter written with very evident care and with every other word capitalized.

Paul B. Driving a large Bunch of logs Down the Wisconsin River When the logs Suddenly Jamed. in the Dells. The logs were piled Two Hundred feet high at the head, And were backed up for One mile up river. Paul was at the rear of the Jam with the Blue Oxen And while he was coming to the front the Crew was trying to break the Jam but they couldent Budge it. When Paul Arrived at the Head with the ox he told them to Stand Back. He put Ox in the the old Wisc. in front of the Jam. And then Standing on the Bank Shot the Ox with a 303 Savage Rifle. The Ox thought it was flies And began to Switch his Tail. The tail commenced to go around in a circle And up Stream And do you know that Ox Switching his tail forced that Stream to flow Backwards And Eventually the Jam floated back also. He took the ox out of the Stream. And let the Stream And logs go on their way.

✝✝✝✝✝✝✝

De Witt Harry:

THE UNDERGROUND RAILWAY

I RECALL as if it were yesterday the time the big blue ox broke out of his corral. Paul was coming out of the front door of the house as the blue streak was going by. He grabbed the ox by the tail and threw him over the house and he landed in the corral from which he had just escaped.

Later Bunyan had trouble with one of the men whom he accused of not being honest. It was then that he originated the saying, "I wouldn't trust that man as far as I can throw a bull by the tail."

Paul was the most kind-hearted man it has ever been my privilege to know. Race, creed or color made no difference to him. He it was who built all those underground railways so popular with the colored population of the south just before the civil war. He later went back and made the tubes smaller so that the Standard Oil Company could use them in transporting crude oil from the wells to the refiners.

✝✝✝✝✝✝✝

Earl Clifton Beck:

PAUL BUNYAN'S BIG OX

Come all you old-time lumberjacks
    Wherever you may dwell,
And listen to me story—
    The truth to you I'll tell.

It's of that grand old lumberjack,
  Paul Bunyan he was called;
He was born up in Wisconsin
  And was thirty-five feet tall.

The winter of the deep blue snow
  He came to Michigan:
He logged along the Saginaw
  And also on the Grand.

And then he got his big blue ox,
  And I've often heard them say
That every day for dinner
  He would eat a ton of hay.

This big blue ox weighed fourteen tons,
  And every time he'd bawl
The earth would shake and tremble
  And the timber it would fall.

He was sixteen feet between the eyes,
  And no matter what you think,
The river went dry for three miles down
  Whenever he took a drink.

One day the ox got ornery
  And met an awful fate:
He slipped and fell and broke his neck
  I'm sorry to relate.

The camp went into mourning,
  Paul Bunyan he got tight
And wept and moaned and howled and groaned
  Till it was broad daylight.

Now I have told you truly
About that big blue ox.
Every word of it is true
You can bet your last year's sox.

For it happened in that winter
When the snow was deep and blue—
I can bring a thousand lumberjacks
Who'll swear this tale is true.

✝✝✝✝✝✝

Lee J. Smits:

PAUL'S NEW YORK TRIP
and The Ostrich Race

He sought other fields to conquer and went to New York. His two blue oxen naturally created a sensation in the metropolis and each day as he led them out onto the streets for exercise crowds of curious spectators marched in procession after the oxen. The throngs became so great that a special detail of police was sent along to preserve order and prevent accident.

The city folk enjoyed watching the two oxen eat and drink. The Big Blue Ox drank fifteen tanks of water a day and the Little Blue Ox drank seven. Paul had to buy up a whole feed store to provision them during his one week in New York. The Little Blue Ox, being smaller, naturally is not mentioned as often as the famous big one, but he did his share of stunts and the two of them were so tall that it took two men standing on ladders to yoke them.

Paul could have made big money in New York if he had charged admission to see the oxen, but it was not his nature to do such a thing. He was noted for his kind heart. That was one reason why everybody liked him. A vaudeville manager saw the financial possibilities of the oxen and offered Paul $50,000 a week to take them on tour. Paul laughed at him and pointed out the fact that no stage in the world was strong enough to hold the two oxen.

Near the end of Paul's week in New York he found a man with a proposition more to his liking. This man had a pair of fast running, enormous sized ostriches, which he claimed could beat any animal in the world in a race. He offered to bet Paul $100,000 his "birds" could win in a marathon against the blue oxen from New York to Seattle. Paul promptly accepted the wager and the details of the contest were arranged.

It was a great day for New York. Thousands thronged about the starting line and looked with amazement on the principals in the race. A mighty cheer went up when the ostriches and the two blue oxen started off in a flash at the crack of the pistol.

There was really "nothing to it." The two blue oxen ran the whole distance from New York to Seattle without stopping for breath. They ran so fast they arrived in Seattle six hours ahead of their shadows. The sad part of the story is that the two remarkable ostriches died half way across the continent. The furious pace set by the oxen broke their hearts.

After the race was won Paul hunted up the ostrich man and collected the $100,000. This money he used to start his camp in the Northwest. He got many huge logging contracts and soon collected a crew of the huskiest men ever seen in any country.

That first winter Paul put in a billion feet of logs. The oxen didn't mind the hard work but demanded all the pickles they could eat. Paul had six teams working day and night hauling in sour pickles for them. The sleigh had forty-foot bunks and they built the loads so high they had to feed the top loaders with food sent up on toy balloons.

FOOD AND THE KITCHEN

Earl Clifton Beck:

PAUL BUNYAN

Paul Bunyan, the lumberman, came from St. Paul.
He owned a big ox that was eleven feet tall.
He mowed down the trees as the farmers mow hay,
And the crew was at work before break of day.
Chorus.
        Down, down, hi-derry down.

I lived in Bay City; no work was in sight;
My board bill was due, and I had to take flight.
My clothes they were torn; I was known as "the scamp."
It was poverty drove me to Paul Bunyan's camp.

I got to Paul Bunyan's that very same day,
Climbed up in his barn and lay down in hay.
With some Peerless Tobacco I did my pipe tamp,
And I smoked away trouble at Paul Bunyan's camp.

When I got to the camp I asked for a job.
Paul Bunyan he met me with a wink and a nod.
My two eyes were black, and I looked like a tramp,
But he says, "You're right welcome to Paul Bunyan's camp."

They called me next morning before three o'clock:
"Get up, you old bum, and pull on your socks.
When you work for Paul Bunyan you don't sleep all day;
And you feed his big ox or you don't get your pay."

I went to the cook shack; 'twas forty rods long.
We all commenced eating at the sound of the gong.
We drank black coffee, ate the breast of a sow;
The pancakes were turned with a big sidehill plow.

With a ham strapped to each foot a big black coon
Greased that griddle from morning till noon.
We had to eat pancakes twice every day,
And at nine in the evening we rolled in the hay.

I went to a skidway the logs to roll down
With a big Highland Hoosier that they called John Brown.
He was big and was strong and was known as a champ,
Was that hog-headed Hoosier at Paul Bunyan's camp.

The trees were all cut and lay on the ground;
We needed a river to run the logs down.
Paul's ox was a big one, of tons he weighed three,
And he plowed a deep ditch for the Big Manistee.

Paul Bunyan quit logging when his muley ox died.
He had a big tent made out of its hide.
With the ox yoke for a pillow he smokes his big pipe
And he dreams of the river he made in one night.

✝✝✝✝✝✝✝

James Stevens:

THE BLACK DUCK DINNER

THE GREAT COOKHOUSE which so ennobled and cheered Paul Bunyan's loggers on their Sundays was the grandest and best planned affair of its kind ever heard of. The dining hall was so commodious and had so much room between the tables that four-horse teams hauled wagonloads of salt, pepper and sugar down the aisles when the shakers and bowls were to be filled. Conveyor belts carried clean dishes to the tables and returned the dirty ones to the wash room. The long-legged flunkies wore roller skates at mealtime, and the fastest among them could sometimes traverse the dining hall in forty-seven minutes.

But it was the kitchen, the powerhouse of this vast establishment, which had the most interest. This domain, ruled by the temperamental culinary genius, Hot Biscuit Slim, was as large as ten Ford plants and as noisy as the Battle of Gettysburg. The utensils that hung on its walls, from the steam-drive potato mashers and sleeve-valve, air-cooled egg beaters to the big armorplate potato kettles, the bigger force-feed batter mixers and the grandiose stew kettles, in which carcasses of cattle floated about like chips in a millpond when beef dinners were being prepared—these polished utensils glittered even when the ranges were smoking their worst at hot cake time.

Paul Bunyan had devised the monorail system for this kitchen, and overhead cranes rattled about at all hours, carrying loads of dishes from the Dishwashing Department to the Serving Department, loads of vegetables and meats from the Supply Department to the Preparations Department, and loads of dressed food from the Preparations Department to the Finishing Department. The dishes were washed on a carriage like the log carriages of modern sawmills. The head dishwashers jerked levers that threw heaps of dirty dishes from the conveyor belts to the carriage, then the carriage was shot forward until the dishes struck a sharp-edged stream of soapy water that had dropped one hundred feet. The clean dishes were bucked off on live rolls, and the head dishwasher shot the carriage back for another load. Some of the clean dishes were run through dry kilns, and others were piled for air-drying by Swede dish-pilers, who wore leather aprons and mittens and could pile sixty thousand dishes per pair in twelve hours.

A list of the marvels of Paul Bunyan's kitchen would fill a book as large as a dictionary. Elevators whirred between the kitchen and the vegetable bins, and a wide subway held four tracks that led to the fruit and vinegar cellars. A concrete chute carried the coffee grounds, eggshells and other waste to the kitchen yard, and from morning till night it roared like a millrace. Billy Puget, boss over the scraper gang, often had to work his mules and men fourteen hours a day in order to keep the kitchen yard cleaned of coffee grounds and eggshells.

Paul Bunyan's loggers had little understanding of the tremendous organization that was required for the operation of such an establishment as the cookhouse. They thanked old Paul for feeding them so well, and they agreed that Hot Biscuit Slim was a powerful good cook. Less fortunate loggers of to-day think of Paul Bunyan's camp life as a dream of bliss, and they are sure that if they had been there they would have worshiped Paul Bunyan. His own loggers, however, took the cookhouse glories as a matter of course, and they never realized what inventiveness, thought and effort were needed to give them such Sunday dinners and such Sunday afternoon dreams and content.

Nor did Paul Bunyan expect shouted praises and thanks from his loggers. He gave so much to them because he expected much from them. He worked his men twelve hours a day, and, had they thought about it, they would have been astounded by any idea of working less. And they would have been perplexed by any other scheme to ease their lot. If there were not to be great exertions, they would have asked, why their sturdy frames, their eager muscular force? If they were not meant to face hazards, why was daring in their hearts? A noble breed, those loggers of Paul Bunyan's, greatly worthy of their captain! He himself told them in a speech he made at the finishing of the Onion River Drive that they were "a good band of bullies, a fine bunch of savages." I should like to quote this speech in its entirety, for it celebrated the accomplishment of a historical logging enterprise, and it was a master oration which showed the full range and force of Paul Bunyan's oratorical powers. But as nine days and eight nights were required for its delivery, it is obvious that no publication save the *Congressional Record* could give all of it. It was at this time that Paul Bunyan served his great black duck dinner.

The speech ended on a Tuesday, and until the following Saturday morning there were no sounds save the snores of weary men and the scratching of the sleepless Johnny Inkslinger's fountain pen. By Saturday noon he had a time check and a written copy of the oration for every man in camp. After dinner the Big Swede, using a fire hose, a ton of soap, and a tank of hair tonic began to give the blue ox his spring cleaning, and Johnny Inkslinger turned in for the three hours of sleep which he required each week. Paul Bunyan was arranging his personal belongings for the move to a new job and musing on his recent accomplishment. He had never driven logs down a rougher or more treacherous stream than Onion River. And the hills over which the timber had been skidded were so rocky and steep that they tried even the strength of the blue ox. Worst of all was the rank growth of wild onions that had covered the ground. They baffled all attempts to fell the trees at first, for they brought blinding floods of tears to the loggers' eyes and made their efforts not only futile but dangerous. When the Big Swede was standing on a hillside one day, dreaming of the old country, he failed to observe a blinded logger come staggering up the slope, and he did not hear him mumble, "This looks like a good stick." Not until the logger had chopped a notch in the leg of his boot had the Big Swede realized his peril. Paul Bunyan, baffled by such incidents, was about to abandon the whole operation when the alert Johnny Inkslinger heard of the failure of the Italian garlic crop. He quickly made a contract with the Italian government, which sent over shiploads of laborers to dig up the wild onions and take them home as a substitute for the national relish. When this had been accomplished it was possible to log off the country.

There had been other difficulties to overcome, too, and as Paul Bunyan spread out a tarpaulin and prepared to roll up his boots and workclothes, he remembered them and praised the saints that they were ended. The next job offered the best promise of easy and simple logging of any he had ever encountered. For miles the land rose in gentle slopes from a wide and smoothly flowing river; there was no brush or noxious vegetation among the clean, straight trees; and, best of all, the timber was of a species now extinct, the Leaning Pine. The trees of this variety all leaned in the same direction, and it was thus possible to fell them accurately without the use of wedges. Paul Bunyan was sure of a season's record on this new job. He thought of the fresh brilliancy it would give his fame, and like a row of snowy peaks glimpsed through the spaces of a forest, his teeth glittered through his beard in a magnificent smile. But another thought quickly sobered his countenance. "Those good bullies of mine!" The words came in a gusty murmur. He dropped the tarpaulin and strode over to the cookhouse. Hot Biscuit Slim, the kitchen chief, came forth to meet him. There was a knowing look in the cook's eyes.

"It's to be a great Sunday dinner to-morrer?" he asked, before Paul Bunyan could speak.

"The greatest Sunday dinner ever heard of," said Paul Bunyan. "I want this to be remembered as the noblest meal ever served in a logging camp. My loggers shall feast like the victorious soldiers of old time. It is a natural privilege of heroes to revel after conquest. Remember, as you prepare this feast, that you may also be making immortal glory for yourself."

"You jest leave it to me, Mr. Bunyan!" answered Slim. "If the baker'll do his part with the cream puffs, cakes and pies, I promise you I'll make 'em a meal to remember. First, oyscher stew, an' then for vegytables, cream' cabbage, of course, mash' potatoes an' potato cakes, lettuce an' onions—"

"No onions!" thundered Paul Bunyan. There was a terrific crash in the kitchen as hundreds of skillets and kettles were shaken to the floor.

"Uh—I forgot," stammered Hot Biscuit Slim. "Well, anyway, they'll be oyscher soup, vegytables, sauces, puddin's, hot biscuits, an' meat in dumplin' stew an' mulligan stew, an' they'll be drippin' roasts, all tender an' rich-seasoned —oh, the meat that I'll give 'em! the meat—" he paused sharply, shivered as though from a physical shock, and misery glistened in his eyes—"only—uh—only—"

"Only you have no meat," said Paul Bunyan gently.

"I'm admittin' it," said Slim wretchedly. "Honest, Mr. Bunyan, no matter how I try I jest *can't* remember to order meat, 'specially for Sunday dinner. I can remember vegytables, fruits an' greens easy as pie, but, by doggy, I always forget meat. I ain't pertendin' a cook's worth keepin' who can't remember meat, no matter how good he is at a fixin' it. I wouldn't blame you if you fired me right off, Mr. Bunyan."

Hot Biscuit Slim leaned against the toe of the hero's boot and wept.

"That means I must rustle deer and bear," said Paul Bunyan patiently. "Well, bear meat and venison will make a royal feast when they have passed through your kettles and ovens. Light the fires, go ahead with your plans; you may yet make history to-morrow!"

He turned away, and Hot Biscuit Slim watched him worshipfully until he was a dim figure on distant hills.

"The best friend me an' my pap ever had," he said. "I'd do anything for a boss like that. I'll learn to remember meat, by doggy, I will!"

Rumors of the marvelous dinner that was being planned reached the bunkhouses, and the loggers indulged in greedy imagining of the promised delights. The day went slowly; the sun seemed to labor down the western sky. Before it sank soft clouds obscured its light, bringing showers and early shadows.

At the approach of darkness Paul Bunyan began his return march to the camp. He was vastly disappointed by the meager results of his hunt. Although he had gone as far as the Turtle River country, he had snared but two deer and three small bears. These only filled a corner of one pocket of his mackinaw, and they would provide but a mere shred of meat apiece for his men. Paul Bunyan did not feel that he had done his best; he was not one to rest on feeble consolations. As he journeyed on he was devising other means to carry out his plans for a memorable and stupendous feast. And ere he was within an hour of the camp the Big Swede was unconsciously outlining the solution of the problem for him.

The Big Swede went to the stable some time after supper to see that Babe was at ease for the night. The clouds were thinning now, and when he opened the stable door soft light poured in on the blue ox, making lustrous spots and streaks on his sleek sides. He turned his head, his bulging blue eyes shining with gentleness and good-will, and his tongue covered the foreman's face in a luscious caress.

"Har noo," remonstrated the Big Swede.

As he solemnly wiped his drenched face he sniffed the fragrance of Babe's breath and stared with a feeling of envy at the clean, glowing hair. When he had finished his inspection and left the stable, it was evident that he was wrestling with some laborious problem. His whole face was tense with a terrific frown; his memory groped among the shadows of some distant happening; he scratched his sides vigorously and breathed deeply of the air, sweet with the odors of washed earth. The purity of the spring weather, the fresh cleanliness it gave the world, and the aroma and sleekness of the blue ox, had brought the Big Swede to face his own sore need of a washing. He dreaded it as an ordeal, an exceptional and hazardous undertaking, and for that reason he wished that he might accomplish it immediately. He wandered aimlessly on, tormented by an unaccustomed conflict of the soul and the flesh, and at last he came to the edge of a cliff. He stared in surprise at the appearance of a lake below. He could not remember so large a body of water near the camp. But the Big Swede had no room for more than one emotion at a time, and a violent resolve now smothered his surprise.

"Yah, aye do him noo," he muttered.

He disrobed swiftly and ran to a rock that jutted from the cliff. Swinging his fists he leaped twice into the air; the second time he flung himself outward in a magnificent dive, his body made a great curve, and then, head first, he plunged downward. But there was no tumultuous surge and splash of waters as a climax of this splendid dive. Instead, the Big Swede's head struck white canvas with a dull, rending impact. For he had mistaken Paul Bunyan's tarpaulin for a lake! The force of his plunge drove him through the canvas and half-buried him in the soft earth underneath. His arms were imprisoned, but his legs waved wildly, and his muffled bellows shook the earth. A prowling logger saw what seemed to be shining marble columns dancing in the moonlight and felt the ground trembling under his feet.

"It can't be," he thought bravely.

Just then the Big Swede made another heroic effort to yell for help, and the logger was shaken from his feet. He jumped up and ran to Johnny Inkslinger with an alarming tale of dancing ghosts that shook the earth. The timekeeper, after sharpening twenty-seven lead pencils to use in case it was necessary to make a report on the spot, started with his medicine case for the place where the logger had directed him. When nearly there he remembered that he had failed to bring his ten gallon carboy of alcohol, which, next to Epsom salts, he considered the most important medicine in his chest. He ran back for it, and by the time he finally reached the Big Swede, that unfortunate's bellows had diminished to groans, and his legs waved with less and less gusto. After thoroughly examining and measuring the legs, Johnny deemed the proof positive that they belonged to the Big Swede. Then he got busy with paper and pencil and figured for half an hour. "According to the strictest mathematical calculations," he announced, "the Big Swede cannot continue to exist in his present interred, or, to be exact, half-interred condition; consequently he must be extricated. I have considered all known means by which this may be accomplished, I have figured, proved, and compared results, and I have arrived at a scientific conclusion. I direct that the blue ox and a cable be brought here at once."

When the loggers had obeyed this command, Johnny made a half-hitch with the cable around the Big Swede's legs, which were waving very feebly now, and in two seconds, amid a monstrous upheaval of dirt and a further rending of the canvas, the Big Swede was dragged out. For a few moments he spat mud like a river dredge; then the timekeeper proffered him the ten gallon carboy of alcohol. It was drained at a gulp, and then, with aid from Johnny Inkslinger, he was able to stagger to the camp office. When Paul Bunyan reached the camp, the Big Swede was lying on his bunk, bundled in bandages from head to foot. Johnny Inkslinger was still busily attending him; bottles of medicine, boxes of pills, a keg of Epsom salts, rolls of bandages, and surgical implements were heaped about the room. The timekeeper gave a detailed account of what had happened, and then Paul Bunyan questioned the victim, who answered briefly, "Aye yoomped, an' aye yoomped, an'— *yeeminy!*"

Johnny Inkslinger gave his chief a voluminous report of the Big Swede's fractures, sprains and contusions.

"He is also suffering from melancholia because he is still unwashed," said Johnny. "But I think I'll restore him. I've dosed him with all my medicines and smeared him with all my salves. I'd have manipulated his spine, but, confound him, he strained his back, and he threatens violence when I touch it. But I have many formulae and systems. He shall live."

"Surely," said Paul Bunyan. "A man is the hardest thing to kill there is."

Knowing that the Big Swede's wounds were nothing in comparison with the ones which he had received in the Dakota battle, Paul Bunyan worried no more about his foreman. He stepped from the camp office, plucked up a young pine tree and brushed his beard, thinking again of his unrealized plan. He remembered the wordless dejection of Hot Biscuit Slim on receiving the scanty supply of deer and bear meat. He determined that the Sunday dinner should yet be as he had planned it; otherwise it would be a bad augury for great achievements in his new enterprise. He thrust the tree into his shirt pocket and walked slowly towards his outdoor headquarters, pondering various schemes that came to mind.

When he reached the white sheet of water he was astonished by its deceptive appearance. It had a silvery glitter in the moonlight, for its surface still held the moisture of the showers. Small wonder, thought Paul Bunyan, that the Big Swede had dived into it; never was a lake more temptingly beautiful—seemingly more deep. He was gazing at the torn canvas and the huge cavity made in the ground by the Big Swede, when he heard a great chorus of shrill and doleful voices in the sky. He looked up and saw an enormous host of black ducks in swerving flight. They had lost their way in the low-hanging clouds at dusk, and now they were seeking a resting place.

Here, thought Paul Bunyan, is a noble offering of chance. Was a black duck more acute than the Big Swede, that the bright, moist canvas would not deceive him also? And once deceived, would not the ensuing dive be fatal? Wasn't a black duck's neck of more delicate structure than the Big Swede's, and wouldn't it surely break when it struck the tarpaulin? This variety of black duck grew as big as a buzzard, and here they were so numerous that clouds of them darkened the moon. Now to deceive them. Paul Bunyan could mimic the voices of all the birds of the air and all the beasts of the fields and woods, save only that of the blue ox, who always replied with a jocular wink when his master attempted to simulate his mellow moo. In his moments of humor Paul Bunyan declared that he could mimic fish, and one Sunday when he imitated a mother whale bawling for her calf the loggers roared with merriment for seventeen hours, and were only sobered then by exhaustion. His voice had such power that he could not counterfeit the cry of a single small creature, but only the united cries of flocks and droves. So he now mimicked perfectly the chorus that rang mournfully in the sky, and at the same time he grasped the edge of the tarpaulin and fluttered it gently.

The effect was marvelous. Now indeed was the canvas a perfect imitation of water. Had you been standing by the sole of Paul Bunyan's boot and seen the gentle flutter you would have been sure that you were watching a breeze make pleasant ripples on the surface of a lake. Ere long the black ducks were enchanted by the sight and sound, and Paul Bunyan heard a violent rush of air above him as of a hurricane sweeping a forest. A vast dark cloud seemed to plunge out of the sky. Another instant and the canvas was black with feathered forms. Paul Bunyan grasped the four corners of the tarpaulin, swung the bundle over his shoulder and strode home to the cookhouse. Hot Biscuit Slim was called forth, and when he saw the mountainous pile of black ducks that filled the kitchen yard he became hysterical with delight. He called out the assistant cooks, the flunkies and dishwashers, and, led by Cream Puff Fatty, the baker, the white-clad underlings streamed for eleven minutes from the kitchen door. The chief cook then made them a short but inspiring speech and fired them with his own fierce purpose to make culinary history.

Paul Bunyan listened for a moment, and then sought repose, with peace in his benevolent heart.

All night fires roared in the ranges as preparations went on for the great dinner. The elevators brought a load of vegetables every minute from the deep bins, potatoes were pared and washed, kettles and roasting pans were made ready, and sauces and dressings were devised. The black ducks were scalded, plucked and cleaned by the Preparations Department, and by morning the cranemen were bringing them by the hundreds to the Finishing Department, where the kettles and pans were waiting for them.

Most of the loggers stayed in their bunks this morning, and those who did come to breakfast ate sparingly, saving their appetites. Time passed quietly in the camp. The loggers washed and mended their clothes and greased their boots, but they did not worry themselves with bed-making. The other Sunday morning chores finished, they stretched out on their unmade bunks and smoked. They were silent and preoccupied, but now and again a breeze blowing from the direction of the cookhouse would cause them to sigh. What enchantment was in the air, so redolent with the aroma of roasting duck and stewing cabbages, so sharply sweet with the fragrance of hot ginger and cinnamon from the bakery where Cream Puff Fatty fashioned his creations! A logger who was shaving would take a deep breath of this incense, and the blood would trickle unnoticed from a slash in his cheek; another, in his bunk would let his pipe slip from his hand and enjoy ardent inhalations, blissfully unaware of his burning shirt; yet another, engaged in greas-

ing his boots, would halt his task and sit in motionless be-
atitude, his head thrown back, his eyes closed, quite
unconscious of the grease that poured from a tilted can into
a prized boot.

At half past eleven the hungriest of the loggers began
to mass before the cookhouse door, and as the minutes
passed the throng swiftly increased. At five minutes to noon
all the bunkhouses were empty and the furthest fringe of
the crowd was far up Onion River valley. The ground shook
under a restless trampling, and the faces of the loggers were
glowing and eager as they hearkened to the clatter and
rumble inside the cookhouse, as four-horse teams hauled
in loads of salt, pepper and sugar for the shakers and bowls.
Then the loggers began to stamp and shout as they heard
the flunkies, led by the Galloping Kid on his white horse,
rushing the platters and bowls of food to the tables. Tan-
talizing smells wafted forth from the steaming dishes. The
loggers grew more restless and eager; they surged to and
fro in a tidal movement; jests and glad oaths made a joyous clamor over the throng. This was softened into a universal sigh as the doors swung open and Hot Biscuit Slim,
in spotless cap and apron, appeared wearing the impressive
mien of a conquering general. He lifted an iron bar with
a majestic gesture, paused for dramatic effect amid a
breathless hush, and then struck a resounding note from
the steel triangle that hung from the wall. At the sound a
heaving torrent of men began to pour through the doors
in a rush that was like the roaring plunge of water when the
gate of a dam is lifted. The chief cook continued to pound
out clanging rhythms until the last impatient logger was
inside.

Then Hot Biscuit Slim reëntered the cookhouse. He was
reminded of a forested plain veiled in thin fog as he surveyed the assemblage of darkly clad figures, wreathed with

white and fragrant blooms of steam. His impression was made the more vivid when the loggers plunged their spoons into the deep bowls of oyster soup, for the ensuing sounds seemed like the soughing of wind in the woods. The chief cook marched to the kitchen with dignity and pride, glancing to right and left at the tables that held his master-work. He asked for no praise or acclaim; the ecstasy that now transfigured the plainest face was a sufficient light of glory for him.

The soup bowls pushed aside, the loggers began to fill their plates, which were of such circumference that even a long-armed man could hardly reach across one. The black ducks, of course, received first attention. And great as the plates were, by the time one was heaped with a brown fried drumstick, a ladle of duck dumplings, several large fragments of duck fricassee, a slab of duck baked gumbo style, a rich portion of stewed duck, and a mound of crisp brown dressing, all immersed in golden duck gravy, a formidable space was covered. Yet there was room for tender leaves of odorous cabbage beaded and streaked with creamy sauce; for mashed potatoes which seemed like fluffs of snow beside the darkness of duck and gravy; for brittle and savory potato cakes, marvelously right as to texture and thickness; for stewed tomatoes of a sultry ruddiness, pungent and ticklish with mysterious spices; for a hot cob of corn as long as a man's forearm, golden with sirupy kernels as big as buns; for fat and juicy baked beans, plump peas, sunny applesauce and buttered lettuce, not to mention various condiments. Squares of cornbread and hot biscuits were buttered and leaned against the plate; a pot-bellied coffee-pot was tilted over a gaping cup, into which it gushed an aromatic beverage of drowsy charm; a kingly pleasure was prepared. More than one logger swooned with delight this day when his plate was filled and, red-faced, hot-eyed, wet-lipped, he bent over it for the first mouthful with the joy of a lover claiming a first embrace.

In the kitchen the chief cook, the baker and their helpers watched and listened. At first the volume of sounds that filled the vast room was like the roar and crash of an avalanche, as dishes were rattled and banged about. Then the duck bones crackled like the limbs of falling trees. At last came a steady sound of eating, a sound of seventy threshing machines devouring bundles of wheat. It persisted far beyond the usual length of time, and Hot Biscuit Slim brought out his field glasses and surveyed the tables. The loggers were still bent tensely over their plates, and their elbows rose and fell with an energetic movement as they scooped up the food with undiminished vigor.

"Still eatin' duck," marveled Hot Biscuit Slim.

"They won't be more'n able to *smell* my cream puffs," said the baker enviously.

The loggers ate on. They had now spent twice their usual length of time at the table. Each plate was in a dark shadow from tall rows of slick black duck bones and heaps of corn cobs. But——

"Still eatin' duck," reported Hot Biscuit Slim.

That no one might see his grief Cream Puff Fatty moved to a dark corner. He was now certain that none of the loggers could have room for his pastries. They ate on. They had now spent three times their usual length of time at the table. The baker was sweating and weeping; he was soaked with despair. Then, suddenly:

"They're eatin' cream puffs!" cried Hot Biscuit Slim.

Cream Puff Fatty could not believe it, but a thrill of hope urged him to see for himself. True enough, the loggers were tackling the pastries at last. On each plate cream puffs the size of squashes lay in golden mounds. As the spoons struck them their creamy contents oozed forth from breaks and crevices. Stimulated by their rich flavor, the loggers ate on with renewed gusto. They had now stayed four times as long as usual at the table. Other enchantments still kept them in their seats: lemon pies with airy frostings, yellow pumpkin pies strewn with brown spice specks, cherry pies with cracks in their flaky crusts through which the red fruit winked, custard pies with russet freckles on their golden faces, fat apple pies all odorous with cinnamon, cool, snowy cream pies, peach cobblers, chocolate puddings, glittering cakes of many colors, slabs of gingerbread, sugar-powdered jelly rolls, doughnuts as large around as saucers and as thick through as cups, and so soft and toothsome that a morsel from one melted on the tongue like cream. So endearing were the flavors of these pastries that the loggers consumed them all.

Cream Puff Fatty and Hot Biscuit Slim solemnly shook hands. There was glory enough for both of them.

At last there were no sounds at the tables save those of heavy breathing. The loggers arose in a body and moved sluggishly and wordlessly from the cookhouse. They labored over the ground towards the bunkhouses as wearily as though they had just finished a day of deadening toil. Soon Onion River valley resounded with their snores and groans. . . .

At supper time, when Hot Biscuit Slim rang the gong, Cream Puff Fatty stood by his side. This was to be the supreme test of their achievement. For five minutes the chief cook beat the triangle, and then a solitary logger appeared in the door of a bunkhouse. He stared at them dully for a moment and then staggered back into the darkness. This was indeed a triumph! Great as other feasts in the cookhouse had been, never before had *all* the loggers been unable to appear for supper. This was a historic day. Cream Puff Fatty and Hot Biscuit Slim embraced and mingled rapturous tears. It was their high moment. They would not have traded it for all the glory that was Greece and the grandeur that was Rome. . . . They had intimations of immortality. . . .

✞✞✞✞✞✞✞

Constance Mayfield Rourke:

PAUL'S BIG GRIDDLE

ONCE THE King of Sweden drove all the good farmers out of the country and a Senator from North Dakota he wanted all the fine upstanding timber cleared off the whole state so as to make room for them, so he asked Paul Bunyon for to do the job and Paul he took the contract. Paul cut lumber out in North Dakota at the rate of a million foot a hour, and he didn't hardly know how to feed his men, he had so many in the camp. The worst trouble was with his hot-cake griddle. It weren't near big enough though it were a pretty good size. The cookees used to grease it with telephone poles with bunches of gunny sacks on the end, but it weren't near big enough. Paul knew where he could get a bigger griddle but he didn't hardly know how to get it to the camp. When it was got up on one aidge it made a track as wide as a wagon road and it were pretty hard to lift. So Paul he thought, and finally he hitched up his mule team. That mule team could travel so fast when they had their regular feed of seven bushels of wheat apiece that nobody couldn't hold them, and Paul had to drive them to a flat-bottomed wagon without no wheels. This time Paul hitched a couple of these here electro-magnets on the back and he drove off to where the griddle was, and he swung them magnets round till he got the griddle on its aidge, and then he drove off lippity cut to the camp, and he got the griddle a-going round so fast he didn't hardly know how to stop it, but he got her near the place where he wanted it, and then he let her go by herself, and she went round and round and round and round, gittin' nearer and nearer the center, and finally she gouged out a hole big enough for a furnace and settled down on top. Then Paul he built a corral around the griddle and put a diamond-shaped roof over it, and built some grain elevators alongside, and put in eight of the biggest concrete mixers he could find. Long in the afternoon every day they'd begin to fill the elevators and start the mixers, and then the cookees would grease the griddle. They all had slabs of bacon on their feet and they each had their routes. Paul he fixed up a fence of chicken wire round the aidge, in case some cookees didn't get off quick enough when the batter began to roll down, so's they'd have some place to climb to. When the batter was all ready somebody on the aidge used to blow a whistle, and it took four minutes for the sound to get across. Then they'd trip the chute, and out would roll a wave of hot-cake batter four feet high, and any poor cookee that was overtook was kinda out of luck.

Paul's cook shanty was so big that he had to have lunch-counters all along the wall so's the hands could stop and get something to eat before they found their places or else they'd get faint a-looking for them. Paul he had the tables arranged in three decks, with the oldest hands on the top; and the men on the second deck wore tin hats like a fireman's with little spouts up the back, and away from the third deck Paul ran a V-flume to the pig-pen, for Paul he did hate waste. The problem was how to get the grub to the crew fast enough, because the cookees had so far to go from the cook-shanty that it all got cold before they could get it onto the table. So Paul he put in a stop-clock ten foot

. . . he got the griddle a-going round so fast he didn't hardly
know how to stop it. . . .

across the face so as he could see it any place in the eating shanty, and he got in one of these here efficiency experts, and they got it all timed down to the plumb limit how long it ought to take to get that food hot to the table. Then Paul he decided to put in some Shetland ponies on roller skates for to draw the food around, and everything seemed fine. But them ponies was trotters and they couldn't take the corners with any speed, and Paul he had to learn 'em how to pace, and a whole lot of victuals was wasted while he was a-learnin' of them, and Paul was losing time and he knowed it. So finally he done away with the ponies and put in a train of grub-cars with switches and double track and a loop at the end back to the main line, so that when the cars got started proper they came back by themselves. And Paul put in a steel tank especial for the soup, with an air-compressor cupola, six hundred pounds to the square inch, and they used to run the soup down to the men through a four-inch fire hose which the feller on top used to open up as he came through.

✝✝✝✝✝✝✝

Esther Shephard:

THE CAMP ON THE BIG ONION

THE TIME I first went to work for Paul was the winter he was loggin' on the Big Onion.

I'd been workin' for old man Gilroy for a good many winters and then finally when he went broke, I thought here's my chance to go to work for Paul. I'd been hearin' about him, of course, for he'd been loggin' on Smith's Neck, down Lake Erie way, a year or two before that and on the Little Gimlet where it empties into the Big Auger, and so when

I heard he was up on the Big Onion that fall I went up there to go to work for him—there wasn't hardly a logger in Michigan but what was workin' for Paul that winter. The only job Paul had to give me was helper to the stable-boss to start with, for the first couple of months, but then afterwards I was one of the regular fallers.

It was sure a tough job, that first job I had, and I never wanted it again, for Bill, of course, like always, was takin' care of the Blue Ox; and he was an awful animal to take care of. It seems sometimes we was out pretty near all night workin' away with that critter, for naturally I was supposed to be helpin' Bill, though he didn't really want me and kind of told Paul so after a while, I guess, and so Paul put me on with the woods gang. But then, even if it was tough, bein' out early that way give me the chance to see the men comin' down for their hotcakes in the mornin', and I guess maybe that was worth somethin'—I know I wouldn't of missed it for a good deal. And then it give me the chance to get acquainted a little bit with Babe too, and kind of give me the run of things at camp.

Paul's camp was so big it was kind of hard for me to get used to it at first—for I hadn't had no experience with loggin' on that kind of a scale—till after a while I kind of learned to find my way around between the buildin's and teamsters and cattle and cooks and everybody.

The number of men in Paul's camp was never correctly counted that I know of, for there was always too many there, and too many goin' out and comin' in all the time for any one ever to be able to count 'em. But one time Paul made a kind of an estimate for a report he had to make to the goverment. They'd asked for figgurs and he said he'd try to get 'em for 'em.

So then he told the chief clerk to count 'em up but after he'd been tryin' for a couple of weeks, runnin' around all over, Johnny come back and told him it couldn't be done.

"There's too many goin' and comin' all the time," he says.

"Well, count the cattle, then," Paul says. "I know there's about five men for every yoke of cattle. That's what I always figgur on anyway. You can give 'em the report on that."

And, "Go on," he says to Windy, who was turnin' the grindstone for him that day, behind the cook-house, where he was sharpenin' up his ax.

But Johnny didn't have no better luck countin' the cattle, for they was goin' and comin' too, and there was a lot of 'em and some of 'em was always bein' killed off for the cook every meal and new ones comin' in from the stockyards.

And so in a couple of days he come up to Paul again and he says, "I can't count 'em, Paul."

That time Paul was just startin' down the road with the Blue Ox to take some logs down to the landin', and I know he didn't like to stop, but he did, though, for just a minute.

"Whoa, Babe!" he hollers.

"I tell you what," he says to Johnny, "pile up the yokes and measure 'em, and figgur from that. It won't be just exactly right, but it'll have to do. We can't waste any plaguy more time with it. We got loggin' to do." And he went on down the road.

And so Johnny, the chief clerk, got the straw boss and some of the rest of us to help him, and we went out there and piled the yokes up, and when we got it done we measured 'em and found we had just exactly three hundred and seventy cords. Figgurin' so many to the cord, and then five men to each yoke, like Paul had said, Johnny could make up the figgurs that was sent in to the goverment.

But of course then that was countin' only about one-third of 'em. In Paul's camp was where the three-shift system was invented, and so we always had one shift in camp, one goin' out to work and one out in the woods, and by measurin' the yokes that way you couldn't only get but one-third of 'em at a time, naturally.

That first fall I was workin' for Paul was when he got the big hotcake griddle. Always in the woods in them days the boys was mighty fond of hotcakes—just like men are pretty generally anywheres, I guess—and if there was anything could be said for Paul it was that he tried to treat his men right. And so, naturally, he wanted 'em to have hotcakes if there was any way he could fix it, and then besides, the way he ate 'em afterwards, he was more'n a little fond of 'em himself.

That spring on the Big Onion we had an awful lot of trouble with the garlic that growed there where Garlic Crick joins the Big Onion River—a kind of V-shaped tract in there along the loggin' road, that was just full of it. The cook tried to use it all up seasonin' the soup but the Frenchies wouldn't stand for it in their pea-soup after the first week, and even with that he only got the top layer off and then there was four more layers growin' under that one. It beats all how thick that wild garlic can grow when it gets a good start. Everybody that even went by that place was seasoned so strong there wasn't nobody else could live with him and, worst of it, he couldn't stand to live with himself even. And we pretty near just had to break up camp, but then Paul heard that the Italian garlic crop was goin' to fail that year and so we grubbed up the whole piece, every last layer of it, and shipped it all to Italy and that way we got rid of it at last; just in time when a good many of us was goin' on the drive anyway, though.

Taggert Ted Brown:

CHRISTMAS ON THE BIG ONION

CHRISTMAS MUST BE properly observed even in his big rough-and-tumble logging camp, so decided Paul Bunyan, the famous Big Boss of many an old time timber-cutting in the Wisconsin North Woods. He must have a real Christmas celebration for his lumberjacks. Paul had two thousand men in his camp on the Big Onion that winter, the winter of the Blue Snow.

Some say that Paul got the idea of a Christmas celebration from a German fellow who came to his camp to sell hospital tickets to the men, while others assert that he borrowed the plan from a tract given to him by a wandering sky-pilot. But that is neither here nor there, and of no great consequence, anyway. The day before Christmas, so one of the old river pigs yarns, Paul shouldered his huge axe and strode forth into the woods to pick a suitable Christmas tree. With him went his favorite oxen, Babe and Benny. All three tramped through the pines toward the Pyramid Forty. Now the Pyramid Forty, in Section 37, was a forty of land shaped like a pyramid, with a heavy forest of timber on all of its sides. It was so high that to see to its top "took a week." It was "as far as twenty men could see." Several lumberjacks became permanently blind in just trying to see halfway up. Paul Bunyan and his crew labored all one winter in trying to clear this forty. From it they cut one hundred million feet of lumber. Some of the men got one short leg from working all winter on one side of the slope. When they finally reached the top of the pyramid in their cutting, the stumps at the bottom had already sprouted and shot up young trees seventy feet in height. When Paul Bunyan at last logged off this forty he hitched his oxen to it, dragged it to Lake Superior and sunk the pyramid in its waters. Geologists will probably never find any trace of it.

Well, on the very crest of the Pyramid Forty, Paul found just the big pine that he wanted. With one mighty blow he felled this woodland giant. The oxen hauled it down the steep slope to camp.

With the tree over his shoulder Paul waded out into the very center of Pea Soup Lake and there set it up. It was a cold day and the water immediately froze about its butt and held it fast. Incidentally, you have no idea what a remarkable lake Pea Soup Lake was. Its history goes something like this. One of Paul's tote teamsters was one day driving across this frozen lake with a load of peas when the ice suddenly crashed, drowning the oxen and spilling the peas into the water. It was a sad loss, for the peas were badly needed. But Paul arose to the occasion. He dammed up the lake outlet and fired the slashings which he had caused to be piled around the shore. Joe, the cook, threw in a quantity of salt and pepper. So Paul boiled the water in the lake and the camp had good pea soup with an *oxtail* flavor all winter. When the men were cutting timber at a distance, Joe's assistants got the soup out to them by freezing it into sticks and pieces of rope. Some of the men drilled holes in their axe handles and filled these with soup. Their hands on the axe handles kept it warm until required for food.

After Paul had set the tree in Pea Soup Lake it froze upright and solid. The great fir towered above all of the surrounding scenery. Paul now summoned all of his handy men. With the help of Joe Muffraw, the camp cook, his camp foreman, Black Dan McDonald, and his favorite lumberjacks Jim Liverpool, Dutch Jake, Red Murphy, Yellow Head,

Curley Charley and Patsy Ward, Bunyan set to work to properly decorate the tree. Muffraw and his colored assistants brought along from the big cook shanty three logging sleds loaded to their tops with choice hams. These Paul had decided to substitute for candles to illuminate the Christmas tree. Jim Liverpool, the famous jumper, who had once cleared Lake Superior in three and a half jumps, winning a Congressional medal for his great feat, was ordered to jump into the tree and hang the hams from the limbs. Black Dan, the foreman, assisted Jim, Paul tossing the hams to them with sweeps of his mighty arm. A few of the hams they failed to catch, and greasy spots on the landscape of some northern counties show where these fell.

These men set in to work hanging the hams in the early morning. So numerous were the branches and so thick the foliage of the tree that when two of Muffraw's helpers went up with the men's lunch at noon, they got lost. Joe had to send two of his big trained chipmunks to trail the blacks. One never was found. These chipmunks Joe had fed on prune stones thrown out from the kitchen and they had in a few weeks grown as big and fierce as tigers.

Big Ole, the camp blacksmith, was busy most of the morning with his sledge and punch punching holes in the doughnuts which were to be hung on the tree. Iron balls were painted a red color to represent cherries, or gilded to simulate oranges. These weighed twenty pounds apiece. A huge silvered ox-shoe was hung on the tip of the tree.

Paul ordered ten thousand popcorn balls to be suspended from his Christmas tree. It was the duty of Joe Muffraw to fill this large order and Joe undertook the job without a whimper. He hit on the scheme of setting fire to three forties of timber slashings, and then throwing forty tons of shelled corn on the hot ashes. The noise of the popping corn was deafening. When it was all popped Joe had old Brimstone

Bill drive out the big oxen, Babe and Benny. With old Bill speeding them up with a flow of his choicest cusswords, Babe kicked the popcorn into balls and Benny rolled them past Joe and his assistants who shoveled molasses over the huge spheres as they went by. These popcorn balls were simply thrown into the tree and stuck on its branches where they hit. At these points some were unrolled to make popcorn strings and garlands and these were draped from limb to limb.

It was a hustle and bustle all day long to get that big tree dressed for the celebration. Some of the lumberjacks got pretty well tired out. Hels Helson, the Big Swede, fell asleep under its branches and Babe, the big Blue Ox, mistook his blonde head of hair for a bale of hay and ate it nearly bald before he awoke. Hels was forever suffering from ox bites.

On Christmas eve, the light from the thousand blazing hams on Paul Bunyan's tree was seen for two hundred miles away. That night two thousand lumberjacks from Paul's Big Onion camp gathered on the ice about the big tree. It was time for merriment and rejoicing. French Pete brought his company of fiddlers, accordion and jews-harp players, there was a five-gallon jug of Kentucky tanglefoot and a two-foot plug of Star tobacco for every man, the gift of good Paul Bunyan. The singing, dancing and horseplay lasted for an entire week. No one thought of retiring to the bunkhouses. The big celebration might have lasted longer but the hams on the tree finally burned out.

Of the lumberjacks who worked for Paul that memorable winter none who are now alive will ever forget the Christmas tree on the Big Onion.

Dell J. McCormick:

THE RED RIVER CAMP

THEY GATHERED their axes and saws and loaded the wagons. Paul had Ole the Blacksmith put wheels under the kitchen and dining room and even under the bunkhouses where the men slept at night. Paul tied them together with strong logging chains, and Babe the Blue Ox pulled the camp houses after him as if they had been so many toothpicks.

When they arrived, the first thing Paul set out to do was to build the largest logging camp in the world. People for miles around came to see it when it was finished. It was so big that when it was breakfast time in the kitchen, it was dinnertime in the blacksmith shop at the other end of the camp.

Every day more men joined the camp of Paul Bunyan. Finally, there were so many that Paul had them work in three shifts: one group working in the woods, one going and coming from the woods, and a third at camp, eating.

Paul bought a great watch so that everybody would know when it was mealtime. It was four feet across the face and tied to his trousers pocket with a logging chain. Of course it cost a lot of money, but Paul said it gained enough time in the first three days to pay for itself. At dinnertime Hot Biscuit Slim would blow a huge dinner horn. It was so large and made such a noise that he knocked down two hundred trees and started a windstorm on the Gulf of Mexico. After that, they decided not to use it. Later, they sold it, and the tin was used to put a new roof on the Capitol at Washington.

It was a very busy camp. Hundreds of men, called swampers, cut paths through the woods. Then the sawyers came and sawed the trees down. As the trees fell, you could hear the men shouting, "Timber!! Timber-r-r!!" to warn the others. Another crew cut the trees up into logs. Then Babe the Blue Ox pulled them down to the river where they were left until spring and then floated down the river in great rafts to the waiting sawmills.

Paul Bunyan finally invented the double-bitted ax with a blade on each side so his men could work twice as fast. Paul himself cut down the largest trees. Sometimes he chopped so fast his ax became red-hot and had to be dipped into a lake of cold water every five minutes to cool it off.

Ole the Big Swede proved to be the best blacksmith on Onion River. When he started to shoe a horse, he would take the animal right up into his lap like a baby. Then he would turn the horse on its back and nail the shoes on. He never took more than ten minutes to shoe a horse.

He once made a set of great iron shoes for Babe the Blue Ox. They were the largest shoes in the world. They were so heavy that when Ole carried one of them from the black-smith shop he sank two feet in solid rock at every step!

Day by day the camp covered more ground until the men had to take a week's food with them when they walked from one end of it to the other. Even the smokestack on the kitchen was so high they had to have it hinged in the middle to let the clouds go by. The dining room tables were two miles long, and the cookhouse boys wore roller skates so they could serve the food quickly.

Everything was on a huge scale. Even the crumbs that fell on the floor were so large that the chipmunks who ate them grew as large as wolves. They chased all the bears out of the country. Later the settlers who came shot them for tigers! Every morning after breakfast it took a crew of thirty men to dispose of the eggshells, coffee grounds, and prune pits that were piled outside the cookhouse window.

Finally, all the logs were cut and floated down the Onion River to the mills, and Paul decided to move on into a new country which lay directly to the west. The new country was later known as the Red River Valley.

The Red River got its name from Paul's camp. It seems one of Paul's cookhouse boys drove a ketchup wagon in the dining room. Every meal the men ate so much ketchup that the boy would only get halfway around when his wagon would be empty.

This made him so angry that one day he tipped the ketchup wagon over and left camp. The ketchup ran down into the river and colored the water red, and to this day that part of the country is known as the Red River Valley.

When Paul moved his camp into the new country, he found that the dining room was still too small for all his men. Every day dinner would be from two to three hours late. Paul was angry and shouted, "Hot Biscuit Slim!" Three men who were standing beside him were blown over by the force of his voice. They rolled over and over and lit on their feet running and never stopped until they were well out of the reach of his voice.

Hot Biscuit Slim, the cook, came on the run. Paul said, "I want a larger kitchen where two hundred cooks can work at the same time. Also build a larger dining room. Make the tables six miles long! Yesterday the men sat down to dinner and it was lunch time the next day before the food arrived. By that time the biscuits were cold, and who wants cold biscuits?"

So they cleared the forests for miles around and built a huge kitchen and dining room. The blacksmith, Ole the Swede, made a huge black kettle. It held eleven hundred gallons of soup.

Then the cook house boys on roller skates brought in more large platters of food.

When Hot Biscuit Slim made soup he rowed out into the center of the kettle with boatloads of cabbages, turnips, and potatoes, and shoveled them into the boiling hot water. In a few hours they had wonderful vegetable soup.

Next the blacksmith made a ten-acre griddle pan for hot cakes. Hot Biscuit Slim strapped flat sides of bacon on the feet of the cookhouse boys. They skated back and forth over the huge griddle until it was well greased.

They thought it was great fun and played tag and crack the whip. The griddle was hot, and they sometimes fell and burned their trousers. When the griddle began to steam it became so foggy no one could see across it.

Every Sunday morning for breakfast Paul's campers had hot griddle cakes. They were so large it took five men to eat one. Paul himself ate twelve or fourteen. The cookhouse boys worked all day Saturday mixing dough and bringing in huge barrels of maple syrup.

Sunday dinner, however, was the biggest meal of the week. Hot Biscuit Slim would cook the very best soup, the finest vegetables, and the nicest spring chickens.

One Saturday he said to Ole the Big Swede, "Tomorrow, I am going to have the best Sunday dinner of the year. When the men are through eating my hot biscuits with jelly, spinach, cucumbers, young red radishes, and chicken pie, they won't be able to eat a mouthful of dessert."

Cream Puff Fatty, who made the desserts, overheard this. He was very angry, for his pride was hurt. "So Hot Biscuit Slim thinks they won't eat any dessert. We shall see!" said he.

Cream Puff Fatty called the dessert boys together and said, "We will make cream puffs that will melt in your mouth! Light creamy ones with whipped cream a foot high! We shall see if they refuse to eat dessert!"

The dinner hour arrived. The men sat down and started to eat. Soup, vegetables, and salads disappeared as the men ate and ate. When the chicken pie arrived, they were almost full.

"Oh look! Chicken pie!" they shouted. They ate the chicken pie. Then the cookhouse boys on roller skates brought in more large platters of food.

"Hot biscuits and jelly! Hurrah!" they cried. They ate the biscuits and there didn't seem to be room for another mouthful of food. Cream Puff Fatty was in despair. He looked down the long dining room. The men were almost finished. It looked as if they couldn't eat another mouthful.

"Now is the time, boys!" cried Cream Puff Fatty. The dessert boys strapped on their roller skates and started down the long tables.

"Cream puffs! Cream puffs!" the men shouted as they saw large plates of fluffy white cakes topped with whipped cream. With a shout they picked up their forks and started eating again. Not a man left the dining room! Every single cream puff was eaten!

"Three cheers for Cream Puff Fatty!" yelled the men. The fat little dessert cook had tears of joy in his eyes. "It was a wonderful dinner!" said Cream Puff Fatty as he shook hands with Hot Biscuit Slim.

PAUL'S FELLOW WORKERS, PALS AND FRIENDS

Glen Rounds:

JOHN INKSLINGER

SOON AFTER Ol' Paul invented mass production in the logging business and got the system to working right, he found himself in a peck of trouble. It seems that the logging went so fast he couldn't begin to keep up with his office work.

At that time there were no figures as we know them now. So he has to do all his figuring in his head and keep all his records there too. It takes eight days and forty-seven hours to figure the payroll alone, and that's only the beginning. There are the commissary accounts, the logging records, hay and grain bills, and a thousand and one other things.

His fingers get blistered from counting on them, but he doesn't stop, and new blisters form and push the old ones back towards his wrists, and still he keeps on counting. Finally the tips of his fingers are blistered clear to his elbows. Luckily, they have time to get well by the time they reach the elbows, so go no farther. But strain as he may, he can never get more than half done.

In desperation he takes some time off and goes up to the North Pole, where he had left the Day-Stretcher he'd invented when he was logging off the Arctic. (Afterwards he'd sold it to the Eskimos, they being so pleased with the long nights it gave them.) Arriving there, he gives old chief Fancypants a broken jackknife and a lead quarter to stretch a sackful of days he's brought with him. He only has them stretched to twice the usual length, being as how he's in quite a sweat to get back to camp, and doesn't want to wait.

As it turns out, this is just as well, for he finds that when he tries to use them he's worse off than before. Naturally, if he was getting behind with the figuring when he worked an ordinary day, it stands to reason that working twice as long a day, he'd get just twice as far behind. And that's exactly what happened, so after a few days he has to give the idea up.

However, he doesn't throw those extra long days out. But being very thrifty, he ships them to a second-hand dealer in the East who has been peddling them out ever since. Perhaps you yourself can remember days that seemed endless, especially of a Monday. If so, you may be sure that it was just one of those days. Almost every school and business has a supply of them.

But to get back to Paul's problem. He's in a stew, sure enough! It looks as though he'll have to invent mass production for figuring the same as he's done for logging. But seeing as how it takes a certain amount of time for even Paul to invent inventions, and him being so busy, he thinks he'll first look around camp and see if he can find someone who can help him.

Here he runs into trouble. He finds a top loader who can figure a little, but Shot Gunderson, the woods boss, insists that he can't be spared from the woods, seeing as how he hasn't any too many top loaders as it is. Then there's the fellow in the cookshack helping Hot Biscuit Slim, who's been heard to say he can both spell and cipher. But

Slim lets it be known, in no uncertain terms, that dreadful things will probably find their way into the food if his helpers are interfered with. And not even Paul dares rile a camp cook.

So it looks like the only thing left is to try and teach Backward Bill Barber, the bull cook, to figure. You see, a fellow that's no good for anything else is given the job of carrying wood and water for the cooks, and looking after the bunkhouses. He's called the bull cook, for no good reason that I ever heard of. Naturally he can very easily be replaced, so Backward Bill gets the job. It's surprising how often people like Backward Bill get put into important jobs because they can be so easily replaced where they are.

For a while he seems to do all right. But soon Paul discovers that his figures never come out in anything but odd numbers, and finds that Bill has had a finger cut off at some time, which throws his counting into nines instead of tens. Being an odd number, nine is much harder to figure with than ten. So that finishes Backward Bill as a figurer.

Next Ol' Paul tries a crude system of bookkeeping by means of notches chopped in trees. On one tree he chops payroll notches, and on another commissary bills, and so on. For a time he keeps a crew of men busy chopping notches as he calls out the numbers. He gets so he can call out three numbers at once, and that's something not everyone can do. This system works fairly well for a time, although Paul hates to keep so many men out of the woods. But these men, not being real figurers, make many mistakes. A notch-chopper chopping payroll notches'll climb a timber record tree by mistake, or a commissary notch-chopper'll get onto a hay and grain tree, and soon the records get as badly mixed as before.

So again he's right back where he started from. He's losing sleep and weight from worrying, and even then he isn't really getting it all done, as he's so busy with other things. And he has so many notch-chopping crews out that he's kind of lost track of them and isn't at all sure that he's called them all in. He's haunted by the fear that maybe he's left a crew out in the woods somewhere to starve.

For a while he thinks seriously about going back to the great cave where he grew up, and spending the rest of his life whittling. I think this was the only time that any problem threatened to be more than Ol' Paul could solve. He kept getting thinner and thinner, and he didn't even have the heart to comb his great beard any more. It is said that the mess-hall was thrown into an uproar one morning at breakfast when two full-grown bobcats chased a snowshoe rabbit out of his whiskers. But that may or may not be true.

He gets in the habit of roaming the woods at night, with the faithful Ox at his heels, just worrying. One morning, finding himself in a part of the country that is strange to him, he decides to explore a little before going back to camp. (Although he doesn't know it, he is near Boston, which everyone knows is the seat of Learning, Culture, and Baked Beans. However, it is unlikely that he'd have cared even if he had known, as he's already learned practically everything there is to know. He's not interested in culture, and beans are no novelty to a logger.)

About ten-thirty he's sitting on a low hill, resting, when he's startled by a yell that uproots trees all around him. Up to that time he's supposed that he's the only man that can holler loud enough to knock down trees, so he's more than somewhat curious.

He stands up and steps over a couple of small mountains, and gets the surprise of his life. Sitting on a hill is a fellow almost as large as Paul himself. He has a high, smooth forehead, and instead of wearing a fur cap he's bareheaded, which even then was a sign of high learning. But the thing that takes Paul's eye is the collar. It is very high, stiff, and pure white, and looks very uncomfortable. (It is said that after he went to work for Paul he kept a crew of thirty-nine men busy every Sunday white-washing it.)

The strange giant is busy scraping the limestone bluff on the other side of the river with a jackknife the size of a four-horse doubletree, scattering the pieces for miles around. When the rock is smooth enough to suit him, he takes an enormous pencil from behind his ear and starts writing down columns of queer marks with it. The pencil is over three feet in diameter and seventy-six feet long—the first one ever used.

Paul stands around, first on one foot and then on the other, waiting for him to look up so he can find out who he is and what he's doing. But it seems that the fellow has just invented concentration and is busy practicing it as he works. So of course he never bats an eye when Paul shuffles his feet, knocking down thirty-five acres of standing timber. Nor does he seem to hear when Paul says, "Reckon as how it's goin' to be a mighty dry summer if it don't rain soon." As I said before, he was concentrating, and concentrating is a mighty exacting operation when it's done right.

After a while, however, he finishes what he's doing and turns around to look at Paul. But he still says nothing, and Paul says the same thing, as the white collar has him impressed more than somewhat. So Paul gets out his can of Copenhagen and offers the stranger a chaw; then they both sit and squirt tobacco juice at ants for a bit until they raise the river almost to flood stage. After they discuss the chances of rain, Paul asks him what he's doing with the marks on the cliff. (He thinks maybe they're some kind of pictures.)

The fellow tells him he's Johnny Inkslinger and those are figures. But naturally Paul knows that figures are something that you think but can't see.

"Them is figures, and I'm sole owner and inventor of them," Johnny insists.

He shows Paul a little of how they work, even working out a couple of problems that Paul thinks up, and finally convinces him that they really work. Then Paul wants to know what he figures, and is completely flabbergasted when Johnny tells him that he just figures for the fun of it, as he has everything that needs figuring all figured.

Paul can't imagine a full-grown man sitting around all day figuring just for the fun of it, but Johnny tells him that he always liked it. As he grew older he got dissatisfied with just figuring in his head as everyone else did, so one day he sat down and instead of just sitting, he sat and thought about what he could do to make figuring more fun.

Finally he hit on the idea of inventing figures that could be seen as well as thought. He worked for many months, and the result was a system whereby he could not only figure anything, but see the figures at the same time. Moreover, figures figured this way could be written down in books and saved for future reference. (This is the system now used in all our schools.)

As you can well imagine, Ol' Paul is pretty excited by this time. Here is mass production in figures, the same as he has in logging. And the fellow seems to be a real artist, so probably could be hired for practically nothing. If he can get Johnny to work for him his worries will be over and he can get out in the woods again. So he puts on the expression a man wears when he holds a royal flush and wants to give the other fellow the impression he's bluffing on a pair of deuces, and asks Johnny how he'd like to have a job figuring for him.

Johnny reckons that would be mighty fine, but that he's a poor man and can't afford such luxuries. Finally Paul convinces him that he means it when he says that he'll furnish him with all the figuring he can do, besides giving him books to write them in, and pay him thirty dollars a month. He right away starts off for camp at a run, he's that anxious to begin work. He was the first bookkeeper in history, and his job with Ol' Paul lasted for many years, to the great advantage of both.

✝✝✝✝✝✝✝

Dell J. McCormick:

JOHNNIE INKSLINGER
and His Magic Pen

ONE DAY a visitor asked Paul how many men were in the camp. Paul didn't know. There was Hot Biscuit Slim and his two hundred cooks. Ole the Big Swede, Blackie, Tiny Tim, and hundreds more.

Paul tried to count them one day at dinner, but they kept coming and going for hours. He asked Cream Puff Fatty how many desserts he had made. "Eight thousand," said Cream Puff Fatty.

"Good!" said Paul. "Then we must have eight thousand men."

"No," said Cream Puff Fatty, "because some of the men don't eat desserts, and Ole the Big Swede eats seven, except when it is strawberry shortcake. Then he eats ten."

So Paul gave up even trying to count the men and sent for Johnnie Inkslinger to do the arithmetic for the camp. Johnnie Inkslinger was the best bookkeeper in the North Woods—a tall sad-looking man with a bald head. He always wore a large pair of eyeglasses perched at the end of his long, thin nose.

He added and subtracted and multiplied endless rows of figures day and night. He became the fastest bookkeeper in the world and never made a mistake. One night he counted all the stars in the sky and never missed one. Johnnie Inkslinger kept track of everything, even down to the last ear of corn in the kitchens.

His magic pen never ran out of ink. A long rubber hose connected it to a ten-gallon barrel of ink, and that is how the fountain pen was invented. Johnnie Inkslinger wrote so fast that the barrel of ink had to be filled every two days.

"You are using too much ink," said Paul one day. "We cannot buy it fast enough." So Johnnie Inkslinger thought of a plan. He quit dotting his "i's" and crossing his "t's" and from then on saved nine gallons of ink a week.

Johnnie Inkslinger invented new ways of adding and subtracting that are used to this day. He wrote every number down twice so as not to make a single mistake.

He also invented the mistake eraser. This was a large rubber sponge to be rubbed over a page of figures. It erased only the mistakes and left all the rest of the figures as they were. Johnnie finally had no use for it as he made no mistakes. He gave it to Hot Biscuit Slim.

Hot Biscuit Slim used it for a while, but he never liked it. The magic sponge erased almost every figure he made. He gave it to Ole the Big Swede. Ole tried it just once and it erased the whole sheet of paper until there was only a blank space where all the figures had been. It seems Ole was very poor at arithmetic, and no matter how many times he added two and two it always came out six.

Johnnie Inkslinger once tried to figure out how much it cost to feed Babe the Blue Ox, but he finally had to give it up. Every time he added up the figures he found that Babe had eaten another barnful of hay. Then he would have to start all over again. This made him so angry that he told

Paul he would quit doing arithmetic forever. Nevertheless, Johnnie Inkslinger remained with Paul during all his years of adventure in the woods.

✤✤✤✤✤✤

James Stevens:

HELS HELSON

"WE HAVE just begun to fight," the boss logger declared to Hels Helson and Johnny Inkslinger. "Keep saying it there!"

Hels Helson was the most obedient of foremen. Every minute for three hours he repeated the watchword.

"We have yust begin to fight, you bat you!" roared Hels, shaking his right fist and gazing heavenward, as Paul Bunyan himself had done. "Yust begin to fight, yesiree!"

At last Hels unwittingly roared and posed before Babe the Blue Ox. Babe thought he was being challenged, and promptly charged. The Big Swede was hit so hard in the rear that his hip pockets were knocked over his shoulders and far into the woods. Hels hunted the pockets for a week, the watchword forgotten—and also the feeding of the Blue Ox. This neglect of Babe led to the first perilous event in the life of the newly made peninsula.

Paul Bunyan was too much occupied with preparations for a Fourther July celebration to notice what had occurred. On the eve of the anniversary of the entry of the Saginaw and the finding of Liberty Paul had a huge stack of scatter-cannon shells and a pyramid of cannon balls ready for his jacks to perform with on the morrow. He hoped with all his heart that the lads would find some fun and consolation out of a riproaring Fourther July. The preparations made, Paul retired to his oldest and easiest private padded hill for a fair night's rest.

In the meantime Hels Helson was returning with his recovered hip pockets. He had discovered a bevy of bears using them for caves. The bears trailed him home, whimpering and moaning, sorrowful over losing such powerful-smelling abodes. In vain the Big Swede hooted and shooed them back.

"Go back to the voods, you fool bars, you!" hooted Hels. "You tank you keep may pockets foor caves all summer noo?"

But the bears stubbornly followed. At last Hels Helson paused to think what might be done about the bears. For three hours he stood scratching his head and thinking, with no other effect than that of a headache. Then Hels noticed that the bears were no longer about. Chuckling with relief, he tramped on for camp. Little did Hels Helson dream that the bears had crawled up his legs while he was trying to think and were even now snuggled in the depths of his hip pockets. Indeed, Hels did not discover their presence until the following year, when he took his regular spring bath. Then a turning out of his hip pockets revealed seventeen big bears and thirty-four cubs. Only a Hels Helson could have carried such a bevy of bears in his hip pockets without knowing he had them.

🌲🌲🌲🌲🌲🌲

W. B. Laughead:

BIG OLE

Big ole was the blacksmith at Paul's headquarters camp on the Big Onion. Ole had a cranky disposition but he was a skilled workman. No job in iron or steel was too big or too difficult for him. One of the cooks used to make doughnuts and have Ole punch the holes. He made the griddle on which Big Joe cast his pancakes and the dinner horn that blew down ten acres of pine. Ole was the only man who could shoe Babe or Benny. Every time he made a set of shoes for Babe they had to open up another Minnesota iron mine. Ole once carried a pair of these shoes a mile and sunk knee deep into solid rock at every step. Babe cast a shoe while making a hard pull one day, and it was hurled for a mile and tore down forty acres of pine and injured eight Swedes that were swamping out skidways. Ole was also a mechanic and built the Downcutter, a rig like a mowing machine that cut down a swath of trees 500 feet wide.

❦❦❦❦❦❦❦

James Stevens:

PEA SOUP SHORTY
and Sourdough Sam

AFTER PAUL BUNYAN had invented logging and brought hosts of little loggers over to Real America to fell trees and drive logs down the rivers, his most baffling problem sprang from the fact that little loggers could not live on raw moose meat as he did. They required cooked food; consequently Paul Bunyan was compelled to build a cookhouse and import cooks. His first cookhouse was a crude affair without any notable mechanical equipment. And his first cooks were men without talent or experience. But Paul Bunyan's loggers were hardy men whose appetites had never been pampered, and no one complained of the camp fare until Pea Soup Shorty took command of the cookhouse.

Pea Soup Shorty was a plump, lazy, complacent rascal, and he made no attempt to feed the loggers anything but hard-tack and pea soup. He even made lunches for them by freezing pea soup around a rope and sending the loggers' lunches out to them in sticks like big candles. Even then the loggers did not complain greatly. Not until the winter in the Bullfrog Lake country were they heard to cry out against their food. That winter Shagline Bill's freight sleds broke the ice on the lake, and the season's supply of split peas was lost in the water. Pea Soup Shorty did not try to originate any new food for the loggers; he simply boiled the lake water and served it to them for pea soup. Then the bunkhouse cranks began to growl; and finally all the loggers revolted against Pea Soup Shorty; and they declared against pea soup also. Paul Bunyan had to look for another kitchen chief. Old Sourdough Sam was his selection.

The Bunyan histories tell that Sourdough Sam made everything but coffee out of sourdough. This substance is really fermented dough, having the rising qualities of yeast. It is said to be an explosive. Modern camp cooks are always at great pains to warn the new kitchen help away from the sourdough bowl, telling them of the sad accident of Sourdough Sam, who had his left arm and right leg blown off in an explosion of the dangerous concoction.

The old cook brought this misfortune on himself. Sourdough was his weakness as well as his strength. Had he been content to keep it only in the kitchen, where it belonged, and to develop it simply as a food, he, and not his son, Hot Biscuit Slim, might be remembered as the father of camp cookery, even as the mighty Paul Bunyan is venerated as the father of logging. But Sam was prey to wild ideas about the uses of his creation. He declared it could be used for shaving soap, poultices, eye wash, boot grease, hair tonic, shin plasters, ear muffs, chest protectors, corn pads, arch supporters, vest lining, pillow stuffing, lamp fuel, kindling, saw polish and physic. One time he came into the bunkhouse with a chair cushion made out of sourdough. As bad luck would have it, Jonah Wiles, the worst of the bunkhouse cranks, was the first man to sit on it. He always sat hard,

and when he dropped on the new chair cushion, he splashed sourdough as high as his ears. Jonah Wiles was fearfully proud of his mackinaw pants, for they were the only pair in camp that had red, green, purple and orange checks. Now the bursted cushion was splashed over all their gaudy colors. Sam apologized humbly and begged the privilege of washing them. His rage showing only in the glitter of his beady blue eyes, Jonah Wiles stripped off the smeared pants and handed them over to the cook. Sourdough Sam recklessly washed them in another of his creations, sourdough suds. Not a thread of color was left in the prized pants; they were a brilliant white when they were returned. The old cook brought them back reluctantly and he was tremendously relieved when Jonah Wiles did not tear into him with oaths and blows. But Jonah Wiles was different from other loggers in that he always concealed even his strongest feelings. So he put on the pants without saying a word, though he was blazing with wrath inside. His rage against the cook was aggravated when his mates began to call him "the legless logger," because of his invisibility from the bottom of his coat to the tops of his boots when he tramped to work. The brilliant white pants did not show at all against a background of snow.

⁜⁜⁜⁜⁜⁜

Lee J. Smits:

VICTOR, THE FIRST HIGH CLIMBER

Victor was nine feet across the shoulders and the width of a razor blade between the eyes (as a good high climber should be). He had a 16-pound double-bitted ax with a rope handle, and just swung it in a circle as he went up. When he started cutting, you couldn't see the sun. He used no safety rope—just a hog hook in his left hand and the ax in his right. He took the 1,600 pound bull block up with him, tied to his belt.

✟✟✟✟✟✟

W. B. Laughead:

JOE MUFRAW,
the One Named Pete

When a man gets the reputation in the woods of being a "good man" it refers only to physical prowess. Frequently he is challenged to fight by "good men" from other communities.

There was Pete Mufraw. "You know Joe Mufraw?" "Oui, two Joe Mufraw, one named Pete." That's the fellow. After Pete had licked everybody between Quebec and Bay Chaleur he started to look for Paul Bunyan. He bragged all over the country that he had worn out six pair of shoe-pacs looking for Paul. Finally he met up with him.

Paul was plowing with two yoke of steers and Pete Mufraw stopped at the brush-fence to watch the plow cut its way right through rocks and stumps. When they reached the end of the furrow Paul picked up the plow and the oxen with one arm and turned them around. Pete took one look and then wandered off down the trail muttering, "Hox an' hall! She's lift hox an' hall."

PAUL'S ADVENTURES
WITH CONTEMPORARY HEROES

Leigh Peck:

PECOS BILL MEETS PAUL BUNYAN
and Starts a New Ranch

EVEN THOUGH Pecos Bill was boss of all the cowhands on the ranch, and had the very finest horse in all the world to ride, and had invented so many new things, he was not satisfied. He wanted to start a new ranch. A small place of just a few hundred thousand acres would do to begin with, he thought. Whenever he had a little time to spare, he rode out on Lightning [his horse] looking for a good place to start a ranch. In those days, there was plenty of land that anyone could have simply by claiming it. But Pecos Bill did not want just an ordinary ranch. He wanted the very best ranch in all the world.

Finally in Arizona he found the very piece of land that he was looking for, with grass taller than a man's head for the cattle to fatten on, creeks fed by springs of pure water for them to drink, and a few trees along the banks of the creeks, for shade in the heat of the day. The land was level except for one mountain. This mountain was tall and quite steep near the top. A very queer kind of birds, seen nowhere else in the world, made their nests among the rocks on the upper slopes of the mountain. They had to lay square-shaped eggs, because round eggs would have rolled right down the mountain.

Pecos Bill thought that this mountain would be just right for his headquarters ranch. The cattle could always find on it the climate they liked best. In cold days they could graze at the foot of the mountain, but in hot weather they could move up near the top, where it would always be cool. They could even have sunshine or shade, just as they wished, for one side of the mountain would be sunny while the other side was in the shade. It would not be likely to rain on both sides of the mountain at once, either, so the cattle could almost always keep dry. Certainly, the wind could not blow from more than one direction at once, and the cattle could always find a sheltered place where the wind was not blowing on them.

There was just one thing wrong with the mountain. It was covered with trees, huge tall trees, clear up to the rocky top. There was not room to ride a horse through the close-set trees, and certainly no room for cattle to graze there, or for grass to grow. Pecos Bill thought and thought, but he could not think of any way to clear the mountain of those trees. He hated to give up and admit there was anything that he could not do. Again and again he rode back to look at the mountain, and try to figure out some way to clear it for his headquarters ranch.

Then one day, imagine his surprise and anger when he found someone else on his mountain! A hundred men were at work at the foot of the mountain putting up a big bunkhouse and a big cookhouse. They did not look like cowboys at all, and they did not have any cattle with them—except for one huge blue-colored ox. He was a hundred times bigger than any steer Pecos Bill had ever seen before, and he ate a whole wagonload of hay at one swallow!

Pecos Bill did not stop to think that he was only one man against a hundred men, and that the huge ox could kill a man by stepping on him. He rode right up to the camp and asked, "Who is in charge here?"

"Paul Bunyan," answered one of the men.

"I want to talk to him," said Pecos Bill.

The man called, "Paul," and there walked out from among the trees the very biggest man in all the world—as big for a man as the Blue Ox was for a steer. Now Pecos Bill himself was a fine figure of a man, six feet two inches high, straight as an arrow and as strong and limber as a rawhide lariat. But this Paul Bunyan was so tall that his knee was higher than Pecos Bill's head! He had a long, dark beard. He wore flat-heeled, broad-toed boots, not like cowboy boots at all. He wore no chaps, and instead of a leather jacket he wore a queer woolen jacket of bright-colored plaid.

But if Pecos Bill was startled, he did not show it. He asked very firmly, "What are you doing on my mountain?"

"This is my mountain now," Paul Bunyan announced. "I've already settled on it."

"That makes no difference. I laid claim to this land long ago," Pecos Bill argued.

"Where's the law that says it's yours?" demanded Paul Bunyan.

"Here it is!" exclaimed Pecos Bill. "This is the law west of the Pecos," and he laid his hand on his pistol.

"That's not fair!" cried Paul Bunyan. "I'm not armed. In the North Woods, we don't fight with pistols. We fight with our bare fists or with our axes."

"Very well," agreed Pecos Bill. "I'll give you the choice of weapons. I have no axe, but I'll use my branding iron to hit with."

Now the branding iron that Pecos Bill carried that day was what is called a running iron. It was only a straight iron bar with a crook on the end of it. Cowboys heat the end of a running iron and draw letters on a steer's hide as you would draw with a piece of crayon on paper.

Pecos Bill heated the end of his branding iron on a blazing star that he had picked up the time the stars fell. He always carried it about with him in his saddlebag, so as to have a fire immediately whenever he needed one. Then the fight started.

Paul Bunyan hit at Pecos Bill so hard with his axe that he cut a huge gash in the earth. People call it the Grand Canyon of the Colorado River now.

Pecos Bill swung his red-hot iron, trying to hit Paul Bunyan, until the sands of the desert were scorched red-colored. That was the beginning of the Painted Desert out in Arizona.

Again Paul Bunyan tried to hit Pecos Bill and hit the ground instead. The queer rocks that are piled up in the Garden of the Gods in Colorado were split up by Paul Bunyan's axe in that fearful fight.

Pecos Bill's iron, instead of cooling off, got hotter and hotter, until the forests in New Mexico and Arizona were charred. These trees, burnt into stone by the heat from Pecos Bill's running iron, are called Petrified Forests now.

But neither man could get the better of the other. For the first and only time Pecos Bill had met his match. And it was the first and only time that Paul Bunyan's crew had seen a man that could stand up to him.

Finally they both paused to get their breath, and Paul Bunyan suggested, "Let's sit down and rest a minute."

"All right," agreed Pecos Bill, and they sat down on nearby rocks.

As they sat resting, Pecos Bill asked, "Stranger, why are you so anxious to take my land away from me? Isn't there plenty of other land in the West, that you could have just by laying claim to it?"

"Land!" exclaimed Paul Bunyan. "It's not the land that I want!"

"Then why are we fighting? What do you want?" inquired the surprised Pecos Bill.

"Why, the trees, of course," Paul Bunyan explained. "I'm no rancher. I have no use for land, any longer than it takes to get the timber off. I'll log the trees off that mountain, and then I'll be through with it. I'm a lumber man."

"Why didn't you say so at first?" exclaimed Pecos Bill. "You are more than welcome to the trees! I've been trying to find someway to get them off the land, so that the grass can grow and my cattle can graze here."

"They'll be off in a few weeks," promised Paul Bunyan, and the two men shook hands.

Pecos Bill and Paul Bunyan were good friends after that, each respecting the other for the fight that he had put up. Pecos Bill had his cowboys drive over a herd of nice fat young steers, to furnish beef for Paul Bunyan's loggers while they were clearing off the trees. When Paul Bunyan and his men were through, they left standing their bunkhouse and their cookhouse and the Blue Ox's barn, ready for Pecos Bill's outfit to move in.

✤✤✤✤✤✤✤

Margaret Prescott Montague:

THE WORLD'S FUNNY BONE

Did any of you folks ever hear tell of Paul Bunyan, that wonderful lumberjack they got up North somewheres? They say he kin burl a log so fast he'll skin it right outer its bark, and then run to shore on the bubbles. Well, we got a mighty logger right here in West Virginia, by the name of Tony

Beaver, and the tricks he pulls off sure air all outer the common. He has his log camp up Eel River, and I'm aiming now to tell you all erbout the time them two great fellers, Tony Beaver and Paul Bunyan, met up face to face. That sure must er bin sompen to see! And outer it, too, come the biggest kinder eye opener for Tony and Paul both.

The first news Tony Beaver's crew had of Paul Bunyan was one time when a strange logger come by the Eel River camp singing a little song:—

> Paul Bunyan growed a mighty tree,
> Its branches scratched the sky;
> And when he felled the doggoned thing
> It ripped a hole on high.

"Hey, stranger!" Big Henry, one of Tony's stoutest hands, yells at him. "That song's all right, but you got the names twisted. It wa'n't no Paul Somebody growed that tree; it was Tony Beaver hisself, and well I recollect the time."

"I never heard tell of no Tony Beaver," says the stranger, "but Paul Bunyan I know well, being one of his hands. In Paul's camp now," he says, setting down on a stump and biting him off a chaw of terbacker, "they got a griddle for frying the batter cakes the fellers eats so big that the onliest way they kin grease the thing is to have six men skate over it with a slab of fat meat on each foot."

"Welcome to Eel River!" says Big Henry. "It's right here in Tony Beaver's camp you belong—only first you got to git them names straight."

"I hate to git things wrong," says the stranger, looking like he was doing his best to hit the truth; "and it's a fact I made a slip when I said Paul Bunyan needs six men to grease that there griddle. It's really eight he uses, and in a pinch I've seen as many as ten er twelve hands skating over it, with them slabs of bacon on they feets. It sure is hot work fer the fellers! Every slide they make they leave a trail of smoke behind 'em, and they have to keep stomping they feet *all* the time to stomp the flames out."

"Look a-here, stranger, didn't you hear me say that was Tony Beaver you was talking erbout?" says Big Henry, gitting mighty restless.

"Paul Bunyan is the man I'm speaking of," says the tother, buttoning up his mouth in a right stubborn way.

"That's a —" says Big Henry, and sidesteps. "That's a —" he says ergin, riding right up to the word and jumping off jest in time.

"If the word yer aiming at is 'lie,' hit it!" says the stranger, standing up kinder dangerous.

"Well," says Big Henry, knowing he has to be polite to company, "we don't have to *say* nothing erbout lies in this camp, for Tony Beaver's got a trick for ketching 'em. He's invented him some sticky lie paper that ketches lies as fast as fly paper ketches flies. Wait, and I'll show you!"

With that he goes into the bunk house, and comes back with a great roll of that thar lie paper. Thar was two or three ole lies still hanging on to the thing, and if thar's one thing worse-looking 'an a fresh lie, it's a ole one.

"Here, now, we'll jest see what's what!" says Big Henry, swishing the paper all erbout in the air whar the stranger'd been talking. But no, sir! He didn't ketch nary ernother lie.

"Hey! Looks like I've been telling the truth all erlong!" says the strange hand, kinder tickled, and some s'prised too. "Or else sompen's the matter with the paper—mebbe you fellers in this camp has sorter overworked it."

"Sompen's wrong, sure," says Big Henry, mightily outdone. "Thar, now!" says he, looking down the trail. "Here comes ole Preacher Mutters! He's got all kinds er book sense if he ain't got no other kind. Mebbe he kin straighten things out. Hey, Brother Mutters!" he bawls. "Did you ever hear tell of a feller by the name of Paul Bunyan?"

The ole preacher claws his fingers through his beard fer a spell, looking as earnest as a billy goat. "It's *John* Bunyan you mean—him as writ that holy book, *The Pilgrim's Progress*," he says, rolling back his eyes, and tipping up his chin to let them pious words trickle down his throat, like a ole hen drinking.

"That's news to me," says the stranger. "Paul mought of had a brother by the name of John, but I never heared tell of him. The Bunyan I'm speaking of," he says, gitting into his stride ergin, "has the biggest bees a feller ever did see. Each one of 'em's big as a full-grown ox, and Paul crossed 'em a while back with a gang er moskeeters, and the offsprings of that wedding is the awfulest critters a person ever did see, fer they has stings both before and behind."

"That sure don't sound like nothing I ever heared tell of John Bunyan," says the preacher, shaking his head mightily mystified.

"Looks like the bunion's on the tother foot, then," says the stranger, acting smart.

"It ain't no Paul Bunyan, ner no John neither—it's Tony Beaver! And I'm here to tell the world so!" says Big Henry, jumping up.

But it was the stranger got in the furst lick. "*Paul Bunyan!*" he says, putting his fist in the word, and landing it on Big Henry's jaw.

"*Tony Beaver!*" Big Henry bellers back at him, placing his name on the tother's nose.

"Hol' on, brothers! Hol' on!" says the preacher, reaching out and trying to peacify the two. But pore ole feller! *Bang!* he got a *Paul* on the side of his head, and next a *Tony* tuck him in the chist, bowling him over on the ground with the wind knocked outer him.

He lay thar for quite a spell gaping up at the sky. "No," he says at last, kinder talking to hisself. "No, that Paul Bunyan surely ain't no kin at all to John."

But jest erbout then Tony Beaver hisself happens up on the scene, toting a little boy on his shoulder what's a great buddy of his'n.

"Here, now! Here!" he says. "What's all this erbout?" With that he scoops ole Brother Mutters up off'n the ground, steps right in betwixt the two fighting fellers, and had everything ca'med down jest in no time.

"But look a-here, Tony," says Big Henry, still all worried up. "Here's a strange hand telling some of your doings, and tacking 'em all on to a logger by the name of Paul Bunyan— or mebbe his furst name's John."

"No, *sir*! It ain't John Bunyan!" says Brother Mutters, feeling hisself all over to see was he fatally busted.

"You all oughter see that blue ox, Babe, of Paul's," says the strange hand, going right erlong like nothing hadn't happened. "He measures all of forty-two axe handles and a plug of terbacker acrost his forehead—forty-two, that is, of Paul's axe handles; that 'ud be erlong erbout one hundred and seventy-five of any common hand's. An' his nose is so fer away from his years he can't hear heself snort."

"Well, *that* ain't nothing," chips in the little boy setting up on Tony Beaver's shoulder mighty proud, fer he jest thinks Tony Beaver makes the world go round. "Tony, he's got him a yoke er steers so big it takes a crow a week to fly betwixt the horns of one of 'em."

"Shake, young feller," says the stranger. "If yer needing a job, I'd be glad to take you up to Paul; he's looking fer stout fellers like you right this minute."

"I thank you," says the little feller, all swelled up, "but I got jest erbout all I kin han'le right here he'ping Tony out."

"I've heared tell of that Paul Bunyan afore now," says

Tony, scratching his year more like he was some kinder varmint than a human. "If he's the great logger you say he is, tell him to come on up Eel River, and him and me'll have a contest and find out which is the best feller."

"That's the very trick!" Big Henry hollers out.

"All right, I'll take your word to Paul—*he'll* show you all sompen," says the stranger, laying back his years, and making ready to shoot fer his own shanty.

"Tony Beaver'll show *him* sompen!" the little feller hollers after him, cocking up his head, and flapping his arms like he was a rooster about to crow.

Well, it wa'n't hardly no time after that 'fore Paul Bunyan come up Eel River with a whole parcel of hands from his camp. Thar was Charlie the Swede, Big Ole, and a heap more, besides Johnny Inkslinger, Paul's timekeeper, with his fountain pen as big as a saw log—no, I dunno's it's quite *that* big.

Well, sirs! When they met, Tony and Paul sure did set a swift pace in manners!

"Welcome to Eel River, Mr. Bunyan," says Tony.

"Pleased to meet you, Mr. Beaver," says Paul. "Me and my crew put out the minute I got your word, but mebbe I'm a bit late gitting here. What's the time?"

"It's any time you say, Mr. Bunyan," says Tony.

"How's that, Mr. Beaver?" says Paul.

"Jest like I say—name the time you want, and it's your'n."

"Well, I *was* aiming to hit your camp at sunup, but now looks like it's nigh midday," says Paul.

"Sunup she shall be!" says Tony. With that he reaches in his pocket and hauls out a handful of time, and *swish!* thar she was right back at sunup ergin, with the dew fresh on the grass, and all the little birds chirping up to sing.

"That's a mighty handy trick," says Paul. "Inkslinger, make a note of that."

The timekeeper laid aholt of his pen, and the scratch-scratching of it was like a million katydids ripsawing on **they** hind legs in fall weather.

"We had bad luck with the time in our camp the winter of the blue snow," says Paul. "There was mighty little forage that year, and Babe, that ox of mine, busted into the granery where the time was kep' an' chawed it all up 'fore we could make him quit—all, that is, 'cept the leap years. Even Babe couldn't stomick *them*."

"My time is yours, Mr. Bunyan. Jest help yerself; take right smart, take darned nigh all," says Tony, showing his manners.

"I thank you," says Paul. "I fetched you a present of a couple of my bees. The pair of 'em'll make you a ton er honey a month. Here, Ole! Fetch up them bees!" he hollers out.

Big Ole brung the bees up, and I wished you could er seen 'em! Each one of 'em was as big as a ox, and they was loaded down with log chains to keep 'em from flying erway.

"We had 'em check they stings with the timekeeper while we was traveling," says Paul. "But Johnny Inkslinger's got 'em labeled which ones goes behind and which before, and kin slip 'em in whenever you say."

Tony casts his eye over 'em, and they sure did give him back a mighty mean look, with both of 'em buzzing like a sawmill cutting through white oak.

"Well," he says, "let's git better acquainted afore we give 'em back they weepons."

After that the stunts betwixt Paul Bunyan and Tony Beaver commenced. But pshaw! It looked like thar wa'n't a pin to choose betwixt the two of 'em. If Tony Beaver tore a white oak up by the roots and pitched it acrost Eel River, Paul Bunyan'd pull up a red oak and toss it over the ridge. And if Paul set the calks of his boots nigh fifty feet up in the face of a cliff, Tony'd jump across Eel River and back ergin without tetching ground on the tother side. So thar they was wasting a lot er sweat and nothing gitting settled. But d'reckly all hands got to noticing that that little boy belonging to Tony's camp kep' a-hollering all the time for Tony no matter which feller done the trick. "Aw, look at Tony Beaver jumping acrost Eel River! Aw, look at Tony stomping his boots up yander on the rocks!" he'd holler.

That made Paul's hands kinder mad. "Look a-here, young feller, your man ain't doing it all! That was Mr. Bunyan what set his calks in the face of the cliff," Big Ole tells him.

The little feller looks at him kinder big-eyed and s'prised, and then he says, "Aw, you fool me!" an' kep' right erlong hollering, "Looky! Look at Tony!" fer everything that happened.

But Paul hisself didn't git mad. He looks at the little feller fer a spell, and then he throws back his head and busts out with a great big round "Haw, haw, haw!"

"What's hitting your funny bone, brother?" Tony asks him, for by now the two of 'em was gitting mighty friendly.

"Thar's a big laf coming from somewhers," says Paul, kinder sniffing the air like he was a hound dawg. "I can't tell whar it's heading from, but when she busts she sure will be a big one. I'm funny that way," he says; "I kin sense a joke and commence to laf when it's still all of ten miles off—be damned if I can't! *Aw—oh!*" he says, clapping his hand to his mouth, "I didn't go to let that word fly out before the little feller!"

"Take it back then, brother!" says Tony.

"How kin I? I spit that word out so hard it's nigh half a mile down the skidways of the past by now."

"I kin git it back fer you!" says Tony, bawling to his hands to fetch him around his riding horse.

Now that nag of Tony's sure is swift, but it ain't so much its swiftness that's peculiar as the way they got him saddled. Tony had a chore boy in his camp a while back what appeared to be jest a fool fer want er sense, and one time the feller fetched the horse round with the saddle facing the tail. "I saddled him thataway so's you could ride both going and coming," he says, his mouth gaping open at his own smartness.

"Well, thar ain't one grain er sense to that," says Tony, "and jest fer that very reason I b'lieve it's true." With that he jumps on the beast, and dogged if he couldn't do jest like the fool said, ride both going and coming. It sure is a swift way er traveling, and the onliest way I know of that a person kin be in two places at onct.

Well, Tony jumps on his beast now, and takes out *pluckety-pluck* after that cuss word Paul had let fly. Riding thataway, it wa'n't hardly no time 'fore he come up with it. But course I don't have to tell none er you all that if thar's one thing a cuss word hates worse'n another it is to be taken back once it's loose. So, with Tony right atop of it, that word turned a kind of a summersault, and tuck back up the road ergin, its years laid flat, jest scooting fer—Well, to name the place that "damn" was heading fer I'd have to let out another cuss word, which I ain't aiming to do; so I'll jest say it was making fer home, and let it go at that.

"Thar she goes! Head her off! *Head her!*" Tony bawls, checking up his horse, and turning erbout with the gravel flying off into the bresh, and the trail smoking behind him.

All hands from both camps spread out acrost the road whooping and hollering fer all they was wurth. But, with them hollering in front, and Tony whooping up behind, that "damn" word commenced to squawk and to fly like a skeered guinea hen. All hands made a jump fer it, but it sailed right over the heads of everyone 'cept Paul. He give sech a master leap that it landed him atop of a white oak tree, and from thar he bounded over on to a low-hanging cloud, ketching that cuss word on the way.

"Aw, *looky*! Look at Tony up in the clouds!" the little feller screeches out, dancing eround and all carried erway.

"That ain't Mr. Beaver up yander; it's Mr. Bunyan," Paul's hands hollers back at him, clean outdone.

Well, *sirs*! Things sure commenced to look bad fer Paul. That cloud had been jest drifting erlong, hanging low in a kind of a doze, but when Paul landed down on it, all so sudden, it give a great bound, and headed fer the sky like a skeered racer, with Paul hung up on it, and no way er reaching ground ergin. More'n that, the cloud was right thin, and it looked like, heavy as Paul is, he mought fall spang through it any minute. Every step he tuck he went down waist-deep in the thing; and it's the truth, time and ergin the fellers seen his boots come dangling through the bottom side of the cloud with nothing but air betwixt them and deestruction. All of Paul's hands sets up a turrible yammering, hollering up at him to "take keer" and "mind out" and "don't fall," and all like that, like the feller would fall if he could he'p hisself. Tony's hands, wanting to show they manners, they hollered too. Johnny Inkslinger, what's the greatest cal'ulator the world has ever knowed, unlimbered his fountain pen and commenced to figger out the distance from the ground, Paul's weight, and all like that, so's they'd know how bad he'd be busted when he drapped.

"Git ready fer the wurst, boys, fer he'll be nothing but fractions when he hits," he says, figgering and sniffling, with the ink and tears all spluttering out together.

But erbout then Big Ole lets out a great yell. "It's all right! Ole Paul's all right! He's kicking him up a thunderstorm!" he hollers.

Sure 'nough, when the hands looked they seen that Paul was milling 'round in the cloud, trompling on it and teasing it, making the thing so mad that it was gitting blacker and blacker, till d'reckly it all fires up and busts out in er

turrible storm, swearing and spitting out thunder and lightening at him. Paul waits jest long ernough to pick him a good
streak of lightening, and then he slides to the ground on it
all safe and sound, 'cept his pants was some scorched, and
a person could smell singed whiskers. But the cuss word, it
was burnt to a crisp.

"I have to thank ole Pecos Bill for that trick," says Paul,
breshing hisself off. "Bill, he's that great cattle man they
got down in Texas. He kin take a cyclone by the year, ride it
acrost three states, and slide to ground on the lightening
whenever he gits ready."

"I knowed you was all right, Tony. I knowed you'd slide
down on the lightening streak," says the little feller.

"Now look a-here, Buddy, you got to git things straight,"
says Tony, kinder worried. "*That's* Mister Bunyan," he says,
pinting at Paul, "and *this* here is me. It was him, not me,
slided down on the lightening streak."

The little feller looks at him mighty earnest, doing his best
to onderstand, but in the end he says, jest like he had afore,
"Aw, you fool me!"

At that Paul Bunyan lets out ernother great crackling laf,
shrugging up his shoulders, and rubbing his elbows erginst
his ribs. "That big laf's gitting closer, I kin feel it tickling
my funny bones," he says.

Tony Beaver looks and looks at the little feller in a kind
of a daze.

"Well, I will be dogged!" he says, like big news had struck
him.

"Haw, haw, haw! Do you reckon it kin be true, brother?"
says Paul.

"Well, thar's one way to find out. Come on, let's take it!"
says Tony. With that he takes the little boy up on his shoulder, and, not saying nothing to the tother fellers, him and
Paul went off into the bresh together.

Tony, he led along through the woods till they come to a little clear spring running out from under the roots of a maple tree. "Now, then, Buddy, you work us a charm," he says to the little feller. With that he breaks off a switch from a witch-hazel bush like what you've seen a water doctor use, and gives it to the young-un to whip through the spring fer a spell. Then he says to Paul, "Look, brother, and tell me what you kin see." And standing right side by side they both of 'em looked down into the water.

"I see myself and nobody else," says Paul. "What do you see, brother?"

"I see myself and nobody else," says Tony.

So thar you see how it was: after the little feller had charmed the water it showed 'em the truth,—what the young-un had sensed all erlong,—that Tony and Paul was one and the same feller, only dressed up in different bodies, and going under the name er Paul Bunyan in one part er the world and Tony Beaver in ernother. Did any of you folks ever meet yer very own self right face to face? Well, I ain't neither, and I know mighty well I ain't craving to. You'd think it would be a powerful awesome sight, but dogged if it tuck them two fellers thataway.

"So you're me and I'm you!" says Tony with a great "Haw, haw!"

"I'm you an' you're me, and I wouldn't be s'prised if ole Pecos Bill from down yander in Texas wasn't mixed up with us, too," says Paul. "An' what did I tell you erbout a big laf coming?"

With that the two of 'em jest laid back, whooping and hollering and laffing fit to bust the sky wide open. They did sorter try to check theyselves up and not act too much like fools fer wanter sense, but the big laf had struck 'em; one of 'em 'ud holler out, "You're me!" and the tother 'ud answer back, "I'm you!" and off they'd go ergin: "Haw, haw, haw!"

Well, er course all that whooping and carrying on fetched the tother fellers loping into the woods, hollering to know what was the joke, like hounds on a hot trail. By that time it sure looked like Paul and Tony hadn't got no sense at all, fer they was carrying on like they was making theyselves acquainted with theyselves. "Mr. Beaver, meet Mr. Beaver," Tony 'ud say, and Paul 'ud answer back, "Mr. Bunyan, shake hands with my friend Mr. Bunyan," and off the two of 'em would go ergin in the craziest laffing a person ever did hear, with the little feller jumping up and down, hollering, "Aw, look at Tony introducing hisself to hisself!"

Well, course none er the hands could make head ner tail outer the thing, but d'reckly the big laf struck them, too, and seemed like the more they didn't know what it was all erbout the more tickled they got. One feller'd holler out to another, "Hey, Buddy! What's the joke?" And the tother'd answer back, "I'll be dogged if I know!" And then the whole shooting match'd go off ergin, whooping and laffing, laying up erginst stumps, and holding on to they sides.

Well, now, er course when a whole parcel er folks gits to laffing beyond theyselves thataway they is running a turrible risk er hitting the world's funny bone, and everybody knows when that happens the world can't hold the laf in and it comes shaking out in a earthquake that's liable to crack a smile a mile wide. So when Paul and Tony commenced to feel the earth heaving up in a kind of a giggle, with a deep far-off growl rumbling up through it, they knowed mighty well what they was heading fer.

"Hey, brother, mind out er we'll have the world laffing with us d'reckly!" Tony sings out. "An' more'n that, my jaws is commencing to hurt," he says.

"That's bad! Haw, haw, haw, haw! That sure is bad!" Paul hollers back. "Here, you fellers, quit this foolishness now and sober down like I'm doing," he says, holding on to a sapling and laffing so hard a person could see the lafs running up the tree and giggling out through the leaves. "Here, quit, I say, and think er sompen solemn!"

"A toothache's a solemn thing; let's think of that," says Charlie the Swede.

"A stomickache is more solemn," says Big Henry, doing his best.

But at that all the Eel River crew jest fell over on the ground laffing, fer if there's one thing that is comical it's Big Henry when his vittles turns erginst him. "Aw, Tony, make him quit! Don't let him say nothing like that if yer aiming to git us checked up! Aw, my jaws, my jaws!" they hollers out, and the world itself rumbled out ernother long "*Ho! Ho! Ho-o-o-o-o!*"

"Here, Inkslinger, git to work now and figger out how long it'll be 'fore the world busts out with that laf!" Paul hollers to his timekeeper.

Johnny Inkslinger sets to work, figgering and laffing as best he could, and d'reckly he gits out, "Mr. Bunyan, sir— Haw, haw, haw! Excuse me. Haw, haw! As nigh as I can figger it the world'll bust out laffing inside of the next fifteen minutes, thirty-three seconds, and sixty-seven hundredths of a second. Haw, haw, haw!"

"You hear that now, Mr. Beaver!" says Paul, reeling up to Tony, and skeercely able to stand fer laffing. "The world's going to bust wide open inside of the next fifteen minutes if we don't all git together and think up sompen solemn."

"Well," says Tony, easing hisself down on a stump, 'cause by now his legs had done failed him, "the solemnest thing we got in this camp is ole Brother Moses Mutters, the preacher feller."

"Send fer him, then!" says Paul. "Send for him quick afore the world busts!"

So, running and laffing, Big Henry and the Sullivan feller

puts out after the preacher, and all the tother hands fell over on the ground and jest fa'rly give up, whooping and hollering, holding on to they sides, and complaining erbout they jaws, with the world frisking up beneath 'em, shaking out little giggles ahead of the big laf like you've seen dust devils scooting along in front of a big windstorm. Then d'reckly here come Big Henry and Sullivan back ergin, still running and laffing with the ole preacher hustled erlong betwixt 'em. The ole feller stood up thar in the midst of all them crazy hands, clawing his fingers through his beard and looking like a scan'alized billy goat.

"Thar, now! Didn't I tell you he was solemn? Aw, my jaws, my jaws!" says Tony.

"It ain't my jaws, it's my stomick hurts the most! Aw, haw, haw, haw! He's the solemnest thing I ever seen in all my life!" Paul says.

"*Yes!* Go on and laf!" the ole preacher bellers at 'em, all fired up, and gitting inter his stride. "Laf yer silly heads off, but some day you all will find out that this world is but a desert dreer."

"Aw, my soul! Don't she look like it right this minute!" Jack Sullivan sings out, and "*Ho! Ho! Ho-o-o-o-o-o!*" come that deep rumble from the world, fer seemed like having itself called a desert dreer tickled it all up and down the bed rock of its ribs.

The ole preacher was kinder startled when he heard that long "*Ho! Ho! Ho-o-o-o-o-o!*" But he tuck a brace and sets out ergin. "Don't you know that hell is right down *thar*?" he says, stomping his foot on the ground, and "*Whoof!*" says the world back at him, giving a kind of a giggle and a buck-jump.

"Hey! What's *that*?" says the ole feller, jucking up his foot mighty quick.

Well, all hands knowed doggoned well what it was, and

they sure didn't want the thing to bust through, but having the world sassing back at the preacher thataway, and him jucking up his foot so quick jest after locating hell right under it, got 'em more tickled 'n ever, so's they jest couldn't speak fer laffing. More'n that, Jack Sullivan jumps his feets up, too, like Brother Mutters had done, and sings out, "*Ouch!* My foot's hot, too! What erbout your'n, Buddy?"

"They's on fire!" says Big Henry, and after that them two big idgits went off in a crazy kind of a dance, jucking up they feets and shaking 'em in the air like they was walking on a hot griddle. It sure was scan'lous, and course it didn't do nothing to sober down the tothers.

"Aw, my jaws! My jaws!" says Tony.

"It'll be more'n yer *jaws* that'll hurt bimeby!" the preacher yells at him. "Hell—hell—*hell*—" he says, and thar he hung up dead with a kind of a guggle, his face drawed up and his throat working like he was fighting fer all he was wurth to git his words out.

"*Aw, my soul!* Look a-yander! The ole feller's going to laf!" Big Henry bawls, all dumbfoundered. At that all hands ketches aholt of they breath and jest looks and looks with all the looks they had, fer it sure was a awesome sight.

"Hell—" Brother Mutters commences ergin, making a brave fight fer it. "Hell—h-e-e-*el*—he—he—*he*—HE—" But, puff as he would, pore ole feller, he jest *couldn't* make the grade, and in another pair er seconds he busts all ter pieces,— "He, he, he! Aw, ho, ho! He, he, he! Haw, haw!"—crackling out the awfulest laffing a person ever did hear. He stands up and lafs fer a spell, but d'reckly his knees broke under him, and he flops down on a log; but even that wa'n't enough, and in the end the ole feller jest sprawls right out on the ground, whooping and hollering and laffing.

Well, sirs! That done the trick, sobering up the tother fellers in a hurry, fer thar wa'n't no living man had ever heard the preacher laf afore and it sure was a turrible solemn sound. Even the world itself swallowed back its giggles, with the long rumble of the big laf dying down and down in the distance. All hands commenced to tell the news of it to one another. "Ole Brother Moses Mutters is laffing," they'd say, passing the word from mouth to mouth like they was awestruck. Thataway it got turrible solemn to 'em, and d'reckly they give way under it.

"Aw, my soul! Jest look a-yander now at ole Brother Mutters!" Jack Sullivan says, breaking down, and hunting him his bandanna.

"I jest can't *stand* having him laf! Make him quit, Tony!" Big Henry bawls, sniffling and sniffling, and wiping his nose acrost his sleeve.

"Brother Mutters is laffing, and he'll *never* tell us no more erbout he-hell," says Jack Sullivan.

"Ner erbout the devil! Seems like I jest can't git erlong t'out the devil!" Big Henry bellers, carrying on like he was losing his blood brother.

And thar you see how it was: none er the Eel River crew had ever set much store by hell and the devil, and all like that, as long as they had it, but now when it looked like it was slipping from 'em they sets up a turrible lamentation—ain't that jest like human natur?

"Here, *quit* that! Don't you know this world is a desert dreer like you allus said?" Big Henry yells at the preacher. But "Haw, haw, haw!" was all he got back from the ole feller. "He never laffed afore in all his life, and he's sixty-three if he's a day. Make him quit, Tony! I jest *can't stand* this!" Big Henry blubbers.

"You say he's sixty-three and never laffed afore?" says Johnny Inkslinger. "Then, as nigh as I kin figger it, he'll have to go on laffing day and night fer three weeks, five days, sixteen hours, thirty-three minutes, and forty-seven seconds afore he gits hisself laffed up to date and kin quit. No, hol' on a minute! I made a bad mistake," he says, scratching out some figgers. "He'll have to laf fer three weeks, five days, sixteen hours, thirty-three minutes, and forty-five seconds and a half, 'stead of forty-seven seconds like I said at furst."

And that's jest *exactly* what the ole feller done. He kep' right erlong day and night with that awful dry crackling laf till the very second and a half Johnny Inkslinger had figgered out, and then *bang!* he stopped dead, and went on back to being jest as solemn as he ever had been.

Well, anyhow, him laffing jest in the nick er time like he done got all hands and the world itself outer a turrible fix. But what it was hit the world's funny bone and started the big laf in the furst place none er the hands ever did know. The nighest any of 'em ever come to tetching the truth was when Paul Bunyan and his crew was leaving the Eel River camp.

"Well, good-bye, Tony Bunyan," Paul says with a grin.

"Aw, Paul Beaver, don't start nothing like that now, er you'll have us all off ergin," Tony answers him back.

PAUL AND THE ANIMAL KINGDOM

Earl Clifton Beck:

PAUL AND THE GIANT MOSQUITOES

B OYS, DID I EVER tell you about the time I drove the Naubin-way over to Paul Bunyan's camp on Big Manistique Lake? Boys, I want to tell you there's some dandy mosquitoes over in that swamp even now, but the modern mosquitoes are nothing like their ancestors.

Well, just as I was pulling into Paul's camp that day I heard some terrible droning noise like one of these modern airplanes. Even Paul, big as he was, seemed excited and yelled to me to hurry into his office. So I knew something was wrong.

Then Paul told me that some of the big mosquitoes was loose. He had trapped them several years ago, because they was bothering his cattle. Paul told me that two mosquitoes was trying to kill his prize heifer. They had the critter down and was trying to drag it off, he said, when along came a really big mosquito. The big mosquito simply killed off the other two, picked up the cow, and flew away. So Paul decided then and there to put on a campaign against them. He and his men trapped several of them in live traps, he said, and the rest got scared and flew away.

But this day, when I come to visit Paul, some of the mosquitoes had broken loose. We barred the doors when we heard the mosquitoes droning overhead. They were landing on the roof. I shook like a leaf, but Paul wasn't scared. Overhead I heard a terrible cracking and looked to see swordlike weapons piercing the roof. Paul said they were mosquito stingers. So he grabbed his sledge and clinched those stingers like a carpenter clinches a nail. Next day he put twelve of his star lumberjacks to executing mosquitoes on that roof. He said he was through showing kindness to the mosquitoes. It didn't pay. They'd stab you in the back.

🌲🌲🌲🌲🌲🌲

W. B. Laughead:

THE GIANT MOSQUITOBEES

HAVE YOU EVER encountered the Mosquito of the North Country? You thought they were pretty well developed animals with keen appetites, didn't you? Then you can appreciate what Paul Bunyan was up against when he was surrounded by the vast swarms of the giant ancestors of the present race of mosquitoes, getting their first taste of human victims. The present mosquito is but a degenerate remnant of the species. Now they rarely weigh more than a pound or measure more than fourteen or fifteen inches from tip to tip.

Paul had to keep his men and oxen in the camps with doors and windows barred. Men armed with pike-poles and axes fought off the insects that tore the shakes off the roof in their effort to gain entrance. The big buck mosquitoes fought among themselves and trampled down the weaker members of the swarm and to this alone Paul Bunyan and his crew owe their lives.

Paul determined to conquer the mosquitoes before another season arrived. He thought of the big Bumble Bees back home and sent for several yoke of them. These, he hoped would destroy the mosquitoes. Sourdough Sam brought out two pairs of bees, overland on foot. There was no other way to travel for the flight of the beasts could not be controlled. Their wings were strapped with surcingles, they checked their stingers with Sam and walking shoes were provided for them. Sam brought them through without losing a bee.

The cure was worse than the original trouble. The Mosquitoes and the Bees made a hit with each other. They soon intermarried and their off-spring, as often happens, were worse than their parents. They had stingers fore-and-aft and could get you coming or going.

Their bee blood caused their downfall in the long run. Their craving for sweets could only be satisfied by sugar and molasses in large quantities, for what is a flower to an insect with a ten-gallon stomach? One day the whole tribe flew across Lake Superior to attack a fleet of ships bringing sugar to Paul's camps. They destroyed the ships but ate so much sugar they could not fly and all were drowned.

One pair of the original bees were kept at headquarters camp and provided honey for the pancakes for many years.

🌲🌲🌲🌲🌲🌲🌲

Charles O. Olsen:

PAUL BUNION GETS A BEAR HIDE

Paul Bunion went a-hunting,
In his forty-dollar shoes;
He packed a pot of honey,
And some dynamite and fuse.

He rolled himself a very fine pill,
From tar-paper and snus,
When all at once he spied a bear
And—hell just busted loose!

He smeared his shoes with honey,
Just to lead the bear along;
A-puffing on his home-made pill
And a-whistling of a song.
He honey-smeared the dynamite
And lit the little fuse;
Then laid it gently on the ground
And left it with adieus.

The bear enjoyed the sweetness
'Til the dynamite went "bang."
Then Paul just skinned him neatly,
(And he whistled while he sang).
But, loggers, heed the moral
Of the poor fool bear that died,
And when you hunt for honey,
Why—be careful of your hide.

Larry Freeman:

PAUL BUNYAN
and the Dreadful Whirling Wimpus

Paul bunyan, the master-logger of all time, the leader of the hardest, toughest band of rough-and-ready, red-blooded, "snuss"-chewing, whisker-growing, ear-chewing bullies that ever chopped, sawed, felled, bucked and trimmed a stick of timber, was bored. Badly bored.

It was a new experience for Paul Bunyan. Never before had he lost the feeling of vigor, the red-blooded itch to be at work with his bullies in logging off the Pacific Northwest and the North country. Never before had he lost the zest for work in these countries. Let a new timber country be found and it was "roll out or roll up, you bullies."

One by one he had cleared the countries, the Minnesota country, the Michigan country, the Dakota country, the He-Man country between the Cascades and the Rockies, the Snake River country, the Coos Bay country, the Big Berry country of Puget Sound. But now there had come to him a new sensation, one of dullness, of boredom. There was beginning to be a sameness to the logging off of these countries of white pine, fir and spruce. Was his soul craving new surroundings, different environment?

Thinking these troublesome thoughts, Paul Bunyan sat on top of a mountain, pondering this new and different feeling. Paul Bunyan, the master-logger, losing his feeling of being the greatest logger because his timber operations were proceeding too smoothly, and too monotonously? He pulled up a young fir tree from the side of the mountain and scratched his head with it. Then he stroked his curly beard with it.

His problem would have stumped an ordinary logger. But Paul Bunyan was no ordinary logger. He was the greatest man in the timber country for ideas.

When his loggers had given up on The Mountain That Stood On Its Head because they couldn't saw and chop while hanging by their heels, Paul had solved that problem. He had loaded his diamond-studded, double-barreled shotgun (the barrels of which were used as smokestacks in his first sawmill) with sheet iron by the thousands of pieces. He had fired it. The sheet iron severed the trees at their stumps and they dropped to the ground, their tops in the soil, their trunks sticking heavenward. Then his loggers had cut them at the top very easily. No problem was too big for Paul Bunyan, who carried an extra logger in the pocket of his mackinaw and whose boot calks left holes in the ground that were taken for stump holes when the farmers, or scissor-bills, came in later years.

So he sat and pondered. Suddenly he thought of Hot Biscuit Slim, the cook, who had come up from the Corn Pone country. He called Slim to him from the cook shanty several miles below. His voice shook the fir trees to the base and loggers working many miles down the valley stopped, took a new chew of fire-cut, and glanced up to see if thunder clouds were gathering.

In an hour or two Hot Biscuit Slim came panting up the mountain.

"You called me, Mr. Bunyan?" he said, reaching up and tugging at the lace in Paul Bunyan's boot, for the master-logger still sat, staring into space, his forehead puckered in valleys. He looked down, then picked up Hot Biscuit Slim and set him on his knee.

"Hot Biscuit Slim," he said, "I heard you telling once of the timber down in the Corn Pone and Swamp countries. What about it? Is it good enough, big enough, to take my band of bully loggers down there to get it?"

Hot Biscuit Slim was elated. It had been a long time since he had left the Corn Pone country and he had a strong hankering to see his old friends. His face crinkled into smiles.

"Oh, yes sir," he answered. "It's fine tall timber. Straight, too. There's yellow pine and oak and cypress, all fine timber, sir, and very little underbrush in the pine country."

And Hot Biscuit Slim told him how, if they struck off down across the He-Man country, they would first come to the East Texas country, full of good pine.

Paul Bunyan slapped his thigh and the jar nearly shook poor Hot Biscuit Slim off his knee. Paul caught him in his hand, steadied him and set him gently on the ground.

"Ho, then," roared Paul Bunyan, "we'll be off to the Texas country." And Hot Biscuit Slim ran happily off down the mountain to spread the news among the loggers.

Hot Biscuit Slim did not tell Paul Bunyan about the Dreadful Whirling Wimpus. The cook had not been in Paul's camp long. He did not know of the master-logger's power to conquer any obstacle, from upside-down mountains to unruly bulls of the woods like Hels Helsen. He was afraid to tell Paul Bunyan about the Dreadful Whirling Wimpus of the Texas country because he thought Paul might not go down there if he did. And Hot Biscuit Slim wanted very badly to see his old friends.

In his heart Hot Biscuit Slim knew, if they went to the Texas country, that Paul Bunyan would sometime meet the Dreadful Whirling Wimpus, and he was afraid that when that happened, Paul Bunyan might be devoured and then the logging industry would decline and decay and disappear.

The camp buildings were put in line and fastened together ready for the move to Texas. Babe, the Blue Ox, who measured seven axe handles and a plug of chewing tobacco between the horns, and was Paul Bunyan's beast of all work, was hitched to the skids of the first shanty and the camp was ready to be moved.

"Fellers, this is a Great Moment for us," Paul Bunyan said. "We are going to extend our holdings until the Paul Bunyan timber rights stretch from Maine to Puget Sound and from Canada to the Gulf of Mexico," he said. He was an able orator as well as a master-logger and knew the power of inspirational speech before workers. Thus, Paul Bunyan was also the first Rotarian. The move to the South started.

Now, while Hot Biscuit Slim had heard of the Dreadful Whirling Wimpus, he had never seen it. No one had ever seen the Dreadful Whirling Wimpus. No one knew in what shape or form it appeared. However, from hearsay and reports based on the horrible results of an encounter with the deadly monster, he was said to be a gigantic ape-like creature with great long hairy arms and enormous paws.

There was a reason why no one had ever seen the Dreadful Whirling Wimpus. He whirled so fast that he could not be seen, but only heard. He whirled in the middle of paths and trails and roads. All that was known about him was that there would be heard a tremendous whirring noise, a loud and constant whirring, as he spun and spun. Whirling dervishes were as slow and awkward as Eastern tourists saddling up on a dude ranch, compared with the Dreadful Whirling Wimpus.

He fed especially on tourists. He relished them, although he would not step aside to let any human being pass him on a path as he whirled.

When the tourist sauntered down a path upon which the Dreadful Whirling Wimpus whirled, he was mystified. He saw nothing. He thought of a great swarm of bees as he heard this great whirring. But he could see nothing. Right into the arms of the Dreadful Whirling Wimpus he walked and it was all over with the unsuspecting tourist. He was simply whirled to death. Then, it is told, the Dreadful Whirling Wimpus bent his huge arms up toward his mouth and licked what remained of the tourist off his paws.

When Paul Bunyan's band of bully loggers reached the Texas country they set to work immediately to log it off, while the master-logger oversaw the job. Paul Bunyan was a mighty man. He was a strapping giant of a man. A week after he stomped through the timber his crew of 10,000 heard the echo of his bootsteps crashing through the timber. It was that long between his steps and the echo at his camp.

On cloudy, rainy, or foggy days Paul Bunyan could not stomp through the woods to cruise his timber. He was too tall and mighty, and on such dark days he could not see the ground. There was always the danger of stepping on a stray logger.

So, on gray days Paul Bunyan spent his time near camp or in a mountainous cave whittling young pine tree butts to a sharp point for toothpicks, or combing his beard with a tree.

Before the loggers had been in the Texas country long a cloudy spell set in. Paul Bunyan was forced to sit idle for several days. When the sky cleared one morning he set out, eager to be exploring this new country.

Unconscious of any danger, Paul Bunyan swung down a path. The master-logger of all time was on the same path with the Dreadful Whirling Wimpus, which revolved more furiously than ever. The deadly monster, which had devoured untold numbers of tourists and common people, lurked squarely in his path. What would happen? Was there to be a struggle of Titans, a crashing of bodies, an horrific impact and fight that would give the sanguinary historians of the centuries to follow something to write about?

Paul strode on. Thump, thump, thump, his calked boots sounded on the path. The Dreadful Whirling Wimpus whirled faster, faster, faster. They were almost together now. And then——

Right into the arms of the Dreadful Whirling Wimpus Paul's steps took him. He walked on without a quiver. There was no hesitation in his step. Never even an harassed glance or frown came down from the mighty man.

After inspecting half a dozen counties of timber, Paul Bunyan returned to camp. As he lay down that night in his one-man bunkhouse which stretched past all the other camp buildings he felt a slight itching on his leg.

He rolled down his green wool socks and peered at his leg. His shin, he found, was slightly skinned, as if some fine sandpaper had been rubbed across it.

How many thousands of tourists and wood hikers had been revolved to their doom on the paws of the creature before Paul Bunyan's shin was skinned, no one knows. There is no table of statistics to show the mortality rate from the paws of the Dreadful Whirling Wimpus.

But Paul Bunyan, master-logger of all time, had met the Dreadful Whirling Wimpus, and with that encounter ended the monster and his human feasts.

🌲🌲🌲🌲🌲🌲🌲

James Stevens:

THE DISMAL SAUGER

NIGHTFALL in the pine woods, and a campfire in the shadows. It is an hour for those with hearts young enough to enter Storyland, the country of imagination. In that country

Paul Bunyan is the American brother of Hercules, Goliath and Gargantua. The forest is Paul Bunyan's home. For the greater part of a century woodsmen have recited his wonderful deeds and amazing adventures. Their stories are the American pictures of the Never-Never land.

At the campfire Old Larrity, the woodsman, speaks to a boy perched on the pine log beside him.

"So long ago," speaks Old Larrity, "in a time too far to be counted in years, Europe was all one kingdom. The ruler of it was called Pete the First. At the same time America was ruled entirely by the good and great Paul Bunyan—a man so great, indeed, that he combed his hair with a pine tree. Always and ever with Paul Bunyan was Babe the Blue Ox, king of timber beasts.

"No man, not even the Injun, knew the American wilderness till Paul Bunyan and Babe came with the winter of the Blue Snow. Them times the young ox was a hunter. Such a fine nose he had that once he started from the bones of a moose that had died of old age, and he back-tracked the beast to the place of its birth. But the Blue Ox was best as a pointer. One July, indeed, he froze into a point for so long and so hard that all the woods for a mile about was frostbitten, and the porkypine's quills turned into icicles.

"Most carnivore-us and bloodthirsty of the timber beasts in them far away times was the rabbit. Then that animal was the original ring-tailed roarer. Panthers was its favorite prey, the which the rabbit would snare with its long, ropy ring of a tail, and then kick to death with its hind feet. So the panther grew the small head it has to this day, to slip from the rabbit's tail twists. And the rabbit, to deceive Paul Bunyan and the Blue Ox, began to hide its tail, to squeak pitiful, pretendin' to be shy and afeard. So at last the rabbit really got to be that way. 'Twas of the rabbit the poet wrote:

Oh, what a tangled web we weave
When first we practice to deceive!

"The worst huntin' for Paul Bunyan and the Blue Ox was after the dismal sauger of the swamps and the happy hodag of the hills. There was no dismaler sound on the wide earth at all, than the drip-drip-drip of scummy swamp water from the sauger's cypress hair. When they heard it, Paul and Babe always got so sad they wanted to die. But when they heard the hilarious huck-a-haw-huck-a-ho of the hodag, then they would roll in stitches and fits. Of course the hodag and the sauger were natural enemies, and kilt each other off at last.

"The biggest bears of the woods were small game to Paul Bunyan. One winter an orphan cub could find no warm hollow anywhere for its long sleep. For weeks the little bear prowled forlorn, then it was lost one night in what seemed a jungle of black thickets. But the jungle was warm, so the cub curled up. The next spring Paul Bunyan felt a scratchin' under the great chin of himself. He let out a roar. 'Somebody has been sleepin' in my beard, and here she is!' With that, Paul Bunyan plucked a scared young bear from his beard. He did it no harm but from then on Paul Bunyan kept a close winter watch on his whiskers."

✤✤✤✤✤✤✤

W. B. Laughead:

NIMROD BUNYAN AND HIS DOGS

WHAT IS CAMP without a dog? Paul Bunyan loved dogs as well as the next man but never would have one around that could not earn its keep. Paul's dogs had to work, hunt or catch rats. It took a good dog to kill rats and mice in Paul's camp for the rodents picked up scraps of the buffalo milk pancakes and grew to be as big as two-year-old bears.

Elmer, the moose terrier, practiced up on the rats when he was a small pup and was soon able to catch a moose on the run and finish it with one shake. Elmer loafed around the cook camp and if the meat supply happened to run low the cook would put the dog out the door and say, "Bring in a moose." Elmer would run into the timber, catch a moose and bring it in and repeat the performance until, after a few minutes work, the cook figured he had enough for a mess and would call the dog in.

Sport, the reversible dog, was really the best hunter. He was part wolf and part elephant hound and was raised on bear milk. One night when Sport was quite young, he was playing around in the horse barn and Paul, mistaking him for a mouse, threw a hand axe at him. The axe cut the dog in two but Paul, instantly realizing what had happened, quickly stuck the two halves together, gave the pup first aid and bandaged him up. With careful nursing the dog soon recovered and then it was seen that Paul in his haste had twisted the two halves so that the hind legs pointed straight up. This proved to be an advantage for the dog learned to run on one pair of legs for a while and then flop over without loss of speed and run on the other pair. Because of this he never tired and anything he started after got caught. Sport never got his full growth. While still a pup he broke through four feet of ice on Lake Superior and was drowned.

As a hunter, Paul would make old Nimrod himself look like a city dude lost from his guide. He was also a good fisherman. Oldtimers tell of seeing Paul as a small boy, fishing off the Atlantic Coast. He would sail out early in the morning in his three-mast schooner and wade back before breakfast with his boat full of fish on his shoulder.

About this time he got his shotgun that required four dishpans full of powder and a keg of spikes to load each barrel. With this gun he could shoot geese so high in the air they would spoil before reaching the ground.

Tracking was Paul's favorite sport and no trail was too old or too dim for him to follow. He once came across the skeleton of a moose that had died of old age and, just for curiosity, picked up the tracks of the animal and spent the whole afternoon following its trail back to the place where it was born.

The shaggy dog that spent most of his time pretending to sleep in front of Johnny Inkslinger's counter in the camp office was Fido, the watchdog. Fido was the bugbear (not bearer, just bear) of the green-horns. They were told that Paul starved Fido all winter and then, just before payday, fed him all the swampers, barn boys, and student bullcooks. The very marrow was frozen in their heads at the thought of being turned into dog food. Their fears were groundless for Paul would never let a dog go hungry or mistreat a human being. Fido was fed all the watch peddlers, tailors' agents, and camp inspectors and thus served a very useful purpose.

🌲🌲🌲🌲🌲🌲

Charles E. Brown:

PAUL'S CHICKENS

PAUL BROUGHT a flock of chickens to his camp on the Big Auger River. His men were fond of hen fruit, and many eggs were used by the cook in preparing other food. The chickens, which were a special breed imported from China, did very well. When the supply of chicken food was low, the cook experimented with mixing sawdust with their grain. It seemed to increase their laying. Then the cook fed them only on sawdust. After a week or two of this sawdust diet the fowls still layed; but they layed knotholes instead of eggs. In the end Paul found it cheaper and easier to grow eggplants for his camp. An infirm lumberjack gathered the eggs from these plants every day.

✢✢✢✢✢✢✢

W. B. Laughead:

LUCY THE COW
and Benny The Little Blue Ox

Lucy, Paul Bunyan's cow, was not, so far as we can learn, related in any way to either Babe or Benny. Statements that she was their mother are without basis in fact. The two oxen had been in Paul's possession for a long time before Lucy arrived on the scene.

No reliable data can be found as to the pedigree of this remarkable dairy animal. There are no official records of her butter-fat production nor is it known where or how Paul got her.

Paul always said that Lucy was part Jersey and part wolf. Maybe so. Her actions and methods of living seemed to justify the allegation of wolf ancestry, for she had an insatiable appetite and a roving disposition. Lucy ate everything in sight and could never be fed at the same camp with Babe or Benny. In fact, they quit trying to feed her at all but let her forage her own living. The Winter of the Deep Snow, when even the tallest White Pines were buried, Brimstone Bill outfitted Lucy with a set of Babe's old snowshoes and a pair of green goggles and turned her out to graze on the snowdrifts. At first she had some trouble with the new foot gear but once she learned to run them and shift gears without wrecking herself, she answered the call of the limitless snow fields and ran away all over North America until Paul decorated her with a bell borrowed from a buried church.

In spite of short rations she gave enough milk to keep six men busy skimming the cream. If she had been kept in a barn and fed regularly she might have made a milking record. When she fed on the evergreen trees and her milk got so strong of White Pine and Balsam that the men used it for cough medicine and liniment, they quit serving the milk on the table and made butter out of it. By using this butter to grease the logging roads when the snow and ice thawed off, Paul was able to run his logging sleds all summer.

Because he was so much younger than Babe and was brought to camp when a small calf, Benny was called the Little Blue Ox although he was quite a chunk of an animal. Benny could not, or rather, would not haul as much as Babe nor was he as tractable but he could eat more.

Paul got Benny for nothing from a farmer near Bangor, Maine. There was not enough milk for the little fellow so he had to be weaned when three days old. The farmer only had forty acres of hay and by the time Benny was a week old he had to dispose of him for lack of food. The calf was undernourished and only weighed two tons when Paul got him. Paul drove from Bangor out to his headquarters camp near Devil's Lake, North Dakota, that night and led Benny behind the sleigh. Western air agreed with the little calf and every time Paul looked back at him he was two feet taller.

When they arrived at camp Benny was given a good feed of buffalo milk and flapjacks and put into a barn by himself. Next morning the barn was gone. Later it was discovered on Benny's back as he scampered over the clearings. He had outgrown his barn in one night.

Benny was very notional and would never pull a load unless there was snow on the ground so after the spring thaws they had to whitewash the logging roads to fool him.

Gluttony killed Benny. He had a mania for pancakes and one cook crew of two hundred men was kept busy making cakes for him. One night he pawed and bellowed and threshed his tail about him till the wind of it blew down what pine Paul had left standing in Dakota. At breakfast time he broke loose, tore down the cook shanty and began bolting pancakes. In his greed he swallowed the redhot stove. Indigestion set in and nothing could save him. What disposition was made of his body is a matter of dispute. One oldtimer claims that the outfit he works for bought a hind quarter of the carcass in 1857 and made corned beef of it. He thinks they have several carloads of it left.

Another authority states that the body of Benny was dragged to a safe distance from the North Dakota camp and buried. When the earth was shoveled back it made a mound that formed the Black Hills in South Dakota.

✤✤✤✤✤✤✤

206 PAUL BUNYAN AND SWEDE CHARLIE†

*Legends
of
Paul
Bunyan*

ONE FOURTH of July, when it was 90 in the shade, Paul Bunyan and Swede Charlie were out hunting the Wiskerwoo bird so that Paul could give the feathers to the head dish manicurist of the camp cook shack.

It was a cloudy day and suddenly, without warning, it began to snow. The flakes—each as big as a dinner plate—came down so fast that they piled up at the rate of two feet a minute.

They were in danger of being buried alive, but the quick wit of Paul saved them. Telling Charlie to follow him Paul swiftly climbed up from one flake to the next.

They went up at such speed that they soon lost sight of the ground. But suddenly they discovered that they could go no higher—it had stopped snowing—so they had to float down on the snow.

After floating down for a half hour they reached the earth again. But they could see nothing but snow—even the highest trees had been buried.

While they were wondering what to do the sun suddenly came out again and the snow began to melt.

It melted so swiftly that the first thing they knew, Paul found himself standing on the ground at the foot of a dead spruce, while Charlie was left hanging to its topmost branch.

Charlie was caught in the branch and could not climb down so Paul pulled over the tree so that Charlie could step off.

Just then Paul saw a fine specimen of the Wiskerwoo bird

† From *4-L Bulletin*, September 1919.

that had been hiding under the roots of the spruce. They caught the beautiful bird and gave the feathers to the dish manicurist.

✿✿✿✿✿✿✿

Thomas G. Alvord, Jr.:

THE BOBCAT AND THE MOON

It was springtime on the Neversink;
    The frogs, the whole night long,
Croaked ever their persistent croaks
    And gargled freakish song.
The still night air was laden sweet
    With odors of the spring,
While all about the loggin' woods
    That night there seemed to cling
The spirit of the springtime, and
    The world seemed all in tune
With the music of the marshes and
    The glimmer of the moon.

For hours the jacks had been asleep,
    Paul Bunyan and his crew,
All dreamin' 'bout their pay checks
    Which were soon a-comin' due,
And of times that were a-waitin' down
    In town of Chickadee,
Where the creeks were flowin' cider,
    And the pie was given free.

Now it happened that a big bobcat—
    The wild and woolly kind—

Was a-prowlin' 'round the camp that night
  To see what he could find,
A-snoopin' 'round most leisurely,
  A-sniffin' here and there,
And a-rubbin' up ag'in the barn
  A-slickin' up his hair.
The big full moon, a disk of gold,
  Had climbed the mountain steep,
And sat a-gazin' thoughtfully
  At all the world asleep,
While the bobcat there on the earth below
  Just purred a bit, and sat,
And wondered what upon the earth
  The moon was lookin' at.
At last old Bob decided that
  He'd like most awful well
To climb upon the bunk-house roof
  And sing a little spell,
And so he yawned a dozen times,
  To loosen up his jaws,
And scratched the earth a trifle
  To sharpen up his claws,
Then leapin' up and off the ground,
  Kerwizz—up through the air,
He lands—kerthunk—upon the roof,
  And sits a-smilin' there.

Old Bob then crawled along the ridge,
  A-talkin' as he stalked,
As well as vicee versee like,
  A-stalkin' as he talked.
He made investigation of
  The pipe, which still was warm,

And learned by rubbin' 'gainst it that
    It wouldn't do him harm,
So he found in that old smokin' pipe
    A friend and company,
And therefore started singin', as
    He thought that possibly
His new found friend would much enjoy
    A solo sweetly sung,
A selection from, "Al Stove-a-door,"
    In choicest feline tongue.
For hours he sat upon that roof
    A-yowlin' out his soul,
But wishin' someone down below
    Would feed the stove some coal.

Now, Bunyan, lyin' there in bed,
    Had listened for an hour
To that 'ar feller's constant yowl,
    And everlastin' meower,
In hopes old Bob would go away,
    And cease his serenade,
And find some other distant roof
    Where he might promenade.
But seein' that no thought like that
    Was in that bobcat's head,
Paul rolled himself reluctantly
    From warm and cozy bed,
Pulled on a pair of loggin' boots,
    And cautiously he crept—
So's not to waken up the men
    Who still dreamed on, and slept—
And searched about that big dark room,
    A-feelin' this and that,

In hopes of findin' somethin' he
    Could fling at that damn cat.

Now it happened that old Tom, the cook,
    That noon of previous day,
Had sent out to the men at work,
    Some sixty miles away,
Among the noonday victuals, such
    As beans, and pie and meat,
A batch of "sodee" biscuits that
    A buzz-saw couldn't eat.
Why, even Paul with jaws like steel
    Could no more make a dent,
In those round cast-iron biscuits, which
    Old Tom the cook had sent,
Than you, or I, could mar, or dent,
    By chewin' night and day
On a cannon ball, or cobblestone,
    Or a grindstone, we will say.
The jacks had been quite angry, and
    They thought themselves abused,
But Paul could only see the joke,
    And felt a bit amused.
Said he, "Don't throw those cakes away;
    "We'll fetch them back to camp,
"And feed them all to Tom, himself,
    "And watch him get a cramp."
So the jacks all had a laugh at that,
    And saw some future fun,
And crammed those cast-iron biscuits in
    Their pockets, every one.
Well, it happened that the jacks forgot,
    Before the close of day,

About revenge upon the cook,
  And how they'd make him pay,
And so they left their biscuits, which
  They couldn't eat at all,
In the pockets of their mackinaws
  A-hangin' on the wall.

It suddenly occurred to Paul,
  A-searchin' in the dark,
That if these biscuits he could find
  He'd surely hit his mark;
And luckily he found a coat
  Containin' three or four,
Besides another hangin' near
  With twice as many more.
So gatherin' up a plen'shush load,
  He crept across the floor,
Stepped out into the moonlight, and
  Behind him closed the door.

There perched upon the bunkhouse roof
  Still yowled that pesky cat,
A-yowlin' sentimental yowls,
  The while he perched and sat.
Through tear-blurred orbs he saw the moon,
  And told the world his woe,
While little did he then surmise
  What waited him below,
Then—ZIP! and SWEEZE! He felt the breeze
  Of somethin' flyin' by,
And then—KERBING! Some awful thing
  Kerslapped him in the eye,
And before he knew just what or who
  Had knocked him scootin' high,

*The
Animal
Kingdom*

He found himself a-steerin' toward
    The moon up in the sky.
Paul knocked the breath right out of him,
    And with it knocked his tune,
And cat and biscuits, each in turn,
    Struck—THUG—upon the moon.

And so you see what caused the dents
    And holes upon the moon;
It was all because that bob-tailed cat
    Persisted with his tune,
And thus provoked hot-tempered Paul
    To throw those cakes at him
With such extreme efficiency,
    And acc'racy and vim.
Those biscuits struck with awful force
    Upon the old moon's face,
And those that missed and made no dent
    Went sailin' on through space.
They're goin' yet fer all I know,
    And can fer all I care,
A-ever swishin' on, and on,
    Through space I know not where.

❦❦❦❦❦❦❦

Wallace Wadsworth:

THE HUGAGS

Paul left his old camp in Maine very early in the morning, and so anxious was he to get located in his new camp that he hurried along at quite a fast pace, so that he arrived on the banks of what was afterwards called the Red River along about sunset of that afternoon. Most of his men kept up with him pretty well, but some of the stragglers didn't arrive until along some time the next morning.

Paul saw at once that he would be able to work very fast in clearing off this level land. "These pines must be a new variety," he said to the Big Swede. "I have never seen any quite like them before. Do you notice how none of them stand up straight, but all lean the same way? I think I'll give them the name of 'Leaning Pines,' and notify the tree experts back East so they can write about them in books." Indeed, there was something very peculiar about the big trees that covered the land so thickly, for they all leaned at just exactly the same angle toward the south.

Ole, however, shook his head over what Paul had said. "Ay tank they bane ordinary White Pines," he disagreed. "Ay tank Hugags make 'em lean that way." It so happened that this time Ole was more right than Paul, for the leaning trees were not a new species at all. Their strange peculiarity had been caused, as the Big Swede suspected, by the Hugag, a frightful looking but entirely harmless animal which was then to be found in great numbers in the Dakota woods.

The Hugag was quite large, with a body like a buffalo, and often weighed as much as two tons. Its head and neck were absolutely hairless, its wrinkled ears flopped downward, its bushy tail waggled constantly, and it had long muscular lips which prevented it from feeding on grass or other low-growing herbage, but which were of the greatest use—like the trunk of an elephant—in stripping from trees the bark and twigs which were its usual food. Its greatest oddity, though, was its legs. They were long and stiff and perfectly straight, being entirely without joints in them, and since they therefore could not be bent the Hugag could never lie down as other animals do. It lived its whole life, waking and sleeping, upon its feet. Occasionally one would by some chance fall or be thrown to the ground, and as it could not bend its legs to get to its feet again, it was then perfectly helpless and soon died of fright or starvation.

Its strange manner of sleeping was the cause of the leaning pines. When it wanted to take a nap, it would face the west and lean its left side against the trunk of a pine tree, brace its hind legs firmly but never ceasing to mark time with its splay-footed front ones, hang down its head and close its eyes, and in this manner it would rest comfortably. Countless Hugags had followed these exact habits through many centuries, and the pressure of their weight against the trees of the Dakota woods had after many years caused all the pines to lean toward the south in the manner which had at first deceived Paul.

The uniform slant of the trees was a great aid in cutting them, for they all fell in exactly the same direction without any guidance on the part of the cutters. Paul was therefore able to use his great three-mile saw to the best advantage. When its blade passed through the forest, it ate its way through the thousands of trunks in its path like a mowing machine in a hay field, and left the trees lying evenly side by side in windrows on the ground, ready to be cut into logs and snaked away.

Paul was so strong that he did not have to have much help with the big saw, and he usually put the Little Chore Boy on the other end to balance it down. He didn't care whether the Little Chore Boy did much saw work with the other end or not, and he never said anything when the youngster would hang onto the saw-handle and ride back and forth as the blade cut through the trees, but he did occasionally get a little angry when the lad thoughtlessly allowed his feet to drag on the ground.

✝✝✝✝✝✝✝

Charles E. Brown:

BILLY THE GOAT
and Paul's Pigs

A GOOD FRIEND presented Paul Bunyan with a goat. This was a kind of animal Paul had no experience with. Paul kept him tied near the bunkhouse. After this rambunctious animal had butted the daylights out of everybody and everything within reach, he was turned over to the tender mercies of Brimstone Bill.

Bill at first tried to control Billy with kindness. But it was just no go. After he had butted Bill right over the roof of the stable, and nearly caused his death on several other occasions, Bill learned that it was always best to have an axe or peavey handle handy when near Billy.

One day Bill tied Billy out to feed in a clearing. There was a big rock. The goat thought that it was an enemy and ran to butt it. The rock never moved. This angered Billy and he went back to butt it again. Bill watched the goat butting the stone for some time, then he went to dinner at the cook shanty. When he returned to the battleground, an hour later, the fight was still going on. Billy was gone, all but his tail, and that part of him was still running at the big rock and butting it.

Pork was a very important article of food at Paul Bunyan's camps. In order to always have on hand an abundant supply of pork Paul kept a large drove of hogs. These were in Brimstone Bill's keeping. This job was wished on Bill, and he couldn't object. He kept the pigs in log pens, but they were always burrowing out and getting away into the woods. Bill and his helpers undertook the job of building a hog-proof fence around the pens. Before starting this work Bill's men somehow managed to get hold of a keg of "Hudnut's Budge."

As a result of their inebriated condition they built the crookedest and craziest fence that human beings ever erected. Paul Bunyan was very much disappointed in this barrier when he saw it. Just the same the fence proved to be very effective. The hogs would burrow under it. Then, because of its crooked and bewildering nature, they would burrow right back again. So it held the pigs after all. They never knew were they in or out of the enclosure.

. . . *they built the crookedest and craziest fence that human beings ever erected.*

PAUL'S GREAT INVENTIONS

W. J. Gorman:

PAUL BUNYAN
Invents a Few Things

Paul Bunyan invented the doughnut, with the assistance of his cook, Flap Jack Slim. To tell the whole truth it was a bit of an accident. Slim, who was strong on sourdough, let a cauldron boil over. The liquid dough poured out on the 10 by 20-acre range at the main cookery; it flooded around the 5,000-gallon tea boiler. When the boiler had been removed, Paul gazed at the round hole in the center, pried the big biscuit off the range, trimmed the edges around with a broadaxe and rolled the doughnut out to the bush where the men acclaimed it as a new confection worthy of the traditions of the camp. After that the cookees could be seen every day laboriously wheeling them out for lunch. Eventually the size was modified 110 diameters for home use.

As a matter of fact one of Paul's principal troubles was supplying his men with a variety of food. The camp cranks were as hard to please then as now and after a few weeks of a new dish they would demand something else. This chronic dissatisfaction was responsible for another invention—corned beef. The particular winter which saw this delightful dish introduced found Paul and his gang logging in Algoma. They were a long way from their meat depot, which was in Kansas and occasionally there was a hitch in the line of communication, resulting in meatless days. The old practice of driving the beef up on the hoof had its draw-backs; the steers were two years on the way and had to feed en route. So Paul consulted Johnny Inkslinger and the Big Swede and they decided to put up a cannery in Kansas, and send the Blue Ox down once a year for a sledge load of meat. They had to pioneer in the packing industry. When they were through contriving the Kansas cowboys simply drove the steers in one door and the corned beef tumbled out the other, all canned. A man named Fray Bentos was boss of the works and to this day you will see his name on corned beef cans. This factory had some novel features. It was seven storeys high. The steers went in on the ground floor; tails, all ready knotted, flew out an opening on the second storey; beefskin moccasins rained down from the third; bones, neatly wrapped in bundles, were lowered from the fourth storey; mattresses stuffed with hair bounced down from the fifth; condensed groans, in five pound pack-ages, fell from the sixth and from the top storey emerged the canned meat products. Fray Bentos was the only man on the job and he never did have time to find out what hap-pened to the horns which disappeared in the process mysteriously.

The tails could be had with one, two or three knots as desired; they were sold to fiction writers for plots. The bones were eagerly sought by the darkies of Dixie. Mattresses and shoepacks went to Paul's camp. The condensed groans were shipped to New York for use in the vaudeville industry.

Another of Paul's troubles arose from the rapidity with which he and his gang logged off the country. One winter, while working in the Cigarette Grass valley, the crew had such a splendid camping ground that they protested against moving. So Paul tried various schemes to keep in touch with his forest operations. Farther and farther each day the men had to walk to work. Eventually it was necessary to put on two shifts, one at work and one walking to work. Later three shifts were required, one walking to work, one working and the other walking back. Finally the distance from camp became so great that all the men were en route and those going out only reached the bush in time to turn around and come back, so that not a single tree was cut. Paul moved the camp with the Blue Ox, as usual and in order to make up for lost time he tried to make an arrangement with the moon to shine every night; but China protested and this scheme came to naught. About this time he had the Big Swede travel to the North Pole to investigate the Northern Lights. He reported back, saying that they were unreliable and anyhow it would take six months to move them down.

This was the winter that Paul contrived the chain axe with four blades. The loggers swung them around in a circle and cut four trees at once. The first day they used the new tool no chips fell, but the third day they started to come down, burying the men. Logging was greatly speeded up that year by Paul's invention of the grindstone. Prior to that the men used to have to roll a boulder down a mountain, following it with the blade laid on the stone to sharpen it. And when they were logging in level country they used to have to bore a hole in a stone, fit it with shafts and run it around, with the men following and taking turns in laying their axes on for grinding. Paul perceived that it would be much simpler to set the stone in a frame and do all the sharpening right in the camp.

Wallace Wadsworth:

THE GRINDSTONE

Paul occasionally got out his three-mile crosscut saw, and with the Little Chore Boy holding down the other end, he also felled vast stretches of the leaning pines. He had so many other things to look after, however, that he worked with his saw only part of the time, trusting to the Seven Axmen to do most of the felling, and well did they live up to his faith in them. It is said that his crews cut over a million feet of logs a day during that winter in the Dakotas, and most of this work was done by the Seven Axmen. Each of the Axmen had five fleet-footed helpers who did nothing but carry dulled axes back to camp and bring out fresh, keen ones again.

The problem of keeping the Seven Axmen's blades sharp was at first a troublesome one. There were no hills in the Dakotas steep enough for them to sharpen axes as they had done in Maine, and so a new way had to be found. "Well," said Paul to himself, "since we can't use stones as they roll down hill, why can't we have a big stone that can be turned while it stays in one place?" So he smoothed off a great flat piece of rock, shaped it perfectly round, and made a square hole for a handle in the center so that it could be swung up onto a trestle and turned by hand. Thus was the problem solved by Paul's invention of the grindstone, a most valuable invention as everyone will agree.

He had bad luck with the first two grindstones he made, though. The first one he laid aside after shaping the stone as he wanted it, intending to put the handle on it after he finished making a trestle to hold it. While he was working on the trestle, Hard-jaw Murphy, one of his men, came around the corner of the tool-house smacking his lips and picking his teeth with a peavey. "That's a mighty good brand of cheese you're getting for this camp now, Mr. Bunyan," he grinned. "I jest found a hull cheese back yonder a piece, and et it all up," and he winked his eye in high good humor, proud of having gotten ahead of the camp steward who was very watchful of victuals between meals.

"Cheese!" exclaimed Paul, rather put out. "That wasn't a cheese, you dunderhead. That was my new grindstone!" and as punishment he set the astounded logger to shaping another stone just like the one he had made away with.

The second grindstone was soon finished and mounted, and it was a very large affair. It did the work of sharpening tools quickly and well, and was very popular with all in camp except the Little Chore Boy, whose task it was to turn it. He finally got so tired of sharpening axes with it that one day he became very angry and threw it out of sight.

Paul came along a few minutes later and saw that his new invention was missing. "What has happened to the grindstone?" he asked in surprise.

"I got tired of turning the thing, so I threw it away," said the Little Chore Boy, sullenly. Indeed, he had flung it so hard and thrown it so far that it had sailed clear across Minnesota and landed in northern Wisconsin, where it sank deep into the earth, digging an enormous hole. The great scar it made when it fell later filled with water and became Grindstone Lake, as anyone can easily see from a map.

"Oh, well, it doesn't matter very much that it's gone," said Paul, his eyes twinkling. "It was getting too small to do the work, anyway." So the Little Chore Boy didn't gain anything, after all, for the very next day Paul made a new grindstone that was much bigger and harder to turn than the other one had been. It is said that this new one was so big that every time it turned around three times it was pay-day again.

In all of Paul's work in the Dakotas Babe, as always, proved of great help to his master. There were some districts which were far from any stream that was big enough to float logs, and so Paul thought of a way to use the Great Blue Ox's tremendous strength in getting this timber nearer water. He would hitch Babe to a full section of land and drag the whole thing, trees and all, down to the river right handy to the camp. There Paul's men would cut the timber from it, pile the logs on the banks of the stream, and then Babe would haul the cleared square mile of land back to its proper place again. In this way Paul was able to log sections that he otherwise never would have bothered about, and never would have been able to touch without the unique assistance of the Great Blue Ox.

It took Babe just one day to haul six sections of land down to the river, and then take them back again after the trees had been cut off. That made thirty-six sections a week. The first week, however, that this plan was put into use Paul had the ox haul Section Thirty-seven down the last thing on Saturday night, intending to leave it there over Sunday and clear it off the first thing on Monday morning. On Sunday the river rose, washed the section away, and it has never been found since. That is why all government survey maps today show only thirty-six sections to a township, as Paul Bunyan lost Section Thirty-seven and never recovered it again.

And so, his mighty crew working in all directions with a vigor and efficiency that has never been equaled, Paul Bunyan progressed rapidly through the winter with his task of logging off the Dakotas. Finally, as spring came on, he suddenly discovered that all the big timber of the two states had been cut off and that some of his men had even worked down into Nebraska and Kansas, clearing off all the trees as they went. Hastily ordering everyone to cease work, he reassembled his men once more at the big camp to await his next orders.

Throughout the Dakotas all the timber that was now to be found was a few patches, here and there, of small trees not big enough for logs. He looked around for a market for these, and found it with a railroad that was just being built across the country. The railroad needed wooden ties for its tracks, so Paul turned most of his men into tie-hacks, or tie-cutters, and proceeded to dispose of all his small timber in the form of railroad ties. He trained the cutters to climb the trees with forty-pound broadaxes strapped to their feet like skates, scoring great slashes in the sides of the trees as they went up. Once at the top, they would slide down again, the heavy blades on their feet slicing off the wood on opposite sides of the trees, hewing two flat faces at once so that the timber was just of the right thickness. After they had learned, also, to cut off a tie every eight feet as they slid down, they worked very fast, having only to climb up a tree and slide back down in order to manufacture it into railroad ties.

Finally, even all the small trees were used in this manner, the ties hauled away, the logs delivered long ago to the sawmills, and the camp cleaned up. Nothing was left of the great forests that had stood on these vast stretches of fertile land excepting the stumps, and Paul soon got rid of them. He picked out the very strongest men in his crew and armed them all with heavy wooden mallets. Then, he himself leading the way, they started out. One blow was enough to drive the biggest stump far down into the ground, and so *thump! thump!* faster than anyone could count, Paul's men pounded all the stumps out of sight into the earth. It was only a day or two until there was not a stump left in sight, nor a tree either—nothing but miles and miles of rolling plains where once the forests had stood and the Hugags roamed. The work in the Dakotas was finished and Paul Bunyan was ready to move on to other fields.

Dell J. McCormick:

THE SAWMILL That Ran Backwards

BY EARLY SPRING Paul had the finest lot of logs in the country, but the regular sawmill refused to cut them because they were oversize. The log carriage could only handle logs up to fourteen feet through. Of course Paul's logs were much larger than that. In fact he threw away anything under six feet as being fit only for fence posts. There was only one thing to do: buy out the mill and rebuild one large enough for the great logs he had cut.

Paul as usual decided he would do everything on a grand scale so he built a sawmill with six complete floors and a huge band saw running clear through the building from the top to the bottom. It cut logs on every floor and had teeth on both sides so he could saw the logs both coming and going.

The first trouble they had was with the smokestacks. They were so high they had to be hinged to let the clouds go by. This took a lot of time and he finally put three men on each stack with long pike poles and they pushed the smaller clouds out of the way. It was quite a nuisance though, because it took a man so long to climb to the top that it was time to come back to supper before he was half-way up.

Paul hired an Englishman by the name of Higgenbottom

as millwright to make sure the machinery was put in according to directions. Higgenbottom claimed he knew all
about sawmills and could put them together blindfolded.
Ole the Big Swede claimed he must have put this one together that way. Everything went wrong from the very
start. Paul gave him a free hand, and he connected up saws
and belts and pulleys all over the place. There were so
many gadgets nobody even knew what they were for. By

the time it was completed everybody was disgusted, but
Paul told the Englishman to go ahead and get steam up
for the opening day.

Paul was quite excited and told the chief engineer to
blow the whistle. Higgenbottom had forgotten to install a
whistle, so Paul grabbed an old bugle that was around
camp and put it to his lips. He blew a great blast on the
bugle that could be heard at Vancouver, B. C. In fact he
blew it with such force he straightened every kink in the
bugle until it was as straight as a flute. The machinery
started moving, and the men leaped to their places.

The strangest thing began to happen! Instead of turning out lumber the mill began to take in sawdust and turn it back into logs. Vast piles of sawdust began to disappear and out of the other end of the mill, instead of finished lumber, came a steady stream of logs. Soon the millpond was full of logs and they started to pile up on the opposite bank. The sawdust disappeared into lumber planks and the planks into logs—just the opposite to what should happen in a well regulated sawmill. They soon found out the trouble. Higgenbottom had connected everything up backwards!

Paul was very angry over the whole thing by this time and shouted to the engineer to shut down. He had all the logs he could handle already, and this crazy sawmill kept turning out more and more logs. He sent for the Englishman, but Higgenbottom had already left camp by the time they got the machinery stopped.

After trying to straighten it out without success, Paul finally gave it up as a bad job and took down the entire mill. The huge band saw was cut up into smaller pieces and used for currycombs, and the leather belting made a new set of harness for Babe the Blue Ox. Paul decided from that time on he would let the sawmill men run their own mills as they saw fit.

✝✝✝✝✝✝

Thomas G. Alvord, Jr.:

PAUL BUNYAN'S MUZZLE LOADER

Regardin' Bunyan's famous gun,
About which few have heard,
It was a gunsmith's work of art
Designed for bear or bird,

A muzzle-loader made in France,
   Its barrel Swedish steel,
Its trigger guard and firin' pin
   Of wrought iron made in Kiel.
It measured eighty feet in length,
   And had a mammoth butt
Carved out of one gigantic log
   Of seasoned butternut.
The front sight on the barrel was
   A ship's keel painted white,
A set of moose horns mounted aft
   Served well as hinder sight;
While a lofty pine shucked of its bark,
   And shorn of limb and knot,
Made a ramrod used for drivin' home
   Both powder-charge, and shot.

The barrel, since its bore was smooth,
   Permitted one to use
A load of nails, or cannon balls,
   Whichever one might choose,
And though black powder served quite well
   To speed shot in its flight,
Paul found that "bug" would do, as well,
   But pre-ferred dynamite,
So when it came to range of ball
   'Twas governed by his views
Regardin' how much dynamite,
   Or powder he should use.

Paul often times shot ducks and geese
   In Texas, on the "Red,"
While he, a thousand miles away,
   Up north on watershed,

A-top a stump sat comfortably,
　　Dry-shod, and watched his hound,
A-wadin' water to his tail
　　In huntin' 'round an' 'round,
In effort to retrieve such fowl
　　As he had, by mistake,
Killed farther south in Texas, down
　　On Fort Worth's private lake.

I reckon, though, the longest shot
　　That Bunyan ever made
Was when he went a-huntin' moose,
　　And had to climb, and wade,
The Rockies in Alaska, and
　　That duck pond, Great Slave Lake,
When one day he sat dryin' out,
　　And watchin' bannock bake,
At a certain choice volcano in
　　The Northland, farther west;
When he spies a moose bird swipin' chuck;
　　And stuffin' level best—
A feature which annoys old Paul,
　　And causes him to shoot
That thievin' little devil, in
　　The act of takin' loot.

It's difficult to swaller hull
　　This rather weird account,
But facts is facts, and must prevail,
　　And truth is paramount.
In shootin' that 'ar moose bird, it
　　Requires Paul's aimin' high,
With his musket pointed anglin' up,
　　In favor of the sky,

And bein' so, the bullet busts
  Right out across the ocean,
Around the earth, and back to where
  Originates a notion
That his hindquarters has been jabbed
  With somethin' powerful hot,
In the region, special, where he sits,
  But for a time will not.

You can bet that ever after that,
  When shootin' heavy loads,
At angles some to skyward, that
  Old Paul when they explodes,
Immedjit steps to right or left,
  The purpose in his mind
A-bein' to avoid a slug
  That's sneakin' up behind.

✟✟✟✟✟✟

Dell J. McCormick:

PAUL BUNYAN'S WATCH

PAUL HEARD one day that they were going to tear down the old courthouse at Tacoma, Washington, so he told Johnnie Inkslinger to go over and put in a bid for the outdoor clock on the tower.

"If it keeps good time maybe Ole the blacksmith could make it into a watch for me," said Paul.

Johnnie got there just as they were about to wreck the building and told the contractor what he wanted. The contractor was glad to see Johnnie because he couldn't figure out how to get the clock down from the tower. It was too heavy for his men to move. He thought he would dicker with this lumberjack who seemed to want it so badly.

"Well, that's a pretty nice clock, and we're proud of it," said the contractor. "Ain't another like it 'round here for fifty miles. Of course it hasn't run for fourteen years, but that makes it just like a new clock. How about fifty dollars?"

Johnnie finally found out that the contractor would pay that much just to get it off the building, so he agreed right away before he changed his mind. It took Babe the Blue Ox just two hours to lower it down with a block and tackle and before evening they had it all crated for the journey back to Paul's camp.

Ole the Big Swede was the best blacksmith in the woods and he went right to work making it into a watch for Paul. He always liked to tinker with things like that. One year up at Red Bottom Lake he made a patent alarm clock. Every morning the bull-cooks would go through the bunkhouses yelling,

"Hit the deck. Roll out or roll up. Day-y-light in the swamp!" Ole never liked that method of waking the men. He said it was old-fashioned. He decided to invent an alarm clock instead that would do the work faster and better.

It was quite a machine and had several pulleys and counterweights. When it started ringing it rang for twenty minutes and then beat a gong. At six o'clock if anyone was still in bed it threw rocks at them. Several tardy sleepers were seriously injured, and Paul finally had to discard the idea.

Ole went right to work on the tower clock and inside of three months he and his helpers had the huge watch ready. When it was all finished and placed in a shiny new case it was about fourteen feet in diameter. The minute hand was six feet long and made of the finest steel Ole could buy.

Paul was pleased with the job and always wore it in his pants pocket with a thirty-foot logging chain tied to a big ring at the top.

It made so much noise at first it drove three men stone deaf and scared all the deer out of the woods. Ole finally put a crew of oilers and greasers working on it until it was as quiet as any watch, and you could only hear it ticking about a quarter of a mile away. Of course with the wind in the right direction you could still hear it five or six miles

away. It was a stem winder and took a donkey engine to wind it. That wasn't so bad though as they only had to wind it twice a year—Fourth of July and Christmas.

It finally stopped one winter when Paul was logging up on the Big Auger and he sent it back to Ole to have it fixed. When all the wheels and fittings were laid out on the ground they covered two and a half acres. It really was a miracle he ever got it together again, but he finally put it together and had a hundred and forty-seven parts left over, including two large circular gears that nobody had ever noticed before. Three helpers climbed into the watch and oiled and greased every moving part. When the back was clamped back in place it ran perfectly except for a slight squeak down in the lower left-hand corner. Ole crated it for shipment back to Paul up the Big Auger.

The next morning he went out to give the watch a final looking-over and nail the cover on the wooden case. Before he got the first board nailed in place, however, he heard a strange sound. A voice seemed to come from the giant watch.

"Let me out of here, you thick-headed idiot!"

Ole dropped his hammer. It was the first time any watch had ever talked back to him. He eyed it strangely. He looked under the watch. He walked around it. There was nobody but himself.

"Must have been yust the wind," said Ole as he picked up the hammer again. A watch couldn't talk! It was absurd. All a watch could do was tell time. He nailed another board in place.

"Drop that hammer, you big lummox, and let me out!"

It was the watch again! He refused to answer. What if someone came up and heard him talking to a watch? They'd think he was crazy. Ole dropped the hammer and fled. He didn't stop until he was safely back in the blacksmith shop. There he sat down to recover his breath. He was still trying to figure it out when Johnnie Inkslinger came along. He had his great notebook in his hand and he looked puzzled.

"Maybe the watch bane talkin' to Yunny Inkslinger too, by Yimminy," thought Ole.

But Johnnie Inkslinger had other things on his mind.

"I've been waiting for you, Ole. We can't find Pete Larsen, that helper of yours. He wasn't in the bunkhouse last night and he didn't show up for breakfast this morning. If he quit camp, why didn't he call in at the office for his money? Have you seen him around?"

Ole scratched his head.

"Last night yust as we quit work on the watch he was with me and we was greasing the watch and he was inside oiling the main spring and——"

Suddenly Ole remembered.

"By Yimminy! Pete, he bane still in watch, I bet you!"

Ole started running back to the watch. With Johnnie's help he pried off the back cover of the huge watch and looked into the darkness.

"Hey, Pete! Was you down inside there?"

Out crawled the poor helper, covered from head to foot with oil and grease.

"I was yust oiling the main spring," said Pete, "when these fellars put the cover back on before I could yump out."

🌲🌲🌲🌲🌲🌲🌲

Thomas G. Alvord, Jr.:

BUNYAN'S
Intra-National Harvester [1]

One morning after breakfast, while most privately engaged,
   Paul Bunyan gave some study to a certain crumpled page
Of a catalogue displaying certain articles for sale,
   By the famous Seers & Sawbuck, doin' business through
      the mail.
There was everything from baby chicks to elephants and
     mice,
   To be obtained at discount, at a most attractive price;

But the article which caught his eye on this one page
　　—eighteen,
　　Praised the notable performance of a certain farm
　　　　machine,
Which not alone cut wheat and oats, and bunched it where
　　　　it fell,
　　In long and lengthy windrows, but progressed with speed
　　　　as well.
Thought Paul, indeed 'tis admirable, and worthy of much
　　praise,
　　And a very marked improvement over tools of other days,
And I am much inclined to think—although much thinking
　　hurts my head—
　　That while some care to harvest grain I'll harvest trees
　　　　instead,
For this thing might cut stalks of spruce, of hemlock and of
　　pine,
　　Providin' that it's some enlarged and altered in design.

While thus absorbed, he visualized expansion wide and
　　grand,
　　In colossal undertakings, then he took his rule in hand,
And spreading out a tracing sheet, with care he straight-
　　way drew
　　A plan superbly accurate from every point of view.
And now, thought Paul, arising and admiring blcck and line,
　　My judgment tells me I've produced a workable design.
This newer plan, with parts enlarged, I'll send to Mr. Seers,
　　And have him build a harvester with more substantial
　　　　gears,
And I'll warrant when in action it will cut more spruce
　　and pine
　　Than all the crews I've ever worked, yes, all of them
　　　　combined.

After much communication, and the passing of some weeks,
    Paul received a bill of lading, and so hurriedly he treks
To the nearest railway station to unload this juggernaut,
    Which for weeks has rendered restless nights and days of
        heavy thought.

At last this noble vehicle, comprised of paint and springs,
    Stands ready for its launching, and the praise of jacks and
        kings;
And Paul, mechanically inclined, proceeds to make inspec-
    tion,
    Demands a heavy head of steam, and by his own elec-
    tion,
Ascends the steps, takes wheel in hand, and 'midst the
    loudest cheers,
    Pulls throttle wide, and lets her go, by slippin' in the gears.
A thunderous roar—the clank of steel—a grinding of her
    parts—
    A cloud of steam, of blackest smoke—a rushing stream
    of sparks,
And out upon the countryside, regardless of direction,
    This mammoth thing of noise and steel, in passing
        through the section,
Lays low in perfect windrows, on the left and on the right,
    Not only saw-log timber, but most everything in sight.
But when it came to stoppin' it Paul realized too late,
    After grabbin' gates, and gadgets, which would fail to
        operate,
Except to furnish further speed, that he and Mr. Seers
    Had overlooked the feature of providin' breechin' gears,
That, therefore, since this wild machine refused to slacken
    down,
    It might be wise to migrate some, and leave the bloomin'
    town.

First he navigated up and down the greater part of Maine,
    Then westward through the mountains of the Allegheny
        chain;
Swerved south and took his bearing on a single standin' pine,
    Where it stood alone at South St. Joe, and make a straight
        beeline,
And missing it by inches, still went on a-chargin' west,
    Through the foothills, up the Rockies, and along the
        highest crest;
Passed on, and on, and westward, over desert, plain and
    stream,
    Until at last:—a splash—a crash—tremendous cloud of
        steam—
And Bunyan and his harvester plunge roarin' in the Bay,
    Which marks the western terminus of the well-known
        Santa Fe—
A right-o'-way which, by the way, keeps well to Bunyan's
    trail,
    And over which we ride today in luxury by rail.
Now it might be thought that Bunyan felt himself some
    taken back,
    But not at all, he only grinned and started to re-track;
But while he hiked those many miles to camp, back east
    in Maine,
    He recalled his morning's solitude, when his overactive
        brain,
And the picture of a harvester upon a crumpled page,
    Had led him to originate the marvel of the age.

Ray S. Owen:

PAUL BUNYAN
the Surveyor Extraordinary

IN READING over the literature recently published regarding the renowned early Wisconsin character, Paul Bunyan, it was the occasion of considerable surprise to find that nothing was mentioned of Paul's famous exploits as a land surveyor.

The old lumber companies had to hire surveyors to survey and compute areas of timber land, fractional sections and townships, but the process was slow and expensive, entailing as it did the clearing of lines and measurement of bearings and distances, as well as laborious computation by a hot fire in the evenings, after a day's survey in the cold, with the attendant drowsiness and errors.

The work dragged so that Paul was appealed to for aid. He had had some experience in engineering office work and bethought himself of the planimeter. His plan was to planimeter the land directly, but he was not able to find a planimeter on the market large enough for his purpose, so he concluded to build one. He had some trouble in finding a suitable wheel but finally procured a quarter-mile race track in fair condition, round, with a good outside edge. He then got a couple of pieces of the state line between Wisconsin and Michigan, one of these was 10 miles long and the other about 8. He put the race track up on edge and attached it to the end of the longer piece of state line, using as bearings, balls from the Cannon Ball River.

For the tracing point he found a 200-foot pine, and fastened it to the 10-mile arm, with the smaller end down.

Another similar tree was used for the fixed point at the end of the shorter 8-mile arm. The joint where the short arm joined the long arm, was improvised with the steel axle of an overshot water wheel, 25 feet long and 8 inches in diameter, as the pin.

The perimeter of the wheel was graduated into 100 parts, by marking the roadway with strips of white pancake batter, 1 foot wide. This took 10 barrels of wheat flour, and each lumberjack in camp had one pancake less for breakfast the next morning, after which a new supply of flour was obtained.

He selected Section 37 of Town 41 North, Range 10 East, to use in calibrating the planimeter. He soon had the length of arm adjusted to read acres direct. He then rigged up a saddle for the blue ox with a socket attached to the saddle horn and into this was set the tracing point.

The method used was to set up the instrument within a few miles of the area to be surveyed, then with the tracing point in the socket on the horn of the saddle, he would mount the blue ox and ride carefully around the boundaries of the land.

The arms cleared the tops of trees and hills and he was able to proceed at the rate of about 2½ miles an hour; thus with the necessary setups and readings he was able to obtain the area of a section of land to 1/100 of an acre in about 2 hours. A township would take him a full day.

He surveyed all the townships of Price County in just five weeks. It was with the aid of this instrument that Paul was able to calculate the length of the Round River. He had some difficulty in lubricating the joint at the junction of the two arms, but it was solved for a time by butchering a fat hog, and attaching the carcass to the top of the 8-inch iron pin. The combination of the frictional heat and sun's rays then melted the lard which ran down the pin and supplied lubrication as needed.

Paul used this machine successfully for many years. When he took the contract to log the state of North Dakota he used it in making his estimates, but lack of hogs enforced a too rigid economy in lubrication and as a result of an overheated bearing the machine caught fire and burned up.

Paul always intended to return the state line when he got through with it, but the fire made it impossible. This eventually caused a dispute and a lawsuit between the two states, and it was not until the summer of 1929 that the position of the old state line was relocated.

❦❦❦❦❦❦❦

John Lee Brooks:

PAUL BUNYAN IN THE OIL FIELDS

PAUL BUNYAN, though not by any means "America's only folk-hero," is easily our most versatile. In addition to his logging, he has muscled-in on other trades. He appears among the tank-builders, erecting a tank so high that a hammer dropped off the top wore out two handles before it hit the ground. Among the old-style truckers he is noted for his skill in being able to wield a forty-foot blacksnake whip out of a covered wagon. The telegraph construction men speak with great pride of his building the Mason and Dixon Line and of his working so fast that his ground crew had to shoot him the insulators out of a machine-gun.

I have told elsewhere (*vide* Texas Folk-Lore Society Publication VII) how Paul came south to the oil fields and soon became a phenomenal driller and operator. He developed new methods such as rolling up the drill stem on a huge drum, and he invented new tools and equipment, giving them appropriate names like "headache post," "bull-wheel," and "calf-wheel," and "lazy-bench." Everything he did, in fact, was super-colossal!

Paul Bunyan at work was something! His rig and gears were so big that, although he lived twelve miles from the lease, he rode to the job by hopping on the rocker-arm of a pump as it went back and forth. His drilling engine had a fly-wheel that took thirty days to make one revolution. The drill-stem, which was flexible, was so heavy that the engine required twenty-four gears to handle it. The derrick was appropriately large: the derrickman went up to his post as a bridegroom and was a grandfather before he came down. His meals were shot up to him out of an anti-aircraft gun. The rotary table was so wide that the backup man had a tent right on it; if he hadn't he could never have got back on time to set the slips. On one occasion Paul determined to break his record for height. He built the structure up, up, up until it became so tall that he and his crew moved to heaven and lived there while they finished their work. Paul decided to drill a well worthy of his derrick. He reached China and stopped.

When Paul attempted other types of work, he was equally terrific. The pipe-liners, the roughest crew to be found in the oil fields, tell of Paul's big camp for which he laid a pipeline to furnish buttermilk for his men. According to them, his tongs were so heavy that it took four ordinary men to lift them. One day when he was setting up the joints on the twenty-four-inch buttermilk line to the camp, he absent-mindedly turned over the pump stations for a hundred miles before he realized that the joints were tight. Work like this hardly brought the sweat, but, if the day was hot, he might wipe the perspiration off his brow with one of

Barnum and Bailey's old circus tents, which was the only thing he could find adequate for a handkerchief. If he got hungry, the café manager had practically a government contract! He kept a whole batch of meal-tickets for Paul, and instead of punching them he simply tacked them on the wall and shot them with a shotgun.

Paul had one disappointment in life: his son Rufus was not up to what he should have been in size, measuring only nine feet between the eyes and forty-four feet from nipple to nipple in the chest. But Paul let him play around the rig for amusement until one day the boy got too close to the injectors of the boiler and was sucked in. When his father found him, he was bobbing around in the gauge glass, and Paul in disgust took him out and wrung his neck for a runt.

These various manifestations of Paul Bunyan evidence his virility and show he is thoroughly and typically native. To American laborers in many fields, he's the super-hero— adaptable, aggressive, unstoppable, the champion at all weights.

✲✲✲✲✲✲✲

PAUL BUNYAN IN TEXAS†

TEXAS FOLK CULTURES are generally expressing themselves in new forms instead of dying. The oil field workers, for example, have borrowed the lumberjack hero, Paul Bunyan, and are now converting him into a gigantic figure of the derricks. A typical story is that of Paul's great posthole deal. Once while he was drilling for oil at Breckenridge, he struck a dry hole. Furious, he smashed the derrick with one blow

† From *Texas Guidebook* (American Guide Series).

of his fist. Then he saw an advertisement for 10,000 post-holes wanted by a rancher in the Panhandle where "the wind blows prairie dog holes inside out." So Paul hitched a chain to the dry hole, pulled it up and, realizing that the hole was too long to handle in entirety, he cut it into proper lengths, shipped the pieces to the Panhandle and made a fortune. Another time, he built a pipe line from his Texas ranch to the Chicago stockyards and pumped his cattle through it, but the pipe was so big that half-grown year-lings would get lost in the threads and starve to death before they could get out.

PAUL'S VEGETABLES

James Stevens:

THE OLD HOME CAMP

THE OLD HOME CAMP of Paul Bunyan, was in the Smiling River country; it lay in a great plain, between this sunny stream and the flowered banks of Honey Creek, which lazed on past the camp ere it joined the river. When the sun got low in the West, the shadow of old Rock Candy Mountain crept over the camp. On hot summer days the frost-hued mountain was a freshening sight; at night it looked like a huge dish of white ice cream. Raspberry trees covered its lower slopes, and in the Junetime they were heavy with berries as big as apples. The lemonade springs bubbled from among these trees, and their waters rippled through blossoming strawberry bushes as they coursed towards the river. In the twilights of the fruitful season the songs of the jaybirds that nested in the raspberry trees sank to a soft and sentimental chorus; and their slumbrous melodies, mingled with the cheery "jemine-e-es" of the jeminy crickets that lived among the strawberry bushes, made a beauty of sound harmonious with the spirit of eventide.

The old home camp had been built in the midst of a grove of maples. It had been deserted for seven years, and only a few moss-covered bunkhouses yet remained. Some bare sections of land, deeply corrugated, showed where the great cookhouse had stood; and trails that had been packed by the trampling of thousands of calked boots were still marked through lush growths of grass.

Paul Bunyan's farm was the source of his supplies; it was ruled by John Shears and worked by the scissor-bills. It covered the rich bottom lands below Honey Creek, and it extended for miles over the bordering hills. Huge red clover blooms tossed and nodded on crowns and slopes when the warm June breezes blew. When the two happy but sensitive bees, Bum and Bill, had got enough honey from them to fill the thirty-five hundred barrels which were required for the loggers' hot cakes each winter, John Shears and the scissor-bills mowed the hay and baled it. Then the milk cows were pastured on the stubble until wintertime. They did not have such grandiose names as are given to cows nowadays—no one in Paul Bunyan's time would have thought of naming a kind, honest heifer Wondrous Lena Victress or Dairylike Daffodil Sweetbread;—they were simply called Suke, Boss, Baldy and S'manthy, but they were queenly milkers. Boss was the great butter cow; John Shears had only to put salt in her milk, stir it a bit, let it stand for a while, and he would have tubfuls of the finest butter in the land. Suke's milk made wonderful bubbly hot cakes. Baldy's milk never soured, and it was especially good in cream gravy. S'manthy's milk was pretty poor stuff, but she had a vast hankering for balsam boughs, and in the winter she would eat them until her milk became the most potent of cough medicines. It saved Paul Bunyan's loggers from many an attack of pneumonia. The grand flocks of poultry, which were ruled by Pat and Mike, the powerful and bellicose webfooted turkey gobblers, performed marvels of egg-laying and hatching. The snow hens, for example, would lay only in the wintertime; they made their nests in the snow and laid none but hard-boiled eggs. There were great vegetable gardens in the bottom lands; there the parsnips and carrots grew to such a depth that the scissor-bills had to use stump-pullers to get them out of the ground. It took two men an hour and a half to sever the average cabbage from its stalk. The potatoes grew to such a size that Paul Bunyan invented the steam shovel for John Shears to use in digging them out. In the chewing tobacco patch the tobacco grew on the plants in plugs, shreds and twists, and it was highly flavored by the natural licorice in the soil.

✝✝✝✝✝✝✝

Earl Clifton Beck:

THE LEAD PENCIL PLANTS

ONE YEAR Paul had me set out eight hundred acres of lead-pencil plants. Well, pretty soon the lead pencils come up eight inches high and started to rubber.

But that wasn't the only crop we got off that eight hundred acres. The blossoms was such a pretty red and blue color that the blackbirds used to come to pick 'em off. Well, I loaded up Paul's old cannon with birdshot and shot the feathers off all them birds. We got so many that we started up a feather-bed factory. Well, sir, every spring after that them birds came back after more blossoms, and we got another crop of feathers.

✝✝✝✝✝✝✝

Earl Clifton Beck:

THE TOBACCO VENTURE

ONE YEAR when I was runnin' Paul's farm, I planted eighty acres of tobacco just across the fence from a big cabbage field. Well, first thing we knowed, a big flock of grass hoppers came in and et up most of the tobacco. Then the darn things'd set on the fence and spit tobacco juice all over them cabbages, till Paul figgered they was a total loss.

Well, sir, a idee hit me. We pulled them cabbages, ground 'em up, and made the best grade of Copenhagen.

✝✝✝✝✝✝✝

Constance Mayfield Rourke:

THE GIANT CORNSTALK

ONCE PAUL PLANTED a grain of corn and it grew so fast that nobody could see the top. Big Swede Charlie climbed up it to have a look at the country but he couldn't climb down again because she grew faster than what he could slide. After a while Paul he decided that Charlie must be getting hungry so he got out his shotgun. Usually he loaded her with a dish-pan full of powder and brickbats, but this time he rammed her full of dough-god biscuits, and they must have kept Charlie a-going for a while, because later when the corn begun to get ripe a lot of little corncobs begun to drop down, showing that Charlie was eating the corn. One day the commanding officer of the Great Lakes Naval Station come round all fixed up with ribbons on his uniform, and he says to Paul,

"Sir, I got orders for you to cut this here cornstalk down."
Paul says, "That ain't got nothing to do with me. The President of the United States or the Secretary of War or Admiral
Dewey can't make me cut down that there cornstalk ef I don't
want to." "But," says the officer, "the roots of this here cornstalk go down so deep and spread out so wide that they reach
in under Lake Michigan on the one side and in under Lake
Huron on the other, and the level's goin' down so fast it in-
terferes with navigation." So Paul he decides to cut down the
cornstalk, and he sends for his best broadax men, and he
signals for them to begin a-chopping by shooting off his gun.
But the cornstalk grew so fast they couldn't chop twice in the
same place and they couldn't make a chip. So Paul he goes
to the logging railroad and he rips up a rail out of the wreck,
and it were a quarter of a mile long and foot square, and he
makes a cable out of it and ties it in a knot around the cornstalk, so the faster she grew the more she cut herself, and
finally after a long while she began to topple over. They had
to warn the people which way she was going to fall, and the
logging engineer he had to get off two miles before he could
sight the top of her with a telescope and see which way she
was leaning; and they could hear the wind a-whistling
through her two and a half days before the top of her ever
struck the earth. They never did find out just how tall she
were even when the dust was all cleared away for she was all
ravelled out by the wind, falling. One ear of corn drove plumb
down into the earth and stuck so tight Paul couldn't get it
out even with his blue ox hitched to it, so he hitched up his
mules, but then he only got the cob, and the grains filled up a
well forty foot deep.

✵✵✵✵✵✵✵

Harold Titus:

THE GIANT CORNSTALK

Tʜɪs ɪs the story that Black Joe told:

"Now, this here mule team of Paul's was a right good pair. They done a lot of work an' Paul he treated 'em right, allus cattelatin' it was best policy to be good to stock. When they was workin' hard it cost a lot to keep 'em up fer sure, but when they was just standin' in th' barn he only fed 'em four bushels of corn to th' feed.

"Paul fed 'em hisself, when he wasn't away, an' when he was gone Swede Charley looked atter 'em—along with th' ox-team, little Babe an' her mate. You heerd tell 'bout *that* team, ain't you?

"My God, Taylor, don't you know nothin'? This here was a good team, too. Never seen 'em myself, but I knowed a chore boy who worked for Paul th' winter of th' blue snow, an' *he* was a tellin' as how little Babe was four ax-handles wide atween th' eyes——"

He spit and wiped his chin.

"One day when Paul was loggin' off Section Thirty-Seven, he was feedin' th' mules an' he sees what looks like a good-sized kernel of corn. Might' good-sized kernel, all right. Paul, he was allus lookin' atter good things, so he stuck her in his vest pocket an' didn't give it to th' mules.

"Atter dinner he was rummagin' round fer a toothpick an' locates this here kernel o' corn. He was out behint th' barn jus' then an' so he kicks a hole in th' ground an' plants her—

"That was th' big barn. See, Paul he kep' a lotta teams on th' haul which meant pret' big barn. Big job, cleanin' this here barn an' Paul was great for this—now, efficiency. So he had th' barn set on wheels an' moved it along every day, 'stead of a-cleanin' her out.

"That night a settler drives in to talk to Paul 'bout some cord wood. He was thar awhile an' 'long 'bout dusk he goes out fer to start home—

"In a minute he was back an' says to Paul that his team's got away.

" 'So?' says Paul, 'Where'd you leave 'em?'

" 'Out tied to that air telephone pole behint your barn,' gesturing.

" 'They ain't no telephone pole thar,' says Paul.

" 'Sure they is,' says the settler.

"So Paul goes out to investigate. He an' th' settler walks aroun' behint th' barn an' th' settler says to look thar; thar she is. Paul looks an' blinks because b' God, his corn had sprouted an' this here telephone pole was his cornstalk!

"Well, it was a pret' high cornstalk by then an' Paul leans back to look up an' see how high it was an', b' gosh, what's he see but that air team an' wagon belongin' to th' settler away up thar, most outta sight. Th' stalk had growed up an' took th' whole shebang along!

"Now Paul he knowed he's got fer to get this here team down, so he sends fer Swede Charley an' says, 'Charley, you climb up an' ontie that air team.'

"So Charley he spits on his hands an' starts up. Darn good climber, Charley; he climbs pret' darn fast, an' he gits away up thar an' then they see him makin' funny motions, wavin' his arms an' such, an' th' boys begin to wonder what's up.

"Well, Paul he figgers it out. Charley can't make it an' 's tryin' to slide down, but this gol-darn stock's growin' up faster 'n he can slide down an' he keeps right on' goin' outta sight.

"Now, this 's pret' serious, thinks Paul, Swede Charley up thar an' goin' higher; what's goin' to happen to him? He'll starve, won't he?

"So Paul runs to th' cook shanty an' gits a lotta biscuits an' into th' van where he keeps his shotgun.

"Pret' good gun, this here one of Paul's. Fair-sized gun, too. Paul he used to load each bar'l with a dishpanful of powder an' brick bats an' he'd shoot her first east an' if he didn't git game thar, he'd shoot her west; allus got game one place or t'other.

"So Paul loads her with biscuits an' shoots both bar'ls up toward where Charley's went, most outta sight by then. And they knowed Charley'd have somethin' to eat ontil they could git him down.

"Th' settler he walks home an' Paul he goes to bed, thinkin' 'bout that air team an' Charley. Nothin' he can do till mornin' but when mornin' comes, th' top of that stalk, th' team an' Charley is all clean outta sight—

"Paul he gits right worried. Atter a few days they commences to find dead crows in th' swamp. Crows kep' fallin' down plumb dead an' nothin' but skin an' bones. Lot o' crows. Paul he figgers that air out, too. This here team's died up thar an' th' crows has started up atter 'em for a nice meal, but they's starved to death on th' way!

"Now this here cornstalk gives no sign of slowin' up. She grows over ag'in' the barn an' they have fer to put th' barn on another set o' wheels so's it'll run sideways. Then she grows ag'in' th' men's shanty an' they has to put that on wheels too, an' th' cornstalk keeps crowdin' 'em apart ontil they has to string a telephone line atween th' barn an' shanty to communicate ready-like.

"Paul he's pret' worried. Never seen nothin' like this here afore. One day a man drives into camp with a feather in his hat an' gold buttons on his coat an' solid gold medals on his

"Now this here cornstalk gives no sign of slowin' up. . . ."

chist an' gold things on his shoulders. He's got a sword an' stripes on his pants an' shiny boots an' he carried a big paper all stuck over with red sealin' wax an' blue ribbins. He walks up to Paul.

" 'You Mister Bunion?' he asks, an' Paul he 'lows how he is. 'Well I gotta warrant for your arrest from Congress,' he says.

" 'Warrant?' says Paul, surprised-like. 'From Congress? What for? An' who are you?'

" 'I'm th' Admiral of th' Navy,' says th' gent, 'an' this here cornstalk's got its roots into Lake Huron on one side an' Lake Michigan on th' other an' she is suckin' the water up so fast that all th' boats is aground!'

"Now Paul, he ain't no mean talker, so he argufies with this here Admiral an' promises him he'll get this here cornstalk out th' way. Th' Admiral he don't want to leave it that way, but Paul he's done a lotta loggin' fer Congress, y' know, an' he stands pret' well. Yup. He logged off North Dakoty. See, when th' Governor who was a reformed Swede found out th' King o' Sweden was drivin' all th' good farmers out an' that they was comin' over here, he wants 'em in Dakoty. But they wa'n't no place for 'em, then, so th' governor gits Congress to say it'll log off th' state an' Congress gives th' contrack to Paul an' makes good, which gives him a pret' fair stand-in—

"Well the Admiral he goes off an' Paul, he sets down to think. He's gotta cut that damn cornstalk down somehow, but it's a big job. He thinks an' thinks an' then he sends for th' Tie-Cuttin' Finn an' says—

"Tie-Cuttin Finn? Never heerd tell on him?"

He clicked his tongue in disgust and sighed.

"Well this here Finn, he was th' best broadaxe man Paul ever had, but he ain't quite so good as Paul wants at that, him havin' a big tie contrack. So Paul he gits an idea. He rigs a thirty-pound broadaxe on each of th' Finn's feet like skates." He drew up a foot to illustrate. "Straps 'em on good an' solid. Then th' Finn goes into th' cedar swamp. He goes up a tree, usin' these here axes for climbers, scores goin' up, gits to th' top, slides down, hews two faces on th' way an' knocks off a tie every eight feet—

"Well Paul, he calls in th' Tie-Cuttin' Finn an' tells him to pick out fifty of th' likeliest-lookin' broadaxe men in camp, which th' Finn does. He takes 'em into th' swamp an' fer a month he teaches 'em ontil he's got fifty of th' best axe-men that ever spit on a hand.

"Then one mornin' bright an' early they all come out, axes all sharp, stripped to their shirts an' lines up roun' th' corn-stalk.

"Paul he gits the dinner horn from th' cook shanty— Ever hear 'bout that dinner horn? Nope? Huh! Well she's a good one. Has to have a good one y'know, 'cause he runs a big camp an' th' men git scattered a long ways by dinner time, but nobody but Paul can blow this here horn. The sound carries all right when Paul blows her, but it's kinda expensive 'cause every time he blows he knocks down 'bout 'leven acres of standin' timber.

"Well, Paul, he gits these here men all strung 'round th' cornstalk an' he blows th' horn for 'em to start. They slam into th' stalk good an' heavy, fifty of 'em, each sinkin' his axe to th' eye—but—" He sighed and paused. "You see, their chop-pin' don't do a dime's worth of good, 'cause this here damn stalk grows so fast that they can't hit twice in th' same place to git a chip off.

"Bad," he muttered. "Pret' bad, with Congress waitin' fer to arrest Paul an' ruin his reppetation.

"So Paul, he does some more thinkin'. Now you recalled 'bout Paul's big sawmill. Pret' good-sized mill. Right *fair* mill. She'd cut a million feet an hour. To keep this mill in logs he had to build a pret' good railroad. Light steel wouldn't stand his trains 'cause they had to load fairly heavy, so Paul had some special steel made, mite heavier 'n anythin' they'd ever used loggin'. Each rail was a quarter-mile long an' a foot square on th' end.

"Now this road, good as she was, couldn't quite keep th' mill in logs. The' was a Scotchman engineer on th' loggin' train an' he used to roll 'em in pret' fast, but Paul he ain't satisfied, an' he laces into th' Scotchman one day an' tells it to him good an' hard an' says to put on a little steam, wood's cheap, an' travel some. That made the engineer mad—'cause he thought he'd been doin' pret' good. So when he goes out with his empties to th' bankin' ground he opens her wide an' she goes so damn fast that th' draft picks up th' steel an' ties an' rolls 'em up behint an' over th' way car ontil railroad, train an' everythin' 's junk.

"Now that air railroad she was Paul's first big failure; gettin' rid of this here cornstalk's th' other. So he natterly thinks 'bout both, an' that gives him 'n idee. He goes over to this here junk pile an' commences pullin' her apart.

"Quite a job, with them quarter-mile rails, but by-an'-by he gits a few pulled loose an' straightened out an' puts 'em over his shoulder an' walks back to camp.

"That evenin' atter supper he takes a look at th' cornstalk, which is a right good-sized stalk by then. He takes these here rails an' knots 'em together, strings 'em aroun' th' stalk, ties 'em up tight in a knot an' stands back an' says: 'There, durn ye, pinch yerself off!' Which the stalk perceeds to do.

"Well she pinches all right. They can hear her crackin' over in Wisconsin.

"Then Paul he thinks to hisself, what'll happen when she comes down?

"So he sends fer his surveyor an' puts him out 'n th' brush with his transit to watch th' top of this here cornstalk. They strings a telephone line out to th' place an' th' surveyor camps there. Th' stalk keeps growin' an' snappin' an' atter a while th' surveyor he telephones an' says she's commencin' to sag.

"Paul he sends his men out into th' clearin' to warn th' settlers an' gets 'em all outen th' way. Everybody's pret' much excited.

" 'She's commencin' to sag somethin' bad,' telephones th' surveyor. Everybody gits away back—an' looks— They can see her quiver an' quake an' by-'n-by they can hear her top whistlin'."

He spat.

"Yes, sir, they heerd that top whistlin' four days afore she hit th' ground!"

He stopped with a nod and tightening of his lips.

"Four days," repeated Joe, seriously. "An' no wonder! Why, Paul, he figgered out that about a mile 'n half of that air top had frazzled out on th' way down!

"They went out to look th' thing over atter she was safe down an' up pret' well toward what was left of th' top end they found 'n ear of corn. Pret' sizeable ear, this here was, and it was druv straight into th' ground by th' stalk.

"Paul he scratched his head an' thinks he better git that air ear out. So he goes gits th' mule team 'nd builds a stump puller. He has to build a pret' big stump puller all right. He rigs her up good an' strong an' hooks on th' mules an' pulls on that cob an' when he gits her up he has 'n eighty foot well, all cobbled up with kernels.

"Yup, Paul was quite a lad. He never let anythin' interfere with his work."

PAUL MADE GEOGRAPHY

G. C. Morbeck:

*Paul
Made
Geography*

PAUL BUNYAN: an Authentic Account of His Prehistoric Activities

PAUL BUNYAN is as old as the earth itself. His activities on this terrestrial ball antedate those of any other living being. Bunyan's life has been an open book to foresters and woodsmen since the dawn of history. It was generally believed that Paul, his blue ox Babe, and his faithful crew, roamed the earth long ages before the usual run of mankind, commonly known as the public, had lost their tails and had a lick of sense, but it could not be definitely proved. It had almost been proved on many occasions, but there was always that something about the story which savored of fiction which finally carried it out of the realm of absolute fact.

Recently, however, there has been unearthed a perfectly authentic account of Bunyan's life which sheds much light on his prehistoric activities. Paul was a great traveler. Since he could not himself write, he dictaphoned extended accounts of his doings during the early period of his life. Centuries later the wax records were dug up by the Egyptians, who, fearing that the precious words might eventually become lost, had them carved on wooden paddles which were carefully hidden away in the dry, among the dead ones in the pyramids.

When the Indians decided to cast their lot on American shores they took many of the wooden pages of this great literary effort with them, using them for propelling their canoes across the great Atlantic. In the course of time the paddles became widely scattered, and soon all were lost, hence the early doings of Paul Bunyan have until now been a closed book.

Last year "Doc" Hough, a forestry student of archeologic proclivities, discovered near the site of our forestry summer camp at Pelican Lake, Minnesota, during one of his probing sessions, probably the only one of these historic paddles in existence. Fortunately, it was a "summary" paddle and in order that no harm might come to it, though all the others be destroyed, this one was well preserved by soaking in the blood of 13 mosquitoes which inhabited the country in those early days, and whose juice was highly antiseptic.

The paddle showed evidences of great age. Upon it was packed very closely weird symbols in an unknown tongue. For a long time the hieroglyphics remained the mysterious sensation of the lumbering world. Councils were held, and grave and learned heads pored over the unusual writings, but to no avail.

Finally when hope was all but abandoned it was suggested by one, Martin, well known among Ames foresters as the living embodiment of the three wise men, that a thorough search be made of the vicinity where the board was found, for clues which might lead to the solution of the mystery. Foresters pawed the earth, pulled up trees by main strength, overturned rocks, split the air with ill-smelling phrases, and tore their hair in their frantic efforts to discover something tangible which might aid in the translation of the mystic characters. Other foresters set themselves apart and waited for divine revelation of the strange writing, but none came.

After many days of strenuous work, their labors were rewarded. A diligent searcher after truth and knowledge, one Trenk, discovered a circular crystal-like object, thick at the center and tapering at the edges, which upon cleaning and polishing proved to be the base of a bottle very common in the days B. P. but now almost extinct. When held just the right distance from the paddle, the "mystery words" were instantly transformed into the language of the realm. Careful peering through the glass by one, Pickford, of good eyesight, has resulted in a very accurate translation, which proved to be nothing less than an authentic account of Paul Bunyan's origin and his activities upon the earth when it was yet young. Attesting the correctness of the manuscript is Paul's right thumb print with its hard lines which mark the character of a true woodsman.

The entire autobiography cannot be set down here; only the principal events in a busy life will be related, and these in an impersonal way.

Paul Bunyan was, is, and ever more shall be. He was the Creator's messenger at the time the earth was built. After about the third day of the creation there appeared in the great sea patches of land, some large, some small, scattered promiscuously about, without order or sequence. Later some were made to rise and spread out, joining with others to form the great continents. The Creator was pleased with His work so far, but in a day or two He became weary of looking down across great areas of trackless wastes. In spite of the rain which fell in abundance nothing grew, and the land remained desolate and unpleasing to the eye.

There was really small wonder for this condition, for how could anything grow without first being planted? So the Creator called to Paul and bade him forest the waste places with every manner and kind of tree until the earth should present a canopy of green beneath which the ground could not be seen. This was Paul Bunyan's first great lumbering job, for doesn't one have to plant trees before one can log them, in regions where there were no trees before? Most assuredly. So Paul entered upon the great task laid out for him. Filling a number of sacks with miscellaneous tree seeds from the great storehouses, he descended to earth to begin his operations. Paul landed in the spot now known as the Garden of Eden. He tarried here for some time, resting from the long journey through space which he had just completed. He lunched upon the fruits brought with him, scattering the inedible portions here and there indiscriminately, as men in playful moods are sometimes wont to do. Presently he picked up his sacks and began his labors.

Paul started eastward scattering seeds broadcast as he went. To the north and to the south flew the light seeds, carried to the remotest parts by the gentle breezes sent to aid in their dissemination. The heavy seeds did not carry so far, hence we have through Asia the coniferous forests in the north and the south fringed by the oaks and other deciduous trees of the heavy seeded varieties. When the Pacific had been reached and the job finished in this direction, Paul retraced his steps to the Garden and, taking a fresh lot of seeds, set out to plant Europe. The method pursued was as before, and we have the central forests of hardwoods, flanked on either side by vast coniferous woods. Reaching the Atlantic, Paul again returned for more seed to seed up areas to the south and the islands of the sea. When this job was completed Paul tarried again to rest in the Garden before returning to his accustomed place. To his surprise there were no forest trees to be seen in the whole region, but rather a great variety of fruit trees laden with luscious fruit of every description. While Paul outwardly admired and loved the fruit dearly, yet inwardly he was greatly peeved at making the colossal blunder of having accidentally broadcasted the seeds of fruit trees, where seeds of forest trees should have been sown.

Looking down again upon the earth Paul noticed land across the sea, heretofore unknown to him, and upon examining it closely found it to be as bleak and barren as the eastern continent had been, so he again took up his sacks of seeds and descended to earth to finish the job. Landing upon the shores of Virginia he travelled westward scattering seeds as before, the light seeds being carried north and south, the heavier seeds falling nearer; hence we have the great northern coniferous forest, and the great southern pine woods with the magnificent hardwoods of oaks, walnut, hickory and other deciduous species occupying the space between.

When Paul arrived at the Mississippi he was about out of seeds, and the remaining few were scattered far and wide to the right, the left, and in front; hence the origin of the fringe forests of the midwestern states.

Bunyan's job was not yet finished. He returned again with seeds, but on account of the great bulk and weight of the heavy acorns, walnuts, hickory nuts and the like he took with him on his last journey only the lighter varieties. In due time he arrived at the Mississippi and crossed it going westward. Here Paul pulled his first real blunder. He sadly miscalculated the distance he had broadcasted from his station east of the river, and didn't begin to sow until he had traversed a considerable distance. The result is the great treeless plains. Paul has never recovered entirely from the remembrance of this error of judgment.

Continuing westward, he scattered seeds far and wide in every direction, being rather careful however that the supply should last out the job. Consequently the Rockies were seeded at the rate of one pound per acre. When Paul arrived at the top of the Cascades of Oregon, he was surprised at seeing stretching before him the great Pacific in all its majesty. Having but a few miles farther to go, and with an abundance of seed remaining, Paul scattered his treasure with a lavish hand. You know the result. The Pacific Coast forests are the finest in the world.

Paul Bunyan's first great job was finished. Travelling leisurely back across America he was greatly struck with the beauty of the new found land and longed to take up his residence here, but duty called him home. Upon returning to the Garden from which he usually ascended, Paul debated long and hard upon the proposition as to whether or not he should return. He finally decided that the earth was a pleasant place to live, and since the forests were now about grown there would be need for his services in transforming the great trees into commodities useful in the building of the great civilization which was soon to appear upon the earth.

Paul was decidedly lonesome during the first 300,000 years, for there were in all this time no human beings upon the earth to enjoy the blessings which were being stored up in abundance for the use of man. The first 300,000 years are always the hardest. Life for Bunyan was just one thing after another, though it was made somewhat easier through his close association with the old blue ox which he captured when very young, and which he trained into a very useful adjunct in his subsequent logging operations.

Once upon returning to the Garden of Eden, after a long trip of inspection through his Asiatic woodlots, Paul noticed forms of life closely resembling himself, scampering about among the vines and the fig trees. Coming closer they proved to be men like himself, only of course of much smaller stature. Paul was greatly delighted at his discovery, and made haste to inquire who they were and from whence they came, and if they knew anything about logging.

Paul picked out 23 Abel-bodied men discarding the Canebearers since logging is not a gentleman's game, but rather one where brawn counts, though it is true brains are sometimes useful in the industry. Not one of the bunch had ever logged. By consistent and persistent training Bunyan soon had a crew that knew the top end of a log when both ends were in sight. Also by scientific feeding the majority were brought to a size Paul thought necessary to logging in those primal days. Every man was 9 axe handles tall and 2 axe handles between the eyes.

Bunyan was now ready to take on any logging job which presented itself. At first business was dull and Paul, his blue ox and his 23 immortals simply lay around waiting for the world to grow up, and populate itself. This was a slow and tedious task as so many people died in those days. Paul became wearied and his crew impatient.

After thousands of years of waiting, people began to see joy in the world and demanded things even beyond Paul Bunyan's power to supply. Joy rides on great prehistoric animals, jazz music and riotous living, together with the general disregard of God's laws, brought the people of the earth into great disfavor of the Almighty. Noah and his immediate relatives were the only ordinary mortals spared in the great catastrophe which overwhelmed the earth as a punishment for man's disobedience.

Noah was directed to build an ark and come in out of the rain which was to follow, and take with him fair samples of all the living things which roamed the earth in order that life might again function when the waters ceased. Noah needed timber, and that badly. Also men who could build the ship. After considerable discussion as to the price, Paul Bunyan landed the job on a cost-plus basis, since it was the first work of the kind ever done, and labor conditions were so very unstable, since steamfitters and plumbers were even then on strike for higher pay and better working conditions.

Paul built the ark. His blue ox and 23 immortals worked hard and long, bringing logs from the ends of the earth, hewing them and laying them in position in the great ship with infinite care. Paul had one great advantage on this particular work. Had he not planted the trees with his own hand? He had, and therefore he knew where every one was, its kind, diameter breast high and its clear length. By referring to his card index he could locate kinds and dimensions precisely. The blue ox and "Lightning Bill" did the rest, and soon there was assembled just the proper amount of material of the right sizes to complete the job. Paul and the immortals and the blue ox then retired to the high mountains and tall timber until the shower passed over, and travelling was again safe upon the earth.

Paul was out of his element somewhat when he built the "Hanging Gardens" for the King of Babylon, but the job was everlastingly good, and the remains of the great structure are to be seen to this day.

The masterpiece of his early work was Solomon's temple. Long years did he labor on the plans for the great structure, and long years did he and his faithful crew work in its construction. The great cedars of Lebanon were brought down on an ice road to Jerusalem, the blue ox bringing 32 at a time, making two trips daily.

When the temple was finished Solomon looked it over and remarked in a rather casual way that it was about the most beautiful piece of work he had ever observed, and he was some observer and a good judge of beauty, as history attests. Not one of his 600 wives disagreed with him on the three general propositions stated above.

Paul and the blue ox Babe were impatient at the enforced idleness due to a general business depression which followed the completion of the temple, but the 23 immortals were glad to get a chance to rest. Life had been strenuous with them and they greatly enjoyed the few days' vacation which was given them by their magnanimous lord and master. Paul had plenty of time to think over matters which interested him, and many times swore loudly when he recalled turning down the contract to build the pyramids. No, sir, and Paul told them so in emphatic language; so they hired local labor, and see what they have. After only 4,000 years the pyramids actually show traces of wear.

While resting on the upper slopes of Mount Lebanon one beautiful spring day, Paul observed smoke in the distance to the westward. Pointing the telescope of his hand compass in that direction his sharp eye detected men busily engaged in clearing land. Bunyan saw a chance to get out from under the idleness he so greatly detested. Calling his trusty crew from the various pleasures and games in which they were wont to engage when not at their usual labors, to-wit: poker, cooties, etc., Paul set forth on a long journey. After two days of incessant travelling, the Bunyanites arrived at their destination, and what do you suppose they found? The "Twins" clearing away the trees and brush in order that Rome might be invented. Being nourished by a wolf, they believed themselves possessed of unlimited power and strength. Paul showed them up quickly and they cowered under his native sarcasm.

The job interested Bunyan, and since he and his stalwart mates were itching to work, not forgetting, of course, Babe, Paul made the wolfish pair a proposition, that he would take over the job of logging the site of Rome, if they would populate the land as fast as it was cleared. Paul worked slowly and carefully, while the twins at top speed "Shanghied" every human being they could locate and brought him to Rome. The population grew—doubled, trebled, quadrupled and chin doubled, but there was always room for more. Two million people inhabited Rome, yet the suburbs could accommodate twice the number; and then the twins gave it up.

Not so with Paul, however. Having caused the building of a great city, he saw great profit in supplying it with wood. Paul dug his bean hole on the island of Sicily, and set his range and hot water barrel south of Naples. From this headquarters camp he logged all Italy. Did he do a good job? He always does. Italy looked like a well-shined boot when Paul finished and it remains exactly so today.

When logging was completed the crew moved on. Paul did not take his "bean hole" with him as was his usual custom, since he was going to make a long journey, and it would be difficult to carry. Likewise he left his range and hot water barrel behind, for the crew travelled light. Paul was usually a good woodsman, but in his haste he forgot to extinguish his fires, and the bean hole burned, and the cookstove smouldered, in spite of the strenuous efforts of the local inhabitants to extinguish the flames.

Finally in desperation, the great Roman legions were called out to quell the fires. Armed with shovels the thousands piled loads upon loads of earth upon the offending utensils, but to no avail. Messengers were sent to implore Paul Bunyan to return and help them out, but he and his immortal 23 and Babe, the blue ox, were already in America, the land of their dreams, and could not be induced to again cross the seas. Meanwhile earth was piled higher and higher upon the great flaming mass, in a mad effort to stem the conflagration. After many days of almost superhuman effort the fires were subdued. They were not fully quenched, however, and to this day Mounts Vesuvius and Etna remain as monuments to Paul Bunyan's disregard for the first principles of good logging,—be careful with fires in the forest.

Dell J. McCormick:

PAUL BUNYAN
Digs the St. Lawrence River

ONE SUMMER Paul decided to leave the North Woods and go back to Maine to visit his father and mother. When he arrived, they talked about old times, and Paul asked about Billy Pilgrim, the biggest man in that part of the country.

"What is this Billy Pilgrim doing?" asked Paul.

"He is digging the St. Lawrence River between the United States and Canada," said Paul's father. "There was nothing to separate the two countries. People never knew when they were in the United States and when they were in Canada."

Paul Bunyan went to see Billy. He found that Billy Pilgrim and his men had been digging for three years and had dug only a very small ditch. Paul laughed when he saw it.

"My men could dig the St. Lawrence River in three weeks," said Paul.

This made Billy angry for he thought no one could dig a large river in three weeks.

"I will give you a million dollars if you can dig the St. Lawrence River in three weeks!" said Billy Pilgrim.

So Paul sent for Babe the Blue Ox, Ole the Big Swede, Brimstone Bill, and all his woodsmen.

Paul told Ole to make a huge scoop shovel as large as a house. They fastened it to Babe with a long buckskin rope. He hauled many tons of dirt every day and emptied the scoop shovel in Vermont. You can see the large piles of dirt there to this day. They are called the Green Mountains.

Every night Johnnie Inkslinger, who did the arithmetic,

275

Paul Made Geography

would take his large pencil and mark one day off the calendar on the wall.

Billy Pilgrim was afraid they would finish digging the river on time. He did not want to pay Paul Bunyan the million dollars, for at heart he was a miser. So he thought of a plan to prevent Paul from finishing the work.

One night Billy called his men together and said, "When everybody has gone to bed we will go out and pour water on the buckskin rope so it will stretch, and Babe the Blue Ox will not be able to pull a single shovelful of dirt!"

The next day, Babe started toward Vermont with the first load of dirt. When he arrived there, he looked around and the huge scoop shovel was nowhere to be seen. For miles and miles the buckskin rope had stretched through the forests and over the hills.

Babe didn't know what to do. He sat down and tried to think, but everyone knows an ox isn't very bright; so he just sat there. After a while the sun came out and dried the buckskin and it started to shrink to normal size.

Babe planted his large hoofs between two mountains and waited. The buckskin rope kept shrinking and shrinking. Soon the scoop shovel came into view over the hills. Then Babe emptied it and started back after another load.

In exactly three weeks the St. Lawrence River was all finished, but still Billy Pilgrim did not want to pay Paul the money.

"Very well," said Paul, "I will remove the water!" So he led Babe the Blue Ox down to the river, and Babe drank the St. Lawrence River dry.

Billy Pilgrim only chuckled to himself for he knew that the first rain would fill it again. Soon it began to rain, and the river became as large as ever.

So Paul picked up a large shovel.

"If you do not pay the money you owe me I will fill the river up again," said Paul.

He threw in a shovelful of dirt. He threw in another and another, but still Billy Pilgrim would not pay him the money.

"I will pay you half your money," said Billy.

Paul again picked up his shovel and tossed more dirt into the river.

"I will pay you two thirds of your money," said Billy.

Paul kept throwing more dirt into the river until he had thrown a thousand shovelfuls.

"Stop! I will pay you all your money!" cried Billy.

So Paul Bunyan was finally paid in full for digging the St. Lawrence River. The thousand shovelfuls of dirt are still there.

They are called the Thousand Islands.

✢✢✢✢✢✢

Genevieve Murray:

PAUL BUNYAN
Logs Off Eastern Montana

THE WINTER that Paul Bunyan had the contract to log off Eastern Montana was an exceptionally bad one. It began in the early fall with a steady rain which increased so that it wrecked Paul's bunkhouse on Indian Creek by raining down through the chimney faster than it could run out the open doors and windows. Then it turned cold. It was so cold that the ten men who took care of Babe, Paul's big blue ox, had to make her drink anti-freeze solution of alcohol and glycerine. That was the time that Babe got delirious and pulled part of the Beartooth Plateau a hundred miles to the north and so made the Crazy Mountains. It was during this cold spell that the flames in Paul's big cookstove froze stiff and Paul had to detail four men to thaw them out with hot water.

The Missouri River kept rising around Paul's camps and so he sent five men and a boy down the river to find what was holding the water. They found that the Yellowstone had frozen fast to the Missouri and that it could not be moved. But Paul knew at once what to do. He called in all his men from the upper camps and set them to making snowshoes for Babe. It took one tamarack, two spruce and the skins of twenty-two mules to make one shoe. They ran out of mules and Paul had to lead Babe out with three shoes and one brush pile to hold her up.

Paul threw three half hitches around the Yellowstone just below the lake and hitched Babe on. In thirty minutes Babe had pulled the Yellowstone out of the Missouri, but in so doing had dragged the upper part of the river so that it cut a gash half a mile deep in the river bed. Paul folded the slack of the river into the upper and lower falls and started for home.

In crossing Alum Creek Babe broke through the six-foot crust and got her snowshoes wet. They shrank to less than one-tenth of their natural size, and Paul was forced to spend the rest of the winter there. It was at this time that he built the hot springs in order to keep warm and Babe got so used to the heat that she couldn't stand any cold. Every time she saw a cloud she started to shiver so hard that the trees all rocked and pinched the saws and axes so tight that the men had to lay off until Babe got over the chill. So Paul decided to send Babe to his son in Texas.

By spring Paul had finished logging off Eastern Montana and he started to move his outfit over onto the Blackfoot before the snow would leave. He detailed twenty men to take Babe and skid a plow across. While they were coming through the Dearborn country a chinook hit them, and Babe started out on the run. But the chinook traveled so fast that while Babe was able to keep on the snow, the plow dragged in the dirt. Babe's speed was so great that she cast a shoe and killed seven men, and Paul had to grab the plow and stick it into the ground. But Babe didn't stop until she reached the Blackfoot, and the plow scooped out a furrow that they call Limestone Canyon.

✝✝✝✝✝✝✝

De Witt Harry:

THE JAPANESE CURRENT

ONCE AGAIN turning to the fascinating adventures of Paul Bunyan on this coast and his intimate connection with so many of the natural marvels now existing we have what is vouched for as the true reason for the Japanese Current, that warm stream that keeps the north Pacific almost like a tropical sea.

The winter of the blue snow, when the great blue blanket lay 50 and more feet deep on the Cascades, Bunyan and the blue ox were sent to remove the snow. Paul lost the ox several times when he would fall into drifts and could not be seen on account of the blending of the color. Bunyan had to have a place to dump the snow, so put it all in Crater Lake, the blue ox dragging a huge scraper that held 29 tons at a time, and the waters have remained blue in the crater from the melted snow.

This was hard exhausting work and Paul and the ox would go out each night and cool off in the ocean. On one of their swims the ox went out so far that he lost sight of land and as Paul had forgotten his compass, they started to swim. Knowing that they would reach some country if they kept it up long enough, Paul held onto the ox's tail and Babe swam so fast that he scorched the water and it boiled and steamed behind them. Swimming is just like walking—if you go long enough

you'll travel in a circle, and this is just what Paul and the ox did, for they came in sight of the Cascade Mountains the next morning after having been in the water all night, came ashore and had to go right to work without any rest.

⁑⁑⁑⁑⁑⁑⁑

DeWitt Harry:

PAUL AND THE PACIFIC OCEAN

THERE HAS BEEN considerable said about Paul Bunyan digging Puget Sound but no one has offered the true reason. I am probably the only living person who can truthfully relate just why he should dig this hole.

Paul had taken a contract for the construction of Mount

Rainier and Mount Hood and one or two other Pacific Northwest scenic resorts, and having several large crews of men working on these different jobs he was rather hard put on just how to handle the weekly wash.

At this time I was engaged in the laundry business in Seattle and we being on rather friendly terms, Paul came to me and told me of his dilemma. I explained to him that my facilities were altogether too limited to handle such a large contract and told him about the size vessel it would take to take care of such a wash as he would have. He thought for a moment and then said, "I can easily take care of that."

He motioned for the "Big Swede" to bring the Blue Ox to him and then and there dug the Puget Sound. I explained to him that the vessel he had so easily contrived was plenty large for the purpose and that the cold water with which it immediately filled would be all right for the breakdown and rinsing purposes but that we would have to have warm water for suds. He immediately walked over and kicked out the partition between the sound and the Pacific, making what is now called the Straits of Juan de Fuca. We used the cold water in the sound during the day for the breakdown and at night when he watered the Blue Ox he drove him a little farther out into the Pacific and diverted the Japan Current into the sound. Thus we made our suds at night and rinsed our clothes during the day, having hot and cold water alternately.

This scheme didn't work very long until we began to hear complaints from countries bordering on the Pacific. The men worked so hard at their tasks that they perspired freely and the continual rinsing of this perspiration from their clothes made the water thick with salt and as our tub was flushed out daily, the Pacific was in turn made salty which rendered it no longer fit for drinking purposes. This was one of the topics the Japanese had up with Charley Hughes during their last conference. They blamed us for the salt being in the Pacific and wanted us to remove it.

To make a long story short we had to give up handling this contract and the men had to do their own washing or get married and let their wives do it. When down at the beaches you have undoubtedly noticed the snowy caps and breakers. The foam on these is the last remnants of the suds from our big wash for Paul Bunyan in Puget Sound.

☘☘☘☘☘☘☘

DeWitt Harry:

CRATER LAKE
and the Cascade Mountains

Stanley Anderson of Toledo, a one time logger, has unearthed from his grandfather's trunk an authentic record which does not dispute but rather coincides with facts already published concerning Paul's trip west after he had logged off about all the timber in Michigan and the mid-northern states. The record, blue in color, written with the blood of the blue ox in Paul's own handwriting, on the inner bark of a spruce tree, says:

"In the fall of 1869, having observed that the corn was growing tight on the cob and that the migratory geese were flying backward, and knowing by these signs that a severe winter was at hand, I decided to come West, where, I had been told, there remained unlimited timber and there maintained a mild climate.

"Everything went well on the trip. We struck Spokane Falls, where the blue ox became frightened at the roar of the water and ran away with the provision sled and the swamp

. . . Paul started to throw in some rocks to stop the leak.

hook. After tearing some terrible gashes in the face of the earth, the swamp hook finally stuck in the top of the Cascade Mountains and I was able to catch up with that frightened ox. We are now in the depth of the Siletz River forest, where the timber is so big and thick that every time the blue ox starts to run he falls down. I intend to stay here until Babe gets thoroughly familiar with the roar of the ocean."

Mr. Anderson says his grandfather was Paul Bunyan's shoer for the blue ox, that the record was written in blood out of the ox's foot, which was hurt in the run-away and that out of the wound Paul caught several barrels of blood to use for writing purposes, his supply of ink having been among the losses from the provision sled. Mr. Anderson vouches for the facts, handed down by his grandfather, that the ox running away with the swamp hook resulted in gouging out the Columbia River gorge, the tearing down of the Bridge of the Gods, and where the big steel hung up in the Cascades and Paul pulled it out, Crater Lake remains as a permanent mark of the point of the hook. Blood from the wound on the ox came off the hook in the ground and turned the water in the lake the color of indigo. When the swamp hook was lifted, water began pouring in at the bottom of the hole and Paul started to throw in some rocks to stop the leak. He had dropped one rock when he noticed Babe growing nervous at the roar of the ocean and had to abandon the job. The Phantom ship is the one rock Paul dropped.

✤✤✤✤✤✤

James Cloyd Bowman:

THE GIANT REDWOODS

WHILE PAUL was making ready to go cruising, he had another letter from the King of Sweden.

Christiania, Sweden.

Paul Bunyan and Co., Ltd.,
   The North Woods, U. S. A.
Honored Sir:
   Many of my honored subjects who have worked in your camp at one time or another, have returned to the Mother Country, and have told me of your wonderful success as a logger. Accept my congratulations.
   What I am wondering is whether you cannot make room for four or five hundred thousand families from my kingdom. As I said in my previous letter, we are becoming crowded beyond comfort.
   Besides, I have a lot of subjects (I do not call them loyal) who have turned socialist. They wouldn't be happy even in heaven. They are all for radical revolution. They want to reform everything—even their Royal King. You see, I've simply got to do something.
   If you could make room for so many, I would gladly ship them all to you free of charge. Cable me collect.
                    Believe me, most Honored Sir, etc.
                         THE KING OF SWEDEN.

   Paul discussed the letter in detail with Johnny Inkslinger, and they decided it would be best not to answer it until Paul had returned from his tour of exploration. Perhaps he would find the place exactly suited to the king's socialists.
   Paul was up long before day, had on his snowshoes, and had his ax securely packed across his shoulder. He started in a beeline for the mouth of the Columbia River. After he had been traveling two or three hours, he came to a place where there was no longer snow. Paul was in a hurry, however, and so didn't bother about his snowshoes. Along about

noon, the sun beat down so hot that it began to warp his snow-shoes—the left one more than the right.

The result was that Paul was unconsciously thrown off his course, and pulled up about the middle of the afternoon in California, something like nine hundred miles to the south of his original destination.

Paul was not sorry for this, for he came suddenly upon a vast redwood forest. The trees were many times larger than any Paul had ever seen.

"These are man-sized trees, at last, by the holy Mackinaw!" Paul shouted to himself happily.

He tried measuring one of the largest trees, and found that he could just nicely put his arms around it and clasp his fingers on the other side; that is, when he lay down on his stomach and circled the roots.

The temptation was soon so great that Paul took his ax and began to try how many of these trees he could fell at a single stroke. About a half-dozen at a time proved an easy task.

"But they'll never believe me if I tell them about these trees, when I get back to camp," Paul smiled wistfully.

With a careful stroke of his ax, he managed to clip a six-inch cross-section from one of the stumps, and by quartering this carefully, he found that he could carry the pieces comfortably in his mackinaw pocket.

Paul didn't realize he was making such a noise, as the great redwoods crashed to the ground. About the fifth stroke of his great ax brought the government inspector down upon him in a hurry.

"You are under arrest!" the inspector shouted indignantly.

"What for?" Paul asked curiously.

"This is a state forest preserve. Come with me, and I'll teach you 'What for!' "

"I'm sorry, sir," Paul replied. "I'm only a visitor here, and didn't know about your law, as you call it."

" 'As you call it!' " The inspector was furious. "Come with me," he commanded, tugging at Paul's boot-strap.

Paul fumbled a while in his vest pocket, and finally drew out a piece of thick birch bark six feet long and four feet wide, on which was inscribed in Johnny Inkslinger's best penmanship:

> PAUL BUNYAN
> Master Woodsman
> North Woods
> U. S. A.

"Here's my card," he said. "When I return, I'll answer to your law, as you call it."

While the inspector was still marveling at the size of Paul's calling-card, Paul was off on the gallop, and within two hours had reached his destination in Oregon.

Paul sat down on the bank of the Columbia River to pull off his snowshoes, and to cool his feet in the water. He was surprised at the number of fish that constantly bumped his shins.

He put his hands into the water, and caught the fish by the dozen. He made a fire and broiled them. They were good to eat. He put a half-dozen of the largest in his pocket to take back to camp to prove his find.

Paul had thus discovered the Chinook salmon. When he made his discovery known, Big Business commercialized it, and today we all enjoy the salmon of the Columbia River.

On his way home, Paul discovered the vast level stretches of the Dakotas.

"This would make an ideal place for the king's socialist Swedes!" Paul laughed to himself as soon as his eyes fell upon the country.

A few hours later Paul was seated in his barnacle, wiping the sweat from his brow, and relating his discoveries to Johnny Inkslinger. When he told Johnny about the mighty redwood trees, Johnny replied just as Paul had thought he'd do:

"I don't like to contradict you or doubt you, Paul, but it sounds like a slight exaggeration. You can just easily span the roots of the largest trees here, you know, with your two hands."

Paul had been hoping all the while that Johnny would doubt him. He proudly fitted together the parts of the cross-section of the great redwood and laid it on the floor.

Johnny squinted his eyes, picked the pieces up and examined them carefully, and then laid them back in place.

"You can tell me anything you want, after this, and I'll believe you," Johnny drawled dryly.

"But what hurts me most, Johnny," said Paul with a sudden change of expression, "is that we were born too late. Alas! they've already got all the big redwoods safely under lock and key where we can't get at them. If only we'd lived in an earlier age, we could then have found some real logging. We could have had the experience of moving some man-sized logs."

"You're just like a boy, Paul. You're always dreaming about something bigger than you've ever done before. Goodness knows, you're already the foremost logger this side of Kingdom Come."

"Well," Paul sighed, "I guess we'll have to let it go at that."

"But didn't you notice any mountains on the way? I used to read in my geography about what they used to call the Rocky Mountains, if I'm not mistaken?"

"No, I didn't notice any mountains exactly. Now that you mention it, I do remember that I did notice that it was up grade for half an hour at one place, and down grade at another."

"That's a bit marvelous, too," Johnny commented.

"But here and there, and everywhere I went, I did see men

making settlements. Almost every river I crossed was full of logs merrily dancing down to the mills. Everywhere were lumberjacks and logging outfits. It seems that my men have gone out to the four corners of the globe and have started operations resembling my own. I never had dreamed things were going as fast as they are. You know, Johnny, I saw only one place that looked as if there were room for a really big year of logging. This, I believe, is the only place in the world for those socialist Swedes."

"You don't say so!" Johnny exploded enthusiastically.

"Yes, Dakota's the only place for Swedes."

"How so?"

"Well, for one thing, they can have their own way out there without bothering other people."

"I don't know that I quite understand," said Johnny, as he scratched his head learnedly.

"Well, then," Paul laughed, "write this letter, and you will understand."

Paul immediately began dictating:

North Woods, U. S. A.

The King of Sweden, Ltd.,
  Christiania, Sweden.
My Honored King:
  We've got the best place in the world for your socialist subjects (I don't call them loyal, either). There's plenty of room out in Dakota for all you can send. The more the merrier. Send them as soon as you're ready.
  Simply send them postpaid, in care of Paul Bunyan, North Woods, U. S. A., and I'll guarantee you won't be bothered with them any longer. They'll have plenty of room to toot their own horn as loud as Kingdom Come, out where we'll homestead them. You'll be owing me five dollars for each one you send, so the more the merrier.
                    Yours, etc.,
                    PAUL BUNYAN.

Johnny argued an hour with Paul over the wording of one sentence of the letter. Johnny contended, if you allowed the king to send his socialists as soon as he was ready, that the woods would be full of warring socialists before Paul had the trees cut and the land made' ready.

Paul contended that, from all he knew about Swedes,— and he'd had a good chance to observe them about the camp, —it would take the king at least a year to turn around once, and by that time he and Babe could have cleared the whole State of Dakota and a part of Minnesota into the bargain.

And so the letter, in due time, was sent.

Paul began making his plans for moving the camp as soon as his merry men returned from the present drive. The watch-word was now "Dakota!"

✿✿✿✿✿✿✿

THE MOUNTAIN
That Stood On Its Head†

PAUL BUNYAN, the mightiest of all logging bosses, came to the Dakotas to log off the strangest of all forests, on the Mountain That Stood On Its Head. Paul had just obtained the help of Hels Helsen, the Big Swede, whom Paul chris-tened Bull of the Woods and appointed him his foreman. As long as the logging operations were confined to the ground beneath the mountain, the industrious but unimaginative Hels managed the work successfully, leaving Paul Bunyan free to do the book work he detested but which had to be done by someone.

Now the Mountain That Stood On Its Head rested on its peak instead of its base and its slopes flared outward from the bottom, shadowing the ground beneath; and on its slopes

† From *South Dakota Guide.*

the trees grew head-downward with their tops pointing to the earth. The rim, or base, of the mountain was two miles above the plain and on top of this base was another plain, covered with the finest standing timber and one hundred and twenty-seven miles in circumference. There were High Springs in the center forming Lofty River, which tumbled from the rim two miles to the plain beneath in a mighty cataract called Niagara, a name which was later given to a little waterfall along the Canadian border.

Now when the trees beneath the five-mile slope of the inverted mountain had all been logged off, the Big Swede began to have trouble with his loggers. He insisted that they should go on logging the inverted slope just as they would an ordinary one—in other words that they should stand on their heads, supported by wire cables that ran from tree to tree. But while doing this all the dirt and sawdust fell into their mouths and eyes instead of to the ground and the blood ran to their heads and altogether the conditions were so unusual that they returned exhausted from each day's labors. So each day found the work going more slowly until finally there was only one tree cut per man for each seventy-two hours of work. But while the unimaginative Swede was being bested, Paul Bunyan was working out his own solution of the problem.

One morning when Bunyan awoke he found that none of the loggers was starting for the woods. He inquired the reason of the Big Swede and that taciturn individual made a speech of unaccustomed length:

"Aye forgot tal you, Bunyan, but aye goin' move dar camp. No use to try har no moore noo aye tank. Logger can' stan' on head mooch lonker har. Aye don' tank so, Bunyan. We move new yob noo."

Paul Bunyan was enraged both at the Big Swede's assumption of authority and his familiar form of address. Raising his voice in a shout that tumbled the loggers from their bunks,

he ordered them to follow him to the Mountain That Stood
On Its Head. On his shoulder was a double-barrelled shotgun that he had fabricated for the job, the barrels of which
he used later as smokestacks for his first sawmill. In his belt
were cartridges loaded with vast amounts of powder and
with sheets of steel two feet square. Arriving at the base of the
mountain, actually its peak, he took aim along its inverted
slopes and pulled both triggers. A thousand pine trees were
sheared off and dropped straight to the ground, their tops
sticking in the earth and their bare trunks waving helplessly
in the air. All day the mighty Paul cleared the slopes of trees
and at evening a new forest stood beneath the inverted cone,
promising easy work for the loggers on the following morning.

But next day Paul saw the Big Swede going alone to the inverted mountain. With Paul Bunyan in hot pursuit the Bull
of the Woods clambered up the shelving slope, crawled over
the rim and began tearing up the standing pine with his bare
hands. Enraged at this independent logging system, Paul
took a flying leap at the rim but missed his hold and took
considerable of the edge with him in his fall. A second leap
and he gained the upper plain and lay there resting before
what he knew would be the battle of his career. The Big
Swede came toward him.

All day that epic battle raged. The sound of the blows
struck could not be told from thunder and the stamping of
the giants made the earth tremble till the frightened loggers
crawled into their bunks and stayed there. Whenever the
contestants neared the edge, great masses of earth would
crumble off and fall to the plain below. Whole acres of standing pine were flattened as one or the other of the fighters
felled his opponent with a mighty blow. All that day and
all that night the battle raged and finally at sunrise the next
morning there came a shock that overturned every bunk-

house. Shortly afterward Paul Bunyan appeared, carrying on his shoulder the vanquished Bull of the Woods.

"You're going to be a good foreman now, Hels Helsen!"

"Aye tank so, Mr. Bunyan."

"You *know* so, Hels Helsen."

"Yah, Mr. Bunyan."

But the Mountain That Stood On Its Head was no more. That titanic struggle had demolished it and spread it out over the plain. Only a few heaps of blood-darkened dust remained, a series of mounds that are called the Black Hills today.

✝✝✝✝✝✝

THE BLACK HILLS†

Wᴵᴛʜ ʀᴇɢᴀʀᴅ to the physical origin of the Black Hills, there is a wide diversity, not to say conflict, of ideas. According to the Paul Bunyan school of thought, it all came about through that mighty logger's Big Blue Ox, Babe, who was 42 ax handles and a plug of tobacco broad between the eyes. It seems that the Big Blue Ox ate a red-hot stove—a stove with a griddle so big that Paul Bunyan had negro boys with hams strapped to their feet slide around on it and grease it. At any rate as soon as the ox had committed this gustatory indiscretion, he left for parts adjacent, contiguous, out lying and still more distant. It was while traveling the more distant parts, far out on the plains, that the ox finally fell down and died of exhaustion or heart burn or whatever oxen do die of when they eat red-hot stoves. Paul Bunyan, meanwhile, had been in swift pursuit of his pet ox, but he arrived too late to do him any good. He could only weep floods of tears that flowed in all directions and then ran together to form

† From *South Dakota Guide*.

the Big Missouri River. Then he set about burying the ox. It was out of the question to dig a grave big enough to hold him, so Paul began to heap earth and rocks upon him until he had covered all of the mighty bulk, making an immense mound at the place where the ox had died. But in time the rains came and washed gullies in it, and the wind and the birds carried seeds there and the mound became scored with gulches and canyons and covered with trees and grass. And so this great mound of earth and rocks which was heaped up to cover Paul Bunyan's ox became the Black Hills that we know today.

However certain quibbling and hair-splitting scientists reject this reasonable theory altogether. According to them, these so-called "Hills" are in reality an old mountain chain.

⚜⚜⚜⚜⚜⚜⚜

James Cloyd Bowman:

GEOGRAPHY WITH A CAPITAL G

IF PAUL BUNYAN has specialized in any one thing more especially than in anything else it has been in Geography, with a capital G. The following yarn will sufficiently illustrate: One bright spring morning Paul discovered that all the billions of feet of logs that he and his men had cut and dragged down to the banking grounds during the previous winter were landlocked in a lake in Northern Minnesota. Without blinking an eyelash, Paul ordered Ole, his great Swede blacksmith, to make an enormous shovel. Paul took this shovel one morning before breakfast, and started to dig a canal through to the Gulf of Mexico. He took his direction from the path the wildfowl had cleft in the air during their last migration. He shoveled so fast that soon the sun was darkened as if by a total eclipse. The dirt that flew over his right shoulder formed the Rocky Mountains, and what he hurled in the opposite direction (there wasn't room in the sky, you understand, to throw all the dirt one way) became the Appalachians. Paul reached the Gulf at the end of the first day just as the sun was about to set. He flicked a hundred gallons of sweat from his brow with his forefinger, flung his shovel down with a grunt and a smile, and galloped back to camp before the last light was put out for the night. On the way North he dropped one of his mittens by mistake. As the years passed, the sand drifted in about his forsaken shovel, and formed what geographers have since been pleased to call the peninsula of Florida. His mitten, too, filled with sand, formed the entire Peninsula of Michigan—Thumb and all! A pretty fair day's work, this delving out of the Mississippi River, Paul thought, though not really his greatest.

✿✿✿✿✿✿

Dell J. McCormick:

PAUL DIGS PUGET SOUND

Babe the Blue Ox became sick one spring, and Paul knew there was only one thing to do. He decided to move west and let Babe feed on the milk of the Western whale. The whales in the Pacific Ocean were scarce that year, and Babe got steadily worse. Paul started digging Puget Sound as a grave for Babe, but the Ox suddenly got better. Paul didn't know what to do with the big hole he'd started until he met Peter Puget.

Puget suggested they go ahead and finish it and make a nice new harbor for Seattle. In fact, he had a dredge that wasn't working at the time so he took a contract to finish it in one year. Well, Peter Puget and his crew worked all one summer but they couldn't move enough dirt to fill a good-sized sandbox. He was getting very worried so he sent for Paul. The harbor wasn't big enough to float a rowboat. Paul looked it over and made him a promise about the big job.

"I'll take Babe the Blue Ox," said Paul, "and dredge out a Sound that will be the talk of the whole country. When we get through there will be room for a hundred boats to tie up at docks all the way from Tacoma to Bellingham. I need room to float my logs, so I'll do it for half price and we'll call it Puget Sound because you are the man who first had the idea."

All the people roundabout had a meeting and decided to let Paul try it, but everybody thought it couldn't be done. Paul sent for Babe, and Brimstone Bill made a new set of harness for the huge Ox. Ole the Big Swede made a giant scoop shovel. It was of solid boiler plate and took the entire output of all the iron mines that year. The rivets that held it together were so large it took three men to hold them.

When it was all finished Paul hitched Babe to it with heavy logging chains and started to work. Of course he worked with a shovel himself but that was only for rounding off the corners and putting in a few islands where he thought they'd look pretty. Babe did most of the work and never seemed to object, no matter how heavy they loaded the scoop shovel. The first load of dirt was so big nobody wanted it dumped on his property, so Paul had to haul it, finally, way back in the mountains. He dumped it in two piles. By the time the Sound was completed the piles of dirt were so high they could be seen for miles, and they named them Mt. Rainier and Mt. Baker. They are still there and can be seen to this day.

Paul ran into trouble from the very beginning because everybody wanted the Sound to run in different directions.

He stood there and calmly threw in shovelful after shovelful.

The folks down towards Tacoma wanted it extended in their direction. Then someone near Everett wanted a harbor there. It kept Paul hopping trying to satisfy them all, and that's the reason the Sound has so many turns and twists. When he was almost through he suddenly remembered he had promised to dig a harbor for some folks to the south so he scooped out Hood Canal. Funny thing too about that canal; he had just finished it and was turning around when Babe got scared of a girl standing under a red parasol and shied to the left. It made a sort of hook in the canal that is there to this day.

Finally the Sound was completed, and everyone was pleased. Paul told Peter Puget to arrange for a big celebration. They would name it "Puget Sound" on that day. Of course Peter Puget was very proud that the Sound was to be named after him and spent a lot of time getting everything ready, but the settlers had a secret meeting and decided to name it Whidby Sound and even had maps printed with the name in big letters.

When Paul heard about it he was pretty mad and he just went out with his big shovel and started filling it all up again. In no time at all most of the channel was filled in. You can get a good idea of the size of one of Paul's shovels by looking at some of the San Juan Islands. He stood there and calmly threw in shovelful after shovelful of dirt until he had almost a thousand islands dotting the Sound.

A group of settlers finally came to him and promised to change the name back to Puget Sound. He asked them who had wanted to keep Peter Puget from receiving the honor that was due him. They told him it was the people living on Whidby Peninsula. They had planned the secret meeting and decided to be selfish about it and call the new harbor after their own land. They didn't think Paul could do anything about the matter after the Sound had once been completed.

Even after the celebration the Whidby people refused to call it Puget Sound.

"Fill up the Sound!" they cried. "It won't make any difference to us. We can still haul our vegetables and milk to market along the roads."

Paul hated the way they had deceived his good friend Peter Puget so he decided to make them pay for it. At that time Whidby Peninsula was connected with the mainland by a narrow strip of land. Well, Paul just took his pickaxe and cut a narrow passage across the strip of land. The water from the Sound rushed in and filled up the passage with such force that the tides made it almost impossible to cross even in a boat. The Whidby people were cut off from the mainland forever. The channel that Paul cut is filled with raging water to this day and is known as "Deception Pass."

✿✿✿✿✿✿✿

Harold W. Felton:

PUGET SOUND

One day Paul Bunyan thought his ox
    Was going to up and die.
So he picked up a pick and spade
    And a tear drop filled his eye.

And sadly by the sea he dug
    A deep hole in the ground.
But Babe got well. The sea surged in.
    The hole is Puget Sound.

MOUNT BAKER†

Wʜᴇɴ Pᴀᴜʟ Bᴜɴʏᴀɴ was with the Puget construction company and old man Elliott and Mr. Rainier on the contract to dig Puget Sound, the city council of Bellingham sent in to the company and asked them if they couldn't have Paul come up and make a bay for them so the ships from Alaska could get nearer land than they had before. They were willing to pay for it, and Paul went up with the blue ox to dig it for them. But when he got there he found that the land where he wanted to make the bay was held by an old homesteader by the name of Baker, who refused to give it up. Paul offered to pay him three times as much as the farm was worth, but the old man was stubborn and would not give it up anyway. Well, Paul tried several times to argue with him and talked himself blue in the face nearly, and even hired a lawyer who could talk both backwards and forwards, but still the old man wouldn't give in. By that time Paul was getting pretty mad and he went down to see the old man again and they had a row that time.

When Paul dug out the bay he threw the dirt up into a big pile on the other side of the city. It didn't take him long to finish the job.

A couple of months later, after old man Baker had got out of the hospital, Paul met him on the street one day.

"There's your farm," says Paul. "It's all there, I guess. You can name it for yourself if you want to."

And that's how Mount Baker happens to be **Mount Baker**.

† From *4-L Bulletin*, May 1922.

James Stevens:

THE GRAND CANYON

"IN THE LONG ago time of Paul Bunyan all rivers were young and wild," speaks Old Larrity, the woodsman, as the night wind carries the song of a waterfall to the campfire. "Most of them he tamed with his own hands, for the spring log drives. Some rivers though, fought Paul Bunyan to their death, and lakes they became, as rivers ever do when they die. But them are sad stories. 'Tis of rivers alive I tell about, as they were in the times before geography books.

"When Paul Bunyan went to log off Kansas, that country was all mountains. The main river of it followed no valley course at all, but rolled up and down the mountains, over each peak. Sometimes the river would fail at a high peak, and one part would rush on, while the other part would slide back down the mountain for a fresh start. Paul Bunyan bested that river when he learned that Kansas was flat underneath the mountains. He then hitched the Blue Ox to a section at a time, and that way turned the country over. So Kansas is flat to this day, its once proud mountains all underground.

"This was the way the Grand Canyon was made. In its younger days the Colorado River was known as the Old Contrary. The river earned that name for itself because in some stretches it would run a mile wide and a foot deep, while in others the river would turn over on its side and run a mile deep and a foot wide. To make the Old Contrary into a reg'lar respectable river, Paul Bunyan and the Blue Ox went to work with their bulltongue plow. Where the river was a mile deep, they plowed it a mile wide. Where it was a mile wide already, they plowed it a mile deep. Then all was even of course. By rights the Grand Canyon should be called Bunyan's plowin'. It should that."

🌲🌲🌲🌲🌲🌲

Al Schak:

FLATHEAD LAKE

FIERCE, ROARING FLAMES smothered and consumed chunks of tamarack in the big stove that stood near the door of the long bunkhouse. Their heat made an orange pillar of the tin stovepipe, their light set aglow the features of the lumberjacks lying on the floor or leaning against the bunks about the stove. The men's faces stood out against the dark remote interior of the building like deeply cut yellow cameos in a setting of cloudy onyx. A smoky kerosene lamp, suspended, from a wire that crawled down out of the gloom from the ridgepole, dispelled but little of the black haze.

To any person who, when entering, pushed the clapboard door against an elbow or a bare foot, a curse would be the greeting, or in passing the group at the stove brushed too heavily against a rheumatic shoulder. Further dexterity would be required in stooping under the masses of steaming clothing draped over wires and cords close about the stove.

The stench of drying socks and jackets and of stale tobacco smoke was stifling, sickening. In the tiered bunks beyond the heat of the fire smelly blankets cast forth the peculiar odor absorbed from long contact with hot unbathed bodies. The tumbled bedding made a jumble of billows in a sea of streaky black.

Ole's candle, perched on the wooden frame of the farthest lower bunk, made a little pool of light in the gloom. His eyes were fixed upon a fiction magazine which he held obliquely to the candle. A tentative clearing of the throat was his only sign of remonstrance when Two-Fingered Bill, the most stentorian individual in the employ of the lumber company, improvised yarns for the entertainment of his small audience.

And on this night Bill was in fine fettle. A slight thaw had been followed by a quick freeze, making the logging roads dangerous with ice. This was to Bill's liking, and all day he had swayed upon loads of logs and bellowed, and lashed his horses as the sled shot down grades and careened wildly around stumps and rocks and fallen trees. The best skinner in camp, he was, despite the loss of two fingers on his whip hand. And Bill knew it.

"Jumpin' Gee Hosaphat, she shure went fine today!" he whooped. "The snow's as slick's the snow that thawed w'en Paul's big ox laid down to sleep, across the Mission Mountains."

"That was the time o' the blue snow, wa'n't it, Bill?" queried the Duke as he snipped the stub of a brown cigarette through the open draft door of the stove.

"Yah, that were the year o' the blue snow. Ol' Paul ploughed up the big plateau that was here then, an' the tops o' the furrows is wot these here mountains is now. It took 'im all day, an' the blue ox, that'd been pullin' on the plow that Ol' Nick had give to Paul, was plumb tired out. So 'e layed down atween the furrows, an' went to sleep right off.

"Well, it thawed during the night, an' w'en Paul pulled the ox's tail to wake 'im up the next morning there was blue slush everywair. W'en the ox got up an' licked 'is flanks the water began to ooze into the hole in the mud where he slept the night before. The snow kept on thawin', an' finally the water started runnin' down atween the furrows.

"Well, sir, that damn puddle never **did dreen off**, an'

that's how we got Flathead Lake to this very day! The snow was blue, and so was the slush, an' so was the water, an' it's been blue as ink ever since.

"Now then, God, He didn't like to see that big puddle there with nothin' in it. So 'E took a broom an' rammed the handle through the ground right under the Cascades an' the Rockies. The end o' the handle came out where Big Arm Bay is—That's wot made the bay an' Wild Horse Island.

" 'Now,' 'E sez, 'now the sea-devils can come in fr'm the ocean!'

"An' they shure did come in, an' they never got out, either, cuz the tunnel that God made with the broomstick caved in some'rs in Idaho. An' w'en the sea-devils frolic around, then's w'en we have the big storms on Flathead Lake."

"Yee Cly! Can't yous falluhs know anyting to come to bet ven it iss almost time to go to vork?"

This from Ole, who had extinguished his candle and buried his head under a quilt.

"Yur right, Ole, we're all gonna roll in pronto," chirped Blind Eyed Mary, whose eyes were watery from the glare of the fire.

"Say, Beel," wheezed Fat Le Blanc, "for w'y did Mistair Bonyan plough the plateau?"

"W'y, he planted a crop o' tam'rack trees. But there was chaff in the seed—that's w'y we got these here damn lodge-poles."

✝✝✝✝✝✝✝

Dell J. McCormick:

THE SIX MISSISSIPPIS

THE FIRST WINTER Paul spent in Wisconsin he cut so many logs Johnnie Inkslinger couldn't count them all. They filled the riverbanks for mile after mile and in some places were piled so high it took a telescope to see the top logs. Johnnie used to jot the totals down on his cuff as he went from camp to camp, but one day he took his shirt off and Sourdough Sam washed it by mistake, thinking it was his own. From then on nobody knew how many logs there were.

The northern sawmills couldn't handle the output, so Paul decided to drive them down the Mississippi to New Orleans. However, at that time there were six Mississippis, not just one main river as we know it now. They all flowed south, and you couldn't tell one from another. It led to many mistakes, but nothing was really ever done about it until Paul came along.

When spring came he decided to send Big Joe, the river boss in charge of the first batch of logs. The men worked night and day getting the logs in the river, and Paul waved good-by to Joe and his men as they went out of sight around the first bend. Everything went along nicely for the first few days. The river was wide and swift and everybody thought they would soon be in New Orleans, but it turned out later they were on the wrong Mississippi, for it suddenly turned west and wandered all over the state of Texas. Joe and his river crew finally ended up at Albuquerque, New Mexico, and had to sell the logs to the Indians for whatever they could get.

Ole the Big Swede took another bunch of logs down the

East Mississippi but he didn't have any more luck than Joe. The river turned east almost as soon as they started. It cut across Indiana and Ohio. It would flow east for a few days and then it would flow west. Then it doubled back on itself and finally emptied the logs into Lake Michigan fifty miles north of where they started.

In the meantime the sawmill owner in New Orleans kept writing and asking what had happened to the logs he had been promised. Paul was getting madder and madder. He just had to get those logs down to New Orleans somehow!

"The six Mississippis aren't going to keep me from shipping my logs south," said Paul. "I'll show them a thing or two. I'll straighten those rivers out if I have to do it with my bare hands. No river is going to tell Paul Bunyan what to do!"

The next day he chained together a great log boom and started down the third Mississippi himself. Babe the Blue Ox went along and enjoyed himself greatly, walking along the bank breaking up log jams with his great horns.

In a few days the river turned at right angles and headed West, but Paul wasn't to be fooled this time. He called to the men and they stopped the huge raft and tied it tightly to the bank. He then took great logging chains and hitched Babe to the front end. When everything was ready he shouted at Babe, and the great Ox pulled the log raft right out of the river and started across the country back to the main Mississippi.

The logs cut a deep furrow in the ground as the Ox dragged it mile after mile across the prairie. It was a mighty effort but Babe was equal to the task. When they finally launched it again they saw a strange sight. Down the furrow where they had dragged the logs came a rushing stream of water. The first river had followed the newly dug river bed and joined the two Mississippis!

When Paul saw the two Mississippis joined together he had a brilliant idea. Why not do the same to all the six rivers and make the six Mississippis one great river that would carry his logs safely down to New Orleans? It was a huge task but with Babe's help he finally did it. By dragging huge rafts of logs from one river to the other he made new river beds and turned all the rivers into the one great Mississippi as we know it today.

✦✦✦✦✦✦

John C. Frohlicher:

PAUL BUNYAN
and The Forest Service

THE DRIVE was down, an' me'n' Paul Bunyan was a-settin' out in front of the Lake House, back in Sturgeon Bay, Wisconsin, a-whittlin' an' spittin' tobacco juice at the flies that was crawlin' up the posts to the hitch-rail. It was springtime, an' the sun was mighty warm an' we was most asleep when old Joe (I fergit his last name, but he was a Belgian, an' run the hotel) came along an' says: "Paul, here's a letter for you."

Paul takes the envelope an' looks at it mighty curious-like, an' fin'lly cuts it open. He takes out the letter, an' looks at it, an' says to me, says he: "Charley, you read this to me. I lef' my specs in the room." Paul was allus leavin' his specs somewheres.

So I read it, an' it said that the President of these United States had appointed Paul to be Forest Ranger on the Silverbow district of the Lewis and Clark Forest, an' he was to report to his supervisor at St. Paul right away, an' then take charge of the district—it an' all the rights, emoluments an' privilege accruin' thereto. Paul said that he'd never worked for the service, but that he'd try it a whirl if I'd come along to look after the books, sort of.

Well, we paid our reckonin' at the hotel, an' took the Hart boat to Green Bay. There we got on the train an' come west. Paul kept lookin' out of the window at the old cuttin's all the way to St. Paul, an' I saw he was mighty blue. I asked him what was the matter, an' he said that the slashin's an' deserted loggin' camps an' burned stumps an' dried spring-holes was a-lookin' at him an' sayin': "Paul, *you* done this—you an' your men. You cut the big pine. You took the clear logs. You left the tops to rot in the hardwood second growth. You dried up the springs, an' brung in the thistles. You are responsible for the wasted land here." But I told Paul not to fret, that whiskey that's spilled ain't fit to drink, an' that we was goin' into the Forest Service to save the timber an' not to mine it as we had done before.

We pulled into St. Paul an' went right up to the postoffice, where we found old man Raines, who was supervisor of the Lewis an' Clark in them days. The forest run from the Mississippi to the Pacific, an' from the Canady line to the blue grass swamps of Arkansas. Raines was plumb tickled to see Paul, an' he told us that our headquarters was in the village of Butte, which hadn't been discovered by the A. C. M. yet. All there was in Butte was in a ravine called Dublin Gulch, an' our station was there, too. It was a right nice cabin, we found when we arrove. But we traveled ten days through the finest ten-log tree stand I ever saw—all the way from St. Paul to Butte. An' when we got there they wasn't no mountains at all —nothin' but a low ridge extendin' from north to south—like the height of land between Superior an' Hudson's Bay, only not so rough.

In Butte we hired three, four men, an' set them out to build trail an' watch fer fire an' draw pay. Me an' Paul done Public Relations work in Butte, but the Relations got strained; Paul

I saw Paul, his back bowed, his Pulaski swingin' like a flail. . . .

got thrun out of the Hibernian Hall on the twelfth of July. He'd proposed that the folks there give three cheers for William of Orange an' the Battle of the Boyne. So we left Butte an' made an inspection trip—just like Ranger Blue does nowadays. Paul carried a Pulaski tool, which is a combination mattock an' axe, an' I carried a water bag an' a garden rake that the big bugs in Washington had sent to me to fight fires with.

We put out two or three small fires—not over a couple sections, any of them—an' kept a smart lookout for more. The woods was gettin' dryer an' dryer; smoke from a big fire to the east of us piled in front of the sun, an' we was gettin' worried. We talked the situation over, an' didn't decide much until Old Man Raines hisself rode into our camp one night. He had been out fightin' that big fire all alone, because Congress wouldn't appropriate money to pay fire-fighters with. Him an' Paul, they set up all night, tryin' to figger out how to stop that fire, which by this time stretched all the way from Canady to the Gulf, an' which was movin' west at a terrible speed.

Paul smoked an' thought on the question, an' in the mornin' he picked up his Pulaski an' says to me: "Charley, you an' Mr. Raines go back to Butte an' stay there. I'm goin' north."

So I took Raines an' we went back to Butte. The smoke kept rollin' up thicker an' thicker, an' we took lots o' lip from those Butte Micks about inefficiency, graft an' incompetency. But I never said nothin'—I was watchin' the north, where Paul had gone. One mornin', about five days after Mr. Raines an' me had got to Butte, I saw a hill to the north—a regular rough old mountain, an' they hadn't been one there the night before. As I looked at it, it seemed to come nearer, and then I saw that it *was* comin', because its shape was changin', an' it was spreadin' considerable, too. I watched close, an' at last I saw Paul, his back bowed, his Pulaski swingin' like a flail, an' his breath comin' in short gasps. He was scrapin' the surface of the country clean—trees, brush, grass, duff—*everything down to mineral earth*, an' leavin' behind him a bare strip about twenty miles across, an' on the western edge of this strip the scrapin's was piled high.

He never said nothin', but he passed Butte like a fast mail passes a tramp. The fire burned everything clean, up to the edge of the cleared strip, an' then went out. The west edge of the strip came to be known as the Rocky Mountain region, an' there was trees all over that, an' nothin' but grass come up on the burned area, until the Swedes homesteaded North Dakota.

Well, he had gone clean to Alaska before starting work, so's the fire couldn't sneak around the north end of his trench. So the big gun in the Washington office accused Paul of exceedin' his authority an' abandonin' his district in the face of danger, and asked him to resign. I ain't never seen him since.

⁂⁂⁂⁂⁂⁂⁂

Earl Clifton Beck:

HOW PAUL MADE
The Thumb of Michigan

Paul and me was sent over on the Huron shore to estimate some timber. Now it took us a heap sight longer than we had figgered. So we run out of fresh grub. Paul says, "Perry, let's go fishing." Says I, "Where is the tackle?" Well, he went back in the swamp and picked up an old swamp hook he'd seed. We picked up a steel cable on shore for a line; and Paul ketched a pig for bait. Then we built a raft and got on and throwed out our line. Nothing happened till it was most dark. Then we had the dangest strike, hooked onto something, and went sailing out into Lake Huron. All night we went speeding around the lake. Twice we seed the lights of Detroit. Come morning and he tired down and went to the bottom and sulked. We see we was pretty close to where we had started. Paul said, "Perry, you stay here on the raft in case this sturgeon starts sudden. I'll slip on shore and give this line a half hitch around a tree." Well, Paul got to shore all right and tied up that fish. Then I got to shore, and both Paul and me laid down to get some sleep. Those dang Huron Indians picked this spot for a war dance, and Paul and me was waked up with the yelling. Paul said, "Perry, that sturgeon is going to get scared." Just then that line begin to wiggle. And first thing we knowed that fish struck for the Canadian shore. He pulled that tree, soil, and everything right along with him. And ever since Michigan has had a Thumb.

🌲🌲🌲🌲🌲🌲🌲

Harold W. Felton:

NEW YORK BLUES

One day Paul Bunyan sat and thought
  About the world's woes.
He was in New York at the time
  And the tears ran down his nose.

His tears fell down upon the ground
  And flooded through his toes,
And that is why in New York State
  The Hudson River flows.

Earl Clifton Beck:

HOW HUDSON BAY WAS MADE

PAUL, THAT IS, the one I knew, lived in Siberia. One day he climbed a tree during a violent windstorm; after he got to the top it started to blow eighteen hurricanes. After a few minutes Paul and the tree went sailing off into space.

After traveling for days in the air, Paul began to drop. When he hit he made a hole over nine hundred miles long and a good many miles wide. Paul was so tired that he fell asleep before investigating his new surroundings. He had a terrible nightmare that caused him to sweat so much that the hole was filled with water. Years later Henry Hudson found this hole and named it Hudson Bay after himself.

PAUL HAD A WAY WITH WATER

James Stevens:

WHEN RIVERS WERE
Young and Wild

S HAGGY GRAY CLOUDS were drifting between green woods and blue sky. The rainstorm was vanishing but the great bough of cedars and firs still dripped. In the sinks of the forest floor were muddy pools. The creek that ran by the logging camp was in flood. On a fallen log sat an old man and a boy watching the foaming yellow torrent as it roared on.

"I have heard how all rivers were like that in the time far away," said the old one musingly. "In the time of Paul Bunyan that was. Then all rivers were young and wild. I have heard of them all, how they were untamed and without rest in the youth of them. It was Paul Bunyan who tamed the rivers. He was that kind of a man."

Larrity, the old logger, fell silent then and the boy waited, himself silent and unsmiling. They were understanding friends. Seventy-five years lay between the two; but, as wise folk know, the years of life run in a circle, so that the very old and the very young may meet in true friendship. Time has that kindness.

Larrity's days as a working man of the woods were long

since done. For a year now he had lived in the Gavin Timber Company's Columbia River camp as a pensioner. Even the light roustabout work of a bullcook had become too much for him. He would just forget his chores. As the camp foreman said, he had become "fitty." He hardly heard or saw the life about him. He lived in memories.

Now, however, he had a friend, one who would journey with him back to his boyhood, to the time seventy-five years ago when the woods had come to life for him in stories about Paul Bunyan. Jeff Gavin was the ten-year-old grandson of the camp-owner; he had come to spend an afternoon with old Larrity.

"Rivers and rivers and rivers," said the old man. "I have heard Paul Bunyan invented them, but I misdoubt. That he tamed young rivers, breakin' them in for log-drivin' no true logger of even this unbelievin' age would doubt at all. Paul Bunyan did not invent rivers, but them he tamed. Yes, sir."

Larrity's words carried himself beyond years and years to the time when he was but a freckled gosling of a boy in the Michigan woods. It seemed that he and Jeff were perched together on a pile of white pine logs by the Menominee River. White water roared before them. The smells of green pines were in the sunny air. Out of the scene spoke black-bearded Pete Flemmand, telling of the taming of wild young rivers by the great Paul Bunyan. What was his tale, now? . . . Ah, the battle with the Big Auger, that old river story.

"I will tell you of rivers," said old Larrity as Pete Flemmand had said to him seventy-five years ago.

The Big Auger was the youngest and wildest of all the rivers in the time of Paul Bunyan. [So Larrity began the old story.] In that time—so far away that it is not even written down in the history books—most of the young rivers were no worse than wild boys who want their own way.

There were Twin Rivers for example which flowed side

by side and were always wishin' they were not rivers but lakes. Paul Bunyan hardly dared take his eyes off them for they would stop flowin' when he did that. There was Rollin' River which would not run in its valley but was ever sneakin' out to the hills and runnin' up and down them in its flow. There was the river that the loggers called the Ol' Contrary, though it was as young as any except the Big Auger. For a way the Ol' Contrary would run along a mile wide and a foot deep, then it would turn over on its edge, it would, and run a mile deep and a foot wide. There was the Big Onion and the Little Garlic—but there is no limit to the wild young rivers of Paul Bunyan's time which might be told about. Most of them were tamed by the great logger with little trouble for he had a way with rivers, he did.

The Big Auger, however, gave him a tremenjus tussle, for it was the real tough boy among the rivers and the wildest of them all. Besides, it was the most powerful in its amazin' flow. The Big Auger got its name from its terrible twistin' powers. Never would this wild young river flow straight and level in its bed but always it flowed in twists and turns so that the sight of it made one think of a monster auger borin' through the land.

So fierce and savage was the river that its name was given to the fiercest and savagest race of men that ever lived on earth, men of a time far later than that of Paul Bunyan. Big ogres these men are called in the history books; and so are they miscalled, for big augers was the true name of that ferocious race after the wild young river of Paul Bunyan's time.

Paul Bunyan came to the Big Auger country after the spring of the mud rain. He was alone when he first saw the river, for he had just stepped over a mountain and Babe the Blue Ox and his men were left far behind him with the step. With his first look at the Big Auger he at once sat down on the mountain and began to brush his beard with a pine tree. Paul Bunyan always brushed his beard when he was thinkin' and the sight of that river made him think as he had never thought before.

Below him the Big Auger was a welter of white between green bank and green bank, with pine forests slopin' up and away. In the sunlight, however, Paul Bunyan could see through the white welter and behold the body of the river twistin' in its bed, shinin' indeed like a giant steel auger borin' on and on. Paul Bunyan thought deep and brushed hard indeed as he wondered how he could drive logs down such a wild young river as that one.

"But drive logs down you I will or my name's not Paul Bunyan."

And then to his astonishment, and it would have made anyone marvel, that bold bad wild young river talked right back to him. Yes, sir, the Big Auger talked back to Paul Bunyan, as no river had ever dared to do before.

"Be jabbers and be jiggers and bad luck to you, Paul Bunyan, whatever you are," said the impident river, "and you'll drive no logs down me, that you will not!"

"I'm the boss-logger of this country, that's who I am!" roared Paul Bunyan, almost aghast and all at such impidence. "Logs I'll drive down you whatever river you are, and it's never bad luck could be wished on me by the likes of you."

"Ho-ho-ho!" laughed the impident river.

And with that insolent laugh the river gave a stupenjus lep out of its bed, curvin' up its supple spiralin' body, all and all, white foam shakin' from it in festoons, streamers and clouds, shootin' out darts of water which glittered like silver forks in the sunlight. So the river leapt, ravelin', growlin', hissin' as it rose, makin' such a tremenjus fierce spectacle and emittin' such wild sounds as would have shook the heart of one less brave than the mighty Paul Bunyan. Higher and higher it leapt and then the Big Auger, that impident young river, it up and it squirted seventy-seven barrels of water in Paul Bunyan's eye!

That the Big Auger did, then dropped back to its bed and as it twisted and foamed on in its course the river gurgled and chuckled.

Paul Bunyan was so stupefied by the bold and brazen prank of the river that for a long time he could not move from his seat on the mountain. There he was settin' like one carved from solid rock when Babe the Blue Ox mooed over the mountain and behind him the Big Swede, Johnny Inkslinger and the loggers in their bunkhouses mounted on the serpentine bobsled.

For seventeen minutes it was a still picture. Babe the Blue Ox rested his chin on Paul's shoulder, the chin of that noble head which measured forty-two ax handles and a can of tomatoes betwixt the horns. Johnny Inkslinger, the great timekeeper, rested a hand on Babe's back and stared over his spectacles at the amazin' river. The Big Swede, who was never bothered by anything but his feet, sat down by Paul to pull an old tree out of his boot. Behind all, hitched to a cable from the yoke of Babe the Blue Ox, the serpentine bobsled curved along the mountain. From the bunkhouse windows the loggers stared, wonderin' what would happen now. Then Johnny Inkslinger ventured to speak.

"You look drenched, Mr. Bunyan," he said.

He roused himself up now and growled in his beard.

"I'll tame you, me buck of a river," he promised.

With that he gave an order for camp to be made.

So it was done and until time for the drive to begin Paul Bunyan never went near the river but spent his time in the camp and the timber. To the Big Auger he said nothin', he threatened nothin'. And when he was ready for the drive he spoke to the river in a friendly voice:

"Rivers were made for log-drivin'. Will you do your natural labor in peace now?"

"Ho-ho-ho!" laughed the river.

And with that it leapt up to squirt seventy-seven barrels of water in Paul Bunyan's eye as it had done aforetime. But the great logger was now on his guard. He swung his acre of a hand and slapped the impident river sprawlin'. He knocked a dozen twists out of it, that he did. Then what did he do but grab a mountain in both fists, tear it up by the roots and heave it down so it covered Big Auger Valley and dammed the rebellious river's course. Then again said Paul Bunyan:

"Now indeed I will tame you, me buck of a river."

And soon it seemed that the Big Auger was truly tamed. First it lay like a stormy lake against the rock wall of the mountain, its waters heavin' and surgin', rollin' in monster waves against the wall, tossin' up clouds of spray—but ever quieter and calmer that dammed-up river was. At last on a fine eventide the once-wild river was as placid as a pasture pond. Paul Bunyan, always forgivin' and kind, petted the Big Auger, reachin' down his acre of a hand and strokin' the river's back, whisperin' soothin' words as he did so.

The Big Auger seemed to wag its tail and Paul Bunyan, all happy and content, lay down to rest.

Now it was for that which the Big Auger, as cunnin' as it was wild, had waited. The river had found a crack in the mountain and as the great logger rested, the Big Auger quietly began to bore through that crack in the rock wall. The night long the river bored and in the mornin', in the dark drippin' dawn of a day stormy with rain, the river burst free with a roar which made the bunkhouses quake and shivered the timber.

"Ho-ho-ho!" the impident river laughed. "You'll use me for a log drive, Paul Bunyan? Ho-ho-ho!"

The last laugh was choked in the river's throat; for Paul

Bunyan, now rampagin' in the savagest wrath he had ever known, had already seized the Big Auger at its head. Then began Paul Bunyan's greatest battle.

With those mighty hands on its throat the Big Auger whipped itself into a desperate fury. The tremenjus force of its tornado twists tossed Paul Bunyan in the air and wrenched his arms so his joints cracked like strikin' lightnin'. But never did his powerful grip loosen on the Big Auger's throat.

Then the ragin' river tried to grind him down. Down into its cruel sharp rocks the Big Auger ground Paul Bunyan. Such was the drawin' power of its twists that the spikes were yanked from his boots; and then the river ripped off the boots themselves; on the cruel rocks his clothes were slashed to tatters; but ever Paul Bunyan held his grip.

For in grindin' Paul down the wild young river had only played into his hands. Or into his legs, for it was really them. With his feet no longer flyin' in the air from the river's twistin' leps, Paul Bunyan could wrap his legs around the river. Now they were one as they twisted and rolled on down the ragin' river's course.

The shaggy packs of gray clouds were low over the timber, darkenin' the green of all the trees. Out of the dark forest into which they had fled at the first uproar of battle the loggers returned to cheer their leader on. Soaked were the loggers, soaked and drippin' with the water shaken from the boughs of the bull pines by the thunder from Paul Bunyan and the Big Auger. Not a man now brushed the water from his mackinaw and not a man wiped his face, but all stared in wonder and fear at the battle, their eyes unblinkin' as the river made its last desperate try at shakin' Paul Bunyan loose and itself free.

No longer did it grind him down in its course but up in the air it rose, puttin' all its strength in the greatest lep ever seen on this earth. On it rose, chokin' and sputterin', spiralin' in twists and turns, foamin' and frothin', hissin' and growlin' in its fierce rage. But all in vain it was. Strong were Paul Bunyan's arms about the wild young river. And stronger they were as his loggers came out of their fear and cheered their hero on in the fight. Like hooks of steel were Paul Bunyan's legs about the Big Auger.

There was one last grand struggle. The Big Auger humped itself up until it was like a U all upside down and almost touchin' the clouds with Paul Bunyan atop the hump. Tighter and tighter Paul Bunyan drew his arms and legs about the river as the clouds parted for him when his vast back neared them on the risin' hump of the Big Auger. The great logger's legs and arms closed like shears and with a cloud-scatterin' hiss and an earth-shakin' shudder Auger River collapsed, broken in half by Paul Bunyan.

River and hero fell from the clouds together. Like dead pools the two halves of the Big Auger then lay in the riverbed. And like dead Paul Bunyan lay on the riverside.

For three days he lay there and when he came to himself the Big Auger was also in life again and flowin' on. Never again was the river a wild young hellion.

And by this is the famous battle remembered:

Where the river had bored through the mountain there was now a great waterfall. That Paul Bunyan left in peace, namin' it after Niagara, his moose hound who was dead and gone. To this day the waterfall is called Niagara in the geography books. A grand sight it is in this time, but peaceful and calm compared to the flow of the Big Auger in the time when rivers were young and wild.

That was all of that story. At the end of it the boy and the old logger just sat and listened. A brisk wind rushed through the boughs overhead. Voices of the forest, speaking tales that would live as long as men heard the roar of running water and the wind-whispers of trees.

✟✟✟✟✟✟✟

W. J. Gorman:

THE SAWDUST RIVER

WHEN PAUL BUNYAN had logged off the Onion River country, he and the Big Swede, his foreman, made a journey in search of new woods to conquer. They happened on the Leaning Pine country, where the trees stood in lines all along the slope of a mountain. Each and every pine leaned in a northerly direction and the mountain range ran east and west. These were ideal conditions for Paul and his crew. He and the Big Swede returned in high good humor and announced to the gang that the camps would be moved forthwith.

The Blue Ox was harnessed, the sleep camps, cookeries and sheds were hooked together, the Ox hitched on and away they went over hill and valley until they reached the Leaning Pine country. The Big Swede explained to the crew the method of operation. They were to start on the north end and cut the trees which were self-skidding, falling down row on row and rolling into the Hot Water River which skirted the mountain. Now, both Paul and the Big Swede had figured out the logging scheme to a nicety, but they did not investigate the Hot Water River very closely and as a result there was a serious hitch in the season's work. When the time came for the drive, the logs were started off with Paul riding on his raft directing operations. For nine days they went down the stream and suddenly Paul noticed that the front end of the drive had caught up to the rear. He sent the Big Swede to investigate and they found out that the river ran in a circle. This was a catastrophe, the worst since the winter of the Blue Snow, but Paul was not stumped.

He decided to saw the logs right there, and to do this he set up his famous nine-story sawmill. He sent Johnny Inkslinger, his bookkeeper, out to the outside with orders for machinery and saws. The Blue Ox hauled them in. The band saws and circulars ran through the whole nine stories and logs were sawed on every story. The sawdust was blown into the circular river and in time filled it solid. Paul, to amuse his men, brought in race horses, which followed this perfect circular track, getting back to the starting post every Sunday. The only trouble he had all summer was with the hinges on the smokestack, which had to be lowered to let the clouds go by.

At the end of the season the Blue Ox hauled out the season's cut, which was bored into nutmegs and sold in Maine. The sawdust river is being mined today for Dustbane.

⚜⚜⚜⚜⚜⚜⚜

James Stevens:

THE HEMLOCK FEVER

When Paul Bunyan discovered the Onion Pine country, his first act was to pull a 60-foot tree up by the roots to sample its strange and powerful smell. At the third whiff rivers of tears gushed from his eyes and streamed down his beard. They washed out a dozen bears that had been hibernating in his beard all winter.

"I warn't a particle surprised," Paul Bunyan remarked. "Ever since the break of spring my beard has been itchin' me some."

Rivers were young and wild in those days. The Big Auger flowed in a racing spiral down its hard-rock bed. It took Paul Bunyan three months to "rassel the kinks out of the

Auger" and straighten it for log driving. The Big Fraid River was scared to death of the north wind; it would turn tail at the first breath of a Norther and run upstream at 60 miles an hour, carrying Paul's log drives back into the woods. One of Paul's biggest jobs was putting spunk into that coward of a river and making it fight for its water rights against the bully of a wind from the north.

Rubber River was 90 miles wide and five miles long. Paul and Babe together stretched it into a regular stream—but they lost their water-stretchers on the job, and Paul could never make another set that would work. Before he had often amused himself in his spare time by stretching lakes into rivers, and it grieved him sorely when he was obliged to give that pleasure up.

The weather was mighty mean to handle in that time. It was nothing for two winters or two summers to come at once. One Fourth of July all four seasons swooped down at the same time, laying out all of Paul's loggers with pneumonia, spring fever, sunstroke and October pip in a single hour. Some winters it snowed rain; other times the clouds would come on wrong side to and rain up; one spring it rained mud for 40 days and nights.

There were diseases then which, luckily for us, vanished with the Bunyan era. One of the worst was hemlock fever. When that hit a man he was seized with a violent urge to go out and work till he dropped and died. One of Paul's roughest times was when an epidemic of hemlock fever ravaged his camp and he had to chain up all his jacks to save them from working themselves to death.

✟✟✟✟✟✟

Glen Rounds:

BABY RAINSTORM

ONE SPRING, a good many years back, Paul Bunyan had a logging camp on the headwaters of the River That Ran Sidewise. He'd had a profitable winter and the landings were jammed full of logs decked up and waiting for the spring floods to float them down to the mills.

Finally, the weather turned warm and the snow started to melt. A few more days and the big drive would be under way. Then one morning the men woke up to find it raining! Now rain is not so unusual at that time of year, but this was no ordinary rain. No siree, Bob. For where the ordinary rain comes down, this came up. All over the camp, and as far as anyone could see, streams of big raindrops were squirting up out of the ground, sailing straight up in the air and disappearing into the clouds overhead!

And with it came trouble. For, as anyone knows, almost all the rain in this country comes down, so of course we build our houses to take care of that kind of rain, seldom giving the other kind a thought. And that was the case in Ol' Paul's camp. The buildings all had tight roofs that water wouldn't come through, but the floors on the other hand, were made with wide cracks so that water and mud tracked in by the lumberjacks would run through to the ground below.

But now, with the rain coming up, the floors leaked like sieves and the water gathered on the ceilings and couldn't leak out. By the time the men woke up there was four feet of water on the under side of the ceiling of every bunkhouse in camp, and it was getting deeper every minute. The men as they got up had to duck their heads to keep from bumping into the water.

One of the loggers hotfooted it over to Paul's office to tell him about it.

"Paul!" he hollered when he could get his breath. "The rain is a-comin' straight up this morning!"

"Yuh mean it's a-clabberin' up to rain, don't yuh?" Paul asked, as he hunted under his bunk for his socks. "Why the Sam Hill don't yuh learn to say what yuh mean?"

"No sir!" the lumberjack insisted. "I meant jest what I said, that the rain is a-comin' straight up outta the ground and yuh kin take a look fer yerself!"

Ol' Paul finally discovered that he already had his socks on because he'd never taken them off when he went to bed, so he put on his boots and stomped over to the window to see what was what. At first he couldn't believe his eyes, so he put the window up to get a better look, and still he didn't believe what he saw. He tried looking out of first one eye and then the other; then he got out his specs, which he most usually didn't wear except when there was no one around, and clamped them on his nose and went outside to have a good close look. But any way he looked at it, the rain was sure enough coming straight up.

So Ol' Paul and the lumberjack sat down to think about it.

After a while the lumberjack spoke up. "Paul," says he, "a feller is kinda prepared fer ordinary rain, fer all his clothes are made to take care of it, if yuh ever noticed."

"How do yuh figger that?" Paul wanted to know, not too enthusiastically.

"Why a feller's hat sticks out so the rain won't run down his collar, much. And his coat overlaps his britches, and his britches overlaps his boots. It's sorta like he was shingled, if yuh see what I mean."

"Yeah," said Paul. "So where does that leave us?"

"Well, when the rain comes up, instead of down, it falls straight up his britches legs, straight up under his coat, and straight up his sleeve! It's mighty, mighty uncomfortable. Wonder, now, if it wouldn't be possible to sorta shingle a feller backwards, like."

And then they sat and thought some more, since the big bear skin in the middle of Paul's floor kept the rain from hitting them as it came up.

Meanwhile, the lumberjacks over in the bunkhouses, and the stable bucks and the bull cooks and the mess hall flunkeys were all in a very bad humor. The cooks were in a bad humor, too, but camp cooks are almost always that way so nobody noticed any particular difference.

After a while a delegation came to Ol' Paul and told him that he'd better do something about this business pretty soon or they'd all quit and go to work for Sowbelly Burke, his rival.

Ol' Paul assured them that he'd get to the bottom of the mystery as soon as possible, but pointed out to them that it would take time, since nothing like it had ever happened before. That being the case there was of course nothing written in the books about how to deal with it. So he'd have to figure it all out by himself.

Besides, he told them, think of the stories you can tell in the towns this summer, about how you got your drive out in spite of the rain that fell straight up!

But they were still mad and going to quit, so he saw he'd have to take measures pretty quick.

After quite a spell of unusually heavy thinking, he called for Johnnie Inkslinger to quick make out an order to his favorite mail-order house for enough bumbershoots to make two apiece for all the men in camp.

"Bumbershoots?" Johnnie asked. "What's bumbershoots?"

"Why the things folks hold up over their heads when it's raining," says Paul. "I've seen pitchers of them in the catalogues many's the time."

"What you mean is Umbrellas," says Johnnie, who comes from up Boston way and always talks sort of special. "And besides," says he, "they will do no good in this emergency, because they are made for rain that falls down and this rain is indubitably coming straight up instead."

"You go on and do like I say," says Paul. "I cal'late to figger out a way to use 'em by the time I get 'em. Tell 'em this is a hustle up order."

A couple days later the bumbershoots came, two for every man jack in camp, and you should have heard the lumberjacks roar. No self-respecting lumberjack had ever been known to carry one of the sissy things and they weren't going to start it now. They might be all right for city dudes, but not for regular he-lumberjacks! No, sir! They'd quit first.

Ol' Paul went on helping Ole open the boxes and told the lumberjacks just to keep their shirts on a minute till they saw what he had in mind.

As fast as the bumbershoots were unpacked, the little chore boy opened them up an' Ol' Paul took his jackknife and cut the handles off short inside and fastened on a couple of snowshoe loops, instead. When he had them all fixed up he had Johnnie call the roll. As each logger came up Paul handed him a couple of the remodeled bumbershoots and told him to slip his feet into the loops. The first men were a mite shy about the business, but after they had put them on and straddled off, as if they were wearing snowshoes, they found that the bumbershoots did keep the rain from coming up their pants legs. And from then on the men pushed and hollered for the line ahead to hurry up so they could get theirs.

"See there," says Ol' Paul. "I guess I knowed what I was

doing. I don't reckon there is anything sissy about wearing bumbershoots on your feet. And, anyways, we'll call 'em bumbershoes from now on, just to be sure!"

The men all cheered again, and decided not to quit camp after all.

The next morning a friendly Indian, Chief Rinktumdiddy by name, came tearing in to camp wanting to see Paul. He told Ol' Paul that he and another Indian were out hunting the day before and they camped by the mouth of a cave out on the prairie a way. After they'd eaten their supper they decided to explore this cave, so they took along some pine knots for torches, and started out. They went back through the narrow twisting passages for about a half a mile, as near as they could judge, when all of a sudden they heard the awfulest noise they'd ever laid an ear next to. They didn't stop to argue, but tore out of there as fast as they could. They figured that by going in there they had made the Great Spirit mad, and that he it was they heard hollering. So now this Indian wanted Paul to see if he could talk the Great Spirit out of his mad.

Ol' Paul was plumb curious, but from what the Chief told him, he knew the cave was too small for him to get into, and he hadn't Babe along to burrow for him, so he sat still and thought for a spell. Finally, he allowed as how maybe two men listening together could listen far enough back to hear the noise from the mouth of the cave. That sounded like a good idea, but the Indian was plumb scared to go back, so Paul called Chris Crosshaul to go along instead.

The cave wasn't hard to find, and when they got there they both listened as hard as they could and, sure enough, they just about heard the noise. But when they tried listening separately they couldn't hear a sound. (It's a well known fact that two men listening together can hear twice as far as one man listening alone.)

For a while Paul listened to the rumpus he could hear going on back in the cave, and a very curious sound it was, too. It was sort of mixed up with whimpering and whining like a lost puppy, and dribbling, splashing sounds, and a sort of pattering; and, now and again, a hollow booming such as lightning might make if shut up in a cellar.

After a spell of especially hard listening that left them both red in the face and out of breath, Paul turned to Chris and said, "Chris, thet's nuthing in the wide world but a baby rainstorm thet's got himself lost back in this here cave, and now he's bellering fer his maw!"

"Yuh don't say," says Chris, doubtful like.

"Yessir!" says Paul, "and by looking at my pocket compass I've discovered thet the noise is a-coming from right under our lumbercamp! The way I figger it, thet little feller got separated from the rest of the herd and got in here by mistake a while back. Now, he's lost and scared. You jest heerd him whimpering and thundering his heart out back in there. Chances are he's got all upset in the dark there and is raining straight up instead of down and don't know it. We gotta get him outta there."

"Yeah?" says Chris Crosshaul. "It sounds reasonable, but how the Sam Hill we gonna git him out?"

"Well, the way I see it," says Ol' Paul, when they had their pipes going good, "the only way to get thet critter outta there is to call him out. It's a cinch we can't drag him out because there is no way to catch hold of a critter like that. And nobody ever had any luck trying to chase a rainstorm anywheres thet I ever heerd tell about."

"Reckon you're right thet fur, Paul," says Chris, "but I never hear tell of any one that can call a rainstorm, neither."

"That's the beauty of the whole thing," says Paul. "We'll be the first ones to ever do such a thing."

"Jest how do yuh figger to go about it?" Chris wants to

know. "Yuh don't mean yuh kin holler like rainstorms, do yuh?"

"Not right now, I can't," says Paul. "But I figger I kin soon learn how. Yuh see, I know a feller in Kansas City thet will rent yuh all kinds of disguises. I'll git him to disguise me up to look like a rainstorm, then I'll go out and live with a tribe of 'em and learn their language. Should be simple enough, shouldn't it?"

And that's just what he did. He got himself all dressed up in a rainstorm suit till you wouldn't have known him. Then he went out into Iowa where most of the rainstorms summered. He fell in with a big tribe of them, and his disguise was so perfect that they just figured he was a strange rainstorm, maybe blown up from Texas way, and they invited him to stay with them as long as he liked.

He had a mighty fine time all summer, helping the rainstorms to soak open-air political meetings, and the like, although probably he took an unfair advantage at times. He always managed to get the rainstorms to rain on people he didn't want elected, and kept them away from the rallies of people he liked.

But, anyway, late in the summer he came back, and just to show off he was always throwing rainstorm words into his talk, till the lumberjacks scarcely knew what he was talking about. Then one day he went over to the mouth of the cave where the rainstorm was. Getting down on his hands and knees, he put his face up close to the entrance to the cave and imitated the cry a mother rainstorm makes when she is calling her young ones.

As soon as he did that, the noise and thundering and blubbering inside the cave stopped at once. There wasn't a sound to be heard, and the rain, for the first time all summer, stopped coming up around camp.

"See thet," says Paul, with a big grin. And then he hollered the rainstorm holler again, and that little rainstorm came tearing out of the cave as if he'd been sent for and couldn't come. He was just a little fellow compared to what some rainstorms are, and a mite puny-looking from being shut in the dark for so long. He jumped into Ol' Paul's arms and licked his face and rained all over him like an excited puppy dog.

Ol' Paul petted him and talked to him soothingly, till he quieted down, then sent him off down to Iowa where the rest of the rainstorms are. The last we saw of him he was just a little cloud over in the next county, and plumb decked out with rainbows, he was so tickled.

🌲🌲🌲🌲🌲🌲🌲

James MacGillivray:

THE ROUND RIVER DRIVE

WHAT! You never heard of the Round River drive? Don't suppose you ever read about Paul Bunyan neither? And you call yourselves lumberjacks?

Why, back in Michigan that's the one thing they ast you, and if you hadn't at least "swamped" for Paul you didn't get no job—not in no real lumber camp, anyway. You Idaho yaps may know how to ranch all right, or pole a few logs down the "Maries," but it's Maine or Michigan where they learn to do real drivin'—ceptin' Canada, of course.

You see back in those days the government didn't care nothin' about the timber and all you had to do was to hunt up a good tract on some runnin' stream—cut her and float her down.

You was bound to strike either Lake Huron or Michigan, and it made no difference which, 'cause logs were the same price whichever, and they was always mills at the mouth of the stream to saw 'em into boards.

But the Round River drive—that was the winter of the black snow. Paul, he gets the bunch together, and a fine lay-out he had.

They was me, and Dutch Jake, and Fred Klinard, and Pat O'Brien—"P-O-B"—and Saginaw Joe, and the McDonalds—Angus, Roy, Archie, Black Jack, Big Jack, Red Jack, Rory Frazer, Pete Berube—oh, we were there some! They was three hundred men all told.

Canada Bill, he was the cook, and two Negroes were his cookees. We'd a stove, eighteen by twenty, and Joe ust to keep those Negroes busy in the morning, skatin' round the stove with hams tied to their feet, greasin' the lid for the hot-cakes.

And it went fine for a while till one morning "Squint-Eyed" Martin, the chore boy, mistook the gunpowder can for bakin' powder, when the cook told him to put the risen in the batter.

Those coons had just done a double figger eight when Joe commences to flap on the batter. Good thing the explosion went upward so it saved the stove. But we never did find the coons—at least not then—cause that was the winter of the black snow, as I told you.

We'd placed our camp on the river's bank—we didn't know it was Round River then—and, we put in over a hundred million feet, the whole blame cut comin' off one forty.

You see that forty was built like one of them gypsum pyramids and the timber grew to the peak on all four sides. It was lucky, too, that we had such an incline, for after we'd been snowed in, shuttin' off supplies, Double Jawed Phalen got walkin' in his sleep one night and chewed up the only grindstone in the camp. So the boys ust to take big stones from the river's bed and start them rollin' from the top of the hill. They'd follow them down on the dead jump, holdin' their axes on them, which was sharp when they got to the bottom.

We'd a shoot for the timber on all four sides, and when we was buildin' the last one on the west, away from the river, we comes across a deer runway. "Forty-Four" Jones, kind o' straw boss, was buildin' the slide, and he liked game. But he didn't say nothin', though I knowed he had an idea.

Sure enough, Jones gets up early next mornin' and he caught the deer comin' down to drink, and he starts the logs comin' down that shoot and kills more'n two hundred of 'em. We had venison steak all winter, which went well with the pea soup.

That pea soup didn't trouble the cook much. You see, we'd brought in a whole wagon load of peas, and the wagon broke down on the last corduroy and dumped the whole mess over into some springs by the wayside.

The teamster came in sorryful like, expectin' a tote road ticket, but Canada Bill, he says to Bunyan, "It's all right, Paul, them is hot springs." So he puts some pepper and salt, and a hunk of pork in the springs, and we'd pea soup to last us the whole job; though it kept the flunkies busy a-totin' it into the camp.

That Round River ox-team was the biggest ever heard of, I guess. They weighed forty-eight hundred. The barn boss made them a buckskin harness from the hides of the deer we'd killed, and the bull cook used them haulin' dead timber to camp for wood supply. But that harness sure queered them oxen when it got wet. You know how buckskin will stretch?

It was rainin' one mornin' when the bull cook went for wood. He put the tongs on a big wind-fall and started for camp. The oxen pull all right, but that blame harness got stretchin', and when the bull cook gets his log into camp, it wasn't there at all.

He looks back and there was the tugs of that harness, stretched out in long lines disappearin' 'round the bend of the road, 'most as far as he could see. He's mad and disgusted like, and he jerks the harness off and throw the tugs over a stump.

It clears up pretty soon. The sun come out, dryin' up that harness, and when the bull cook comes out from dinner, there's his wind-fall hauled right into camp.

It's a fright how deep the snow gets that winter in one storm, and she'd melt just as quick.

Bunyan sent me out cruisin' one day, and if I hadn't had snowshoes I wouldn't be here to tell you. Comin' back, I hit the log road, though I wouldn't knowed it was there but for the swath line through the tree-tops. I saw a whiplash cracker lyin' there on the snow. "Hello!" says I, "someone's lost their whiplash"; and I see it was Tom Hurley's by the braid of it. I hadn't any more'n picked it up, 'fore it was jerked out of my hand, and Tom yells up, "Leave that whip of mine alone, d—m ye! I've got a five hundred log peaker on the forty-foot bunks and eight horses down here, and I need the lash to get her to the landin'."

They was big trees what Bunyan lumbered that winter, and one of them pretty near made trouble.

They ust to keep a compitishun board hung in the commissary, showin' what each gang sawed for the week, and that's how it happened.

Dutch Jake and me had picked out the biggest tree we could find on the forty, and we'd put in three days on the fellin' cut with our big saw, what was three cross-cuts brazed together, makin' 30 feet of teeth. We was gettin' along fine on the fourth day when lunch time comes, and we thought we'd best get on the sunny side to eat. So we grabs our grub can and starts around that tree. We hadn't gone far when we heard a noise. Blamed if there wasn't Bill Carter and Sailor Jack sawin' at the same tree.

It looked like a fight at first, but we compromised, meetin' each other at the heart on the seventh day. They'd hacked her to fall to the north, and we'd hacked her to fall to the south, and there that blamed tree stood for a month or more, clean sawed through, but not knowin' which way to drop 'til a wind storm came along and blowed her over.

Right in front of the bunkhouse was a monster schoolma'am, what's two trees growed as one, so big she'd a put the linen mills out of business. Joe Benoit and Dolph Burgoyne ust to say their A, B, C's in front of her, and soon learned to swear in English. Whenever we got lost on that pyramid 40, we'd just look around four ways 'til we see the schoolma'am's bonnet, and then we could strike for camp.

You should have seen the big men what Bunyan put on the landin' that spring, when they commenced breakin' the rollways. All six-footers, and two hundred pounds weight. Nothin' else could classify, and the fellows what didn't come up to the regulations was tailed off to burn smudges, just to keep the musketeers from botherin' the good men. Besides the landin' men got a double allowance of booze.

I'll tell you how it come.

Sour-faced Murphy was standin' in the kitchen one day lookin' worse than usual, and first thing the flunky knowed the water and potato parrins in his dish began to sizzle, and he saw right away that it was Murphy's face what was fermentin' them. He strained the stuff off, and sure enough he had some pretty fair booze, which was much like Irish whisky. After that Bunyan takes Murphy off the road and gave him a job as distillery.

She broke up early that spring. The river was runnin' high, and black from the color of the snow, of course, and all hands went on the drive. Bunyan was sure that we would hit either the "Sable" or Muskegon, and he cared not a dam which, fer logs was much the same allwheres.

We run that drive for four weeks, makin' about a mile a day with the rear, when we struck a camp what had been a lumberin' big and had gone ahead with its drive, what must have been almost as large as Bunyan's from the signs on the

banks. They'd been cuttin' on a hill forty too, which was peculiar, for we didn't know there could be two such places.

We drove along for another month and hits another hill forty, deserted like the last one, and Paul begins to swear, for he sees the price of logs fallin' with all this lumberin' on the one stream.

Well, we sacked and bulled them logs for five weeks more, and blamed if we didn't strike another hill forty. Then Bunyan gets wild! "Boys," he says, "if we strike any more of them d—n camps, logs won't be worth thirty cents a thousand, and I won't be able to pay you off—perhaps some of you want to bunch her? Let's camp and talk it over," he says.

So we hits for the deserted shacks, and turnin' the pyramid corner, we who was leadin' butts right into—our school-ma'am! And there at her feet was those two coons what had been blown up months ago, and at their feet was the hams! Then we knowed it was Round River, and we'd druv it three times.

Did we ever locate it again? Well, some!

Tom Mellin and I runs a line west, out of Graylin' some years afterwards when logs gets high, thinkin' to take them out with a dray-haul, and we finds the old camp on section thirty-seven. But the stream had gone dry, and a fire had run through that country makin' an awful slashin' and those Round River logs was charcoal.

****

Douglas Malloch:

THE ROUND RIVER DRIVE

'Twas '64 or '65
We drove the great Round River Drive;
'Twas '65 or '64—
Yes, it was durin' of the war,
Or it was after or before.
Those were the days in Michigan,
The good old days, when any man
Could cut and skid and log and haul,
And there was pine enough for all.
Then all the logger had to do
Was find some timber that was new
Beside a stream—he knew it ran
To Huron or to Michigan,
That at the mouth a mill there was
To take the timber for the saws.

(In those old days the pioneer
He need not read his title clear
To mansions there or timber here.)
Paul Bunyan, (you have heard of Paul?
He was the king pin of 'em all,
The greatest logger in the land;
He had a punch in either hand
And licked more men and drove more miles
And got more drunk in more new styles
Than any other peavey prince
Before, or then, or ever since.)
Paul Bunyan bossed that famous crew:
A bunch of shoutin' bruisers, too—
Black Dan MacDonald, Tom McCann,
Dutch Jake, Red Murphy, Dirty Dan,
And other Dans from black to red,
With Curley Charley, yellow-head,
And Patsy Ward, from off the Clam—
The kind of gang to break a jam,
To clean a bar or rassle rum,
Or give a twenty to a bum.

Paul Bunyan and his fightin' crew,
In '64 or '5 or '2,
They started out to find the pines
Without much thought of section lines.
So west by north they made their way
One hundred miles until one day
They found good timber, level land,
And roarin' water close at hand.

They built a bunk and cookhouse there;
They didn't know exactly where
It was and, more, they didn't care.

Before the Spring, I give my word,
Some mighty funny things occurred.

Now, near the camp there was a spring
That used to steam like everything.
One day a chap that brought supplies
Had on a load of mammoth size,
A load of peas. Just on the road
Beside the spring he ditched his load
And all those peas, the bloomin' mess,
Fell in the spring—a ton I guess.
He come to camp expectin' he
Would get from Bunyan the G.B.
But Joe the Cook, a French Canuck,
Said, "Paul, I teenk it is ze luck—
Them spring is hot; so, Paul, pardon,
And we will have ze grand bouillon!"

To prove the teamster not at fault,
He took some pepper, pork and salt,
A right proportion each of these,
And threw them in among the peas—
And got enough, and good soup, too,
To last the whole of winter through.
The rest of us were kind of glad
He spilt the peas, when soup we had—
Except the flunkeys; they were mad
Because each day they had to tramp
Three miles and tote the soup to camp.

Joe had a stove, some furnace, too,
The size for such a hungry crew.
Say what you will, it is the meat,
The pie and sinkers, choppers eat

That git results. It is the beans
And spuds that are the best machines
For fallin' Norway, skiddin' pine,
And keepin' hemlock drives in line.
This stove of Joe's it was a rig
For cookin' grub that was so big
It took a solid cord of wood
To git a fire to goin' good.
The flunkeys cleaned three forties bare
Each week to keep a fire in there.
That stove's dimensions south to north,
From east to westward, and so forth,
I don't remember just exact,
And do not like to state a fact
Unless I know that fact is true,
For I would hate deceivin' you.
But I remember once that Joe
Put in a mammoth batch of dough;
And then he thought (at least he tried)
To take it out the other side.
But when he went to walk around
The stove (it was so far) he found
That long before the bend he turned
The bread not only baked but burned.

We had two coons for flunkeys, Sam
And Tom. Joe used to strap a ham
Upon each foot of each of them
When we had pancakes each A.M.
They'd skate around the stove lids for
An hour or so, or maybe more,
And grease 'em for him. But one day
Old Pink-eyed Martin (anyway
He couldn't see so very good),

Old Pink-eye he misunderstood
Which was the bakin'-powder can
And in the dough eight fingers ran
Of powder, blastin'-powder black—
Those niggers never did come back.
They touched a cake, a flash, and poof!
Went Sam and Tommie through the roof.
We hunted for a month or so
But never found 'em—that, you know,
It was the year of the black snow.

We put one hundred million feet
On skids that winter. Hard to beat,
You say it was? It was some crew.
We took it off one forty, too.
A hundred million feet we skid—
That forty was a pyramid;
It runs up skyward to a peak—
To see the top would take a week.
The top of it, it seems to me,
Was far as twenty men could see.
But down below the stuff we slides,
For there was trees on all four sides.

And, by the way, a funny thing
Occurred along in early Spring.
One day we seen some deer tracks there,
As big as any of a bear.
Old Forty Jones (he's straw-boss on
The side where those there deer had gone)
He doesn't say a thing but he
Thinks out a scheme, and him and me
We set a key-log in a pile,
And watched that night for quite a while.

And when the deer come down to drink
We tripped the key-log in a wink.
We killed two hundred in the herd—
For Forty's scheme was sure a bird.
Enough of venison we got
To last all Winter, with one shot.

Paul Bunyan had the biggest steer
That ever was, in camp that year.
Nine horses he'd out-pull and skid—
He weighed five thousand pounds, he did.
The barn boss (handy man besides)
Made him a harness from the hides
Of all the deer (it took 'em all)
And Pink-eye Martin used to haul
His stove wood in. Remember yet
How buckskin stretches when it's wet?
One day when he was haulin' wood,
(A dead log that was dry and good)
One cloudy day, it started in
To rainin' like the very sin.
Well, Pink-eye pounded on the ox
And beat it over roads and rocks
To camp. He landed there all right
And turned around—no log in sight!
But down the road, around the bend,
Those tugs were stretchin' without end.
Well, Pink-eye he goes in to eat.
The sun comes out with lots of heat.
It dries the buckskin that was damp
And hauls the log right into camp!

That was a pretty lucky crew
And yet we had some hard luck, too.

You've heard of Phalen, double-jawed?
He had two sets of teeth that sawed
Through almost anything. One night
He sure did use his molars right.
While walkin' in his sleep he hit
The filer's rack and, after it,
Then with the stone-trough he collides—
Which makes him sore, and mad besides.
Before he wakes, so mad he is,
He works those double teeth of his,
And long before he gits his wits
He chews that grindstone into bits.

But still we didn't miss it so;
For to the top we used to go
And from the forty's highest crown
We'd start the stones a-rollin' down.
We'd lay an ax on every one
And follow it upon the run;
And, when we reached the lowest ledge,
Each ax it had a razor edge.

So passed the Winter day by day,
Not always work, not always play.
We fought a little, worked a lot,
And played whatever chance we got.

Jim Liverpool, for instance, bet
Across the river he could get
By jumpin', and he won it, too.
He got the laugh on half the crew:
For twice in air he stops and humps
And makes the river in three jumps.

We didn't have no booze around,
For every fellow that we found
And sent to town for applejack
Would drink it all up comin' back.

One day the bull cook parin' spuds
He hears a sizzlin' in the suds
And finds the peelin's, strange to say,
Are all fermentin' where they lay.
Now Sour-face Murphy in the door
Was standin'. And the face he wore
Convinced the first assistant cook
That Murphy soured 'em with his look.
And when he had the parin's drained
A quart of Irish booze remained.
The bull cook tells the tale to Paul
And Paul takes Murphy off the haul
And gives him, very willingly,
A job as camp distillery.

At last, a hundred million in,
'Twas time for drivin' to begin.
We broke our rollways in a rush
And started through the rain and slush
To drive the hundred million down
Until we reached some sawmill town.
We didn't know the river's name,
Nor where to someone's mill it came,
But figured that, without a doubt,
To some good town 'twould fetch us out
If we observed the usual plan
And drove the way the current ran.

Well, after we had driven for
At least two weeks, and maybe more,

We come upon a pyramid
That looked just like *our* forty did.
Some two weeks more and then we passed
A camp that looked just like the last.
Two weeks again another, too,
That looked like *our* camp, come in view.

Then Bunyan called us all ashore
And held a council-like of war.
He said, with all this lumbering,
Our logs would never fetch a thing.
The next day after, Sliver Jim
He has the wits scared out of him;
For while he's breakin' of a jam
He comes upon remains of Sam
The coon who made the great ascent
And through the cookhouse ceilin' went
When Pink-eye grabbed the fatal tin
And put the blastin' powder in.

And then we realized at last
That ev'ry camp that we had passed
Was *ours*. Yes, it was then we found
The river we was on was round.
And, though we'd driven many a mile,
We drove a circle all the while!
And that's the truth, as I'm alive,
About the great Round River drive.
What's that? Did ever anyone
Come on that camp of '61,
Or '63, or '65,
The year we drove Round River drive?
Yes, Harry Gustin, Pete and me
Tee Hanson and some two or three

Of good and truthful lumbermen
Came on that famous camp again.
In west of Graylin' 50 miles,
Where all the face of Nature smiles,
We found the place in '84—
But it had changed some since the war.
The fire had run some Summer through
And spoiled the logs and timber, too.
The sun had dried the river clean
But still its bed was plainly seen.
And so we knew it was the place
For of the past we found a trace—
A peavey loggers know so well,
A peavey with a circle L,
Which, as you know, was Bunyan's mark.
The hour was late, 'twas gittin' dark;
We had to move. But there's no doubt
It was the camp I've told about.
We eastward went, a corner found,
And took another look around.
Round River so we learned that day,
On Section 37 lay.

PAUL MADE
AND MET THE WEATHER

James Stevens:

THE YEAR OF THE HOT WINTER

No region of Real America, save Kansas, boasted of its weather in Paul Bunyan's time. In the heyday of the mighty logger the climates and seasons were not systematized; they came and went and behaved without rule or reason. There were many years with two winters, and sometimes all four seasons would come and go in one month. The wind would frequently blow straight up and then straight down. Sometimes it would simply stand still and blow in one place. In its most prankish moods it would blow all ways at once. The weather was indeed powerful strange in those days and it got itself talked about. And nowhere were its ways more evil than in Utah.

When Paul Bunyan moved his camp to the state of Utah for the purpose of logging off its forests of stonewood trees he was not careless of the climate; he merely failed to suspect its treachery. Besides, other troubles beset him. The gritty texture of the stonewood timber dulled the edge of an ax bit in two strokes. At the end of their twelve-hour day in the woods the loggers had to sharpen axes for seven hours. They were always fagged out. Then there was only one small river near the forests, and Babe, the blue ox, who had got hayfever again since coming West, drank it dry every fifteen minutes. The loggers thirsted, and they were bedeviled by sand in their blankets and in the beans, for every time Babe sneezed he raised a dust storm that rolled its clouds through the cookhouse and the bunkhouses and covered the great plain and the hills around the camp. A spirit of dark and evil melancholy settled on the loggers.

Paul Bunyan hoped for an adequate water supply from the December snows. And he brought all his inventive powers to the problem of felling the stonewood trees. In eleven days and nights he devised eight hundred and five systems, machines and implements, and from this galaxy he selected a noble tool.

Paul Bunyan's new invention was the double-bitted ax, which is used everywhere in the woods today. Paul Bunyan devised it so that a feller could chop with one blade, then twist the handle and whet the other blade on the gritty stone-wood with the backward swing.

But even with the new axes the logging went on slowly. The camp supply of elbow grease gave out, and the loggers suffered stiffened joints. The December snows were light, and the thirsty blue ox continued to drink the entire water supply. The bunkhouses came to be dens of ominous brood-ing and quiet instead of gay and noisy habitations. Finally the shipment of webfooted turkeys from the Great Lakes arrived too late for Christmas dinner. The loggers became dour, gaunt, embittered men.

Then came New Year's Day and outrageous fortune. When the loggers went to work at the first thinning of darkness they attributed the peculiar oppressive warmth of the morn-ing to an unusual Chinook wind. There was, however, no wind at all. Then the rising sun shot blazing rays into a cloud-less sky. Even then the loggers did not realize that they were witnessing an Event. This was the beginning of a notable year, the Year of the Hot Winter. As the sun climbed higher the heat grew more intense. The Christmas snow had vanished at the first burning touch of day. The ground baked and cracked. The stonewood trees glittered in a fierce light. Each logger threw off his mackinaw, muffler, sweater, stagged shirt, woolen overshirt and undershirt, his paraffin pants, mackinaw pants and overalls and his Arctic socks, heavy wool socks, light wool socks and cotton socks. All heavy clothing was speedily thrown aside, and everywhere in the plain, in the valleys, and on the hillsides were piles of garments, and by each pile a logger toiled, clad only in drawers and calked boots. But still sweat dripped and trickled from their bodies; they labored more and more languorously. Each quarter of an hour the blue ox, with lolling tongue, dashed madly for the river and drank it dry.

Paul Bunyan was distressed by this change in his affairs, but he was not daunted. Confident that his loggers would do their best in the meanwhile, he again retired to solitude, hoping to devise something that would conquer the hostile and unnatural season. He returned with the great timber scythe, with which he could fell a full section of timber with one swing of his mighty arms. Carrying the timber scythe over his shoulder, Paul Bunyan strode toward his camp. His tread was vigorous despite the deadening heat. Benevolent ideas stirred his heart. He himself would do the arduous labor of felling the stonewood trees; the loggers would be asked only to do the lighter work of trimming and bucking the trees into logs. They were a fine bunch of savages; ordinarily they would not allow even Paul Bunyan to do their natural work. Perhaps they would resist such intrusion now. But the great logger was sure of his persuasive powers.

As he neared the camp, busy as he was with philanthropic thoughts, he failed to note an unusual silence in the woods and about the bunkhouses. Not until he saw Babe and the

Big Swede sleeping in the stable was he made aware of the extraordinary. Paul Bunyan went next to the camp office. Johnny Inkslinger, that tower of energy, was sleeping at his desk! His fountain pen had dropped from his hand, and as it was fed by hose lines from twenty-five barrels of ink, a black stream gushed from its point and flooded the floor. A chorus of faint snores came from each bunkhouse. The cookhouse looked gloomy and deserted. In the woods the axes and saws lay where the loggers had left them. For one hundred and seventy-nine minutes Paul Bunyan stood silently in the midst of his camp, tormented by wrath, regret and sorrow. His outfit had failed him. After all these years of comradeship in labor they had allowed a mere hot winter to provoke them into faithlessness. He had left them without an idea that they would be untrue to the job while he was scheming to make it a success. But they had weakened. Very well, he thought, after his brief period of emotion, he would perform their labor for them while they snored. They should awaken to shame.

One stride brought him into the first clearing made among the stonewood trees. Without losing a second, he threw the timber scythe from his shoulder, he grasped its handles, then took a long swing, and the first section of trees thundered to the ground. On he went, making a circular swath. As he stepped with his right foot the sharp scythe blade crashed through the trees on the cutting stroke, and as he stepped with his left he brought the scythe behind him with a vigorous swing. On and on he labored, his steps coming faster as the circle widened. Every seven hours he paused to whet the blade of the timber scythe on a bundle of the stonewood trees which he carried in his hip pocket. The hot winter drove its fires upon him, but his passion of toil repelled them with a stronger flame. The great logger's walk became a run; the dazzling blade of the timber scythe flashed in strokes of inconceivable rapidity; the sections of stone-wood trees fell in a steady roar.

Then Paul Bunyan began to sweat. He had labored before this, but never so savagely, nor in such penetrating heat. Only the man who raises a good sweat for the first time can realize what an astounding store of perspiration the human body can hold. On occasion it gushes from innumerable springs, seeming inexhaustible. It streams down the crevices and valleys of the body and floods the flat spaces; it soaks the clothing and drips to the ground. Imagine then what happened when Paul Bunyan's stored perspiration was unloosed. As he toiled on, ever more fiercely, his sweat flooded his boots, it surged over their tops and foamed towards the ground like two Niagaras. His swinging body and flying arms flung out clouds of spray. These strange waters coursed over the plains in torrents and gathered in heaving pools. The little river was submerged, drowned, exterminated. The waters crept towards the camp. Paul Bunyan, more and more engrossed with his labor as time went on, did not note the rising flood. His circle grew wider and wider. It left the plain and swung around the bordering slopes. Section after section of the trees was felled, only to be covered by water, for the stonewood timber was too heavy to float. But Paul Bunyan labored around and around the circle, quite unaware of the tragical consequence of his efforts.

For five days and nights the loggers lay in their bunks, too lazy to get up to eat, too lazy to do aught but drowse and dream. But at twelve o'clock on the fifth night the waters had reached the bunkhouses, and they learned of their peril. Yells of fear arose from every quarter, and in a few moments the whole camp, with the exception of Babe, the Big Swede, and Johnny Inkslinger, was aroused. Fright made the loggers forget the hot winter, and gave them energy. When they looked out on a vast lake glittering in the moonlight, and saw in the dim distance the twin rivers roaring from Paul Bunyan's boots, they knew that speedy and efficient action was necessary to save their lives. The best swimmers swam out to the tool house and brought back hammers, saws and nails. Each logger then began to build a boat from his bunk, and for three hours they worked feverishly and silently constructing the vessels. When the last one was finished the word was passed along and in a few moments the boats, each one carrying a logger and his blankets, swarmed from the bunkhouses. Before the armada had gone twenty feet the boats all filled with water and sank, while the loggers uttered lamentable cries. These changed to sounds of rejoicing, however, when it was discovered that the water was only waist deep. The loggers rescued their bundles from the boats and scampered to the shore like a holiday host at a beach.

But their joy did not last; it quickly gave way to dread. Paul Bunyan, toiling more desperately every moment, was rapidly moving around the circle. In a short time he would be upon them, and at any instant he might discover the fate of his trees, the flooding of his camp, his complete disaster. The loggers all understood the reason for the mighty man's wrathful labor. Their sense of blame confused them and smothered their native courage. The host began to move over the hills, haltingly at first, and with heads bowed like penitents. Then, as the volleying thunder of Paul Bunyan's timber scythe sounded nearer and nearer, they lifted their heads and struck a faster pace. Then guilty fears possessed them and every logger of the lot began to gallop madly. Someone yelled, "Ol' Paul's a-comin'!" and the warning cry was echoed from thousands of throats all over the hills. The loggers were taken by panic; the runaway became a stampede. By dawn they were making such running leaps that each logger would hit his chin with his front knee and his head with his back heel at every stride. They were so scared that they never stopped until they got to Kansas.

For many days and nights after the stampede of his loggers Paul Bunyan had toiled on, swinging his timber scythe with undiminished rapidity. He had not observed the desertion of his men, or the flooding of his camp, or the fate of the stonewood trees. But at last his energy and strength began to fail, his pace slackened, he swung the scythe with slower strokes, and the intervals between the rolling thunders of falling trees became longer and longer. Then the timber scythe dropped from his hands, and he sank to the ground. Now he saw for the first time the shimmering distances of salt water which covered the stonewood trees and all but the tallest buildings of his camp. For seven hours he gazed on the lamentable scene, then his head dropped to the ground. He was not disheartened; he was only tired. He slept.

Days and nights went by with little change in the unnatural season. The days of springtime came, but here there was no spring. Summer days began, the sultriness of the nights got increasingly heavy and thick, and in the daytime the overpowering blaze of the sun seemed to make the very hills shrink, while the surface of the lake was veiled in steaming mists. The slumbers of Paul Bunyan, Johnny Inkslinger, the Big Swede and the blue ox became so deep that the active careers of all of them might have ended there ingloriously had it not been for Babe's appetite, which always tormented him, sleeping or waking. The Big Swede was couched on the high-piled hay in the manger, and Babe's chin rested on his body. Stirred by a hunger that would not be denied, his jaws began to work mechanically; they closed over the fifty pound plug of chewing tobacco that the Big Swede always carried in his hip pocket, and it was swallowed like a blade of grass.

Babe gasped, groaned, and shuddered; then he lunged to his feet, snorting and bellowing, for chewing tobacco was as poisonous to him as to a circus elephant. He gouged the Big Swede viciously with his horns until he awoke with yells of agony and astonishment. And not until he saw, through the stable door, Paul Bunyan asleep on the far side of the lake did Babe heed the foreman's powerful remonstrances. With a last angry toss of his horns, which threw the Big Swede through the stable window, Babe turned and plunged into the water. So fast did he run that he threw foaming waves to the furthest reaches of the lake. When he reached Paul Bunyan he emitted a joyous bellow and eagerly began licking the great logger's neck. For one hour and twenty-seven minutes Babe assiduously tickled him, and then Paul Bunyan sprang to his feet with a great roar of laughter. He felt strong and fresh; he smiled cheerfully at the blue ox, who capered around him. He straddled Babe and rode him across the lake to the flooded camp.

🌲🌲🌲🌲🌲🌲🌲

W. J. Gorman:

PAUL BUNYAN
The Arctic Explorer

Paul made manys the jaunt up north. In fact he lumbered there and to such good purpose that it is hard to find a tree in areas thousands of miles square. People called them the Barren Lands after Paul and the Blue Ox were through with them. According to his diary he attempted a new method of lumbering, pulling the trees out by the roots, hence there are no stumps left in areas which were once covered by great forests. "Trees around Great Bear Lake were all of six inches at the butt and fifteen feet high," says the epic historian of the woods. "This timber we floated down the Mackenzie River to Herschel Island where we sold it to the Vermont Yankee skippers who used to come in around Alaska for the whaling. The Eskimos in those parts," says Paul, "were blond; they had hooked noses and talked with a twang." Just what the significance of this observation may be, one is left to figure out for himself.

When it comes to matters of weather and temperature we are listening to an expert when Paul speaks. He says: "In the so-called Arctic regions the climate was mild. Even at 50 degrees below zero the water did not freeze and it was only at 90 degrees Centigrade below that we got any relief from the mosquitoes. The bumblebees were also a nuisance. We used to set dead falls for them, cut them up with crosscut saws and use them for Sunday dessert. Bees knees fried were good.

"The butterflies were useful and quite tame. The cookees used to milk them and it was pathetic to see them coming up the lane, laying their heads over the bars and to hear them mooing in the dusk of the evening.

"When we first went to the Arctics the Eskimos lived in stone and timber houses four storeys high but when we logged the country over they had no building materials left. They had to take to the snow and in their dire extremity they learnt a lesson from the bees, building houses patterned after the hive.

"That was the winter of the blue snow and it was a hard one on the natives. They had to stand up twice to cast a shadow and if it had not been for the white foxes they would have starved to death.

"Since we left we have heard that they have built permanent snow houses which they move around with them even in the summer. There may be nothing in this yarn and I personally cannot vouch for its truth. Some say they have no igloos now and that they have even forgotten that they ever had them, which seems strange in a country where there is nothing else with which to build homes except snow.

"When we pulled out we went to the Oregon country and on the way used the Blue Ox to dig the Portland Canal, throwing up the Cascade Mountains in the process."

Thus does the immortal Paul deal authoritatively with contentious matters. It is a pity that the early history of the country—according to Paul—is not put into book form for the instruction and delight of our school children today. Alas, Paul's Blue Ox is dead and gone but bull goes on forever.

🌲🌲🌲🌲🌲🌲🌲

Ida Virginia Turney:

PAUL BUNYAN COMES WEST

PAUL HE COME to Oregon 'round by Californy, 'count o' a mistake, an' that thar blamed trail is follered consid'able yit. Y' see Paul wus a busy man an' when he wus in a special hurry he didn't never stop fer no train; he jist hoofed 'er—in winter he done it on snowshoes. 'Twuz the winter o' the Blue Snow, the same Year's the rain come up from China an' tore all the roots o' the alfalfy up an' the' wuz big floods all over the hull kentry, that year Paul he jist finished up his loggin' job in Dakoty and he thot he'd take a look at the West. 'Nother thing with the trees all gone the weather got awful cold. One mornin' when Paul wuz a-gittin' himself some breakfast he set the coffeepot full o' bilin' coffee on the back o' the stove fer a minute an' it froze so fast the durned ice wuz too hot to handle. Wal, that thar settled it fer Paul—the West fer hisn. When he was leavin' Minnesoty the' wuz a lot o'

. . . it struck awful hard rock an' bounded clean back outn the hole.

snow in the woods yit so he jist stropped on his snowshoes an' struck out straight west. 'Fore long the sun got awful hot an' the dust riz in clouds but Paul he kept a-goin'. Bym-by it got so durned hot it warped Paul's snowshoes somthin' turrible—the left a lot more'n the right—so's he traveled in a arc an' come out at Frisco—nine hundred miles out'n his way an' he lost a hull day by it.

Paul he wuz a-totin' his big pick an' shovel 'long in case he sh'd run right onto pay dirt, an' he come to a place whar he thought he c'd fix a good waterin' place fer Babe. Wal, he dug an' dug till the bottom fell outn that thar hole, an' he wuz so s'prised he let go his shovel an' it dropped clean out o' sight. Paul he jist about give up ever gittin' it back; but in about an hour er so, it struck awful hard rock an' bounded clean back outn the hole an' up in the air more'n a hundred feet. 'Course Paul never could ketch it, fer it wuz all melted; so it's been boundin' up an' down faithful once an hour ever since. Bym-by the Gov'ment named the hole Old Faithful an' put the Yellowstone National Park 'round it.

Paul went 'long totin' jist the pick, but by the aft'noon o' the second day it begun to git kind o' heavy. Then he come to the Colorado River an' he thought he'd wade 'long upstream fer a spell an' cool his feet. He drug the pick 'long behind him fer to ease his shoulder an' it made quite a scratch in the river bed, tho it wuz runnin' thru solid rock. Fust thing Paul knowed he c'd hardly see out. That thar scratch they calls the Colorado Canyon.

✝✝✝✝✝✝

Harold W. Felton:

BABE'S CYCLONES

The blue ox quite unconsciously
   Created quite a wind
When he swished his tail contentedly
   And rolled his eyes and grinned.

Some people think that cyclones are
   The remnants of the gale
That sprang up when the great blue ox
   Swished his curly tail.

✝✝✝✝✝✝

Charles E. Brown:

WRITING HOME

IT WAS SO COLD during one winter at one of Paul's camps that even the fire in the big camp range froze. When a lumberjack wanted to write a letter to his home, he just stepped outdoors and shouted the words he wished to write. These froze solid. He wrapped them up in a gunnysack and sent them home. When the sack arrived, all his folks had to do was to thaw them out in or on the kitchen stove, and they had the letter just as it was spoken.

✝✝✝✝✝✝✝

Wallace Wadsworth:

THE YEAR OF THE HEAVY FOG

THE GREAT LOGGER had hardly gotten things to running smoothly again when the work was once more held up, this time by the coming of the Big Fog. The fog drifted down over the country one night, and for several weeks it was like a thick cottony blanket covering the land. It was so thick that the fish in the river were unable to tell where the river left off and the fog began, and many thousands of them— swimming around in the fog and thinking they were still in the river—became lost in the woods and were left stranded among the trees far from water when the fog finally went down. Paul's men all had to wear mosquito netting over their heads in order to keep the pollywogs out of their faces.

The fog was so thick that while it lasted any cutting of timber was almost out of the question, and so all of the men in camp began devising various sports to help pass the time away. Their favorite game was a fishing contest, which helped to while away many dull hours during the Big Fog.

In this contest several men would carry big gunny sacks to a favorite spot, and stand there, holding the mouths of the sacks wide open. Then they would begin to imitate the cries and calls which the fish made as they swam around through the fog, and the man who enticed the most fish into his bag won the contest.

Once one of the men heard a queer wailing sound some distance away, and thinking that it was some new kind of fish, he began mocking its cries. It came nearer and nearer, and finally he enticed it into his bag. He could tell immediately from the feel of it through the bag that the creature was not a fish, and from the roughness of its loose and bumpy skin he was able very shortly to learn what he had captured. "Hooray!" he yelled to his companions, "I've caught a Squonk!" and despite the poor animal's desperate wailings he bundled it under his arm and hurried with it to the bunk-house. He was greatly excited over his unusual catch, which was indeed a prize, and he looked forward to enjoying the importance which the display of it to his fellows would give him.

The Squonk, which is one of the rarest animals in the woods, is a very shy creature, and its retiring disposition is due to the shame which it feels on account of its unlovely appearance. It has dull red eyes, a long comical nose, and an ill-fitting warty skin, as well as several other blemishing defects, on account of all of which it intensely dislikes being seen. Because it yearns to be beautiful, and yet is condemned to be so fearfully ugly, it is always unhappy and weeps and wails constantly, leaving a trail of tears wherever it goes. So rarely did it ever get near men that the logger who had caught the Squonk was greatly elated, and called all his friends to the bunkhouse to see the queer creature when he put it on view. When he opened the bag, however, there was nothing there except some salt water and bubbles. The poor creature, made more unhappy than ever by being caught, and being so fearful of being seen in all its homeliness, had simply dissolved in tears.

At one time during the Big Fog the mist began to leak through the cook shanty roof, so Paul called out some of his men and set them to nailing on more shingles. When the fog finally cleared away, there was a great crash where the men had done their work, and they saw then what they had done. The thickness of the fog had confused them, and instead of nailing the shingles on the cook shanty roof, as they thought they were doing, they had nailed them out onto the fog itself which, of course, let the new roof collapse when its support began to disappear.

Paul Bunyan finally figured out a way to get rid of the Big Fog. He hitched Babe up to a great plow, made a lot of ditches, and drained the fog right back into the river.

❦❦❦❦❦❦

Dell J. McCormick:

THE POPCORN BLIZZARD

WHEN PAUL BUNYAN had cut down all the trees in North Dakota, he decided to go west. It was summertime, and the forest was sweet with the smell of green trees. The spreading branches cast their cool shadows on the ground.

"We must cross vast plains," said Paul to his men, "where it is so hot that not even a blade of grass can grow. You must not become too thirsty as there will be very little water to drink."

Paul knew it would be a long, hard journey, so he decided to send all the heavy camp equipment by boat down the

Mississippi River and around the Horn to the Pacific Ocean. Paul told Billy Whiskers, a little bald-headed logger with a bushy beard, to take a crew of men and build a boat. Billy had once been a sailor. In a short time the boat was finished and loaded with all the heavy camp tools.

Everyone cheered as Billy Whiskers and his men started down the Mississippi River on their long trip. Billy wore an admiral's hat and looked every inch the sailor, although he hadn't been on board a ship for thirty-five years.

With Paul and Babe the Blue Ox leading the way, the rest of the camp then started across the plains on their long journey west. In a few days they had left the woods and were knee deep in sand that stretched out before them for miles and miles. The sun became hotter and hotter!

"I made some vanilla ice cream," said Hot Biscuit Slim one day as he gave the men their lunch, "but the ice became so hot under this boiling sun that I couldn't touch it!"

Tiny Tim, the water boy, was so hot and tired that Paul had to put him up on Babe's back where he rode the rest of the trip. Every time Babe took a step forward, he moved ahead two miles, and Tiny Tim had to hold on with all his might. Even Ole the Big Swede, who was so strong he could carry a full-grown horse under each arm, began to tire.

There was not a tree in sight. Paul Bunyan's men had never before been away from the forest. They missed the cool shade of the trees. Whenever Paul stopped to rest, thirty or forty men would stand in his shadow to escape the boiling sun.

"I won't be able to last another day," cried Brimstone Bill, "if it doesn't begin to cool off soon!"

Even Paul Bunyan became tired finally and took his heavy double-bitted axe from his shoulder and dragged it behind him as he walked. The huge axe cut a ragged ditch through the sand that can be seen to this day. It is now called the

Grand Canyon, and the Colorado River runs through it.

It became so hot that the men were exhausted and refused to go another step. Hot Biscuit Slim had complained that there was very little food left in camp. That night Paul took Babe the Blue Ox and went on alone into the mountains to the north. In the mountains Paul found a farmer with a barnful of corn.

"I will buy your corn," said Paul to the farmer. So he loaded all the corn on Babe's back and started for camp. By the time he arrived there, the sun was shining again and the day grew hotter as the sun arose overhead. Soon it became so hot that the corn started popping. It shot up into the air in vast clouds of white puffy popcorn.

It kept popping and popping and soon the air was filled with wonderful white popcorn. It came down all over the camp and almost covered the kitchen. The ground became white with popcorn as far as the eye could see. It fell like a snowstorm until everything was covered two feet deep with fluffy popcorn.

"A snowstorm! A snowstorm!" cried the men as they saw it falling. Never had they seen anything like it before. Some ran into the bunkhouses and put on their mittens and others put on heavy overcoats and woolen caps. They clapped each other on the back and laughed and shouted for joy.

"Let's make snowshoes!" cried Ole the Big Swede. So they all made snowshoes and waded around in the white popcorn and threw popcorn snowballs at each other, and everybody forgot how hot it had been the day before. Even the horses thought it was real snow, and some of them almost froze to death before the men could put woolen blankets on them and lead them to shelter.

Babe the Blue Ox knew it was only popcorn and winked at Paul.

Paul Bunyan chuckled to himself at the popcorn blizzard and decided to start west again while the men were feeling so happy. He found them all huddled around the kitchen fire.

"Now is the time to move on west," said Paul, "before it begins to get hot again." So they packed up and started. The men waded through the popcorn and blew on their hands to keep them warm. Some claimed their feet were frost-bitten, and others rubbed their ears to keep them from freezing.

After traveling for a few weeks more, they saw ahead of them the great forest they had set out to reach. They cheered Paul Bunyan who had led them safely over the hot desert plains. Babe the Blue Ox laughed and winked at Paul whenever anyone mentioned the great blizzard.

After reaching the great forest in the Rocky Mountains, Paul sent Brimstone Bill and Babe on to the Pacific Coast to meet Billy Whiskers and help unload the boat. They finally found the ship outside the entrance to the Golden Gate.

"What's the matter?" shouted Brimstone Bill. "Why don't you come in to shore?"

"I can't!" cried Billy Whiskers through a large megaphone. "My ship is stuck fast to the bottom of the ocean."

That seemed very queer to Brimstone Bill, for the water was almost a mile deep out in the ocean beyond the Golden Gate. Billy Whiskers rowed ashore and explained. It seemed they had made a mistake when they built the ship. The men used new, green lumber and it quickly became water-soaked and the boat started sinking. As soon as the water came up to the edge of the deck, Billy Whiskers would put in to shore and build another deck on top of the first deck.

When that became water-soaked he would build still another deck on top of that. When he finally arrived at the

Golden Gate he found he had one hundred and thirty-seven decks on his ship. And all but one of them was under the water!

Of course, with a boat like that, they couldn't go through the Golden Gate, and all the cargo had to be put on rafts and floated ashore. There they loaded everything on the big Blue Ox and were soon back in Paul Bunyan's camp in the Rocky Mountains.

THE SPIRIT OF PAUL BUNYAN
WILL STAY IN AMERICA

Louis C. Jones:

PAUL BUNYAN IS BACK!

We thought that he was dead, but he is back again!
They told us, when the big camps closed or the whistle-punks
    moved in,
He said the hell with it, and slunk away and died.
We should of known it wasn't so.
What clay could hold a man like Paul,
Ol' Paul who laid the prairies clean
And straightened out the Whistlin' River with his blue ox
    Babe?
We should of known that our Paul Bunyan couldn't die.

He came again without our having any word,
Johnny sent no note to put us wise.
The first we heard, the stars were laughin' all along the Milky
    Way
And trees from Maine to Oregon were shiverin' more than
    ever wind could make them do.
Then he was here—
His long, full strides were lopin' over counties at each step,
The mountains bellowed back the echoes of his big bull voice.
He wasn't dead— No, sir!

He'd snoozed a bit, but he wa'n't dead, not by a dam-site.
The bluejay'd waked him up and said that tough jobs waited
Tougher than his greatest in the woods,
And Sam—his uncle—in black need.
It seems some little runt, hog-wild and slipp'ry as an eel, was
    gettin' the whole world by the tail,
And old Sam's friends were in a nasty fix
And Sam himself no longer slept in peace but lay with wear
    open eyes at night.
It wasn't timber needed cuttin' now
Nor ornery rivers to be straightened out,
But guns and planes, and tanks to build
And men to train to run the tarnal things.
Now where the hell was Paul
And what sad day was this when he'd let down a friend?

That's why he's back among us once again.
No bully ever pushed this boy about
And no mad loon's a-goin' to do it now.
He's in the factory towns and in the mines,
He stalks along the regimental streets at night.
He spits upon his hands and adds his weight to ours.

But last night I got an awful start, for I seen him hikin' of
    across the hills.
"Hey, where ya goin', Paul?" I yells.
And all the time I'm thinkin' of the big, the dirty job that
    must be done.
My heart was in my pit until he hollered back,
"I'm fetchin' Pecos Bill who rode the cyclone till she dreened
    out under him and
Big John Henery who beat the steam-drill down.
They're comin' back to work with me for Sam."

Before the night is through, they'll all be back
And as the night-shift starts for home and morning-shift goes
    in to punch the clock
And when the sentries yawn along their posts at dawn,
Just let them listen;
For they'll hear these three beside them, roaring their brave
    belly-laughs into the wind.
They're coming now and stayin' till the job is done, and
    afterward, if we deserve the likes of them.
We thought they all was dead. They ain't.
They're just as live and kickin' as ourselves.
To say the truth out, plunk and plain,
They *are* ourselves,
And so they must remain.

Bibliography

In preparing the following bibliography, I have followed the form used by Miss Gladys Haney in her valuable work published in the Journal of American Folklore (55:155-68. July 1942). I have used the material in Miss Haney's bibliography, as supplemented by Mr. Herbert Halpert in the Journal of American Folklore (56:57-9. January 1943), and have made a number of additions.

I gratefully acknowledge the cooperation of The Journal of American Folklore, Miss Haney and Mr. Halpert. My own contributions to the bibliography have been made with the help of many of Paul Bunyan's friends. I acknowledge specifically the assistance and cooperation of Mr. Charles E. Brown, Mr. James Stevens, and Dr. W. W. Charters.

I. TALES

ANON.: "Traditional Ceremonies in the U.S.: Return of Paul Bunyan." *Reader's Digest,* Vol. XXXVI, No. 214 (February 1940), p. 87. Mention of several of Paul's adventures and an account of the winter carnival in Bemidji, Minnesota.

ANON.: "Paul Bunyan in Oregon." *Oregon Oddities,* November 15, 1939. Mimeograph. 4 pp. Informational Service of Oregon Writers' and Historical Records Survey Projects of the Works Projects Administration of Oregon. A composite of the "key stories" with particular emphasis on Oregon.

BALDWIN, GRACE D.: "Finding Out About Paul." The *Frontier,* November 1924, p. 18. Missoula, Montana, Montana State University: H. G. Merriam.

BARTLETT, WILLIAM W.: "Logging Camp Diversion and Humor." *History, Tradition and Adventure in the Chippewa Valley,* pp. 232–36. Chippewa Falls, Wisconsin: The Chippewa Printery; 1929.

An authentic description of the logging camp background for Paul Bunyan tales is followed by mention of Paul and several of his crew and a description of the hodag hoax perpetrated by Eugene S. Shepard of Rhinelander.

BECK, EARL CLIFTON: *Songs of the Michigan Lumberjacks,* 296 pp. Ann Arbor: University of Michigan Press; 1941. Several Bunyan yarns are included along with other tall tales (pp. 281–90). There are also some tales in verse from oral tradition (pp. 248–60). A few Paul Bunyan drawings are also given.

BINFORD, THOMAS: *Paul Bunyan in the Army. See:* Miller, Bethene.

BLAIR, WALTER: *Tall Tale America,* pp. 167–84; 220–32. New York: Coward-McCann; 1944. Several of the Bunyan stories as well as other tales of American folk heroes.

BOTKIN, B. A.: *A Treasury of American Folklore.* New York: Crown Publishers; 1944. 932 pp. Contains stories, ballads, and traditions of the American people. Foreword by Carl Sandburg. The title describes this book, which contains many tales and references to Paul.

———: "Tall Talk and Tall Tales of the Southwest." *The New Mexico Candle.* New Mexico Normal University, Las Vegas, New Mexico, June 28, 1933. Reprinted in *A Treasury of American Folklore* (pp. 602–3) under the title of "Paul's Oklahoma Farm," as told by Kara Fullerton.

BOWMAN, JAMES CLOYD: *Adventures of Paul Bunyan.* New York, London: The Century Co., 1927. 286 pp. The first Bunyan book to be written especially for children. The author gives a fairy tale setting for the stories, and pictures Paul, who will always be "a boy with a big heart," coming to "free the forests from their long bondage."

———: "Paul Bunyan." *From Indian Legends to the Modern Book Shelf—Michigan Anthology,* pp. 97–100. Edith R. Mosher and Nella Dietrich Williams, editors. Ann Arbor: George Wahr; 1931. Portions of Chapters III and XIII from his book, *The Adventures of Paul Bunyan.*

BRAUN, IRWIN H.: *Laugh and Learn Grammar.* San Francisco: Harr Wagner Publishing Co.; 1941. 311 pp. Grammar lessons from Paul Bunyan stories.

BROOKS, JOHN LEE: "Paul Bunyan: Oil Man," in *Foller de Drinkin' Gou'd,* pp. 45–54. Austin, Texas: Publications of the Texas Folk-Lore Society, No. VII (1928). The author has collected legends making Paul almost as great an oil man as he was a lumberjack.

———: Idem. Reprinted in *Eve's Stepchildren,* L. N. Jones, editor. Caldwell, Idaho: The Caxton Printers, Ltd.; 1942.

———: "Paul Bunyan." The *Saturday Review of Literature,* Vol. XXV, No. 20 (May 16, 1942), p. 10. Short tales of Paul's activities in the oil fields.

———: "Paul Bunyan Goes South." *Literature. A Series of Anthologies —Interpreting Literature,* p. 289. New York: The Macmillan Company; 1943, E. A. Cross, Florence M. Meyer and Emma L. Reppert, 694 pp. Paul in the oil fields.

BROWN, CHARLES E.: *Flapjacks from Paul Bunyan's Cook Shanty.* Madison, Wisconsin: the author, State Historical Society; 1941. 4 pp. Seven key stories are given in brief form.

———: *Paul Bunyan: American Hercules.* Madison, Wisconsin: the author; 1937. 8 pp. More synoptic presentations.

———: *Paul Bunyan and Tony Beaver Tales.* Madison, Wisconsin: the author; 1930. 18 pp.

———: *Paul Bunyan Tales.* Madison, Wisconsin: the author; 1922, 1926, 1927; (with Ted Brown) 1929. 7 pp. Brief sketches of some of Paul's adventures.

———: *Sourdough Sam.* Madison, Wisconsin: Wisconsin Folklore Society; 1945. 4 pp. Tales of Paul and his famous camp cook.

———: *Bunyan Bunkhouse Yarns.* Madison, Wisconsin: Wisconsin Folklore Society; 1945. 4 pp.

———: *Brimstone Bill.* Madison, Wisconsin: Wisconsin Folklore Society; 1942. 6 pp. Tall tales of the exploits of the famous boss Bullwhacker of Paul Bunyan's camps.

———: *Paul Bunyan Classics.* Madison, Wisconsin: Wisconsin Folklore Society; 1945. 8 pp. Some of the more famous stories.

———: *Johnny Inkslinger.* Madison, Wisconsin: Wisconsin Folklore Society; 1944. 4 pp. Deacon seat tales of Paul Bunyan's industrious camp clerk at his Sawdust River camp in Wisconsin.

———: "Yarns of Paul Bunyan's Boyhood." The *Wisconsin Magazine,* Vol. V, No. 3 (March 1927), p. 19. (The author is given as P.E.S. in the publication.) Interesting résumé of some of the tales of Paul's boyhood.

———: "Paul Bunyan's Blue Ox." The *Wisconsin Octopus,* November 1933. University of Wisconsin.

———: "Shanty Boy." Madison, Wisconsin: Wisconsin Folklore Society; 1945. 4 pp. Tales of the great singer, storyteller and dancer of Paul Bunyan's camps.

———: "Ole Olson." Madison, Wisconsin: Wisconsin Folklore Society; 1945. 4 pp. Tales of the Mighty Swede Blacksmith of Paul Bunyan's Wisconsin and other great logging camps.

———: "River Pigs and Bull Punchers." The *Wisconsin Alumni*

Magazine, Vol. XXXII, No. 111 (December 1930), p. 101. Madison Wisconsin: The Wisconsin Alumni Association. Some of the better known tales retold.

BROWN, TAGGERT TED: "Christmas on the Big Onion." The *Wisconsin Octopus,* Vol. XV (1933), pp. 93–4. A fantastic tale of the celebration, with Paul's tree set up in the center of Pea Soup Lake, and lighted with burning hams.

CARMER, CARL: "How Paul Bunyan Straightened the Crooked Road." *The Hurricane's Children,* pp. 164–172. New York: Farrar and Rinehart; 1937. A few adventures are sketched in the author's very readable style, and then he tells of the big party given in Bemidji for Minnesota's most famous citizen.

————: "Paul Bunyan." *America Sings,* pp. 238–41. New York: Alfred A. Knopf; 1942. The rawhide harness story retold.

DAVENPORT, SAMUEL R.: "Tall Timber Tales: A Saga of Paul Bunyan." *Eve's Stepchildren,* Lealon N. Jones compiler, pp. 288–95. Caldwell, Idaho: Caxton Printers, Ltd.; 1942. A story of Paul's Lost Camp told by a French-Canadian lumberjack.

Detroit News (News-Tribune): "The Round River Drive," July 24, 1910, p. 6, illustrated section. The earliest known reference to Paul Bunyan in print. Contains many of the better known tales. This prose version later appeared in verse form in The *American Lumberman,* by Douglas Malloch.

DOBIE, J. FRANK: "Giants of the Southwest." The *Country Gentleman,* Vol. XLI, No. 8 (August 1926), p. 11. Philadelphia: The Curtis Publishing Company.

FEDERAL WRITERS' PROJECT: *A South Dakota Guide* (American Guide Series), pp. 80–82, 170–71. Pierre, S. D.: South Dakota Guide Commission; 1938. An account of the origin of the Black Hills as a burial mound for Babe.

————: *Minnesota* (American Guide Series). New York: Viking Press Inc.; 1938. One wonders if the writers gave Paul his due. On p. 361 mention is made of the statue in Bemidji, and on p. 287, of the fact that the Onion River derives its name from a Bunyan legend.

————: *Oregon—End of the Trail,* p. 81. Portland, Oregon: Binfords & Mort; 1940. A list of the changes Paul and Babe made in the physical features of Oregon.

————: *Texas Guidebook* (American Guide Series), p. 95. New York: Hastings House; Texas State Highway Commission; 1940.

————: *Wisconsin* (American Guide Series), pp. 466, 469. New York: Duell, Sloan and Pearce; 1941.

FIELD, RACHEL (compiler): *American Folk and Fairy Tales*. New York: Charles Scribner's Sons; 1929. 302 pp. A carefully selected group of folk tales. Indian legends, Louisiana folk tales, Southern mountain stories, and tales of Paul Bunyan, Tony Beaver, and Uncle Remus are included.

FINGER, CHARLES J.: *A Paul Bunyan Geography*. York, Pa.: Maple Press; 1931. 39 pp. The book contains but one map, in black and white, with a small number of details. The tales are familiar ones.

Four-L Bulletin: A publication of the Loyal Legion of Loggers and Lumbermen, Portland, Oregon.

Vol. I, No. 7 (September 1919), p. 30. "Paul Bunyan and Swede Charlie have Awful Experience with Midsummer Thaw." A tale with pictures.

Vol. III, No. 5 (May 1921), p. 38. "Paul Bunion Gets a Bear Hide," by Charles O. Olsen.

Vol. IV, (March 1922), pp. 3, 27. Some of the baby stories and how Elmer died of heart failure.

Vol. IV, No. 4 (April 1922), pp. 3, 36. Some Bunyan tales, contributed.

Vol. IV, No. 5 (May 1922), p. 34. More tales contributed by readers. One tale points out that one year Paul lost so much money he had to mortgage the big farm. The farm was so big, that when the mortgage was due on one side of it, it wasn't due on the other side, and so, the mortgage could not be foreclosed.

Vol. VII, No. 7 (March 1925), p. 51. The writer says he never heard of Paul in seven years in the woods.

Vol. VII, No. 13 (May 1925), p. 9. Remarks about Stevens and Shephard books.

Vol. VII, No. 19 (July 1925), p. 35. Review of James Stevens' Paul Bunyan.

Vol. VII, No. 26 (October 1925), p. 43. Cartoon.

FREEMAN, LARRY: "Paul Bunyan and the Dreadful Whirling Wimpus." The *Kansas Magazine* (1933) Annual, pp. 66–8. Manhattan, Kansas: Kansas State College Press, Department of Industrial Journalism; 1933. The hero encounters an awesome Thing.

FROHLICHER, JOHN C. (Jack): "Paul Bunyan and the Forest Service." The *Frontier*, November 1924, pp. 18–20. Missoula, Montana, Montana State University: H. G. Merriam.

GARLAND, ACEL: "Pipeline Days and Paul Bunyan." *Foller de Drinkin' Gou'd*. Austin, Texas: Publications of the Texas Folk-Lore Society, No. VII, 1928, pp. 55–61. New adventures of Paul, told evenings in a pipeline camp.

GORMAN, W. T.: "Grab Samples." The *Northern Miner,* July 23, 1931, p. 12 (Second Section); September 17, 1931, p. 12 (Second Section); October 1, 1931, p. 11 (Second Section); October 22, 1931, p. 11.

HANDY, R. D.: *Paul Bunyan and His Blue Ox.* Chicago: Rand McNally Company; 1937. 64 pp. A ten-cent book worth many times the price, filled with humorous tales well illustrated by the author.

HARRIS, FOSTER: "The Hero of Petrolia." *Adventure,* Vol. LXXIX, No. 3 (August 15, 1931), pp. 116–17. New York: The Butterick Publishing Co.; 1931. Tales of Paul in the oil fields. He is called the patron saint of all oil workers.

HARRY, DEWITT: "The Listening Post." Portland, Oregon: *The Morning Oregonian;* February 7, March 1, 3, 8, 10, 11, 12, 13, 15, 17, 19, 22, 28, and April 2, 1922. Tales contributed by readers.

HAVIGHURST, WALTER: "Immortals in Mackinaws—Paul Bunyan's Crew." *Upper Mississippi: A Wilderness Saga,* pp. 177–83. New York: Farrar and Rinehart; 1937. The setting is given for the growth of the tales, and Paul and his men are characterized.

HOLMES, FRED L.: *Alluring Wisconsin,* pp. 403–05. Milwaukee, Wisconsin: E. M. Hale & Company; 1937. Describes the Paul Bunyan room in the Memorial Union Building in Madison, and the authentic logging camp, with relics, in Eau Claire.

HOPKINS, BERT: "Paul Bunyan, Only True American Myth." The *Wisconsin Magazine,* Vol. I, No. 3 (June 1923), pp. 32–3. Many of the familiar tales are presented in synoptic form, with very little comment—that to the effect that Paul Bunyan is an all-American myth.

HOUGH, DONALD: "The Lost Legend." *Outdoor America,* Vol. II, Nos. 6–10 incl. Chicago, Ill.: Izaak Walton League of America Inc.; 1924. A story in five installments in the issues of January, February, March, April, and May 1924.

JAMES, MARTIN: "A Story About Paul Bunyan," *Jack and Jill,* Vol. II, No. 3 (January 1940), pp. 4–9. Dad gives Ruthie and Zander a not-too-convincing account of the black duck dinner.

JONES, EDWARD R.: *Paul Bunyan, Preface, Prose, etc.* Madison, Wisconsin: Mrs. Edward Jones; 1930. 32 pp.

LANGEROCK, HUBERT: "The Wonderful Life and Deeds of Paul Bunyon." The *Century Magazine,* Vol. CVI, No. 1 (May 1923), pp. 23–33. A sketch of Paul's life with the comment that he is "a wholly American mythical figure, if not the only one."

LAUGHEAD, W. B.: *Paul Bunyan and His Big Blue Ox.* Westwood California: Red River Lumber Company, Eleventh Printing; 1940

40 pp. (First published in 1922.) A cleverly written mixture of source material and advertising for the Red River Lumber Company. The author's illustrations are very effective.

————: "Some Exploits of Paul Bunyan." *Quest*, Max Herzberg, Merril Paine, and Austin Works, compilers. pp. 171–77. Boston: Houghton Mifflin Company; 1940. Some of the tales in the booklet above mentioned are rewritten.

————: "The Marvelous Exploits of Paul Bunyan." *In Our Times* (Source Readers in American History, No. 5), A. B. Hart and J. G. Curtis, editors, pp. 285–93. New York: The Macmillan Company; 1927. A few of the key stories are well told.

LIBRARY OF CONGRESS: Music Division, Folklore Section. Records of Paul Bunyan stories.

"Paul Bunyan Stories," spoken by Crosshaul. Ironwood, Michigan, Alan Lomax, 1938. Record 2423A: the reversible dog tale; mention is made of Babe, Lucy and Benny.

"Paul Bunyan Stories," spoken by Perry Allen. St. Louis, Michigan, Alan Lomax, 1938. Record 2264 B2: "The Round River Drive." Record 2265 B2: Paul used butter for his log skids. One winter the flame in the lanterns froze. The frozen flames were thrown out and when summer came they thawed and caused a great forest fire which was so hot it melted the river. Paul was never able to stretch the river back to its original shape so he did the best he could and joined the two ends together by building the locks that are now at Sault Sainte Marie. Record 2266 B2: Paul as a baby and how he made the tides in the Bay of Fundy.

"Paul Bunyan Stories," spoken by Bill McBride. Mt. Pleasant, Mich., Alan Lomax, 1938. Records 2259 B2, 2260 A1: round stones were used to sharpen axes. Another river was set on fire.

LOWE, BERNICE BRYANT, and SINGER, LELAND W.: *Hello Michigan.* Syracuse, New York: L. W. Singer Co.; 1939. Some Paul Bunyan tales appear on pages 278–83.

MACGILLIVRAY, JAMES: "The Round River Drive." (*See* Detroit News.)

MCCORMICK, DELL: *Paul Bunyan Swings his Axe.* Caldwell, Idaho: Caxton Printers, Ltd.; 1936. 111 pp. Endpapers show a map of the Paul Bunyan country, with new locations for some of the old places. Some of the key stories, with embellishments, are told for children.

————: *Tall Timber Tales.* Caldwell, Idaho: Caxton Printers, Ltd.; 1939. 155 pp. Old tales plus several new ones; illustrations by Lorna Livesley.

McDonald, James J.: "Paul Bunyan." Radio Station WHA, University of Wisconsin, March 22–April 26, 1933. A series of weekly broadcasts including tales of Paul's adventures and helpers and how and why the stories developed.

———: "Paul Bunyan and the Blue Ox." *Wisconsin Blue Book,* pp. 113–28. Madison, Wisconsin: Democrat Printing Company; 1931. An excellent résumé including most of the key stories.

McHugh, Vincent: *Caleb Catlum's America,* pp. 240–51. New York: Stackpole Sons; 1936. Paul and Babe assist in bringing the temperate zone back to where it belongs.

Malcolmson, Anne: *Yankee Doodle's Cousins,* pp. 229–60. Boston: Houghton Mifflin Company; 1941. Paul was born with a beard. Well-told tales. Some of them adapted from James Stevens' *Paul Bunyan.*

Martin, Wayne: "Paul Bunyan on the Water Pipeline." *Folk-Say: A Regional Miscellany,* B. A. Botkin, editor, Vol. I (1929), pp. 50–63. Tales collected by the narrator while employed on a water pipeline in Texas. There is a bibliography which includes Paul Bunyan and other folklore heroes.

Miller, Bethene: *Paul Bunyan in the Army.* As told by John Rogers Inkslinger (pseudonym). Portland, Oregon: Binfords & Mort; 1942.

Miller, Olive Beaupré: "Big Paul Bunyan and His Blue Ox, Babe," and "Paul Bunyan Goes West." *Heroes, Outlaws, and Funny Fellows,* pp. 200–12; 314–32. New York: Doubleday, Doran and Company; 1939. The chief tale is of Little Meery and the poison parsnips; the second chapter includes many of the familiar adventures in Washington and Oregon. Illustrated by Richard Bennett.

Montague, Margaret: "The World's Funny Bone." The *Atlantic Monthly,* Vol. CXL (September 1927), pp. 327–36. An excellently written humorous tale in which Paul Bunyan visits Tony Beaver in the Eel River camp and the two discover that they are "one and the same feller, only dressed up in different bodies."

———: "Paul Bunyan Meets Tony Beaver." *Literature: A Series of Anthologies—Heritage of American Literature,* pp. 538–44. E. A. Cross, Grace A. Benscoter, and William A. Meacham, compilers, 750 pp. New York: The Macmillan Company; 1944. The two great men meet.

———: *Up Eel River.* New York: The Macmillan Company; 1928. 225 pp. Paul meets Tony Beaver in the last chapter.

Morbeck, G. C.: "Paul Bunyan—An Authentic Account of His Pre-Historic Activities." The *Ames Forester,* Vol. X (1922), pp. 100–07.

Ames, Iowa: Iowa State College. An account disclosing how Paul originally planted the world's trees.

Morning Oregonian: See Harry, DeWitt.

MURRAY, GENEVIEVE: "Paul Bunyan Logs Off Eastern Montana." The *Frontier* (November 1924), pp. 20–1. Missoula, Montana, Montana State University: H. G. Merriam.

MURTAUGH, JANET: *Wonder Tales of Giants and Dwarfs.* New York: Random House; 1945. 66 pp. The Paul Bunyan story in this collection starts on p. 27. Illustration by Florian.

NELSON, BRUCE: *Land of the Dacotahs.* Minneapolis, Minnesota: University of Minnesota Press; 1946. How Paul Bunyan accidentally created the Black Hills.

NEWTON, STAN: *Paul Bunyan of the Great Lakes.* Chicago, Illinois: Packard & Co.; 1946. Legends of the wonderful lumberjack Paul Bunyan, told the author by the lumberjacks of upper Michigan.

ORR, MARGARET: "Paul of the North Woods Logging Camp Legend." *Sun Up, Maine's Own Magazine,* May 1932, p. 15. Some of the tales in short form.

OWEN, RAY S.: "Paul Bunyan, the Surveyor Extraordinary." *The Wisconsin Engineer,* Vol. XXXIV, No. III (December 1929), p. 91. A delightfully serious description of the planimeter Paul constructed for his survey-work, using a quarter-mile racetrack for the wheel and a part of the Wisconsin-Michigan state line for the arms.

PECK, LEIGH: "Pecos Bill Meets Paul Bunyan and Starts a New Ranch." *Pecos Bill and Lightning,* pp. 26–36. Boston: Houghton Mifflin Company; 1940. Paul and Bill have a matched fight over a wooded mountain, and learn when it is over that Paul wants only the trees, and Bill, the land cleared for cattle grazing.

RAIHLE, PAUL H.: "Paul Bunyan." *The Valley Called Chippewa,* pp. 38–40. Cornell, Wisconsin: Chippewa Valley *Courier:* the author; 1940. Some interesting tales. The author states that Paul has become a part of the Chippewa Valley.

RAYFORD, JULIAN LEE: "Our Own Gods Are Always Comic." The *American Mercury,* Vol. LX, No. 256 (April 1945), pp. 491–7. The author states that Paul is "far and away the most magnificent, the most superbly typical and creative American ever known."

———: "Paul Bunyan on Saipan." *Esquire,* Vol. XXV, No. 6, Whole No. 151 (June 1946), p. 98. Some tales which the author states were told to him on Saipan.

ROUNDS, GLEN: "Baby Rainstorm." *Story Parade,* Vol. V, No. 4, (April 1940), pp. 35–44. A very modern version of the story of the rain that came up from China.

————: "How Paul Bunyan Lost a Cutting Crew in Kansas and Built the Biggest Dragline Ever Built." *Lumbercamp,* pp. 72–3. New York: Holiday House; 1937. A tale of Paul as a business man.

————: *Ol' Paul.* New York: Holiday House; 1936. 133 pp. Mr. Rounds says he collected the stories and made the drawings at the scene "during the three winters I worked for him." There are new tales and revised versions of the old ones, all told in the writer's forceful manner.

————: "Ol' Paul and His Camp." *Daring Deeds (Happy Hour Readers),* pp. 423–30. Mildred English and Thomas Alexander, editors. New York: Johnson Publishing Co.; 1938.

————: "Why There Are No Trees on the Desert." *A Sub Treasury of American Humor,* pp. 440–43. E. B. White and Katherine S. White, editors. New York: Coward-McCann; 1941. Pages 87–101 from his book *Ol' Paul.* Paul not only removes the trees from the desert but invents dry ice.

ROURKE, CONSTANCE M.: "Paul Bunyon—Lumberjack." *New Republic,* Vol. XXIII, No. 292 (July 7, 1920), pp. 176–9.

SCHAK, AL: "Flathead Lake." The *Frontier,* November 1924, pp. 21–2. Missoula, Montana, Montana State University: H. G. Merriam.

Seattle Star: See Smits, Lee J.

SHAY, FRANK: "Paul Bunyan, Mightiest of Loggers." *Here's Audacity,* pp. 163–225. New York: Macaulay Company; 1930. The tales are told with gusto and the author gives his keen sense of humor full play.

SHEPHARD, ESTHER: *Paul Bunyan.* Seattle: McNeil Press; 1924. 235 pp. A group of the key stories told in appropriate manner, as if by one lumberjack.

————: *Paul Bunyan.* New York: Harcourt, Brace and Company; 1941. 233 pp. The classic will be more popular than ever with Rockwell Kent's illustrations. There are 24 full-page drawings, as well as clever initial letter sketches at the beginning of each chapter.

————: "Paul Bunyan and His Blue Ox." *In Search of America,* edited by Lucy L. Hazard, pp. 252–62. New York: Thomas Y. Crowell Company; 1930. Excerpt from her book.

————: "Paul Bunyan's Cornstalk." *Golden Tales of Our America,* edited by May Lamberton Becker, pp. 301–10. New York: Dodd, Mead and Company; 1929. Three pages of comment by Mrs. Shephard, followed by one chapter from her book.

————: "The Camp on the Big Onion." *Literature: A Series of Anthologies—Understanding Literature,* pp. 412–16. E. A. Cross, Dorothy Dakin, and Helen J. Hanlon, compilers. New York: The

Macmillan Company; 1944. Short tales of the camp on the Big Onion.

SMITS, LEE J.: Tales contributed by readers to a column in The *Seattle Star* (Seattle, Washington) of November 17, 18, 19, 20, 22, 23, 24, 25, 26, 27, and 29, 1920.

STERN, REN'EE B.: "Paul Bunyan, Babe and the Blue Snow." *Book Trails to Turrett Tops*, Vol. V, pp. 156–63. Chicago: Child Development Foundation, Inc.; 1937.

STEVENS, JAMES: "The Black Duck Dinner." *American Mercury*, Vol. II, No. 6 (June 1924), pp. 161–69. A few introductory comments in the first person are followed by pages 95–113 from his *Paul Bunyan*.

———: "The Black Duck Dinner." *America is West*, edited by John T. Flanagan, pp. 18–30. Minneapolis, Minnesota: The University of Minnesota Press; 1945. The *American Mercury* story.

———: *Paul Bunyan*. New York: Alfred A. Knopf; 1925. 245 pp. The book has been reviewed so much as to need few comments. The introduction is of interest, for in it Mr. Stevens gives the French background for Paul, mentions several key stories, and gives Paul first place among folklore heroes. Woodcuts by Allen Lewis.

———: *The Saginaw Paul Bunyan*. New York: Alfred A. Knopf; 1932. 261 pp. Again "new light" is cast on Paul and his men. Woodcuts by Richard Bennett.

———: "The Winter of the Blue Snow" and "The Old Home Camp." *American Folk and Fairy Tales*, compiled by Rachel Field, pp. 225–272. New York: Charles Scribner's Sons; 1929. Excerpts from *Paul Bunyan*.

———: "When Rivers Were Young and Wild." *Woman's Home Companion*, Vol. LVIII, No. 7 (July 1931), pp. 26–27. The story of Paul's taming the Wild Big Auger River, finally forming Niagara Falls from a part of it. His hand-to-hand struggle with the river has a Beowulf-Grendel sound.

———: "The Great Hunter of the Woods." The *Frontier*, Vol. XI, No. 2 (January 1931), p. 129. Missoula, Montana, Montana State University: H. G. Merriam.

———: "The Great Hunter of the Woods." The tale from The *Frontier*, reprinted in *The Best Short Stories of 1931*, edited by Edward J. O'Brien, pp. 258–68. New York: Dodd, Mead and Company; 1931.

———: "Why Poker Was Invented." The *American Mercury*, Vol. XV, No. 58 (October 1928), pp. 129–38. Mr. Bunyan's invention of the great American game and the reasons therefore.

————: "The Dismal Sauger." The *American Mercury*, Vol. VIII, No. 31 (July 1926), pp. 302–7. A tale which does not mention Paul but which describes a great battle between The Dismal Sauger and The Great Hodag, animals of Paul's time and woods.

————: "Love Affair." The *American Mercury*, Vol. VI, No. 22 (October 1925), pp. 161–6. More about creatures of Paul's time and woods.

————: "Bull of the Woods." *Columbia*, Vol. XI, No. 4 (November 1931). New Haven, Connecticut: Knights of Columbus. An analysis of the Bunyan tradition containing some old tales and some less well known.

————: "Paul Bunyan, Hercules of the Timberlands." *Everyweek Magazine*, October 28, 1934. Cleveland, Ohio: Newspaper Enterprise Association. Some tales which are the "hull truth" of the history of Paul Bunyan and his time.

————: "Paul Bunyan, The American Giant Myth." *Everyweek Magazine*. Cleveland Ohio: Newspaper Enterprise Association. November 3, 10, 17, 24 and December 1, 1935. Appeared in various newspapers, one of which was the *Denver Rocky Mountain News*, as a feature supplement. Full pages of pictures by Charles J. Coll, with short tales by Mr. Stevens.

————: "Fishermen's Paradise and the Onion Pines." *Folk-Say, a Regional Miscellany*, pp. 124–41. Norman, Oklahoma: The University of Oklahoma Press; 1931. Fishing on the Ripple River and how Paul's pet trout helped log off the Onion River.

————: "In the Winter of the Blue Snow." *Tales and Travel*, pp. 437–50. *The Child Development Readers*, Julia Letheld Hahn, editor. Boston: Houghton Mifflin Company; 1938. Stories of the Blue Snow, the Coming of Babe and the invention of logging.

————: "Last of the Shanty Boys." *American Mercury*, Vol. LX, No. 258 (June 1945), pp. 725–31. The strings from Paul's Bulgarian zither were used to make the Brooklyn Bridge.

STEWART, K. BERNICE and HOMER A. WATT: "Legends of Paul Bunyan, Lumberjack." *Transactions of the Wisconsin Academy of Sciences, Arts, and Letters*. Madison, Wisconsin: The Academy, Vol. XVIII Part 2 (1916), pp. 639–51. Tales collected from lumbermen of the Middle West and the Northwest are sketched. A discussion of the origin of the Bunyan stories is given, with the conclusion that they are "likely adaptations of tales which have elsewhere an existence in some form," as only a few seem to refer distinctly to lumbering.

THOMPSON, HAROLD W.: *Body, Boots and Britches*, pp. 129–31. Philadelphia: J. B. Lippincott Company; 1940. Several Bunyan stories from Canada and the Adirondacks. Chapters 6, 11, and 12 have tales and discussion of several local folk heroes from New York: John Darling, Bill Greenfield, Joe Call, Cal Corey, "Boney" Quillan. Other tall tales are also given.

TITUS, HAROLD: *Timber*, pp. 215–24. Boston: Small, Maynard and Co.; 1922. The giant cornstalk had a team tied to it when it started to grow. The cornstalk story in detail.

TURNEY, IDA VIRGINIA: *Paul Bunyan Comes West*. Eugene, Oregon: University of Oregon Press; 1919. 34 pp. A chapbook illustrated by pupils in design at the University, under the direction of Helen N. Rhodes.

————: *Paul Bunyan Comes West*. Boston: Houghton Mifflin Company; 1928. 45 pp. The tales collected are "strung together in a continuous narrative," told by Yank who "knowed Paul Bunyan." The artistic and appropriate linoleum cuts are by Helen N. Rhodes.

————: "Paul Bunyan Comes West." *Their Weight in Wildcats*, James Daugherty, editor, pp. 177–88. Boston: Houghton Mifflin Company; 1936. The stories in the 1928 book.

————: *Paul Bunyan the Work Giant*. Portland, Oregon: Binfords & Mort; 1941. 80 pp. The text is brief. The eighty full-page three-color illustrations show vigor and originality.

————: *Paul Bunyan Marches On*. Portland, Oregon: Binfords & Mort; 1942. 80 pp.

————: *A New Literary Type, with Special References to the Tales of Paul Bunyan*. Miss Turney's Ph.D. thesis, revised.

UNTERMEYER, LOUIS: *The Wonderful Adventures of Paul Bunyan*. 131 pp. New York: The Heritage Press; 1945. Some tales retold.

WADSWORTH, WALLACE C.: *Paul Bunyan and His Great Blue Ox*. New York: George H. Doran Company; 1926. 238 pp. Unique in having Paul born "a long time before the Revolutionary War."

————: "Hero of the Lumber Camps." *Literature: A Series of Anthologies—Interpreting Literature*. E. A. Cross, Florence M. Meyer, Emma L. Reppert, compilers, pp. 283–88. New York: The Macmillan Company; 1943. Some of the tales in short form.

————: "The Winter of the Blue Snow." *Making America* (The Curriculum Readers, Vol. V), pp. 205–13. Clara Belle Baker and Edna Dean Baker, editors. Indianapolis, New York: Bobbs-Merrill; 1937. Some of the details of events during the notable winter.

WATT, HOMER A.: "Paul Bunyan Provides for His Crew." *The Rise of Realism*, Louis Wann (editor), pp. 270–73. New York: The

391

Macmillan Company; 1933. Some of the key stories are given, selected partly from the work done by Miss Stewart and Mr. Watt. Paul Bunyan represents the prose folk-tale in Editor Wann's collection.

————: "When Grandpa Logged for Paul." *Literature and Life*. Book III. (Life Reading Service.) Chicago: Scott, Foresman and Co.; 1936. Grandpa tells some Bunyan tales until bed time.

————: *See* Stewart, R. Bernice.

II. POETRY

ALLEN, WILLIAM N.: "The Round River Drive." *Poetry Out of Wisconsin*. August Derleth and Raymond E. F. Larsson, editors, pp. 16–20. New York: Henry Harrison; 1937. Other adventures are given too, but the Round River drive is stressed. This poem and E. S. Shepard's of the same name are very much alike.

ALVORD, THOMAS G., JR.: *Paul Bunyan: A Legendary Hero of the North Woods*. New York: Albert and Charles Boni; 1935. 111 pp. Much like the 1934 book.

————: *Paul Bunyan and Resinous Rhymes of the North Woods*. New York: Derrydale Press; 1934. 137 pp. Although printed in 1934, the rhymes were written and the illustrations drawn more than twenty years earlier, according to the preface. The book contains old and new stories. Paul's companions are all new; the time-keeper is Inkcanblot, and Babe is white.

COFFIN, ROBERT P. TRISTRAM: "Bunyan's Lake." *Primer for America*, p. 68. New York: The Macmillan Company; 1943. How Paul made Moosehead Lake.

————: "Paul's Lullaby." *Primer for America*, pp. 120–21. New York: The Macmillan Company; 1943. The Lullaby Paul's mother sang.

ERICKSEN, MABEL N.: *The Ballad of Paul Bunyan*. Bemidji, Minnesota: the author: 1939. 8 pp. Many of the key stories are well told in rhymed verse.

FROST, ROBERT: "Paul's Wife." *New Hampshire*, pp. 44–8. New York: Henry Holt and Company; 1923. The tale of a dryad sort of wife, told with the poet's usual grace and power.

————: *Collected Poems*. New York: Henry Holt and Company; 1930. A volume consisting of many of the poet's works, including "Paul's Wife."

————: "Paul's Wife." The *Century Magazine*, Vol. CIII, No. 1 (November 1921), pp. 84–8. Apparently the first publication of the poem which later appeared in *New Hampshire*.

JONES, EDWARD R.: *Bunyan's Progress*. Madison, Wisconsin: The author; 1929. 76 pp. Includes adventures in Alaska and Panama as well as the old tales.

JONES, LOUIS C.: "Paul Bunyan is Back!" *New York Times Magazine*, Vol. XC (August 24, 1941), p. 5. An interpretation of Paul Bunyan as the symbol of the loyal American citizen of today, in a fine piece of blank verse.

KNOX, ETHEL LOUISE: "Paul Bunyan's Blue Ox." *Highways and Byways*. The *Child Development Readers*, pp. 58–62. Beryl Parker and Paul McKee, editors. Boston: Houghton Mifflin Company; 1938. A pleasing poem of the Blue Ox.

————: *Ballads of Paul Bunyan*. See Strong, Section IV.

LEIGHTON, LOUISE: "I Hear Paul Bunyan." *Poetry Out of Wisconsin*, August Derleth and Raymond E. F. Larsson, editors, 334 pp. New York: Henry Harrison; 1937. p. 170. A pleasing sound picture of Paul striding at night through the Norway pine forests where he once worked.

MALLOCH, DOUGLAS: "The Round River Drive." The *American Lumberman*, Whole No. 2032, April 25, 1914, p. 33. The *American Lumberman* states that credit for this poem should be given to Douglas Malloch, who was known as "The Lumberman Poet." Mr. James MacGillivray informed Dr. W. W. Charters in a letter dated May 26, 1942, that he and Mr. Malloch wrote this poem together. *See Journal of American Folklore*, Vol. LVII, No. 225 (July 1944).

MORRISSETTE, PAT: "Paul Bunyan: An American Symbol." *Folk-Say, The Land is Ours*, B. A. Botkin, editor, Vol. IV (1932), pp. 274–94. "An attempt to crystallize in one personality derived from American folklore the characteristics of the American people. In the second half of my sequence, I dwell on the theme 'The Resurrection of Paul Bunyan,' or America awakened to the fact that it has despoiled its resources."—p. XIX, Hartshorn thesis (see criticism section), quoting from a letter dated March 14, 1934.

OLSEN, CHARLES O.: "Paul Bunion Gets a Bear Hide." *Four-L Bulletin*, Vol. III, No. 5 (May 1921), p. 38.

RAYFORD, JULIAN LEE: "The Great American Paradise." *Esquire*, Vol. IV, No. 3, Whole No. 22 (September 1935), pp. 68–9. Paul is rough and tough in this poem.

SANDBURG, CARL: *The People, Yes*, pp. 97–9. New York: Harcourt, Brace and Company; 1936. Some of the Bunyan stories are given. The book is important not only as a magnificent example of the literary use of folklore, but also for the large number of folktales given.

SHEPARD, EUGENE S. and KARRETTA G.: *Paul Bunyan—His Camp and Wife*. Tomahawk, Wisconsin: Osborne Press; 1929. 97 pp., the first 45 on the title subject. Several of the key stories; Paul's wife is given credit for bringing him fame.

————: "Round River Drive." *Wisconsin State Journal*, February 24, 1929. See note under William N. Allen.

YATES, PAUL C.: *Paul Bunyan in North Dakota*. El Campo, Texas: El Campo Citizen Press; 1937. 49 pp.

III. DRAMA

CONKLE, ELLSWORTH P.: *Paul and the Blue Ox*. Austin, Texas: the author, Department of Drama, University of Texas. Ms. 1934. Eight scenes, showing the loggers at work and play; the last shows Paul sadly leaving his men who have settled down to domestic life. Dr. Conkle has followed the tradition that one must never tell a Bunyan tale as he has heard it. The premiere was at the University of Iowa in July, 1939.

DAVENPORT, SAMUEL R.: "Sky River Drive." *Midwest Prize Plays*. L. N. Jones (editor). Chicago: Dramatic Publishing Co.; 1938. pp. 68–86. A one-act play. An old logger living with his daughter-in-law and granddaughter is constantly nagged for telling tales of Paul. His hero returns in time to rescue him, as the blue snow falls again. The play won the National Open Folk Playwriting Contest in 1938.

STEVENS, HENRY BAILEY: *Johnny Appleseed and Paul Bunyan*. Boston: Baker; 1930. 92 pp. Three acts with prologue. The play shows Paul in a new role as the villain, while Johnny Appleseed carries off the honors, and an apple tree in full bloom is the main character. The scenes are laid in the Ohio wilderness in the early 1800's.

STOKES, RICHARD L.: *Paul Bunyan: A Folk-comedy in Three Acts*. New York: G. P. Putnam's Sons; 1932. 102 pp. Reviewers call it "fantastic" rather than "folk." The drama is well planned for stage performance and is best suited to a sophisticated audience.

IV. MUSIC

BERGSMA, WILLIAM: "Paul Bunyan, a Ballet for Puppets and Solo Dancers." Rochester, N. Y.: the composer, 18 Upton Park. Ms., 1939. Paul Bunyan's men are the solo dancers in the three-part ballet, with a performance time of thirty-three minutes. James

Stevens' *Paul Bunyan* was used as a source. The premiere was in Rochester, N. Y. in May 1939.

BRITTEN, BENJAMIN: "Paul Bunyan." New York: to be published by Boosey and Hawkes, Inc. Four scenes and a prologue. Mr. W. H. Auden is the librettist. The authors describe their work as a choral operetta with many small parts, rather than the few star roles usually given. Paul Bunyan, who appears only as a voice, is conceived as a "projection of the collective state of mind of a people whose tasks were primarily the physical mastery of nature." The operetta presents in fairy-story form the development of the country from before Paul Bunyan's time until after pioneer days are over. The premiere was at Columbia University in May 1941.

HOWLAND, RUSSELL: "Babe, the Blue Ox." Ann Arbor, Michigan: the composer, Department of Music, University of Michigan. Ms., 1935. A march first played at the University of Wisconsin Paul Bunyan Homecoming in 1935. This selection is the first one completed in a planned suite of five numbers.

KREUTZ, ARTHUR: "Paul Bunyan." A dance poem. For large orchestra. Includes "The Kingdom of Kansas," "Winter of the Blue Snow," and "Paul Bunyan's Dinner Horn." Written in April 1939. New York: Carl Fischer and Co. Rental library.

————: "Paul Bunyan," "Winter of the Blue Snow." Boston: C. C. Birchard and Co.; 1942. Orchestra score.

MANTON, ROBERT W.: Incidental music for H. B. Stevens' *Johnny Appleseed and Paul Bunyan*. Boston: Baker; 1931. The forest motif is prominent, and a genuine pioneer folk tune and an Indian war dance melody are used. Johnny Inkslinger is the violinist.

MOROSS, JEROME. "Paul Bunyan: An American Saga." The ballet was composed for Mr. Charles Weidman who danced Johnny Inkslinger at the premiere at the Theatre Guild, New York City, in October 1935. The sources of the ballet were principally James Stevens' books and the composer's own memory of tales. Mr. Weidman owns the only copy of the ballet.

RICH, JOHN K., ALLAN GRANT and J. E. MADDY: "Paul Bunyan—A Legend of the North Woods." New York: Chappell; 1940. The suite is in four movements (The Great Blue Snow, Paul Bunyan's Education, The Song of the Loggers, and Paul Bunyan's Farewell), arranged for orchestra and chorus.

STRONG, MAY A.: *Ballads of Paul Bunyan*. Philadelphia: Theodore Presser Co.; 1943. 76 pp. Choral cycle for mixed voices and narrator. Ballads by Ethel Louise Knox.

V. ART

AMATEIS, EDMOND: "Efficiency." Attractive figures of Paul, interpreted as a friendly giant, Babe, and the Story Teller, the latter perched on Paul's shoulder. The group appeared above the central door of the Medicine and Public Health Building at the New York World's Fair, 1939–40. There were two other groups: Strap Buckner representing Humility and Johnny Appleseed representing Benevolence. These groups measured approximately 16 x 20 feet, were cast in water-proofed plaster, and weighed four or five tons. It is the belief of the sculptor that the groups were destroyed at the termination of the fair. One reproduction of "Efficiency" is shown on the reverse side of the December 1939 calendar issued by the Wisconsin Anti-Tuberculosis Association, Milwaukee.

AYRES, LEMUEL DELOS, JR.: *A Design Project for E. P. Conkle's Paul and the Blue Ox.* Unpublished M.A. thesis, University of Iowa, 1938.

BARNES, CARROLL: "Paul Bunyan." A 42-inch statue of North Carolina cherry, completed in 1938 and exhibited in both East and West. The sculptor's monumental Paul, 16 feet tall and carved from a redwood log is placed near Sierraden, Mr. Barnes' mountain art gallery, which is a few miles from the entrance to Sequoia National Park.

BARRETT, OLIVER: "Paul Bunyan." Eugene, Oregon: the sculptor, School of Fine Arts, University of Oregon. A model for a statue of Paul Bunyan has been completed.

BOLDEN, JOSEPH: *Paper Trade Journal,* New York, August 8, November 7, 1946. Advertisements of the Mead Sales Co.

GROPPER, WILLIAM: Several of Gropper's works are reproduced in *Fortune* Magazine, July 1944, pp. 148–51.

————: "Paul Bunyan." Reprint in Bulletin of the Metropolitan Museum of Art, Vol. XXXV, Sec. II (1940), p. 17. Paul is shown more than mountain high with a huge tree trunk thrown carelessly over his shoulder. His head is small and the amount of his intellect doubtful, or perhaps the broad grin indicates merely good nature.

HADER, ELMER S.: "Gallery of American Myths." Century, Vol. CVII, 1924, p. 894. A noted illustrator of children's books presents a woodcut of Paul with a huge axe in his hand. His dog Elmer stands at his side holding an ox (surely not Babe?) in his mouth. The artist shows Paul as a giant who "in his own person fulfills the wildest dreams" of the loggers.

HANDY, R. D.: "Paul Bunyan's Pictorial Map of the United States." Chicago: Rand McNally and Company; 1935. The map is in full color, size 28 by 21 inches. Paul and his men are shown forming the physical features of the country. The truthfulness of the pictures is certified by Johnny Inkslinger and Shot Gunderson.

HILDEBRAND, GUSTAVE: Mr. Beck says (op. cit. I) "The Paul Bunyan drawings, including the end papers, were made by Mr. Gustave Hildebrand of the Michigan Art and Craft Project, Detroit. The originals belong to a series of mural decorations executed for the main lobby of Michigan House, in the West Quadrangle of the men's residence halls at the University of Michigan. There are several minor changes, however, in the drawings facing pages 26, 96, and 248."

HUTTON, HUGH: *Paper Trade Journal,* New York, June 20, July 11, October 10, December 5, 1946. Advertisements of the Mead Sales Co.

KENT, ROCKWELL: Illustrations for Esther Shephard's *Paul Bunyan.* New York: Harcourt, Brace and Company; 1941. It is evident that the artist is a Paul Bunyan enthusiast, from the fine character interpretations given in the 24 full-page drawings in the book. The initial letter sketches at the beginning of each chapter are an added attraction.

KREIS, HANS: "Puzzle." *Child Life,* Vol. XV (1936), p. 229. Paul is shown in a thoughtful mood, one snowshoe resting on a rocky ledge while he looks out over the wintry landscape. The puzzle is to find Johnny Inkslinger, Babe, Hels Helson, and the two lumberjacks hidden in the picture.

LEVIT, HERSCHEL: The *Paper Trade Journal,* New York, December 27, 1945, January 24, February 28, March 21, 1946. Advertisements of The Mead Sales Co.

PITZ, HENRY C.: A painting of Paul and Babe reproduced in advertisements of The Mead Sales Co. in *Fortune,* May 1944; *Printers' Ink,* April 21, 1944; *Tide,* April 1944; and other media.

SMITH, EDWARD C.: The *Paper Trade Journal,* New York, April 18, May 16, September 5, 1946. Advertisements of the Mead Sales Co.

UNSIGNED: Statues of Paul and Babe on the lake shore, Bemidji, Minnesota. Paul is 18 feet tall, and Babe is in proportionate scale. In 1937, the year Paul's statue was completed, it was wired so that he could direct the events during the winter carnival. The figure of Babe was completed in 1939. Both are made of concrete and steel, and each weighs about ten tons. Photograph, *Life* Magazine, February 5, 1945, pp. 58–59.

WATROUS, JAMES: Paul Bunyan murals, University Memorial Union, Madison, Wisconsin. The murals are twelve in number, and appear on the walls of "Paul Bunyan's Cookshack." Paul and Babe are prominent. The map of the Bunyan country favors Wisconsin. The appropriate murals were completed in 1936.

WERNER, JACK: "Paul Bunyan Does Some Weeding." Political cartoon in *The Chicago Sun*, reprinted in the *New York Herald Tribune*, July 14, 1946.

VI. CRITICISM

AMES, CARLETON C.: "Paul Bunyan—Myth or Hoax?" *Minnesota History*, Vol. XXI, No. 1 (March 1940), pp. 55–8. The author decides that he is the latter and asserts that "the Paul Bunyan legend is not indigenous to the lumber camps but has been developed and exploited since their day in this section for various purposes, commercial and otherwise," in a letter written November 25, 1941.

See also "The Paul Bunyan Tales." *Minnesota History,* Vol. XXI, No. 2 (June 1940), pp. 176–8. Discussion of the Ames article (*Minnesota History*, Vol. XXI, No. 1, March 1940, pp. 55–8), and some interesting information from W. B. Laughead.

Ibid. Vol. XXI, No. 3 (September 1940), pp. 296–8. Reprints an article by M. M. Quaife in which he contends that the Paul Bunyan legend was introduced into the Michigan-Saginaw River area after the Stevens book.

ANON.: "American Legends." *Life* Magazine, Vol. 18, No. 6 (February 5, 1945), pp. 58–9. Story of Paul and other American folk heroes.

ANON.: "Paul Bunyan—Giant." *Fortune* Magazine, Vol. XXX, No. 1 (July 1944), p. 148. Several of the William Gropper pictures are reproduced. Paul is stated to be a purely American figure, and inspiration for greater tasks to come.

ANON.: *Encyclopedia Britannica*, 14th edition, Vol. IV, p. 393. Discusses origin of the myths and suggests likeness of Paul to Hercules and Thor.

ANON.: "Paul Bunyan by R. L. Stokes." The *Nation*, Vol. CXXXVI, No. 3524 (January 18, 1933), p. 71. Sources are given for the Stokes comedy, which is called "fiercely vernacular and authentically American."

BATES, ERNEST S.: "American Folk-lore." *Saturday Review of Literature*, Vol. II, No. 50 (July 10, 1926), pp. 913–14. High praise is given Percy MacKaye, and regret is expressed for the pseudo-folklore of Ballads and Songs of the Shanty Boy. James Stevens is criticized for his "rendering of the Rabelaisian" Paul Bunyan stories.

and the suggestion is given that collectors follow the method of the Brothers Grimm.

BERTELSON, ERNEST B.: "She Saw the Importance of Paul Bunyan." *Christian Science Monitor* Weekly Magazine Section, June 30, 1945, p. 18. Notes on Esther Shepard's work.

BOWMAN, JAMES CLOYD: "The Paul Bunyan Yarns." *Michigan History Magazine,* Vol. XXV, No. 1 (1941), pp. 25–8. Tales of Paul are given a place as "the most fundamentally American of all our folklore."

CHARTERS, W. W.: "Paul Bunyan in 1910." *Journal of American Folklore,* Vol. LVII, No. 225 (July 1944), pp. 188–9. Discussion of Paul's first known appearance in print and the growth of the legend.

CHASE, MARY ELLEN and FRANCES DEL PLAINE: "Tales and Legends." *The Art of Narration,* pp. 139–156. New York: F. S. Crofts and Company; 1926. Comments on the French Paul Bunyan and how he became a Real American are followed by a reprint of Chapter I from James Stevens' *Paul Bunyan.*

CHASE, STUART: "Paul Bunyan." The *New Republic,* Vol. XLIII, No. 553 (July 8, 1925), pp. 186–7. An appreciation of Stevens' *Paul Bunyan* and analysis of the "golden chunk of almost pure primitive literature." Mr. Chase finds four ideas of significance in the "rush and drive of these tremendous yarns."

DAVIS, M. L.: "James Stevens of Paul Bunyan Fame." *Sunset,* Vol. LXII (May 1929), p. 16.

DERLETH, AUGUST: *The Wisconsin* (Rivers of America Series). New York: Farrar and Rinehart; 1942, pp. 205–217, 255. Paul is compared with Whiskey Jack and the story of the Hodag is told.

DOBIE, J. FRANK: "Paul Bunyan." The *Nation,* Vol. CXXI, No. 3138 (August 26, 1925), pp. 237–8. An assertion that as an American folk creation, Paul's only peer is Uncle Remus, and a criticism of James Stevens' and Shephard's books, with "no abiding enthusiasm for either."

DORSON, RICHARD M.: "America's Comic Demigod." *American Scholar,* Vol. X, No. 4 (1941), pp. 389–401.

HADER, ELMER S.: "A Gallery of American Myths." *Century,* Vol. CVII, No. 6 (April 1924), pp. 891, 894. Paul is stated to fulfill "the wildest dreams of all the loggers."

HARTSHORN, MELLOR: *Paul Bunyan: A Study in Folk Literature.* Los Angeles: Occidental College, M.A. thesis, 1934. 218 typewritten pages. A thorough study of the Paul Bunyan literature up to 1934, with the purpose of determining the significance of the cycle in American folklore. The key stories are presented with footnotes

399

locating them in from one to four earlier publications. An analytical comment is presented for each of the major books. The author concludes that Paul Bunyan "comprehends not only the national humor of exaggeration and fondness for boasting, the realism of the representation of the golden age of logging, but also the self-portraiture of epic scope." There is a carefully annotated bibliography of Paul Bunyan literature and of the background literature of folklore.

HAZARD, LUCY L.: *The Frontier in American Literature.* New York: Thomas Y. Crowell Company; 1927, p. 79. The author comments on the growth of interest in folklore and says Paul Bunyan is now "of the stature of the nation."

HOLMES, FRED L.: "Badger Saints and Sinners." Milwaukee, Wisconsin: E. M. Hale and Co.; 1939. Chapter XXIX, pp. 459–474. A discussion of the authenticity of the Bunyan tales.

J. H. K.: "Tall Tales of the Tall Timber." *Survey,* Vol. LIV, No. 7 (July 1, 1925), p. 408. Stevens has made Paul Bunyan come alive, and just in time, the reviewer says, to preserve the flavor of an age that is passing.

LE FEVRE, LOUIS: "Paul Bunyan and Rip Van Winkle." The *Yale Review,* Vol. XXXVI, No. 1 (Autumn 1946), pp. 66–76. The author says that "Paul represents the American frontier tradition of titanic material achievement."

LITTELL, ROBERT: "Paul Bunyan." The *New Republic,* Vol. XLI, No. 529 (January 21, 1925), p. 234. Favorable comments on Esther Shephard's book and a discussion of the tales as a mixture of ancient mythology, daydreaming, real American humor, and an attempt to impress the credulous greenhorns.

McDONALD, MARIAN J.: *The Legend of Paul Bunyan.* Madison, Wisconsin: University of Wisconsin. A.B. thesis, 1928. 75 typewritten pages. A general discussion of folklore with comments on the Paul Bunyan publications to date.

MACKAYE, PERCY: "A Homer of the Logging Camps." *Bookman,* Vol. LXI, No. 4 (June, 1925), pp. 473–4. Comments on Stevens' and Shephard's books and a discussion of sources, with similarities drawn between European myths and legends and this American tale.

POUND, LOUISE: "Nebraska Strong Men." *Southern Folklore Quarterly,* Vol. VII, No. 3 (September 1943), pp. 137–9. Dr. Pound points out that Paul Bunyan is obviously the progenitor of Febold Feboldson.

QUAIFE, M. M.: *See* Ames, Carleton, C.

RAYFORD, JULIAN LEE: "Paul Bunyan's Kin—Grist for the Dramatist's

Mill." *Theatre Arts*, Vol. XXIX, No. 3 (March, 1945), pp. 161–5. The author states that the whole epic is waiting for the dramatist.

ROTH, HENRY: "Lynn Riggs and the Individual." *Folk-Say, A Regional Miscellany*, Vol. II (1930), p. 386. The author compares Hannie and Texas, in Mr. Riggs' play, *Roadside*, with Paul Bunyan, the "epic character."

ROURKE, CONSTANCE: *American Humor*. New York: Harcourt, Brace and Company; 1931, 324 pages. A scholarly presentation of the development of American folklore. On p. 233 Paul Bunyan tales are characterized as following "the long-established pattern of the tall tale" and as being general rather than "deeply localized."

———: "Paul Bunyon—Lumberjack." The *New Republic*, Vol. XXIII, No. 292 (July 7, 1920), pp. 176–9. An excellent defense of Paul's American origin and mention of the strict lumberjack code which requires that the tales, though about Paul, never originate with him. (The author spells the hero's name with an "o" which is the original French spelling.)

———: "The Making of an Epic." *Saturday Review of Literature*, Vol. II, No. 5 (August 29, 1925), p. 81. One of the best reviews of Stevens' and Shephard's books, calling them both "touchstones for the future."

SHAY, FRANK: "The Tall Tale in America." *Folk-Say, A Regional Miscellany*, Vol. II (1930), pp. 382–5. The author asserts that there is no European background for them, and that our heroes are as American "as our national weakness for boasting." He points out the danger of merging the individualities of the heroes and suggests that authentic tales be gathered soon.

SHEPHARD, ESTHER: "The Tall Tale in American Literature." The *Pacific Review*, Vol. II, No. 3 (December 1921). Some tales are set forth in short form. Paul is called "America's only epic hero since the days of Indian myth-making."

SHERMAN, STUART: "Paul Bunyan and the Blue Ox." *The Main Stream*. New York: Charles Scribner's Sons; 1927, pp. 71–9. Praise for Mrs. Shephard's book and criticism for Mr. Stevens' as lacking the gift "for imaginative and persuasive American lying."

STEVENS, JAMES: "Paul Bunyan Stories." *Saturday Review of Literature*, Vol. III, No. 2 (August 7, 1926), p. 30. A letter in answer to E. L. Bates' article (*see* Bates). Mr. Stevens objects to the term "Rabelaisian" to describe the original Paul Bunyan stories. He asserts that there is no definite body of Bunyan tales and defends his own procedure of never repeating a story he has heard.

———: Reply to "Our Own Gods are Always Comic" (*see* TALES,

RAYFORD, J. L., *American Mercury*, April, 1945.) *American Mercury*, Vol. LX, No. 258 (June 1945), p. 759.

STEVENSON, PHILIP: "Handicraft." *Folk-Say, A Regional Miscellany*, Vol. II (1930), pp. 322–3. The author says that except for Paul Bunyan and Pecos Bill there is no Anglo-American folk art.

TABOR, EDWARD O. and STITH THOMPSON: "Paul Bunyan in 1910." *Journal of American Folklore*, Vol. LIX, No. 232 (April-June 1946), p. 134. Notes of Bunyan tales from diary entries made in 1910.

VAN DOREN, CARL: "Document and Work of Art." *Century Magazine*, Vol. CX, No. 2 (June 1925), pp. 242–4. Mrs. Shephard's book is the former. The critic prefers art, and explains how Mr. Stevens has failed to achieve it.

————: "Paul Bunyan Goes West." *The Roving Critic*. New York: Alfred A. Knopf; 1923, pp. 105–7. Praises Miss Turney's book and wonders whether American imagination will make a Hercules or a Munchausen of Paul Bunyan, or neglect him completely.

————: *The American Novel: 1789–1939*. New York: The Macmillan Company; 1940, pp. 270–1. The critic has decided that Paul is a Munchausen, and the legend is "essentially American in its specific geography, its passion for grotesque exaggeration, its hilarious metaphors, its drawling, unblushing narrative method."

WATT, HOMER A.: *The Rise of Realism*, Louis Wann, editor. New York: The Macmillan Company; 1933. 805 pp. A defense of Paul Bunyan's place in American folklore and a statement of the epic scope of the tales with an added American element, "a conscious comic inflation of both characters and episodes."

VII. RELEVANT LIST

ANON.: "Antoine Barada," *Nebraska Folklore Pamphlets*, No. VIII, Part 2 (September 15, 1937), pp. 9–11.

ATKINSON, ELEANOR: *Johnny Appleseed*. New York: Harper and Brothers: 1915. 341 pp. A well-written biography of the saint of the apple orchards, which "restores him to his time and place and recalls the almost incredible conditions under which he did his inspired task."

BAUGHMAN, ERNEST W.: "Bobby Hayes, Quarry Worker." *Hoosier Folklore Bulletin*, Vol. I, 1942, pp. 75–7.

BEATH, PAUL R.: "Febold Feboldson," *Nebraska Folklore Pamphlets*, No. V (July 1, 1937), pp. 1–12; No. VIII, Part 1 (September 15, 1937), pp. 1–8. Two Nebraska folk heroes.

BLAIR, WALTER: *Native American Humor* (1800–1900). New York: American Book Company; 1937. The introduction (1–162) gives

402

a fine survey of American humor including comment on the relation between the oral and literary tall tale. There is an excellent selected bibliography (163–96). The rest of the book is an anthology of the various types of written humor.

————: *Tall Tale America*. New York: Coward McCann; 1944.

———— and FRANKLIN J. MEINE: *Mike Fink, King of Mississippi Keelboatmen*. New York: Henry Holt and Company; 1933. 283 pp. The story was written after a great deal of research. The epilogue gives an excellent summary of the development of Mike Fink as a folklore hero.

BOATRIGHT, MODY C.: *Tall Tales from Texas*. Dallas, Texas: The Southwest Press; 1934. 100 pp. Contains "A Preface on Authentic Liars" by J. Frank Dobie (vii–xvii), and an analysis of cowboy tales by the author, including the statement that Pecos Bill "is apparently a late development for few of the old-time cowmen have heard of him." A fine collection of tales is given, using a framework of story-telling around a campfire.

BOTKIN, B. A.: *A Treasury of American Folklore*. New York: Crown Publishers; 1944. A complete book of American folklore.

BOWMAN, JAMES CLOYD. *Pecos Bill*. Chicago: Albert Whitman and Company; 1937. 296 pp. The tales are presented in a delightfully humorous style. Mr. Bowman consulted original documents and fabulous story tellers in collecting material about Pecos Bill, whom he calls the best and most characteristic representative of the broad humor of America.

BROWN, CHARLES: *Paul Bunyan Natural History*. Madison, Wisconsin: the author; 1935. 8 pp. Thirty-two animals, "now mostly extinct," are described and classified.

————: *Whiskey Jack Yarns*. Madison, Wisconsin: Wisconsin Folklore Society; 1940, pp. 1–9.

————: *Cousin Jack Stories*. Madison, Wisconsin: Wisconsin Folklore Society; 1940, pp. 1–8.

————: *Old Man River*. Madison, Wisconsin: Wisconsin Folklore Society; 1940, pp. 1–20.

————: *Sea Serpents*. Madison, Wisconsin: Wisconsin Folklore Society; 1942, pp. 1–10.

CARMER, CARL: *The Hurricane's Children*. New York: Farrar and Rinehart; 1937. 175 pp. The tales have a whimsical quality and are told with a keen sense of humor. The best-known folk heroes, Mike Fink, Davy Crockett, Old Stormalong, Pecos Bill, Kemp Morgan, Strap Buckner, Tony Beaver, John Henry, are all included as well as a few newcomers: Ocean-Born Mary, Annie Christmas, Feobold

Feoboldson, and others. Many of the stories have been told over the air on a program called "Your Neck o' the Woods."

————: *America Sings.* New York: Alfred A. Knopf; 1942. 243 pages. Twenty-nine American folk tales, each with a song out of the same background.

CHAPPELL, LOUIS W.: *John Henry, A Folk-Lore Study.* Jena: Fromannsche Verlag, Walter Biedermann; 1933. An excellent and comprehensive study.

CHITTICK, VICTOR L. O. (editor): *Ring-Tailed Roarers: Tall Tales of the American Frontier, 1830–60.* Caldwell, Idaho: Caxton Printers Ltd.; 1941. 316 pp. In the introduction, the editor sketches the growth of tall tales. The remainder of the book is devoted to whoppers. Davy Crockett, Simon Suggs, and Mike Fink are the best-known characters included. A two-page list of tall tales and notes on authors and sources concludes the book.

DAVIS, E. B.: "Paul Bunyan Talk." *American Speech,* Vol. XVII, No. 4 (December, 1942), pp. 217–25. Words used by loggers and their meanings.

DAVIDSON, LEVETTE JAY: "Colorado Folklore." The *Colorado Magazine,* Vol. XVIII, No. 1 (January, 1941), pp. 1–13. Discusses the tall tale in the West with special attention to Jim Bridger.

DAUGHERTY, JAMES (editor): *Their Weight in Wildcats.* Boston: Houghton Mifflin Company; 1936, 188 pp. A collection of stories of Mike Fink, Paul Bunyan, Johnny Appleseed, Davy Crockett, Kit Carson, John Henry, and other frontier heroes. The attractive illustrations are by the editor.

DORSON, RICHARD M.: *Davy Crockett, American Comic Legend.* Rockland, N. Y.: Rockland Editions; 1939. Selections from the old Crockett almanacs and reproductions of many of their illustrations.

FEDERAL WRITERS' PROJECT OF THE WORK PROJECT ADMINISTRATION: *Idaho Lore.* Caldwell, Idaho: The Caxton Printers Ltd.; 1939. pp. 113–40. Tales "tall and broad."

FIELD, RACHEL (compiler): *American Folk and Fairy Tales.* New York: Charles Scribner's Sons; 1929. 302 pp. A carefully selected group of folk tales. Indian legends, Louisiana folk tales, Southern Mountain stories, and tales of Paul Bunyan, Tony Beaver, and Uncle Remus are included.

HALPERT, HERBERT and EMMA ROBINSON: "'Oregon' Smith, An Indiana Folk Hero." *Southern Folklore Quarterly,* Vol. VI, No. 1 (March, 1942), pp. 163–8.

HAVIGHURST, WALTER: *Upper Mississippi: A Wilderness Saga.* New York: Farrar and Rinehart; 1937. 258 pp. The story of settlers on the prairies and woodsmen in the forest, vividly told by the author and beautifully illustrated by David and Lolita Granahan. Part III is called "The Epic of Lumber."

HAZARD, LUCY L.: *In Search of America.* 581 pp. New York: Thomas Y. Crowell; 1930. Many collected tales.

HOLBROOK, STEWART H.: *Holy Old Mackinaw.* New York: Macmillan Company; 1938. 278 pp. A rollicking history of the lumberjacks in Maine, in the Middle West, and in the Pacific Northwest. The first chapter of the book is the Saga of Jigger Jones, one of the last of the authentic old-style lumberjacks.

HOSMER, PAUL: *Now We're Loggin'.* Portland, Oregon: Metropolitan Press; 1930. 210 pp. A series of humorous narrative essays telling of lumbering and the life of lumberjacks.

HURSTON, ZORA NEALE: *Mules and Men,* pp. 129–37 and passim. Philadelphia: J. B. Lippincott Company; 1935. "Big Lies" as told by Florida Negroes; many of them are known by Whites over the country.

JOHNSON, GUY B.: *John Henry: Tracking Down a Negro Legend.* Chapel Hill, N. C.: University of North Carolina Press; 1929. 155 pp. An excellent summary of the research done by the author. Excerpts from letters, and words and music for many of the fifty ballads discovered, are included. The critical bibliography of John Henry lists books, periodicals and phonograph records.

KEARNEY, LUKE SYLVESTER: Lake Shore Kearney (pseudonym), *The Hodag and Other Tales of the Logging Camps.* Wausau, Wisconsin: the author; 1928. A group of tales told in the lumber camps of northern Wisconsin. In some, Paul is mentioned (i.e., The Round River Drive, pp. 18–28.); others are just good yarns, one of them telling of the capture of the hodag and giving a minute description of the fierce beast.

LINDSAY, VACHEL: *Johnny Appleseed and Other Poems.* New York: Macmillan Company; 1928. "In Praise of Johnny Appleseed," pp. 82–92, is written in three parts, with the same vividness that is found in "the Congo."

MACKAYE, PERCY: *Tall Tales of the Kentucky Mountains.* New York: George H. Doran Company; 1926. 185 pp. An excellent collection of old tales, presented in the vernacular of the Munchausen of the Kentucky Mountains, Old Sol Shell.

MCLAUGHLIN, R. P.: "Joe Mafraw." *The Frontier,* Vol. IX, No. 1 (November, 1928). Missoula, Montana, State University of Montana: H. G. Merriam. A woodsman's song picked up in the woods and recorded by R. P. McLaughlin. This is certainly a song about "Joe Mufraw, the one named Pete," who worked for Paul.

MEINE, FRANKLIN J.: *Tall Tales of the Southwest: 1830–1860.* New York: Alfred A. Knopf; 1930. 456 pp. The introduction sketches the growth of the tall tale, and is followed by a large number of the tales themselves, forerunners of Paul Bunyan stories. A helpful brief bibliography is included.

MILLER, OLIVE BEAUPRÉ: *Heroes, Outlaws and Funny Fellows.* New York: Doubleday, Doran and Company; 1939. 332 pp. A Junior Literary Guild selection.

MONTAGUE, MARGARET: *Up Eel River.* New York: The Macmillan Company; 1928. 225 pp. Monologs of Truth-Teller, giving in the "free and easy speech of the West Virginia lumberman," tales of Tony Beaver and his marvelous adventures. In her preface, Miss Montague calls this legend the "only genuine bit of folklore which America has yet produced." The last chapter of the book brings in Paul Bunyan and merges the two heroes into one.

O'REILLY, EDWARD: "The Saga of Pecos Bill." *Century Magazine,* Vol. CVI, No. 6 (October, 1923), pp. 827–33, 1923. The first notice of the "mythical cow-boy hero of the Southwest." Drawings by Elmer Hader.

PECK, LEIGH: *Pecos Bill and Lightning.* Boston: Houghton Mifflin Company; 1940. 67 pp. Attractive illustrations in color by Kurt Wiese. A book written for children, giving in brief form the adventures of this gayest of heroes.

ROUNDS, GLEN: *Lumbercamp.* New York: Holiday House; 1937. 117 pp. The story of a gullible whistle punk at Camp Fifteen, giving the Paul Bunyan atmosphere. The author's drawings and the grained wood back add to the attractiveness of the book.

ROURKE, CONSTANCE: *Davy Crockett.* New York: Harcourt, Brace and Company; 1934. 276 pp. Reviewers praise it highly, both for the delightful style of the telling, and for the scholarly discussion of sources in the fine critical essay at the end of the book.

SENGER, HANK: *A Saga of the Sawtooths.* Caldwell, Idaho: Caxton Printers Ltd.; 1938. Pictures by Nick Villeneuve. Pictures of the wild animals of Paul's time. Verses and tales about them. Paul is not mentioned.

SHAY, FRANK: *Here's Audacity!* New York: Macaulay Company; 1930. 256 pp. Most space is given to Paul Bunyan, but the author has presented vivid pictures of Old Stormalong, Kemp Morgan, Casey Jones, Pecos Bill, Tony Beaver, and John Henry. There is a brief helpful bibliography included.

THOMAS, LOWELL: *Tall Stories, The Rise and Triumph of the Great American Whopper*. New York and London: Funk & Wagnalls Company; 1931. A rich collection of tall tales secured through audience response to a radio program. Of great value for distribution study is the listing of the addresses of all contributors of variants even when their texts are not given.

THOMPSON, HAROLD W.: *op. cit. See* Section I.

TRYON, H. H.: *Fearsome Critters*. Cornwall, N. Y.: Idlewild Press; 1939. More or less scientific descriptions of the animals around Paul. Paul is mentioned on pages 21 and 27.

Acknowledgments

The compiler and publisher wish to make acknowledgment of their indebtedness to the following publishers, authors, newspapers and periodicals for permission to reprint the material included in this anthology:

American Lumberman: for "The Round River Drive" by Douglas Malloch.

The Ames Forester: for "Paul Bunyan: An Authentic Account of His Prehistoric Activities" by G. C. Morbeck. Reprinted by permission of *The Ames Forester* and the author.

D. Appleton-Century Company, Inc.: for excerpts from *The Adventures of Paul Bunyan* by James Cloyd Bowman. The Century Co., New York, 1927.

Albert & Charles Boni, Inc.: for excerpts from *Paul Bunyan: A Legendary Hero of the North Woods* by Thomas G. Alvord, Jr.

The Atlantic Monthly: for "The World's Funny Bone" by Margaret Prescott Montague. Reprinted by permission of *The Atlantic Monthly* and the author.

Charles E. Brown: for excerpts from his articles, leaflets and booklets on Paul Bunyan.

The Caxton Printers, Ltd.: for excerpts from *Tall Timber Tales* and *Paul Bunyan Swings His Axe* by Dell J. McCormick and from *Eve's Stepchildren,* compiled by Lealon N. Jones.

Columbia: for "Bull of the Woods" by James Stevens.

Detroit News: for "The Round River Drive," by James MacGillivray.

Doubleday Doran & Company, Inc.: for excerpts from *Paul Bunyan and the Great Blue Ox* by Wallace Wadsworth. Copyright 1926 by Doubleday, Doran & Co., Inc.

Fortune: for excerpts from "Paul Bunyan—Giant."

The Frontier: for "Paul Bunyan and the Forest Service" by John C. Frohlicher; "Paul Bunyan Logs off Eastern Montana" by Genevieve Murray; "Flathead Lake" by Al Schak and "The Great Hunter of the Woods" by James Stevens. Reprinted by permission of *The Frontier*, H. G. Merriam, and the authors.

Harcourt, Brace and Company, Inc.: for excerpts from *Paul Bunyan* by Esther Shephard, copyright 1924 by Esther Shephard. Reprinted by permission of Harcourt, Brace and Company, Inc.; and for "Who Made Paul Bunyan" from *The People, Yes* by Carl Sandburg, copyright 1936 by Harcourt, Brace and Company, Inc.

Henry Harrison: for "I Hear Paul Bunyan" by Louise Leighton from *Poetry Out of Wisconsin*, edited by August Derleth and Raymond E. F. Larsson.

Hastings House: for an excerpt from the *Texas Guidebook* (American Guide Series).

Holiday House: for an excerpt from *Ol' Paul, the Mighty Logger* by Glen Rounds.

Henry Holt and Company, Inc.: for "Paul's Wife" from *Collected Poems* by Robert Frost.

Houghton Mifflin Company: for excerpts from *Pecos Bill and Lightning* by Leigh Peck.

Journal of American Folklore: for the bibliographies of Gladys J. Haney and Herbert Halpert. Reprinted by permission of the *Journal of American Folklore* and the authors.

Kansas Magazine: for "Paul Bunyan and the Dreadful Whirling Wimpus" by Larry Freeman. Reprinted by permission of *Kansas Magazine* and the author.

Alfred A. Knopf, Inc.: for excerpts reprinted from *Paul Bunyan* by James Stevens, by permission of Alfred A. Knopf, Inc. Copyright 1925 by Alfred A. Knopf, Inc.

Michigan History Magazine: for "Geography with a Capital G," by James Cloyd Bowman.

NEA Service, Inc.: for "The Hemlock Fever," "The Mighty Fisherman," "The Dismal Sauger," and "The Grand Canyon" by James Stevens.

The New Republic: for "Paul's Big Griddle" and "The Giant Cornstalk" by Constance Mayfield Rourke. Reprinted by permission of The New Republic and the Estate of Mrs. Constance D. Rourke.

The New York Times: for "Paul Bunyan is Back" by Louis C. Jones. Reprinted by permission of *The New York Times* and the author.

The Northern Miner: for "Paul Bunyan Invents a Few Things," "The Sawdust River," and "Paul Bunyan, The Arctic Explorer" by W. J. Gorman.

The Oregonian: for "The Big Blow," "The World's Champion Faller," "The Underground Railway," and "The Japanese Current," by DeWitt Harry; "Paul and the Pacific Ocean," as told to DeWitt Harry by W. A. Schaffner; and "Crater Lake and the Cascade Mountains" as told to DeWitt Harry by Bert Geer.

The Red River Lumber Company: for excerpts from "Paul Bunyan and His Big Blue Ox," by W. B. Laughead.

The Saturday Review of Literature: for "Paul Bunyan," by John Lee Brooks. Reprinted by permission of *The Saturday Review of Literature* and the author.

The Seattle Star: for "Paul's New York Trip and the Ostrich Race," told by H. C. to Lee J. Smits; and "Victor, the First High Climber," told by Paul J. Peppets to Lee J. Smits.

Governor M. Q. Sharpe: for "The Black Hills," and "The Mountain That Stood on its Head," from *South Dakota Guide.*

James Stevens: for excerpts from *The Saginaw Paul Bunyan.*

Story Parade: for "Baby Rainstorm" by Glen Rounds.

Harold Titus: for "The Giant Cornstalk" from *Timber.*

Ida Virginia Turney: for an excerpt from *Paul Bunyan Comes West.* Reprinted by permission of the author and the University of Oregon Press.

University of Michigan Press: for excerpts from *Songs of Michigan Lumberjacks* by Earl Clifton Beck.

University of Wisconsin: for "Christmas on the Big Onion," by Taggert Ted Brown, from *The Wisconsin Octopus.*

Wisconsin Academy of Sciences, Arts and Letters: for "Babe and the Log Jam," by K. Bernice Stewart and Homer A. Watt from *1916 Transactions.*

Wisconsin Engineer: for "Paul Bunyan—The Surveyor Extraordinary" by Ray S. Owen.

Woman's Home Companion: for "When Rivers Were Young and Wild" by James Stevens. Reprinted by permission of *Woman's Home Companion* and the author.

411

List of Authors, Publications and Selections

The compiler lists below the titles of the publications from which the selections in this book were taken. The page numbers refer to pages in this volume. In some cases the compiler has given a title to an excerpt or chapter which is not so titled in the original volume, but it should not be difficult for the interested reader to locate the piece and read further on the subject if he consults the volume from which the selection was made. (For names of publishers and publication dates, *see* Bibliography.)

413

414

Freeman, Larry: in the *Kansas Magazine* (1933)
Paul Bunyan and the Dreadful Whirling Wimpus *193*

Frohlicher, John C: in *The Frontier* (November 1924)
Paul Bunyan and the Forest Service *307*

Frost, Robert: *Collected Poems*
Paul's Wife *80*

Four-L Bulletin
Mount Baker (May, 1922) *300*
Paul Bunyan and Swede Charlie (September, 1919) *206*

Gorman, W. J.: in *The Northern Miner* (Column headed "Grab Samples")
Paul Bunyan Invents a Few Things (October 1, 1931) *221*
Paul Bunyan, The Arctic Explorer (October 22, 1931) *360*
The Sawdust River (September 17, 1931) *325*

Halpert, Herbert: in the *Journal of American Folklore* (January 1943)
Bibliography *379*

Haney, Gladys J.: in the *Journal of American Folklore* (July 1942)
Bibliography *379*

Harry, DeWitt: in *The Morning Oregonian* (Column headed "The Listening Post")
The Big Blow (March 22, 1922) *31*
Crater Lake and the Cascade Mountains (told by Bert Geer) (March 10, 1922) *282*
The Japanese Current (March 17, 1922) *279*
Paul and the Pacific Ocean (told by W. A. Schaffner) (March 19, 1922) *280*
The Underground Railway (March 11, 1922) *102*
The World's Champion Faller (March 8, 1922) *48*

Jones, Louis, C.: in *The New York Times* (August 24, 1941)
Paul Bunyan is Back *375*

415